House of Jo'Rae

The Legend of Mistress Mattie and Hattie

Marsha Bullock
3/19/21

Marsha Bullock

Marsha Bullock

This is a work of fiction Names, characters, businesses, places, events and incidents are either of the author's imagination or used in a fictitious manner. Any resemblance to actual person, living or dead, or actual events, is purely coincidental.

For information regarding permission, write:
Marsha Bullock, Author
info@vivdimagination13.com

ISBN-13: 978-1986219976
ISBN-10: 1986219976

House of Fo'Rae

I would like to thank God first for blessing me with the gift of creativity and the gift to write. I dedicate this book to my parents William Bullock and Brenda Bullock. Thank you mama for always being my strength, my encourager, my protector, my proofreader, my biggest critic and biggest fan. You've always been there for me. I could never repay you and I'm forever grateful.

Thank you Daddy for your love and support and for always encouraging me never to be just satisfied with life, always strive to be better.

I would like to thank my two amazing children: Kerwin and Toni, whom I adore. Thanks to Reginald Kindle for all your love and support over the years. Thank you to my family and friends. It's such a blessing to have such an awesome support system.

R.I.P to my grannies Lucille "Lu" Foree who taught me "sometimes you gotta raise a little hell to get a little peace", Mary "Mu" Scott Bullock who taught me to love The Lord always and believe in him. Helen Johnson "Mama" who taught me " be a lady at all times"...

iii

Table of Contents

Prelude

L egend has it, long years ago during slavery, Hattie Mae was the unwilling object of The Master's affection and was subjected to numerous encounters with his wicked sexual habits. She bore him a daughter whom he insisted work in the big house as with Hattie Mae, since Hattie Mae was on the darker side of the spectrum that was unheard of. However, The Master who was king of the castle made it happen.

Over the years, he ordered Hattie Mae to his quarters countless nights. This highly offended his wife who was also his first cousin, Mistress Mattie. Mistress Mattie's father sold her to The Master for a few acres of land and a handful of slaves when she was only fourteen years old. As she aged she became too old for his sadistic needs and was replaced with a countless number of young female slaves including Hattie Mae.

In the Kitchen one day, Hattie Mae noticed the master looking at the daughter she'd had for him, but not like a father would look at his daughter. It was more like a man lusting for a woman. The only problem was she was his blood daughter and barely thirteen. This situation disturbed Hattie Mae a great deal so she went to Mistress Mattie and begged her to send the child away even sell her off. However Mistress Mattie refused. She said that only the master had the right to buy and sell slaves. As the weeks went by Hattie Mae knew it was just a matter of time before The Master would take the young teenager's virginity and ruin her forever, with little to no regard for her being his daughter.

One night, when Mistress Mattie had disappeared on one of her many trips deep in the woods to her cabin (where she claimed she rested from mental exhaustion from The Master and his wicked ways tearing away at her very soul), The Master came down to the slave quarters, but this time he bypassed Hattie Mae and dragged their daughter into the shed where he raped her. Hattie Mae had to restrain herself. Her husband Robert Lee, who was twice the size as the master and could crush his entire skeleton with one blow, wasn't there. He was Mistress Mattie's driver and was waiting in the woods for her. However, he was just a slave and feared The Master's whip. Hattie Mae listened in horror as the young girl screamed out for help. Finally The Master came out of the barn dragging the young teenager, who was soaked in blood and battered and bruised. She was like a zombie in a trance.

The sight of this sent Hattie Mae into a rage. She grabbed an ax that was lying on the barn floor and hacked The master in his back. He fell to the ground in pain then Hattie Mae gave him another whack across the face. Then she gave him another fatal blow to the head. Hattie Mae, who was a butcher by trade then took a meat cleaver and deboned him like he was a piece of meat. She stood there with blood dripping everywhere and carved him apart from head to toe. She had piles of his body spread throughout the barn.

The daughter sat there and watched the entire spectacle, never blinking an eye. In the wee hours of the morning before the sun arose, Robert Lee and Mistress Mattie returned to find Hattie Mae and her daughter doing what looked like a Voodoo Spell over the bones. Hattie Mae had stuck a stick in The Master's head to hold it up. Robert Lee was horrified but, to Hattie Mae's surprise, Mistress Mattie was shockingly calm. She ordered all the slaves to stay in their quarters; anybody found outside would be hung at once. She ordered Robert Lee to clean up the entire mess as she escorted Hattie Mae and her daughter to the big house.

Mistress Mattie cleaned both ladies up and set them on her lounge chair in her room. After Robert Lee had cleaned the barn she ordered him to the big house. She sat down calm and collected. She looked at Hattie Mae and said, "We have a problem. Somebody has to pay for this horrific crime. You know its death to a slave for attacking a white man, let alone a Master." She looked at Hattie Mae then at the teen, who was still in shock, and from her appearance she would never be the same. Mistress Mattie said, "I do understand your pain and suffering, Hattie Mae, nevertheless, somebody has to pay for this."

Robert Lee spoke up he said, "Punish me I'll give my life for them." Mistress Mattie looked up as if she had expected it and was relieved he had said that. It was almost like she was waiting for him to take the blame. Hattie Mae begged and pleaded with Robert Lee but Mistress Mattie seemed to already have a plan. She said that since it was Sunday morning nobody, not even the overseer, would visit the plantation today. She said they had at least until Monday morning to get Robert Lee away from there. Robert Lee looked at Mistress Mattie and said; "You know its death to you if you help us, Why would you?"

Mistress Mattie gave Robert Lee a look that only lovers share. Hattie Mae caught it right away. She wondered what had been really going on all those nights in the cabin on the bayou where Mistress Mattie said she went to rest her mind. Was she really relieving her sexual frustration with Robert Lee? Hattie put the thought out of her mind. She listened to Mistress Mattie unfold her plan. She told Robert Lee that since they were on The Bayou he had a better chance of getting to St Vincent in the Caribbean Islands than he did making it up north.

She went to her desk and wrote him a pass to undock the boat to make it ready for The Master. She told him once he was in the boat he should take off and never look back. She knew he could make the trip because he was a skilled sailor. He had made the trip to St Vincent many times, especially when The Master had too much wine. Plus Mistress Mattie knew Hattie Mae had taught Robert Lee how to read and write. She said by the time all this was revealed he would be in the Caribbean Islands. She gave him a bag of money to use, and said if he were to get away that they'd meet him in the Caribbean a few months later. She told him that he would be free because there was no more slavery there. She said her family owned property there and over the months he should check in to see if they'd arrived.

Robert Lee was astonished by Mistress Mattie's willingness to help them. Mistress Mattie told them they had no time to waste. They quickly set the plan in motion. Robert Lee was gone like a thief in the night and Mistress Mattie went to work on her part of the plan. She stood on the docks and watched the boat depart the harbor. Then she ordered all the slaves to the barn. She told them that something terrible had happened to the master and that if they wanted to keep their families and not be sold off, whatever they thought they knew they better not tell anybody else but God. She told them if they even thought about telling anything they had better think twice and that she'd make sure all their wives and daughters would be sold to slave masters as wicked as her husband.

The slaves did exactly what they were told, The next morning when the overseer arrived he found Mistress Mattie locked in her room and holding a shotgun. She played her part to the fullest. She said she was scared for her life. She told him that Robert Lee had gone mad and killed The Master and fled off into the woods to the north. The overseer sent the dogs out and then sent for The Slave Patrol, after it was all said and done, a reward for Robert Lee's head was posted. Mistress Mattie's brother came down from Texas to run the plantation. Mistress Mattie stayed in her room for three months never leaving for anything. The brother said she was grieving the loss of The Master. There was no word from Robert Lee.

One day Mistress Mattie called Hattie Mae to the master bedroom. She released all the chambermaids from their duties and said Hattie Mae was her new personal servant. Mistress Mattie ordered Hattie Mae to lock the door and pull the curtains then have a seat at the side of the bed. She looked at Hattie Mae with such a sorrowful look. She said, "How have you been? How's the child holding up?" Hattie Mae replied, " She hasn't said a word and I believe she is with child." Mistress Mattie looked up to the sky and said, "Lord why?" Then she rubbed her stomach; she removed the covers and unfastened her nightgown to reveal her stomach.

She looked at Hattie Mae and said The Master hadn't touched me in over a year. Hattie Mae put her head down to the ground. She said, "How then can this be Mistress Mattie?" Mistress Mattie said, "My husband was a sick man. He desired young girls such as yourself and your daughter." She looked at Hattie Mae and lifted Hattie's Mae's face up to look her in the eyes.

She said, "I hated you since you got here, walking around with your voluptuous body, round breast, full lips, and plump ass. I watched my husband lust for you night and day wanting, nothing to do with me. That envy led me to your husband Robert Lee. I figured since you had mine I would take yours. All those trips to The Bayou—I made him take me and I enjoyed every second of it. He was nothing like The Master. He was gentle and strong. She paused for a second and smiled, she said, "And I do declare he had the biggest penis I'd ever seen. I swear it was like a monster." She looked at Hattie Mae and regained her composure. It seemed like the thought of Robert Lee's penis frazzled her a bit.

Hattie Mae looked at the Mistress and smiled, She said "And you're telling me all this because why?" Mistress Mattie said, "Because I want you to suffer and be jealous, because I had him." Hattie Mae replied with, "Well, I'm sorry, Mistress, but I'm far from jealous, I'm actually happy that you enjoyed him so. After what your husband did to me, I couldn't stand my husband's touch. I wasn't good enough for him, so if having you, Mistress Mattie, pleased him then so be it."

Mistress Mattie looked confused and said, "My Lord, you truly loved him. She looked down at the floor and said, "I, too, love him. This is why I helped him hopefully to freedom." She then told Hattie Mae that they were going to leave this godforsaken place and never return. She told Hattie Mae to continue to hide her daughter's pregnancy and that she should begin to pretend she was pregnant. She said they would use a pillow to stuff Hattie Mae's dress that would make it appear she was with child. She said that Hattie Mae and her daughter were to spend all their time in her chambers until she could make arrangements to go to the plantation in the Caribbean.

The plan was Hattie Mae was going to take Mistress Mattie's child and raise it as her own together with Hattie Mae's daughter's child. However Hattie Mae had a different plan as far as her daughter and her unborn child were concerned. The night before they were scheduled to leave for the Caribbean, Hattie Mae mixed up some of her special plant juices and fed it to all The Master's mulatto children. She thought to herself that she wasn't going to leave behind those devil babies. She was going to wipe out The Master's entire bloodline including her very own child. Hattie Mae couldn't bear the thought of her daughter bringing The Master's child into the world. She felt as though they would be cursed with the same demonic thirst for young girls. However, after she had secretly taken out all of the mulattos she went seeking hers. She found her hiding in the woods crying. She finally spoke after months; she looked at Hattie Mae standing there holding a cup of poison for her to drink. She said "Mama, if you want me to die, so be it, I don't want to live anymore no how. I'm ruined for the rest of my life." Then she extended her arm out for Hattie Mae to hand her the cup. Tears rolled down Hattie Mae's cheeks. She put her head down in shame. She poured out the poison, wrapped her arms around her daughter and said, "The ancestors will work it out."

Mistress Mattie, Hattie Mae, and the pregnant daughter boarded a boat bound for the Caribbean and never looked back. Legend said that after slavery was abolished in the United States, Hattie Mae's descendants returned to claim the plantation. Rumor also had it that Hattie Mae's daughter bore twin girls and Mistress Mattie bore a son.

Interlude

As all legends would have it, over the years juicy tidbits of the legend gets either left out or excerpts get added in. The legend of Mistress Mattie and Hattie Mae is no exception.

So let's start with the tidbits that were not so correct, such as the part about Hattie Mae being Gypsy's great grandmother. That's not true. Hattie Mae was indeed Gypsy's ancestor but more like several generations back. Yes, Hattie Mae had the gift to communicate with the dead, heal the sick and sometimes, see into the future. All those gifts were passed down from generation to generation, with Gypsy also having the gift of sight, healing, and communication with the dead.

Legend had it that Robert Lee escaped to St Vincent however this is misunderstood. He actually escaped to St Lucia.

As for Mistress Mattie's brother coming to run The Plantation after his death it was actually The Masters brother who came.

As to any reference to Hattie Mae mentioning God, well that was a misunderstanding too. She was actually referring to her ancestors.

As for the extra add on, that some folks would consider exaggerations. Well, in this case there really aren't any. Some folks say a lot of the story was left out.

Don't fret though: The Legend of Mistress Mattie and Hattie Mae will be told in this uncut version. So let's get started.

House of Fo'Rae

Chapter One:
Bon Voyage

Hattie Mae knew the time was coming near for her and Mistress Mattie to be leaving. Mistress Mattie's baby bump was growing bigger every day, and Hattie Mae's daughter's stomach was getting bigger and her behavior even stranger.

Hattie Mae didn't have time to worry about Mistress Mattie or her daughter. Hattie Mae had work to do.

For months, she had been plotting an escape with a few other slaves.

Hattie Mae didn't feel right about the plan she and Mistress Mattie had made to go to the Caribbean and never return. Also, Hattie Mae was struggling with the plan she had for the late Master Fo'Rae's mulatto children; her daughter included.

Master Fo'Rae was a monster. Hattie Mae could never allow an offspring of his to live and develop the sickness for young girls he had. All his offspring had to die along with him.

Hattie Mae plotted for weeks how to make the perfect escape to the North. She and few other trusted slaves, whom she'd taught how to read English just like Mistress Mattie taught her years ago, were planning to run.

Hattie Mae always thought Mistress Mattie was a strange woman. Some days, Mistress Mattie would go out of her way to be nice to Hattie Mae, and then some days she would be cold and distant.

However, on the days Mistress Mattie was nice, Hattie Mae soaked up all the information from Mistress Mattie that she could such as secret back roads, how to get her hands on a map, and most importantly, where Master Fo'Rae kept the guns.

Hattie Mae mixed up an herb concoction of black pepper, nutmeg, cinnamon, and Cayenne pepper. She also added a pinch of chamomile in the mixture.

Hattie Mae mixed a batch every day, and at night she would sneak off with the trusted slaves and spread it all over the ground along the route the slaves would take to freedom.

The mixture was done to confuse the hound dogs. Dogs disliked the smell of all those spices mixed together. The scent would burn their noses and the dogs couldn't pick up the slaves' scent. Hattie Mae had a special treat for the slave tracking hounds. Since she couldn't get close to them on a daily basis, she convinced Master Fo'Rae's brother that the slave trackers bloodhounds were continually getting loose and biting the slaves.

Master Fo'Rae's brother was furious and had his driver take him to the location where they kept the bloodhounds. He gave the slave trackers a piece of his mind. While Master Fo'Rae's brother was on a tantrum about the cruel and inhuman way the south treated their slaves, the driver that was working with Hattie Mae sprinkled the mixture all over the plantation. He even spread it around the bloodhound's cage, which made the hounds bark and howl.

The slave trackers thought that the dogs' barking was funny. One even said they were barking because they hated niggers just as much as he did.

Hattie Mae laughed to herself because the joke was on the slave trackers.

Hattie Mae got the word from Mistress Mattie that they were leaving. Hattie Mae quickly put her plan into action. Hattie gathered all the slaves who wanted to leave together. She told them that tonight was their only chance to leave. In the morning, she and Mistress Mattie were boarding the boat never to return.

The slaves broke up into groups of three totaling nine in all. Hattie Mae gave them three different routes all to the same place, New York. Hattie Mae had heard Master Fo'Rae's brother repeatedly say that New York City was the safest place on earth for runaway slaves.

The only problem was, when they got there they wouldn't have papers.

As they were plotting the last details, Hattie Mae caught sight of who she considered was a spy. It was Master Fo'Rae's brother's servant he'd brought with him from Texas.

Hattie Mae called him to come out of the shadows of the bushes.

Hattie Mae said, "Show yourself, traitor!"

Those words seemed to provoke anger in him.

He stepped into the light and said, "Surely those words don't apply to me, and a traitor I am not!"

He tipped his hat to Hattie Mae and the rest of the slaves.

He said, "I've come to aid you in your departure."

Hattie Mae replied, "What are you talking about? We're just praising the Lord and praying!"

The Man gave a slight grin and responded, "Now, now Ms. Hattie Mae we all know you don't believe in no white God and you definitely ain't out here praying to him. Now let's stop wasting time. We only got a few more hours to make a distance between these here slaves and those slave trackers."

The slave stopped and said, "Allow me to introduce myself properly, I'm Pierre Cordova."

All the slaves just frowned; they weren't impressed with Pierre Cordova, and they didn't trust him. Hell, he had come here with Master Fo'Rae's brother to keep them in line. All the other slaves had been born on this plantation.

One of the slaves said with disgust, "And what can you aid us with?"

Pierre Cordova said, "Well, I'm glad you asked that."

Then he pulled something from his coat pocket.

All the slaves gasped for air.

Pierre Cordova had paper, ink, and most importantly, he had Master Fo'Rae's brother's seal.

Hattie Mae smiled and simply said, "I won't ask how and why. Let's start writing!"

Hattie Mae wrote all the slaves freedom papers and stamped it with Master Fo'Rae's brother's seal.

That night, as the slaves made their final preparations, Hattie Mae made her rounds to Master Fo'Rae's plantation babies.

It was no surprise to Hattie Mae that none of them had joined the other slaves to escape. In their confused minds, they were under the impression that they were better than the other slaves because they were Master Fo'Rae's children.

Hattie Mae just shook her head. Damn fools really felt like they were a part of the Fo'Rae family. Hell, the late Master Fo'Rae didn't give two rats' asses about them. They were just nigger babies on the plantation. They worked sun up until sun down just like all the rest of the slaves.

It was easy to get them to drink her special blend of herbs. She just started up a conversation and offered them something to drink. One by one they drifted off to their death.

Hattie Mae eased her conscience by telling herself that they all were offspring of the devil Master Fo'Rae, and were better off dead. The world would be a better place without them.

However, when it was her daughter's turn, it wasn't so easy to do. Her daughter hadn't spoken a word since the night Master Fo'Rae defiled her. However this night she spoke up.

When Hattie Mae heard her voice, her love for her daughter wouldn't allow her to harm her. She just held her in her arms and cried.

15

Hattie Mae was confused when she woke up the next morning. She thought that the plantation would be swarming with slave trackers and dogs.

But, that wasn't the case. It was business as usual. The slaves that were left seemed to be confused also.

Hattie Mae didn't even hear all the cries of the mothers of the plantation babies she'd poisoned. Hattie Mae thought for sure their screams alone would wake the nation.

Hattie Mae saw all the slaves who didn't escape moving on about their daily business.

Pierre Cordova walked over to Hattie Mae and said, "Morning, Ms. Hattie Mae. Let me get those bags for you."

Hattie Mae whispered, "What the hell is going on? Why didn't those ignorant fools leave?"

Pierre Cordova smiled and replied sarcastically, "Well, Ms. Hattie Mae, those ignorant fools been done left, hours ago. And those dead bodies you left, well, I took care of those for you. I put them in a shallow grave under the mansion. I figured it served the Fo'Rae family right, to have a bunch of plantation babies haunting their family home."

Hattie Mae was still confused. She couldn't understand why Pierre Cordova was being so helpful. That was until she saw Pierre Cordova gazing at her daughter. Then she remembered he was sweet on her.

Hattie Mae said, "So, why aren't the slave trackers here yet?"

Pierre Cordova smiled and said, "Could have something to do with that bottle of moonshine Master Fo'Rae had me take them last night as a peace offering. Master Fo'Rae felt so badly about how he clowned over at the slave trackers' station, that he sent them a peace offering. Master Fo'Rae and the overseer got drunk last night. Why, they haven't even realized some of the slaves are gone."

Just then Hattie Mae heard the bell ringing signaling that a slave had escaped. The overseer and his sons came running.

All the slaves just lined up. They already knew the drill. To the overseer's count, it was sixteen slaves missing in all.

Hattie Mae had taken out four mulattos, and twelve slaves had escaped.

Now here came all the weeping and wailing from the mammies of the runaway slaves.

However, what happened next shocked Hattie Mae.

Master Fo'Rae's brother told all the slaves to go to their quarters and remain there. He told the overseers to run and fetch the Slave trackers and then he told Pierre Cordova to make sure Mistress Mattie, Hattie Mae, and Hattie Mae's daughter didn't miss the boat.

Hattie Mae saw Mistress Mattie come out of the mansion annoyed by everything that was going on.

Mistress Mattie looked like she was going to faint.

Master Fo'Rae's brother insisted that Pierre Cordova make sure that they made it to the docks safely and on time.

When they were leaving the plantation, Hattie Mae saw the slave patrol. One of the slave patrollers was fussing about the bloodhounds being lazy dogs and something about how they had to catch those niggers before sundown.

Hattie Mae smiled to herself. She had a feeling they'd never catch the runaway slaves. Hattie Mae had made them a map and pointed out hiding resting spots no bloodhound could find.

If the runaway slaves kept up the pace and continued to drown themselves in Hattie Mae's concoction of peppers, they'd make it to New York to freedom.

Hattie Mae overheard the slave trackers say that a few slaves from a neighboring plantation were on the loose.

The slave tracker kicked his foot down and said, "These fucking niggers are getting out of hand. They need to be taught a good lesson."

Then the slave tracker looked over at Mistress Mattie's carriage, he tipped his hat at Mistress Mattie and said, "Good-morning Ma'am. Have a safe trip."

Then he looked over at Pierre Cordova and said, "Well, whatcha waiting on boy? Get a move on and if you see any of your nigger friends. Be a good little nigger and advise them to come on back. Because when I catch them, they gonna wish they'd never been born."

Mistress Mattie looked at the slave tracker with utter disgust and said, "I'm pretty sure they already wish they'd never been born. I'd kindly suggest that you not refer to my servants as "niggers" in my presence. I find it to be tacky and distasteful. As a matter of fact, quite frankly, I'm offended."

The man just replied, "Yes ma'am" and moved on.

Mistress Mattie, Hattie Mae, and Hattie Mae's daughter, whose name was Savanna, made their way to the docks. All three of them were terrified that they'd get caught. Mistress Mattie was trying her hardest not to throw up her morning breakfast of grits and fried fish. Hattie Mae smiled to herself as she watched Mistress Mattie swallow back her throw up and lay her head on the side of the coach window, holding her stomach to absorb every bump the coach rolled over. It seemed like the driver and the horse were having a bad day.

When the coach finally came to a stop at the docks, Mistress Mattie stumbled out of the carriage.

She looked at the driver and said, "Good Lord, surely you don't have to drive this carriage as reckless as you are? What in tarnation is your problem?"

The driver replied, "Why Mistress Mattie, I ain't never drives this old thing before now. I reckon it's just gone take some getting used to, that's all. We gon be fine after a while."

Mistress Mattie started to reply, but the smell of the seawater, combined with the wobbly ride and that fried fish she'd eaten for breakfast had her throwing up all over the docks.

The driver looked at Mistress Mattie, bucked his eyes and clinched his hat close to him.

He said, "We's sick today Mistress Mattie?"

The sight of Mistress Mattie miserably sick brought a smile to Hattie Mae's face. Hattie Mae had purposely made that breakfast; she knew the smell of fish made Mistress Mattie sick to her stomach.

Hattie Mae figured that was what Mistress Mattie got for sleeping with her husband and getting pregnant. To top all that off, Mistress Mattie was making Hattie Mae pretend she was pregnant because she didn't want to bear the shame of having a nigger baby.

Hattie Mae looked over at her mulatto daughter Savanna who was holding her six-month pregnant belly.

Hattie Mae thought to herself, *Ain't that a bitch. Mistress Mattie had been in the woods pleasuring herself with Hattie Mae's husband, Robert Lee. While Mistress Mattie's husband, Master Fo'Rae had been raping Hattie Mae and Savanna, his own blood daughter.*

Hattie Mae shook her head in disgust. She took her mind to a happier time, before the slave traders captured her right outside her village in Sierra Leone. The slave tracker took her and her protector.

Hattie Mae, who was the daughter of a fearless warrior, had always felt protected, except on that day. The strange white-faced men had a weapon

Hattie Mae nor her tribe members had never seen.

Later, on the slave ship, Hattie Mae learned that the strange weapon was called a gun.

Hattie Mae quickly put Africa out of her mind. Hattie Mae had been in Louisiana for sixteen years, ever since she was twelve years old. Hattie Mae put her hand on Mistress Mattie's back and rubbed it. Hattie Mae winked her eye at her daughter Savanna and gave a little grin.

Hattie Mae rubbed Mistress Mattie's back and said, "Now, now Mistress Mattie. Rest your mind. We's gone be alright."

Mistress Mattie gathered herself together. She looked at Hattie Mae and said, "I'm sure we will be, but we would be much better if you would just admit that you hate me for loving Robert Lee."

Hattie Mae just pretended she didn't hear Mistress Mattie.

Instead, Hattie Mae pointed at the nap sack she saw Pierre Cordova hiding under the suitcases.

Hattie Mae looked at Mistress Mattie and said, "Well, looks like we's gon have a stowaway!"

Mistress Mattie held her pearls tight. She said, "Lord, Hattie Mae we don't need this, not today. What are we going to do?"

Hattie Mae replied sarcastically, "Well, Mistress Mattie, seeing as how smart you is, I'm sure you will figure out something."

Then Hattie Mae bent down to pick up her bag.

Mistress Mattie just rolled her eyes at Hattie Mae and proceeded towards the docks.

They saw the crew standing there to greet them. Master Fo'Rae's brother, who was running the plantation now, had sent word down to the docks a few days beforehand. He sent his slave Pierre Cordova, who was on loan from Master Fo'Rae's Spanish friend who lived down in Texas.

Pierre Cordova was at Fo'Rae Manor to improve on Master Fo'Rae's fleet of ships. He was a master navigator.

Master Fo'Rae let him drive the coach to drop off the ladies. Master Fo'Rae knew Pierre Cordova was sweet on Hattie Mae's daughter Savanna.

After Pierre Cordova had unloaded all the baggage into the ship, Pierre went to his hiding place. Pierre Cordova wasn't about to let the love of his life Savanna sail away and never to return to Louisiana.

Hattie Mae made a point of expressing to Pierre Cordova to say his goodbyes to Savanna. She assumed after all that reminding him about saying his goodbyes and rumors from the slave quarters about what happened to Robert Lee. Well, Pierre Cordova had figured that the ladies weren't planning on coming back.

Mistress Mattie looked at Hattie Mae and said, "You do realize that if he stows away, either he is going to drown or starve to death on this journey."

Hattie Mae replied with a sour face, "Love, besides, I begged you to keep Pierre Cordova away from my baby Savanna."

Mistress Mattie responded, "Oh don't be a sourpuss, Hattie Mae. You know that boy has helped Savanna tremendously."

Hattie Mae frowned her lips and said sarcastically, "Yes ma'am you's correct, and please forgive me for underestimating your wisdom."

Then Hattie Mae boarded the ship.

Mistress Mattie replied, "Sassy Heffa," as she walked towards the ship, she stopped when she saw Pierre Cordova.

Mistress Mattie said, "I do declare Pierre Cordova this has got to be your lucky day."

Hattie Mae turned around when she heard Mistress Mattie say that.

Hattie Mae saw Mistress Mattie look into her coin purse and take out a note. She snapped her fingers for one of the slaves to come to her.

Mistress Mattie said, "Run and take this note to Master Fo'Rae. Tell him it's from me."

She told Pierre Cordova that he was going to the Caribbean with her and her crew. Mistress Mattie said she needed her own personal young buck to assist her on this voyage.

Hattie Mae smiled and continued on up the ramp. She was nervous; she felt her stomach start to turn. The last time Hattie Mae had been on a ship she ended up in slavery.

Hattie Mae stopped dead in her tracks when she saw a familiar face sitting in her path. Her knees felt weak. She could hear what he was saying, but she felt like she was going to pass out.

Mistress Mattie said, "Hattie Mae are you okay?"

The man stuck his foot out to block Hattie Mae's way.

Then the man said, "No niggers on the upper decks. Go directly to the lower deck of the ship. You should not be seen or heard unless you are called for. Understand nigger?"

The man looked at Hattie Mae and said, "I bet you remember me don't you?"

Hattie Mae didn't answer, but she did remember him. He was the white man that captured her and took her from her home. Hattie Mae just stood there frozen.

The Man leaned in close to Hattie Mae and yelled, "What are you deaf nigger? You hear me talking to you?"

He rose up his hand as if he was going to strike her, but Mistress Mattie stepped in between them.

She told Hattie Mae, "Be on about your business."

Hattie Mae did as she was told.

Mistress Mattie seemed a little perturbed about how he had spoken to Hattie Mae.

She looked at the man, then pointed to a gold dust carving that was on the floor.

Mistress Mattie said, "Can you read that for me."

The man said with excitement, "Why yes ma'am I sure can. It says "Fo'Rae Dreams."

She said, "And how many Fo'Rae's are aboard this vessel?"

The crewmember seemed to be confused. He replied, "Well, Mistress Mattie, at the moment the only Fo'Rae on this ship would be you and your slaves. That's if you consider them human."

Mistress Mattie said in a harsh tone, "That's right, my ship and my slaves. So for the duration of this trip, you will mind your manners and refrain from being disrespectful to my servants. Now do your job and mind your own business. Hoist your sorry ass up off that chair, pull the anchor up, and get us out of this dreadful place."

He nodded His head, "Yes ma'am," and walked away.

Mistress Mattie insisted that they get a move on. She saw Master Fo'Rae riding in a heated hurry to stop the ship.

Hattie Mae's heart sank to the bottom of her feet. She knew that Master Fo'Rae had figured out their plan.

Mistress Mattie, Hattie Mae, and Savanna all stood on the deck of the boat, waving and blowing kisses at Master Fo'Rae. Mistress Mattie pretended to be completely deaf when Master Fo'Rae said she didn't have the authorization to take Pierre Cordova.

Mistress Mattie looked at the banks of Louisiana fading into the background. She held both Hattie Mae and Savanna's hand.

Mistress Mattie said, "Never come back to this godforsaken place. There's nothing here for you except misery and death!"

As Hattie Mae and Savannah walked towards the slave quarters of the ship, she heard Mistress Mattie say, "No ma'am, we are staying together."

Then Mistress Mattie looked over at one of the ship's attendants who was eyeing Savanna.

It seems as if Hattie Mae had already taken notice of the ship attendant's intentions. Hattie Mae was holding the handle of her hook knife and watching the man as he put all the bags in the room.

The attendant looked at Savannah with a devilish grin and headed for the door. Then he looked up to see Pierre Cordova standing there. Pierre Cordova stood about 6'5, solid, thick, and strong as a Bull.

Hattie Mae could tell that the thin-framed ship attendant was a little intimated by Pierre Cordova's presence. He hurried past him to the deck of the ship.

Pierre Cordova refused to go to the bottom of the ship. He made himself comfortable in front of the ladies' quarters.

The ladies admired Pierre Cordova's chivalry. Hattie Mae knew even though he'd only known Savannah for a short while, he was in love with her.

Hattie Mae pulled out her black bag and got out her incense and candles.

Hattie Mae saw Savannah and Mistress Mattie spying on her.

Hattie Mae said, "Yes, we need the spirits' protection from these heathens aboard this ship."

Mistress Mattie replied, "As much as your Voodoo magic scares the life out of me, I do agree."

Savannah started a fire and lit all the candles.

Both ladies sat in silence as Hattie Mae summoned the spirits to protect them.

Hattie Mae started rambling in her native tongue. Then she walked over to her bag and pulled out several small jars. She searched them until she found the one that was labeled "Black Pig's Blood."

Hattie Mae took a napkin and smeared the blood around the frame of the door.

Mistress Mattie was appalled. She just turned her head swiftly and unpacked her suitcase.

Mistress Mattie started saying a prayer. She asked Savannah to join in.

Savannah refused and looked over at Hattie Mae.

Hattie Mae said, "We will never pray to the same God as our enslaver. What God allows this?"

Mistress Mattie just ignored Hattie Mae and prayed louder.

All of a sudden, Mistress Mattie doubled over in pain.

Hattie Mae removed all Mistress Mattie's clothes and examined her. Hattie Mae had a strange look on her face as she leaned her ear against Mistress Mattie's stomach.

Hattie Mae said, "Tell me again Mistress Mattie when your last menstrual cycle was."

Mistress Mattie's face turned red as fire. She replied, "My dear isn't that a little personal?"
Hattie Mae nonchalantly replied, "Extremely personal," as she stuck her entire hand inside Mistress Mattie's vagina.

Hattie Mae closed her eyes and felt around inside Mistress Mattie's vagina. Hattie Mae removed her hands from Mistress Mattie's vagina and placed her ear back on Mistress Mattie's stomach.

Mistress Mattie was getting a little frightened. She said, "I demand you tell me this instance what's going on. Hattie Mae, you look like you've seen the devil himself."

Hattie Mae replied, "Child, two little devils to be exact. I hears two heartbeats. It appears Mistress Mattie you gone be having two little nigger babies! From my estimation, they gone be here sooner than you expected. You won't make it to the Caribbean in time, these babies is coming soon."

Savannah stood up and held Mistress Mattie's hand. She put her head on Mistress Mattie's stomach and her other hand on hers.

Mistress Mattie said, "Precious little gifts from God that nobody wants. Lord, forgive us for we know not of what we do."

Savannah stood up and wiped the tears from her eyes. She said, "We shall toss them into the sea when they're born. All three of them nobody cares about dead nigger babies."

Needless to say, Mistress Mattie and Hattie Mae both remained silent. Hattie Mae wasn't quite sure how to respond to that. All Hattie Mae knew was no babies were going to be tossed in the ocean on her watch. Hattie Mae suggested that maybe Savannah lie down. Perhaps the motion of the ocean was upsetting her.

Savannah took Hattie Mae's advice and laid down. Later that night Hattie

Mae heard Savannah praying to the spirits to take her baby. Savannah begged the spirits to have mercy on her.

The days and nights on the ship were getting rough. The smell of the ocean and the rough waters made Mistress Mattie and Savannah seasick. Hattie Mae kept guard over them as they slept.

The ship's crew seemed to have gotten the message that no foul play would be going down on Pierre Cordova's watch.

One day when Mistress Mattie and Hattie Mae walked the deck, a crewmember was reading a map. He asked Hattie Mae to hold it up for him.

He said, "Have you ever seen that map before?"

Hattie Mae had never seen a map before, so she replied, "No."

The crewmember replied, "Well, it wouldn't matter, you couldn't read it anyway."

Hattie Mae smiled; she thought, *On the contrary, I can read it. That was the only good thing Master Fo'Rae did for her. Master Fo'Rae taught some of his slaves how to read and write in French. Master Fo'Rae often sent his slaves to do business on his behalf with other French people. However, he always told the slaves to play dumb when dealing with the Americans. He always said Americans weren't to be trusted.*

Hattie Mae hated Master Fo'Rae; everything about him was evil. From the day she came to his plantation to the day she chopped him to pieces, she hated him. Hattie Mae learned very quickly how to handle Master Fo'Rae though. Hattie Mae learned that if she satisfied Master Fo'Rae, he would allow her to do certain things, such as practicing her Voodoo religion, wearing her traditional hairstyles of cornrows, and, when she was alone read all the books in his library.

Master Fo'Rae also allowed her to bathe in the finest of soaps and creams that Hattie Mae made from the herbs and flowers he allowed her to grow.

Master Fo'Rae was so obsessed with Hattie Mae's body and skin that he built a bathhouse just for her.

Hattie Mae frowned when she thought about Master Fo'Rae; his very touch made her sick to her stomach. Hattie Mae reminded herself that what she had done with Master Fo'Rae, she did to survive. Fighting him just left her bruised and beat up. Making peace with what her life had become eased the pain. Plus Hattie Mae had learned all Master Fo'Rae's weaknesses, so when he came to call on her for her services, the entire encounter only lasted a short while. The Master would get so worked up just looking at Hattie Mae, sometimes it was over before it began.

The crewmember pointed to the map and said, "We're somewhere here. We need to go there." Then he pointed to a spot on the map that said St. Lucia.

The crewmember looked a little worried and said, "Let's pray we make it there safe."

As Hattie Mae was helping Mistress Mattie back to her quarters, they ran into the white man that had brought Hattie Mae to America. He looked at Hattie Mae with a devilish grin and said, "I don't think I've ever forgotten what you were doing when I found you in the jungle." Then he looked at Mistress Mattie and said, "You should ask your nigger," and then he stopped and grinned. He continued, "Oh my, forgive my poor manners; I meant to say your servant about what she was doing with her gentlemen friend when I found her." He smiled and said, "It's a fascinating story."

Mistress Mattie was too ill to reply. She just said, "Yes, maybe one day I will. For now, you just stay away from us and mind your business."

Mistress Mattie was having a hard time getting around, Her stomach was getting bigger, and, according to Hattie Mae's predictions, those babies were coming soon.

After Hattie Mae had washed up Mistress Mattie and Savannah whose stomach was also getting bigger, Hattie Mae poured water into a small tub.

She stripped down naked and stood in front of the mirror. She observed herself. Hattie Mae was tall and dark. She rubbed her face with the washcloth and worked her way down her body. She stopped when she got to her breast, she felt somebody watching her. Hattie Mae looked in the mirror to see Mistress Mattie standing behind her.

Mistress Mattie just starred at Hattie Mae.

Hattie Mae pulled her dress off the table and covered her body.

She said, "Mistress Mattie, can I help you with something?

Mistress Mattie calmly replied, "No, please don't cover up. I've always wondered what you looked like under your clothes. I've always wanted to know what you had that I didn't have. Please don't deprive me of this view."

Mistress Mattie slowly reached for the dress Hattie Mae was using to cover her body. She uncovered Hattie Mae's naked body.

Hattie Mae was at a loss for words. She remembered that she was still a slave and Mistress Mattie could have her whipped at any moment. So Hattie Mae stood there naked.

Mistress Mattie stood there unapologetically studying Hattie Mae's body. Mistress Mattie lingered in closer to Hattie Mae; she gently placed her hands around Hattie Mae's waist, then she ran her hand along the curve of Hattie Mae's hip.

Mistress Mattie seemed puzzled. She said, "I've never seen anything quite like it. Your body looks like it was hand carved and your skin is soft as cotton. Looks like it's been drenched in rich dark chocolate."

Mistress Mattie tilted her head to the side as if she couldn't believe what she was seeing.

Mistress Mattie took a deep breath and said, "Well, I guess now I see why Old Master Fo'Rae was obsessed with you."

Mistress Mattie held her stomach and walked back to her bed. She said, "I'd kill for those curves." Then she smiled and looked at Savannah who was witnessing the entire conversation.

Mistress Mattie winked her eye at Savannah and said jokingly, "Well, Hattie Mae are you just going to stand there naked all night or are you going to finish your wash up. Nobody wants to see you naked."

Then Mistress Mattie said, "Hattie Mae be a dear and reach in my grooming kit, grab my beeswax and do yourself a favor darling. Your body might be a work of art, however, your playground area is somewhat of a mess."

Then Mistress Mattie pointed to Hattie Mae's pubic hair.

Mistress Mattie smiled and said, "Looks like a jungle down there, no pun intended. Please wax it all off. No self-respecting lady would be caught dead with all that hair. And I can't bear to look at it for another second."

Savannah and Hattie Mae both laughed.

After Hattie Mae was finished bathing and dressing herself, she sat on the edge of the bed and braided her hair.

Mistress Mattie rubbed her stomach and looked over at Savannah. She took a deep breath and said, "My, we sure are in a predicament, aren't we? You're pregnant with your own father's child, and I'm pregnant with twins by a slave."

Mistress Mattie put her hand on Hattie Mae's hand. She said, "Master Fo'Rae was a horrid person. You two aren't the only ones who suffered at his hands. Remember I'm his cousin. I too came to live with him when I was barely a woman. I was part of a package deal."

Mistress Mattie shook her head with disgust; she said, "My daddy was his uncle. This behavior surely is uncivilized."

All three ladies just laid in the bed trying to forget their memories of

Master Fo'Rae.

Mistress Mattie told Hattie Mae that she was the only friend she'd ever had. Mistress Mattie told them that things were going to be different when they arrived in Saint Lucia. She said Savannah and Hattie Mae would no longer be slaves. She said that they were free to do whatever they wanted.

Then Mistress Mattie looked at Hattie Mae and said, "Promise me that you will always take care of my babies. Never leave them."

Hattie Mae replied, "I promise!"

Mistress Mattie looked out of the tiny window over the ocean.

She said, "I wonder what's become of Robert Lee?"

Hattie Mae and Savannah just ignored that comment; neither one of them wanted to bring up that situation. Mistress Mattie was in love with Robert Lee, who happened to be Hattie Mae's husband.

Mistress Mattie looked at Hattie Mae. She said, "Hattie Mae, please forgive me."

Hattie Mae replied, "There's nothing to forgive Mistress Mattie. Things happen in life which we have no control of. We just make the best of things. That's all."

Mistress Mattie responded, "And what are you making the best of Hattie Mae?"

Hattie Mae knew that Mistress Mattie wanted her to admit that she was mad because she had sex with Robert Lee. However, Hattie Mae didn't see it as something Robert Lee did willingly. Hell, Mistress Mattie had ordered him to do it! Although Mistress Mattie was acting like Robert Lee and she had some torrid love affair. Hattie Mae knew Robert Lee was just following orders. Besides, Hattie Mae had to admit she wasn't that upset. She was a little mad because Robert Lee never told her.

Mistress Mattie said, "Hattie Mae, I know Robert Lee was the love of your life. Say something."

Hattie Mae replied, "No ma'am, he wasn't the love of my life. He was a man that I grew to love after Master Fo'Rae forced me to be with him."

The room was silent. Savannah's eyes glanced over at Hattie Mae. It was like what Hattie Mae said surprised her as much as it did Mistress Mattie, who seemed to be gathering her thoughts together.

Mistress Mattie said, "Come again Hattie Mae. Did you say Robert Lee wasn't the love of your life?"

Hattie Mae replied, "Yes I did, and no he wasn't."

Mistress Mattie responded, "Well, I be damned."

Chapter Two:
Black and White

The trip from Louisiana to the Caribbean usually was only six weeks. However, with the winds, storms, and heaviness of the ship, it was taking a little longer.

They were in their tenth week and one of the crewmembers had died from starvation and lack of fresh water. The wind had blown the ship off course, so they didn't really know where they might end up.

Hattie Mae knew what she said about Robert Lee not being the love of her life was lingering in Mistress Mattie's mind. Hattie Mae always hated that about Mistress Mattie; she was a nosey, inquisitive heffa. Hattie Mae heard Mistress Mattie's voice calling her name. From the sound of it, Mistress Mattie was in a lot of pain.

Hattie Mae hurried over to Mistress Mattie's side. Hattie Mae said, "Mistress Mattie what seems to be the problem?"

Mistress Mattie pulled back the covers to reveal a pool of blood. Hattie Mae kept herself calm. She said, "Well, Mistress Mattie looks like those two little devils is about ready to makes they's way into this here world. Ain't nothing's you or I cans do to hold them back."

Mistress Mattie grabbed Hattie Mae's hand and said, "Hattie Mae, my Lord what are we going to do?"

Hattie Mae quietly locked the cabin door. She made a fire to boil seawater.

Hattie Mae then pulled out some clean sheets, gathered a razor, and then set next to Mistress Mattie.

Hattie Mae said calmly, "What we's gone do is bring these here little precious babies safely into this world."

Hattie Mae looked at Mistress Mattie and handed her a wooden serving spoon. Hattie Mae said, "Now when those pains come, you bite down on this spoon. Try to bear the pain as long as you can. The less screaming and carrying on, the less stress on the babies."

Mistress Mattie's eyes were big as bow dollars. Hattie Mae knew that Mistress Mattie was scared. Mistress Mattie had never had a baby before. She didn't know what to expect. Hattie Mae on the other hand had given birth to, two babies, Savannah and a baby boy, who Master Fo'Rae snatched right out of her arms and sold. Hattie Mae never even got a chance to kiss him and tell him she loved him.

After Master Fo'Rae took Hattie Mae's son, Master Fo'Rae disappeared for months. After his return, He was even more mean and hateful.

While Master Fo'Rae was away selling Hattie Mae's son, Hattie Mae fixed her body to assure she never brought another child into this horrible world. Never again would she birth another one of Master Fo'Rae's offspring.

Hattie Mae wiped a tear from her eyes. She focused back on Mistress Mattie. Mistress Mattie said, "Hattie Mae are you thinking about Claude, your baby son again?"

Hattie Mae gave a little smile and replied, "No ma'am, I leaves the past in the past. I'm focused on these babies right here."

Mistress Mattie doubled over in pain. She bit down on the spoon. Hattie Mae checked Mistress Mattie and said, "It won't be long."

Savanna sat next to Mistress Mattie and held her hand. She said, "Don't fret non Mistress Mattie, mama done delivered plenty plantation babies."

Hattie Mae knew Mistress Mattie was about to fall apart. Hattie Mae decided to tell Mistress Mattie the story behind the love of her life.

She began, "When I was a young girl back in Sierra Leone, my Grandmother taught me everything she knew about medicine, spells, and healing potions. Every day my grandmother taught me a new lesson."
Hattie Mae smiled and said, "In between my lessons, I would watch the warriors practice and dance our tribal dances. I was taken with one who they called Bactou. Oh my, he was a handsome warrior. Bactou was strong as a lion and fast as the great cheetah."

Hattie Mae stopped to compose herself. The thought of Bactou frazzled Hattie Mae.

Hattie Mae said, "I was just a young girl and he was just a few years older than me, but the tribe considered him a man."

Mistress Mattie was so enthralled with Hattie Mae's story she forgot she was in labor.

Mistress Mattie's eyes widened and she said, "Hattie Mae, was that your lover you were in the jungle with when they caught you?"

Hattie Mae replied, "Not the jungle, the bush."

Hattie Mae was a little irritated with Mistress Mattie and the rest of the white folks referring to Africa as some jungle savage place. However she had to stay focused on the babies that were getting ready to pop out of Mistress Mattie any second.

Hattie Mae continued with her story; she said, "As a rite of passage in Africa, men get the foreskin removed from their manly area. Here in the states y'all call it circumcision."

Hattie Mae stopped talking when Mistress Mattie screamed out a bloodcurdling scream. The contractions were getting stronger and coming about five minutes apart. After Mistress Mattie composed herself, she said, "Well, go on with your story Hattie Mae, these babies are gonna be here soon. Oh my and I do so want to hear the ending of your tale."

Hattie Mae said, "All the tribal boys of age would line up naked side by side. An elder would cut the foreskin from each young man's penis with the same knife. After that, they would be warriors. It's a great honor."

Mistress Mattie replied, "Oh my! Without anything to numb the pain and they used the same knife. Lord above how barbaric."

Hattie Mae frowned her face and continued the story.

Hattie Mae said, "Bactou was a true champion. He never flinched, he just stood there."

Mistress Mattie replied, "Wait, how do you know?"
Hattie Mae smiled and said, "Cause I's hiding in the bushes watching."

Mistress Mattie laughed and said, "Why Hattie Mae you little rascal."
Mistress Mattie waved her hands in the air and said, "Finish the story."

Hattie Mae told Mistress Mattie about a week had gone by and Bactou started feeling bad. He had developed an infection from the chief using the same knife. Hattie Mae said Bactou was in an extreme amount of pain and she felt bad for him.

Hattie Mae said, "So I stole some rubbing creams from my grandmother's medicine bag and gave them to Bactou. Bactou insisted I apply it because he was too weak. So every morning, I'd meet him in the bush to apply the medicine. That's what I was doing when the white men catches us."

Mistress Mattie replied, "Catches us, Hattie Mae, you mean to tell me Bactou is in the United States?"

Hattie Mae responded, "No Mistress Mattie. He never made it to The United States. Bactou overpowered the white captors and jumped ship. I's reckoned he'd died or got ate up by a shark. Either way, he ain't never stepped one foot on American soil."

Mistress Mattie grabbed her stomach and screamed out, "Hattie Mae get these things out of me!"

Hattie Mae checked the babies to see a head coming. Hattie Mae told Mistress Mattie to bite down on the spoon and push.

Mistress Mattie gave two pushes and pushed out a little girl. Hattie Mae handed the little girl to Savannah, who cleaned the little girl up and wrapped her in a blanket.

Savannah laid the baby girl in Mistress Mattie's arms. Mistress Mattie was just staring at the baby.

Mistress Mattie said, "She's a dark one, isn't she? I've seen plenty plantation mulattos, and she's by far darker than them all."

Hattie Mae replied, "Well, Robert Lee is pure blooded African. Nevertheless, she is your baby from your body."

Mistress Mattie seemed to be realizing that she was really having black negro babies.

Mistress Mattie handed the baby to Savannah.

Mistress Mattie turned her head from the baby girl. She said, "I can't bear to look at it."

Then all of a sudden Mistress Mattie yelled out, "Lord the other one is coming!"

Hattie Mae told Mistress Mattie to push and sure enough the other one popped out. Hattie Mae hesitated to hand the baby to Savannah this time.

Hattie Mae was just staring at the baby.

Hattie Mae quietly whispered, "It's a boy."

Hattie Mae handed the baby to Savannah, who had the same disbelieving look as Hattie Mae. Hattie Mae reached her hand inside Mistress Mattie and pulled out the placenta.

Hattie Mae took the placenta, wrapped it in a towel and placed it in a large bowl.

Savannah cleaned up the baby boy and wrapped him in a blanket. Savannah handed the baby to Mistress Mattie.

Hattie Mae and Savannah stood there waiting for Mistress Mattie's reaction.

Mistress Mattie refused to hold the baby boy.

She just said, "Please remove them from my sight Hattie Mae. I can't stand to look at them. I've waited years to have a baby and I've had two black ones on this very day. The Lord is just cruel."

Hattie Mae took the baby boy from Savannah.

Hattie Mae said, "Ma'am I think you gonna be wanting to see this here baby."

Hattie Mae set the baby boy on Mistress Mattie's bosom.

Mistress Mattie was about to fuss when she caught a glimpse of blond straight hair. Mistress Mattie held the baby boy up. She removed the blankets and stared at him. Mistress Mattie placed her hand next to the child's cheek to compare their skin color. Then Mistress Mattie bent the back of the baby boy's ears. She was amazed.

Mistress Mattie looked up at Hattie Mae and said, "Why Hattie Mae this baby is as white as pure driven snow?"
Hattie Mae replied, "Yes he is."

Mistress Mattie cried tears of joy. She held on to the white baby boy for dear life. Hattie Mae tried to give her the black baby girl, who at this point was screaming to the top of her lungs. Hattie Mae's guess was the little baby was hungry.

Hattie Mae looked at Mistress Mattie rubbing the baby boy's blonde hair.

Hattie Mae said, "Ma'am I believes this baby girl is hungry and wants to nurse."

Mistress Mattie refused to nurse the baby girl. Mistress Mattie said Savannah could nurse her, since she was carrying a baby her breast were full of milk. Mistress Mattie said that any milk in her breast was reserved for the white baby boy. Hattie Mae enlightened Mistress Mattie that Savannah's milk won't come until after she had the baby.

Hattie Mae was getting a little upset. Then she remembered her slave status. Hattie Mae simply told Mistress Mattie that if she didn't nurse the baby, she was going to die.

As the night wore on, Mistress Mattie rested with the white baby boy by her side at all times. Mistress Mattie never even looked over at the black baby girl who was sleeping in Hattie Mae's arms. Hattie Mae smiled at the baby girl who looked just like Hattie Mae's husband, Robert Lee.

Hattie Mae said, "Rest little baby girl. Hattie Mae is gone look out for you cause yo white Mammy sho ain't."

Hattie Mae took the baby boy while Mistress Mattie was asleep. Hattie Mae couldn't believe how white he was and with blonde hair. He looked just like Mistress Mattie. In all Hattie Mae's years on the plantation, she had delivered lots of The Master's mulatto kids, and none of them had come out this white.

Hattie Mae knew Mistress Mattie had every intention of keeping this white baby boy.

Over the next few days, Hattie Mae waited for the little boy to darken up; however, no such thing happened. He was just as white with curly blonde hair, blue eyes, and pink lips.

Savannah had her baby girl. Savannah's baby looked like any other plantation mixed breed baby.

Poor Savannah was nursing her baby and Mistress Mattie's baby girl. Mistress Mattie was still refusing to have anything to do with the baby girl and acting like the little white baby boy was the best thing since baked bread.

Hattie Mae was up on the top deck when she felt the storm coming. She heard the captain say they were way off course and if they didn't find land soon, they were all going to starve to death or die of dehydration. Pierre Cordova gathered up the last of the supplies he had hidden below. Pierre Cordova told Hattie Mae that the storm was going to be bad. He said all the ladies and those babies better buckle down and find something steady to hold on to. He also said that the supplies were only going to last a day or two.

Hattie Mae saw the white man who took her from her home staring at her. She walked past him, never making eye contact or acknowledging him.

He said, "A few more nights on this ship and I might have to call on you. Let's see if you can give my penis the same treatment you gave your jungle mate."

Hattie Mae replied under her breath, "You would have to add nine more inches to your penis. Surely I wouldn't be able to find such a small penis."

The white man raised up and said, "What did you say to me jungle bunny?"

Just then Mistress Mattie and Pierre Cordova appeared. Mistress Mattie ordered Hattie Mae to tend to those screaming babies.

When the storm started, the ship rocked back and forth. The wind was blowing it like a tiny rag doll. Hattie Mae heard Pierre Cordova calling her name. When she got to the top of the ship, she saw him and some crewmembers frantically trying to get control of the ship.

Pierre Cordova said two of the men had fallen overboard. He said it was just three men left, him, the white man that took Hattie Mae from Africa, and the crewmember that was eyeing Savanna.

All the rain, wind, and seawater were getting stronger. Hattie Mae heard yelling and made her way to the back of the ship. She saw the man that had taken her from Africa holding onto the side of the ship for dear life. The wind had tossed him over, and he had hit his head on the side of the ship. The man said, "Help me please."

Hattie Mae looked around to see who he was talking to because she knew he wasn't talking to her.

Hattie Mae bent down close to him she said, "Well, look-a here. I do believes you in a terrible situation."

The white man replied, "I'll have you hung for speaking to me like that."

Hattie Mae stood up. She grinned and very sarcastically said, "In what lifetime?" She kicked him in the face and said, "You gonna die tonight, but don't fret maybe we'll both get our prayers answered; I pray you come back as a black man. That way you can get treated with the same disrespect you treat us with. Your women can be raped and beaten. You can work from sun up to sun down, and your kids can be sold off to the next plantation."

Hattie Mae took a pole and held it up over him. She could tell he was losing his grip.

Hattie Mae said, "Oh, but don't worry, you'll get your prayers answered too. As a black man you'll have a bigger penis."

Then she took the pole and whacked him across the head. The white man fell into the ocean where Hattie Mae saw something grab him and took him under water.

The storm was strong it almost tore the ship apart. Hattie Mae was scared, but she knew she had to be strong. Hattie Mae ran down below to get a stone out of her black bag. She ran back to the bowel of the ship. She held her stone up to the sky.

Hattie Mae said, "I'm Fatama, from the house of Daramy, from the tribe of Mandinka, You will allow me passage. I will not be stopped."

Hattie Mae started ranting in her native tongue.
Pierre Cordova and the crewmember who was eyeing Savannah just stood there watching.

All of a sudden a burst of light came from the sky, the ocean stood still, and the storm calmed down. A dolphin swam in front of the ship. He seemed to be trying to get Hattie Mae's attention.

Hattie Mae stood still for a second. Then she followed the dolphin's movement with her eyes. She never moved her head. She pointed in the direction of the dolphin that seemed to be leading her. Hattie Mae told Pierre Cordova to follow the dolphin that he knew the way to where they needed to go.

Pierre Cordova and the last white crewmember just followed her direction.

The storm settled down, and they seemed to be sailing smoothly. However, there was no more food or water, and none of them had eaten or had water. Hattie Mae knew they had to eat especially Mistress Mattie and Savannah. They both had to nurse those babies.

Hattie Mae retrieved a bucket she had hidden. It was filled up to the top with ocean water. She stuck her hand in and took out a rag. She unwrapped the rag and looked at Mistress Mattie and Savannah's placenta she had kept.

She kept it in the salt water to keep it fresh. Hattie Mae boiled it up and fed it to Mistress Mattie and Savannah along with some breast milk she made Savannah and Mistress Mattie squeeze in a cup. Hell she figured if it was keeping those babies alive it would keep them alive too. Hattie Mae gave a small piece to Pierre Cordova and the last white crewmember. Hattie Mae told them it was squid that washed up on the boat during the storm.

All the food was gone, and there was no water left. Mistress Mattie was still holding on tight to that white baby boy and praying to her white Jesus. Mistress Mattie still hadn't held her little black baby girl yet.

Savannah was still nursing both baby girls and praying to the spirits to save them. Hattie Mae could tell Savannah didn't really want to be bothered with her baby girl either. Savannah's daughter was a painful reminder of how horrible Master Fo'Rae had been to her.

Hattie Mae knew if they survived this voyage, it was going to be up to her to take care of both those baby girls.

Mistress Mattie had named the little white baby boy Charles Fo'Rae.

However, she never gave the black baby girl a name. As a matter of fact, Savannah hadn't named her baby girl either. So Hattie Mae just called them baby girl one and baby girl two.

Pierre Cordova, on the other hand, had taken a liking to both baby girls. He helped out as best he could. Hattie Mae knew it was Pierre Cordova's interest in the baby girls that kept Savannah in good spirits.

Pierre Cordova told Savannah that he would proudly be both baby girls father. Mistress Mattie didn't seem to have a problem with that at all.

However, she did insist that both baby girls' last names be Fo'Rae.

Mistress Mattie said that both girls were technically still property of House of Fo'Rae.

Hattie Mae frowned her face. She thought to herself, "White folks always so quick to claim their property."

Mistress Mattie looked over at Hattie Mae and said, "Hattie Mae it's safer for them to have the Fo'Rae last name. We don't know what to expect in this new place. Even though there's no slavery in St Lucia, we don't know the treatment of your people. The Fo'Rae name is very powerful in St. Lucia."

Hattie Mae had to agree; even though Hattie Mae had planned to disappear with Savannah and those babies as soon as they reached land.

Hattie Mae's plan was to disappear and never to be seen again.

Although Mistress Mattie claimed to be Hattie Mae's friend, Hattie Mae understood that she was legally Mistress Mattie's property.

Hattie Mae heard Pierre Cordova yelling land. Hattie Mae gave thanks to the ancestors and started preparing to depart the ship. Hattie Mae bundled the babies up and got Mistress Mattie and Savannah together.

When they arrived on the docks, to Hattie Mae's surprise, she saw black sailors there to unload them and help them off the ship.

One of the men who was taken records of the ship and cargo said, "I see two white adults, three negro adults, two negro babies and one white baby boy.

Is this correct?"

Mistress Mattie looked at Hattie Mae in delight. Mistress Mattie replied, "That would be correct."
Mistress Mattie held the white baby boy up and said, "This is my son Charles Fo'Rae."

The man responded, "Well, welcome to St. Lucia Baby Charles. Enjoy your stay."

When they arrived at the Plantation on St. Lucia, Hattie Mae couldn't believe her eyes. The plantation was even bigger than the one in the states. Hattie Mae wasn't saying a word, she was just taking in everything.

Hattie Mae couldn't believe her eyes. She hadn't seen free African people since she was stolen from Africa. A sense of relief came over Hattie Mae. She unpacked her bags and settled the babies down. She looked out of the window over the ocean. St. Lucia was a beautiful place, almost as beautiful as Hattie Mae's homeland Africa.

Over the weeks, Hattie Mae and the ladies were settling down. Hattie Mae took care of the two baby girls, and Mistress Mattie never let baby Charles out of her sight. Baby Charles seemed to be getting whiter. Over the months, his appearance never changed. He kept the blonde hair and blue eyes.

The baby girls never received names. Everybody just referred to them as baby girl one and baby girl two. Hattie Mae was once again enjoying her freedom to come and go as she pleased. Hattie Mae had made friends with the locals. She even met some Africans that practiced the Voodoo religion like she did.

In St. Lucia, Hattie Mae was free to do what she wanted with her time. However, there was still a great deal of hatred for Negros, even though the negros outnumbered any other race. The white man still had the power.

Mistress Mattie kept her word and Hattie Mae and Savannah were free to go their own way. Savannah married Pierre Cordova and stayed on the plantation with Mistress Mattie. Hattie Mae also stayed on the plantation to help out, only now Mistress Mattie paid Hattie Mae an honest wage. Hattie Mae also kept both the baby girls.

Hattie Mae was happy for Savannah when she married Pierre Cordova, but she brewed up a potion and secretly slipped it to Savannah in her tea. After Savannah drank the potion, Hattie Mae stole some of Savannah and Pierre Cordova's personal property. Hattie Mae and her newly found Voodoo practicing friends secretly performed a spell on Savannah to assure she wouldn't bare any male offspring.

Although Pierre Cordova was a great man, Savannah was a Fo'Rae by blood. Hattie Mae didn't want any more males born into Master Fo'Rae bloodline. She couldn't take the chance that they would grow up and have a thirst for young girls as he did.

In the first year of Savannah and Pierre Cordova's marriage, Savannah gave birth to a baby girl. Hattie Mae laughed to herself when Pierre Cordova told Savannah that they would try again for a son. Hattie Mae knew that was never going to happen.

Pierre Cordova got a job on the docks.

Mistress Mattie spent months searching for Robert Lee, without any luck. Hattie Mae had been in St. Lucia long enough to know that if a negro didn't want to be found, he could make that happen. Hattie Mae never uttered Robert Lee's name.

Things in St. Lucia weren't the greatest, but it was one hundred percent better than being enslaved in the United States.

In 1845, five years after they had been in St. Lucia, Hattie Mae arrived home one day to see bags in the entrance of the house. Hattie Mae read the tags on the bags, which read; "Property of Mr. Fo'Rae."

"Damn," Hattie Mae said out loud.

Hattie Mae eased to the door in the foyer. She heard Master Fo'Rae's brother speaking with Mistress Mattie about how she had no right to take Pierre Cordova. He appeared to be very upset.

Master Fo'Rae's brother said, "I had to pay two thousand dollars to Pierre Cordova's owner for compensation for lost property."

Mistress Mattie responded, "Well, I do apologize and I will make sure you get your money back. My plantation here in St. Lucia has done well over the years. As well as my plantation in Louisiana."

Hattie Mae smirked a little. She knew that Mistress Mattie was reminding Master Fo'Rae's brother that she was the legal owner of all the property her late husband left behind.

Master Fo'Rae said a few curse words in French.

He was interrupted by Young Charles Fo'Rae who was now five and still white as snow.

Master Fo'Rae's brother looked at Young Charles and said, "And who might you be young fellow?"

Charles replied, "I'm Charles Fo'Rae." Then he pointed to Mistress Mattie and said, "She's my mother."

Master Fo'Rae's brother was a bit surprised. He responded, "Is that so?"

Mistress Mattie called Charles to come to sit in her lap. She told Master Fo'Rae that she only learned she was pregnant when she was aboard the ship. She said that it was a surprise to her.

Master Fo'Rae asked Mistress Mattie why she'd never mentioned it in her letters.

Mistress Mattie just said it slipped her mind.

As they sat in the living room talking, Hattie Mae went through Master Fo'Rae's brother's bag. She saw court papers ordering Mistress Mattie to return Hattie Mae and Savannah to the United States as property of the Fo'Rae estate. Although the plantations were left to Mistress Mattie because she was Master Fo'Rae's wife at the time of his death, the slaves were purchased with his shipping company's money, which Master Fo'Rae's brother shared half the stocks. So according to United States law, legally Hattie Mae and Savannah belong to Master Fo'Rae's brother.

Master Fo'Rae's brother and Mistress Mattie spoke for a while about family business and how well the cotton fields, sugarcane, and tobacco harvest were going. Master Fo'Rae's brother said that the slaves were reproducing at a pleasantly delightful rate. He said Mistress Mattie had tripled her slaves in the last five years. He also informed Mistress Mattie that he would no longer be able to run her plantation in the states. Either she was going to have to find someone else to run it or sell it.

Master Fo'Rae's brother lit his cigar and took a puff. He blew the smoke out slowly, and then crossed his legs.

He said calmly, "Speaking of slaves. Where is Hattie Mae and Her daughter Savannah? And if I'm not mistaken, weren't they both with child when they boarded the ship?"

Mistress Mattie coughed to clear her throat.

Mistress Mattie hesitantly replied, "I regret to inform you my dear brother in law, but Hattie Mae and her daughter Savannah lost both the babies and as soon as we docked at this very shore. Hattie Mae and Savannah ran away never to be seen again. I do declare it was unfortunate loss for the estate and a blessing at the same time."

Hattie Mae stood in the hallway spying and shaking her head in disbelief.

Hattie Mae thought to herself, *As much as white folks lie and tell stories, Mistress Mattie was terrible at it.*

Master Fo'Rae's brother took another puff of his cigar. He looked at Mistress Mattie and said, "Ran away? You don't say? Well, yes that is unfortunate. However, I received no news of this."

Mistress Mattie had turned five shades of red and her leg started to tremble slightly. She replied, "Oh my, the postal service here is something terrible. It always perplexed me why you never responded to my letter informing you of the situation."

Master Fo'Rae's brother said, "Yes the letter must have gotten lost in the mail. Yet you say it was a blessing also, how so?"

Mistress Mattie replied, "Hattie Mae was a strange one. Always lurking around chatting in a strange language. Collecting chicken bones and pigs blood."

Mistress Mattie stood up and held her heart like the very thought of Hattie Mae annoyed her.

Mistress Mattie turned around sharply and said, "I blame my husband, your brother. He always was so lenient with Hattie Mae. Allowing her to practice her Voodoo, it was nothing but witchcraft, of the devil I tell you. I'm glad she ran away."

Master Fo'Rae's brother cracked a half smile. He said, "You might be correct about that. The very mention of her name back at the plantation sparks frenzy in the slaves. Hell a couple of them begged me not to bring her back."

He looked at Mistress Mattie and said, "Mysteriously the day y'all left, quite a few of the mulattos died. Some folks say they killed theselves, however rumor in the slave quarters was that Hattie Mae killed them all with some strange potion she tricked them into drinking.

You wouldn't happen to know anything about that now would you?"

Mistress Mattie simply replied, "Now how would I know anything about the slaves and their dealings."

Master Fo"Rae's brother smirked and replied, "Right, how could you? Nevertheless somebody buried them under the mansion, imagine that!"

Master Fo'Rae's brother put out his cigar and said,

"Well, Mistress Mattie, the trip here has taken a toll on these old knees."

He bent down and rubbed his knees and legs. Then he said, "If you don't mind Mistress Mattie, I think I'll call it a night."

Mistress Mattie had one of the housekeepers escort Master Fo'Rae's brother to his quarters for the night. When the coast was clear, Mistress Mattie frantically told Hattie Mae to come out of the foyer hiding.

Mistress Mattie said, "Hattie Mae I know you been sneaking about and heard everything! Now I need you, Savannah, and those babies to stay out of sight until he leaves."

Mistress Mattie seemed to be all bent out of shape over her brother in law's presence. One of the housekeepers entered the sitting room to retrieve Mistress Mattie's son, Young Charles. The housekeeper said that Master Fo'Rae's brother wanted to say goodnight to him before he fell off to sleep. Mistress Mattie told the housekeeper she would take him to her brother in law's room.

However, the housekeeper replied, "Ma'am, he specifically said for me to bring the child alone."

Mistress Mattie responded, "Well, then run along, but don't keep him up too long. It's an exhausting trip from the states."

Hattie Mae and Mistress Mattie stood there speculating what the Master's brother might know. Mistress Mattie kept assuring herself that her son

Charles was the spitting image of her and that there were no traces of Negro blood in him. Hattie Mae, on the other hand, was formulating a plan of escape in her mind. It was no way she was going back to the United States to resume her position as slave slash concubine.

No Ma'am, Hattie Mae thought to herself, as she headed towards the quarters where Savannah, Pierre Cordova, and the children were hiding. Hattie Mae told them to be ready to go at a moment's notice.

Hattie Mae wandered off to her cabin where she practiced her Voodoo. Mistress Mattie had given her the old slave quarters to mix up her potions and whatnots. Mistress Mattie said as long as Hattie Mae kept her Voodoo ways out of the mansion and away from her son Charles, she didn't care what she did down there.

When Hattie Mae entered the shed, she heard a noise. She walked in to find Master Fo'Rae's brother waiting on her. Hattie Mae froze in her tracks for a second. Then she scanned the cabin to find something to use as a weapon. Hattie Mae picked up an old broom handle.

Master Fo'Rae's brother smiled and said, "Oh my, the runaway slave has returned to claim her belongings. I see the spirit of Nat Turner still lives on inside you."

He smiled and said, "Now Hattie Mae, have I ever given you any reason to fear me? Here I am coming to pay you a friendly visit and you acting like I'm here to attack you."

Hattie Mae looked the Master's brother in the eyes and said, "I ain't never going back alive. The only way you gone get me back on the ship is in a pine box."

Master Fo'Rae's brother slapped his knee and laughed.

He replied, "You're a feisty little Negro. Relax Hattie Mae; I ain't here to take you back. Hell nobody wants you and your Voodoo anyway. The name Hattie Mae spooks the slaves. How are they supposed to get any work done, when they too scared you gone put a spell on them?"

Master Fo'Rae's brother picked up one of Hattie Mae's voodoo dolls.

He said, "I don't believe in all this Voodoo mumbo jumbo. It's nonsense. Nevertheless, the slaves believe it. So you're not welcome at the plantation in Louisiana."

Hattie Mae was confused, she said, "Well, if you ain't here to take me back, whatcha here for?"

Master Fo'Rae's brother smiled and said, "Now that you've asked, I'll tell you. I was here to check on Mistress Mattie, hell she is the owner of the plantations I manage and my cousin. Not to mention the fact that she was married to my brother."

He smiled at Hattie Mae and said, "I know, a trifling mess right, Kins-folks marrying each other and having babies. It just ain't natural. However, it is what it is. Rest assured, Hattie Mae, I'm nothing like my brother. I have no intentions on humiliating you by forcing myself on you, and I most definitely don't desire young girls. I'm an honest Christian man."

Hattie Mae looked at him. She knew he was up to something. She could see it in his eyes, and his spirit spoke to her.

Hattie Mae said, "You here for that boy! You must be crazy if you thinking for one second Mistress Mattie gone allow you to carry that boy off to The States. Charles is her pride and joy. She would die fighting you for him."

Master Fo'Rae lit up some candles and took out a book. He said, "Hattie Mae, you know what this is? It's a journal of all my brother's thoughts and activities that went on at the plantation in Louisiana. He kept detailed records of all the slave births and deaths. He even made a special column for all the mulatto children he created with the slaves. Funny thing is all those mulatto children died the night you left. All except, well your daughter Savannah and your son Claude."

Hattie Mae got upset by the mention of her son Claude's name. She said, "My son Claude is dead to me, Master sold him off a long time ago."

Master Fo'Rae's brother replied, "You say sold? My dear Hattie Mae, you're sadly mistaken. My brother never sold a slave named Claude. However, I do have a record of him sending a baby boy mulatto named Claude to New York City to be taken care of by some runaway slaves. I estimate Claude to be about eighteen years of age now."

Hattie Mae felt faint; she reached for a chair. She said, "Lies, why would Master send Claude to New York City?"

Master Fo'Rae's brother replied passionately, "To preserve his family name!"

Hattie Mae didn't respond.

Master Fo'Rae's brother said, "I see my answer puzzles you, Hattie Mae. So let me enlighten you. The family name Fo'Rae goes back generations, all the way from France. Family wealth and businesses are passed on to keep the wealth in the families. The last name Fo'Rae is carried on by the male child."

He stopped, seemed as if he was getting sad. He said, "I myself have no offspring. My better half and I can't seem to reproduce."

He opened the journals. He smiled and said, "My brother wrote this all in French, he had such pride in being a nobleman from France."

Hattie Mae rolled her eyes and frowned. She said, "A nobleman he was not! He was an evil demon."

Master Fo'Rae's brother continued on with his conversation. He said, "Read this to me Hattie Mae and don't pretend like you can't read. I know my brother taught you how to read and write in English and French."

Hattie Mae turned the journal around and began to read off a list of family names.

Master Fo'Rae's brother said, "Do you see anything odd about those names?"

Hattie Mae replied," Yes, there are all women's names."

Master Fo'Rae's brother responded, "Yes, you're correct. Not one male offspring to carry on the Fo'Rae name."

Hattie Mae stood up and said, "Until now, Young Charles Fo'Rae. You intend on taking him for yourself to carry on your name."

Master Fo'Rae had a devilish look on his face. He replied, "Yes, I do, Hattie Mae; that is, if the true colors don't start showing."

He winked his eye at Hattie Mae and said, "Get my meaning?"

Master Fo'Rae's brother looked at Hattie Mae and said, "You know Hattie Mae, the slaves talk and they tell a very interesting tale about your husband Robert Lee, Mistress Mattie, and a little cabin down on the bayou. And in my reading through my brother's journals, I came across something else interesting. He wrote that he hadn't had sexual relations with his wife Mistress Mattie in years. So I found it a little odd that she has a five-year-old son. How about you, Hattie Mae, do you find that odd?"

Hattie Mae replied, "Whatcha talkin, it all sounds like lies and foolishness to me. Anyway, if you say that Young Charles ain't Master Fo'Rae's child, whatcha want him for? He ain't no kin to you no-how."

Master Fo'Rae's brother grinned and replied, "See Hattie Mae, that's where you're unmistakably wrong darling. Mistress Mattie is still my first cousin.

So you see Young Charles Fo'Rae is my kinsfolk."

Hattie Mae just stood there trying to figure out how she fitted in the Master's brother's plan.

Hattie Mae replied, "Well, how does all this affect me? What do you want from me?"

Master Fo'Rae said, "I simply want you to watch after Charles until he is of age. I want you to keep a journal of his life and teach him everything you know."

Hattie Mae looked at Master Fo'Rae's brother and said, "Ain't that his mother's job?"

Master Fo'Rae's brother looked at Hattie Mae and replied, "You and I both know Mistress Mattie is as smart as a box of rocks. I promise you, Hattie Mae, if you do this for me I'll bring your boy Claude back to you. Hattie Mae, I'm begging you to help me. Young Charles Fo'Rae is my family's legacy. He will assure that my family name lives on and on."

Master Fo'Rae's brother looked through the journal. He read a few pages. He said, "Hattie Mae, what year were you born in?"

Hattie Mae seemed to be getting annoyed with Master Fo'Rae's brother. She replied, "I was born in the year of 1813. Why is that any concern of yours?"

Master Fo'Rae's brother said, "Did you know that the slave trade in Africa became illegal in 1808?"

Hattie Mae responded, "Really! What does that have to do with anything?"

Master Fo'Rae replied, "Think about it, Hattie Mae. How did the slave trade end in 1808 and you end up on a vessel headed to America seventeen years later and you were only twelve? A slave ship holds over three hundred people. How many other Africans were on the ship with you?"

Hattie Mae thought about it. She couldn't remember a single person on that ship with her except Bactou and the crewmembers. As a matter of fact, it was only a half a dozen people on the ship with her. After Bactou overpowered one of the crewmen and jumped ship, Hattie Mae was the only African aboard.

Hattie Mae replied, "I don't rightly recalls how many people was on the ship. And I don't care."

Master Fo'Rae responded, "Well, let me tell you a story. A long time ago about ten years before you were even born, my grandfather, who started the shipping company, he traveled back and forth from France to Africa importing and exporting all sorts of goods, most of them illegal. My grandfather fell ill one trip on the voyage to Africa. On this particular trip, he took my older brother and me, who you refer to as Master Fo'Rae. We were just teenagers. When we reached the shores, the locals that my Grandfather traded with saw how sick my Grandfather was and took him to this village to pay a visit to the local Voodoo Priestess. The locals believed she could cure anything. This village was a spectacular sight to be seen. Warriors guarded it with their lives."

Master Fo'Rae's brother smiled and said, "And I be damn this Voodoo Priestess could heal anything. She had every herb and root known to man and then some. As my grandfather recovered in her hut, he noticed that the Voodoo Priestess was adorned with precious stones and jewels. The jewels seemed to be of no value to her though. As we walked through the village, we noticed all the tribe members were adorned with the precious stones.

My grandfather asked them where did they find such beautiful stones and they took him to a place where the stones covered the earth. My grandfather's eyes danced with joy at the sight."

Master Fo'Rae's brother looked at Hattie Mae and said, "My people are always looking for the value in everything. Yet your people just see the beauty. No one was laying any claim to the precious stones. It was like all the money that could be made off the stones was unimportant. The chief of the village picked one up off the ground and handed it to my brother and me."
Hattie Mae seemed to be unmoved by Master Fo'Rae's brother's story.

Until he said, ", That Voodoo Priestess was your Ouma."

Hattie Mae's eyes filled with tears over the thought of her Ouma.

Master Fo'Rae's brother said, "Hattie Mae, as a boy I met your Chief. My Grandfather made plenty of trips across the sea and purchased precious stones from him and sold them. However, he never was in the slave trading business. My grandfather was a decent, hard-working man. He had a lot of respect for your chief. My grandfather died shortly after and my brother and I took over the company. My brother secretly got into the slave trading business in America. I had no parts of it, but that's neither here nor there.

Let's get into how you became a part of this story. Well, Hattie Mae, it all began when The Chief found out my brother was in the slave trading business. Also, my brother and your Chief had a disagreement about the diamond mine your village was sitting on. My brother tried to trick him into selling the land, and when that didn't work, he tried to trick him into a trap to capture him and make him part of the slave trade. Well, your Chief's adviser, your Voodoo practicing Ouma, she saw right through my brother. She told your Chief he should not be trusted; for that matter, no white man should be trusted. So your Chief refused passage through his village to any white man. Your Chief sent out an order that all white men be killed on sight. Your Chief sent his warriors out to attack anybody that docked on his shores. He had his warriors destroy our ships and take all the weapons on it. The village was then virtually untouchable. It was only one way in and one way out. Now the warriors had weapons."

Hattie Mae was glued to The Master's brother's story.

He continued and said, "Well, needless to say, that infuriated my brother. He plotted revenge against the Chief of the village and the Voodoo Priestess. My brother couldn't get to the Chief because the Warriors guarded him at all times. However, he followed the Voodoo Priestess and learned her only weakness."

Master Fo'Rae's brother looked at Hattie Mae and said, "Her weakness was you, her granddaughter. My brother plotted until he found a way to get you. He knew if he took you, it would break the spirits of the village."

Hattie Mae looked up with tears running down her face and said, "That day in the bush, he was after me."

Master Fo'Rae's brother picked up the diary and said, "The entire story is in the book."

He set the book on the table and left.

Master Fo'Rae's brother spent a lot of time with Young Charles Fo'Rae while he was there. Hattie Mae watched them together; it appeared that Charles loved the attention. Master Fo'Rae told Mistress Mattie not to worry, that Hattie Mae and her family were free to do as they pleased. He even tore up the court ordered papers for Hattie Mae and Savannah's return and gave them new papers declaring them free just in case anybody tried to drag them back to the states. Master Fo'Rae told Pierre Cordova that he could repay him the money he owed him by coming to work at Fo'Rae Shipping Company.

Master Fo'Rae's brother stayed a month, then he was off back to Louisiana. Before he boarded the ship, he walked up to Hattie Mae and gave her a black journal. He said, "Please fill it with moments from Young Charles's life."

Master Fo'Rae's brother kissed Young Charles goodbye, then he hugged baby girl one and baby girl two goodbye.

As he was boarding the ship, he looked at Hattie Mae, winked his eye and said, "Hattie Mae do keep Charles out of the sun! Oh and please name those little nappy-headed baby girls. Baby girl one and baby girl two is not a suitable name for Fo'Rae children.

Chapter Three:
A Legacy was born

Hattie Mae wracked her mind over the following weeks trying to figure suitable names for Baby Girl One and Baby Girl Two. Hell, they had been calling them that for over five years. They had grown into those names, but Hattie Mae knew the girls were getting older and they had to be named.

Hattie Mae discussed some possible names with Savannah. Her reaction to naming the girls however caught Hattie Mae by surprise.

Savannah said nonchalantly, "I don't necessarily care what you name Baby Girl Two. I mean she is mine but, let's face it, she spends most of her time with you practicing spells and what not. My only concern at this moment is how dark my new baby girl is getting."

Savannah looked at her new infant daughter as if she was offended by her darker skin tone.

She said, "Can you believe how dark she is? Don't you have a potion or some kind of cream that can lighten her up?"

Hattie Mae was stunned and at a loss for words.

She mumbled, "I think her skin color is perfect. She's dark just like her Papa."

Savannah replied, "Yeah, that's the problem. She's a little too dark for my liking."

Hattie Mae decided she was going to disengage from this conversation before she smacked fire from Savannah's color struck ass.

Hattie Mae had noticed over the years how Savannah favored the lighter colored Negros over the darker ones. Hattie Mae knew Savannah felt like she was more important because she was half white. It always puzzled Hattie Mae, because Master Fo'Rae never acknowledged Savannah as his child. To him, she was just another plantation baby that he disrespected.

However, according to Master Fo'Rae's brother, Master Fo'Rae did acknowledge Hattie Mae's son Claude as his. Master Fo'Rae had even sent him away to New York away from the slave trade.

Hattie Mae often wondered what ever happened to Claude. Now she knew, Claude and Savannah looked just alike. Only Claude was darker.

Hattie Mae laughed at the thought of Savannah being the one who was darker. Hattie Mae knew Savannah felt like lighter, closer to white was better because of the way she was raised. All the light skinned slaves worked and lived in the big house and the darker ones went to work in the field.

Hattie Mae knew she was going to have to put Savannah in her place one day but today wasn't going to be that day.

As Hattie Mae was heading to the main mansion, she saw a gentleman walking toward her. As he got closer, she recognized his face.

Hattie Mae said to herself, "Well, I be damned! It's Robert Lee."

Robert Lee ran to Hattie Mae and held her in is arms. He wept tears of joy.

He said, "I thought I'd never see you again wife."

Hattie Mae was speechless. She couldn't believe her eyes.

She said, "But we saw the ship all torn apart on the shore; they said no one survived."

Robert Lee replied, "That's what I made it look like Hattie Mae. I didn't know anything about this place. But I done did good for myself. I gots me a little metal shop, saved up some money, and I gots a little piece of land to build a house on for us and Savannah."

Hattie Mae was still a little taken aback. She knew Robert Lee wasn't fully aware of what had happened since he'd last seen them. So Hattie Mae filled him in on their situation. She told him about Savannah's babies and about his twins he had with Mistress Mattie.

Robert Lee was displeased with that news. He took off his hat, threw it on the ground and kicked it.

Robert Lee said, "No, please tell me this ain't so. White twin babies with Mistress Mattie? No I don't believe you."

Hattie Mae replied sarcastically, "Why the long face? I thought you fancied Mistress Mattie. I mean all that special time y'all spent in the cabin on the bayou."

Robert Lee grabbed Hattie Mae by the shoulder. With tears in his eyes he said, "I never wanted you to know that. I'm so ashamed of myself. Not once was I okay with the goings on in the cabin on the bayou. I did what I was told. Hattie Mae I'm a man, I can't control what my body does when a naked women is standing in front of me ordering me to have sexual relations with her. I does as I was told. But you are the only women I's ever loved."

Hattie Mae felt in her spirit that Robert Lee was telling the truth.

She replied, "Those babies is here. I've grown to love both of them. Question is, what is you gone do. Mistress Mattie is got it made up in her mind that y'all's in love and gone live happily every after."

Robert Lee was disgusted. He said, "Never!"

Hattie Mae replied, "Well, you best be getting on bout yo business because Mistress Mattie is making her way down here."

Then Hattie Mae pointed up the hill at Mistress Mattie who was too far away to get a good look at who Hattie Mae was talking to.

Robert Lee begged Hattie Mae to meet him later. Hattie Mae told him to meet her back at this very spot an hour after sundown. Hattie Mae said Mistress Mattie had her bath, a shot of whiskey and went to bed like clock work every night.

Robert Lee agreed and disappeared into the bushes. Hattie Mae met Mistress Mattie half way up the hill.

Mistress Mattie was too busy blabbering something about Young Charles being sick with a fever and having a skin rash. She was all out of breath hollering. Hattie Mae just calmly walked to the mansion to find both Charles and his sister Baby Girl One sick.

Hattie Mae looked at Mistress Mattie and said angrily, "They both appear to be under the weather. Let me get them some roots from my bag."

Hattie Mae took care of both the children. She placed both of them in the bed. However, Mistress Mattie insisted on rocking Charles in her arms.

Hattie Mae was furious. Hattie Mae got in Mistress Mattie's face and said,

"Did you forget they twins, both of them is your own childrens? It's just not right how you treat Baby Girl One. You acts like she don't exist!"

Mistress Mattie never said a word she just held Charles in her lap rocking.

It appeared that Young Charles had love in his heart for his sister, Baby Girl one, because he held her hand as Mistress Mattie rocked him.

Hattie Mae slammed down the plant roots she had for the children and said, "That should break the fever and heal up the rash. The tea will help them sleep through the night."

Then Hattie Mae stormed away.

Like clock work Mistress Mattie was asleep after she'd bathed and had her shot of whiskey. Hattie Mae cleaned herself up and made her way to where she told Robert Lee to meet her.

Robert Lee was there waiting for Hattie Mae. Robert Lee stood there staring at her. No words were ever spoken. Hattie Mae just grabbed Robert Lee's hand and led him to her shed where she practiced her Voodoo. Hattie Mae knew no one would come near it out of fear.

Hattie Mae stood there in the candlelight taking in the beautiful sight of Robert Lee. Time and freedom had been good to him. He was perfect in every way.

An uncontrollable urge to have Robert Lee came over Hattie Mae. Her body burned with lust. It was like the heat of hell entered her vagina. Hattie Mae couldn't control herself. She had never wanted Robert Lee this bad.

Hattie Mae took her clothes off and lay on the bed with her legs wide open.

Robert Lee said, "Is that an invitation?" as he was removing his clothes.

Hattie Mae had forgotten the touch of a man. After all the horrible things Master Fo'Rae had done to her, she'd lost any desire for men. Being in St.

Lucia seemed to ease Hattie Mae's mind. She felt like a woman tonight and, hell, Robert Lee was her husband.

Hattie Mae took total control of the situation; she straddled Robert Lee and rode him like he was the last man alive. Hattie Mae let go of her fears and horrible memories of past sexual encounters and allowed herself to feel and enjoy every inch of Robert Lee. Just like Mistress Mattie described Robert Lee's penis, yes it was like a monster.

Hattie Mae felt her body trembling. It was a feeling of pleasure she'd never felt before. Her entire body shook with pleasure. Hattie Mae rolled off Robert Lee and just lay there next to him.

Robert Lee was trying to catch his breath. He said, "Well, I guess that just answered my question."

Hattie Mae replied, "What was your question?"

Robert Lee responded, "Well, I was going to ask if you missed me, but I reckon I just got my answer." Hattie smiled and laid her head on Robert Lee's chest. Hattie was getting ready to tell Robert Lee all about what had been happening in the last five years since she last saw him, when Robert Lee held Hattie Mae's hand.

Hattie Mae started to say something when all of a sudden she saw flashes of Robert Lee's life flashing before her eyes. She saw him as an embryo being bred and born to two pure blooded Africans, and then sold as a young man to Master Fo'Rae. She saw him and Mistress Mattie in the cabin on the bayou doing unspeakable things, Hattie Mae saw Robert Lee's trip across the ocean to St. Lucia. Then a horrible feeling came over Hattie Mae and tears streamed from her eyes. She saw Robert Lee laying in a casket and her crying over it.

Hattie Mae closed her eyes tight to try to clear her mind, but the vision continued. The last thing Hattie Mae saw in her vision was her childhood love Bactou.

Hattie Mae jumped up clear out of the bed. Hattie Mae was horrified. Shaking and trembling she couldn't form a sentence. Hattie Mae had heard her grandmother back in Africa speak of visions when she was a child, however, she had never had one before. Normally it was just a feeling she got when something was wrong.

Hattie Mae heard her grandmother's voice say, "Your gift is getting stronger child. Don't fight it. Don't try to change what you've seen. It's already done."

Hattie Mae screamed out, "No, I don't want the gift."

Robert Lee was a little startled; he got up to see who Hattie Mae was talking to. Robert Lee looked at Hattie Mae shaking in the corner of the little cabin.

He said with great concern, "Hattie Mae, who might you be speaking with?

Cause if I'm not mistaken you and me is the onli-est ones in this cabin."

Hattie Mae composed herself. She knew she couldn't tell Robert Lee what she just saw and heard. He'd for sure think she'd gone mad.

Hattie Mae simply replied, "No-one, I'm just tired, that's all. We can rest here until morning. Then we can figure out this mess."

Hattie Mae was scared to close her eyes. She kept her eyes open as long as she could. Hattie Mae always knew she had the gift; she was just unaware of how powerful her gift was becoming.

Hattie Mae touched Robert Lee's hand again to see if she could get another vision, but no such luck. Hattie Mae pondered the vision over carefully in her mind. Then she remembered seeing Robert Lee as a baby, then as a young man, then finally dead in his casket and her crying over it. Hattie Mae remembered what Robert Lee was wearing in the casket. She looked on the floor to see Robert Lee's clothes.

Great spirits, Hattie Mae thought to herself, *those are the same clothes.*

Hattie Mae lay restless all night. She lit her burning oils to calm her mind, but it didn't work. She could feel the presence of death all around Robert Lee. Hattie Mae dreaded this feeling. She knew it was nothing she could do to stop death.

Then Hattie Mae remembered what her grandmother used to say, "You can't stop death, but sometimes he does show up to give you a warning to get your house in order."

Hattie Mae figured that vision was her warning. Hattie Mae was bracing herself for another vision. When she was a child, her grandmother told her this would happen. Hattie Mae's grandmother also told her to just accept the visions as a gift from the spirit world and be honored that they chose her.

Savannah was standing outside Hattie Mae's cabin when she walked out in the morning. Hattie Mae was taken by surprise by Savannah being there because ever since they came to St. Lucia, Savannah had lost her interest in Hattie Mae's Voodoo.

Savannah looked at Hattie Mae and said, "Whatcha hiding Mama? I have been watching you from a distance all night. Ever since you come to me wanting to name dem baby girls. I saw you go in that cabin with a man, but it was too dark for me to make out who he was."

Robert Lee opened the cabin door, smiled and said, "It's me baby girl, yo Papa. I came to get my favorite girls!"

Savannah's face lit up with joy. Hattie Mae hadn't seen her that happy in years. Savannah ran to Robert Lee and embraced him.

Savannah said, "We thought you was dead!"

Hattie Mae let Robert Lee and Savannah have their moment. Hattie Mae was still a bit upset about her vision. Then she remembered the last thing she saw in the vision, Bactou. Hattie Mae wondered why in the world would she be seeing Bactou.

Savannah insisted that Robert Lee meet her husband Pierre Cordova and her babies. Hattie Mae cooked them up some breakfast and they all enjoyed each other's company, until Baby Girl One appeared at the door, standing there looking like the spitting image of Robert Lee.

Hattie Mae called Baby Girl One over to the table.

Baby Girl One said, "Mama Hattie Mae, Mama Mattie said she needs your help as quickly as possible, Young Charles is still with fever and she said bring all your potions and roots with you. Mama Mattie is in a terrible way, so do you mind if I stay down here for a spell?"

Hattie Mae smiled and replied, "Of course not baby. Come have some breakfast and visit with Savannah and her babies."

Baby Girl One looked over at Robert Lee then back at Hattie Mae and said, "Mama Hattie Mae, who's this man?" Then she pointed to Robert Lee.

Robert Lee stood up and said, "I's yo Papa; Robert Lee."

Baby Girl One looked confused. She looked up at Hattie Mae and said,

"But I don't have a Papa, Mama Hattie Mae."

Hattie Mae picked Baby Girl One up and took her over to Robert Lee and said, "Why Baby Girl One, all us got a Papa, and Robert Lee is yours."

She handed Baby Girl One to Robert Lee.

Robert Lee held Baby Girl One in his arms tight as he could and said, "Never in my life did I think I's have a blood kinsman. I don't rightly know what to say."

Hattie Mae looked over at Savannah, who didn't seem to be feeling this family bonding session between Robert Lee and Baby Girl One. Hattie Mae could feel the jealousy exuding from Savannah's eyes. If looks could kill, Baby Girl One would be dead.

Robert Lee looked up to witness Savannah's displeasure also.

Robert Lee motioned for Savannah to come to him. He hugged both Savannah and Baby Girl One and said, "Praise Allah, I gots both my baby girls with me."

Baby Girl One reminded Hattie Mae of why she was at Savannah's doorstep to begin with. Hattie Mae grabbed her bag.

Hattie Mae looked at Robert Lee and said, "Come on, we best get this family reunion over with. I don't know what's gonna happen, but ain't no sense in prolonging your reunion with Mistress Mattie."

Robert Lee, Hattie Mae, and Baby Girl One made their way to the mansion. Hattie Mae heard Mistress Mattie's voice fussing about Young Charles as she entered the mansion.

Baby Girl One took off up the stairs running and screaming, "Mama Mattie, I got a Papa."

Mistress Mattie replied, " Of course you do child, everybody does. Now, did you go and fetch Hattie Mae like I told you to?"

Baby Girl One responded, "But my Papa is here!"

Mistress Mattie froze still. She slowly turned around to see Robert Lee standing in the bedroom door.

Hattie Mae watched Mistress Mattie's reaction. Mistress Mattie's face lit up like her white Jesus himself was standing in the frame of that door. However Mistress Mattie contained her happiness. There were several upstairs maids cleaning and how would it look if the Mistress of the house ran into the arms of a black man. Hell the housekeepers were already questioning why Baby Girl One was calling Mistress Mattie, Mama Mattie, when supposedly Hattie Mae was her mother. One of the housekeepers had even mentioned that it was odd that Baby Girl One and Young Charles had the same birthday and seemed to be thick as thieves.

Mistress Mattie composed herself and said, "Oh my Robert Lee, you sure are a sight for sore eyes. I would love to sit and chat with you, but right now my son Charles is in an awful way. He's had a fever all night."

Mistress Mattie appeared to be overwhelmed with the return of Robert Lee and with Young Charles being sick. Mistress Mattie called for the housekeeper to bring her a glass of water.

Mistress Mattie looked over at Hattie Mae and said, "Please tell me you have something in your bag to break this fever for good."

Hattie Mae responded," Mistress Mattie why don't you rest a while? I'll stay with Young Charles. He'll be just fine. The illness just has to run its course."

Mistress Mattie hesitated at first then agreed to rest a while. As she walked past Robert Lee, she said, "Welcome back."

Robert Lee heard Baby Girl One whisper to Young Charles, "That's our Papa!"

Young Charles was too sick to respond.

Robert Lee walked over to the bed. He watched Hattie Mae give Young Charles some medicine.

Robert Lee just stared at Young Charles. Hattie Mae knew Robert Lee was thinking that this white child couldn't possibly be his. If Hattie Mae hadn't seen both of those babies come out of Mistress Mattie's body, she wouldn't have believed it either.

Robert Lee held up his hand to look at a mark he'd had on the inside of his hand since birth. Then he picked up Young Charles' hand to observe that Young Charles had the same mark.

Robert Lee said, "My father had the same mark on his hand. He called it a birthmark. My father said all the male children in his blood line had it."

Hattie Mae was trying to listen to what Robert Lee was saying, but she was distracted by a dark shadow hovering over Robert Lee and Young Charles.

Hattie Mae got an alarming sensation that the dark shadow was death!

She walked down to Mistress Mattie's room. She could hear her crying as she soaked in the tub. Hattie Mae heard Mistress Mattie praying to her white Jesus, begging and pleading him to break the fever.

Hattie Mae knew Young Charles was sicker than they'd expected. Plus Hattie Mae had seen the black shadow of death hovering over both Young Charles and Robert Lee.

Hattie Mae stopped abruptly in the hallway. She felt a sharp pain in her head. Hattie Mae gripped the side of the door to keep her balance.

Hattie Mae got another vision. This time she could see a casket, but it was a small casket. One you would use for a child.

She ran down the hallway to check on Young Charles whose fever hadn't subsided yet.

Hattie Mae also felt the presence of death in the room. Hattie Mae felt bad.

She suspected Young Charles might be leaving this lifetime soon. Hattie Mae knew that if anything happened to Young Charles, Mistress Mattie was going to fall apart.

Hattie Mae could still hear Mistress Mattie crying.

Hattie Mae looked at Robert Lee and said, "You should go to her and comfort her. It's y'all's child she's crying over."

Robert Lee replied, "And say what to her?"

Hattie Mae looked down at the ground, she slowly looked up and said, "Say or do whatever you have to, to make her feel better." Robert Lee was shocked. He responded, "Come again Hattie Mae?"

Hattie Mae said, "You heard me. Go to Mistress Mattie comfort her the way any man would comfort a women who loves him. Take her mind off of Young Charles."

Robert Lee replied, "Let's me be clear, Hattie Mae. You want me to go have sexual relations with Mistress Mattie to ease her mind. Hattie Mae how dare you ask something likes that of me. What are you now, a Madame?"

Hattie Mae simply responded, "Please do this for me."

Robert Lee was utterly appalled. He walked back and forth across the floor.

He stopped and turned to look at Hattie Mae. They both could hear Mistress Mattie crying.

Robert Lee sheepishly said, "Alright, Hattie Mae, I'll do it for you, but only if you promise to come with me and stay with me."

Hattie Mae thought about it.

Robert Lee said, "It's the only way I'll do it. If you come be by my side as my wife again."

Hattie Mae listened to Mistress Mattie crying.

Hattie Mae looked at Robert Lee and said, "Okay, I'll leaves with you, but only after this baby is better."

Then Hattie Mae pointed to Young Charles.

Robert Lee slowly walked to the room where Mistress Mattie was. Hattie Mae sent all the housekeepers away for the night. Hattie Mae sat with Young Charles while Robert Lee comforted Mistress Mattie. It was only a short while that Robert Lee had been in the room when Hattie Mae heard Mistress Mattie's headboard frantically hitting the wall and Mistress Mattie moaning with pleasure.

Young Charles seemed to be getting sicker. Hattie Mae called for Savannah to sit with Young Charles while she went to retrieve some herbs from her voodoo cabin.

Savannah looked at Hattie Mae and said, "Town folks is dying from this plague. Mama, I know you can fix this. You knows everything there is to know about herbs and spells. Even the dark spells. I seen all the books you have hidden in your cabin."

Hattie Mae seemed to be frightened of the very word dark spells.

She looked at Savannah and said, "Don't you ever mentioned dark magic again. Never! And stay away from my cabin and my books. They's not for you."

Savannah replied, "But, mama, it's Charles. He's family. Wouldn't you do anything to save him?"

Hattie Mae responded, "Anything but step into the dark side of Voodoo. There's always a price to pay. Savannah if I ever hear you speak of such a thing again, you'll be sorry!

Hattie Mae turned to exit the room when she saw Mistress Mattie standing in the doorway listening to the conversation.

Hattie Mae walked past Mistress Mattie. Hattie Mae didn't even look at her; she could smell Robert Lee all over Mistress Mattie. Even though Hattie Mae all but forced Robert Lee to pleasure Mistress Mattie she didn't want to look at her because Hattie Mae knew what was coming: the death of Young Charles.

Hattie Mae went to find Robert Lee, who was at the lake washing the scent of Mistress Mattie off of him.

Robert Lee looked at Hattie Mae and said, "It would behoove you, Hattie Mae to be on bout yo business. I'm powerfully tired and at this moment the very sight of you sickens me."

Hattie Mae started to say something, but Robert Lee turned his back on her.

Hattie Mae made her way to her cabin where she found Mistress Mattie looking through all her books.

Hattie Mae said, "Mistress Mattie, can I help you with something?"

Mistress Mattie replied angrily, "Why yes you can, Hattie Mae. I heard you and Savannah talking. I know you have something in one of your little books that can help my son Charles."

Mistress Mattie begged Hattie Mae to do what-ever she could to save Charles, but Hattie Mae refused.

Hattie Mae said, "Mistress Mattie you don't understand. You cants cheat death. When death comes it's your time. It's nothing you can do about it."

Mistress Mattie frantically grabbed Hattie Mae and screamed, "You see death on Charles?"

Mistress Mattie was hysterical; she started pulling down all Hattie Mae's books and reading through them. Hattie Mae finally got Mistress Mattie to settle down. Mistress Mattie slammed the cabin door as she left. Hattie Mae had an uneasy feeling that Mistress Mattie left with something.

 The next morning, there was no change in Young Charles. Mistress Mattie had Savannah sit with Young Charles. Mistress Mattie said she had an errand to run. Before Mistress Mattie left, she told the housekeepers to leave. She said she didn't want more germs around Young Charles. Mistress Mattie also told Baby Girl One not to leave the mansion, which was odd because normally Mistress Mattie didn't care what Baby Girl One did.

Although she was her mother, Baby Girl One spent most of her time with Hattie Mae.

Hattie Mae just figured Mistress Mattie was being revengeful because she wouldn't help Young Charles, but like Hattie Mae said, you can't cheat death.

Hattie Mae spent the day cleaning up her house and catering to Robert Lee, who was still pissed about Hattie Mae insisting on him having sex with Mistress Mattie. Hattie Mae told Robert Lee that she owed Mistress Mattie that because Mistress Mattie gave them their freedom. Robert Lee begged to differ. Robert Lee said Mistress Mattie hadn't given them a damn thing.

Hattie Mae was just about to go to the well for water when Baby Girl Two entered the house.

Baby Girl Two said, "Hey Mama Hattie Mae, I just saw your friend leave Mistress Mattie's house. Looked like she was visiting with Young Charles and Baby Girl One."

Hattie Mae felt her heart drop to her knees.

Hattie Mae said, "What friend baby?"

Baby Girl Two said, "Your friend that you trade herbs with. Her and Mistress Mattie covered up all the mirrors with black sheets so the spirits couldn't get in them."

Hattie Mae felt faint. She knew Mistress Mattie had gotten one of her friends to tap into the dark magic. Hattie Mae dropped everything and took off running towards the mansion. Robert Lee and Baby Girl Two took off behind her.

Hattie Mae was running so fast she was out of breath. Something unexplainable came over Hattie Mae. She felt a strong surge of power flowing through her body. Hattie Mae stretched out her hands and the doors of the Mansion flung open.

She saw Mistress Mattie standing at the top of the stairs.

Mistress Mattie said devilishly, "You're too late, Hattie Mae."

Hattie Mae bent down and held her knees to catch her breath. She screamed out, "What have you done?"

Mistress Mattie coldly replied, "I did what I had to do to save my boy." Hattie Mae ran up the stairs to the children's room.

She held her stomach and cried. Hattie Mae saw the burnt candles, blood and animal carcass. Hattie Mae looked over to see Young Charles resting comfortably his fever was gone and he appeared to be perfectly fine. Hattie Mae was scared to look over at Baby Girl One.
 She slowly turned to see the dark shadow lifting off Baby Girl One's body and disappear in the ceiling.

Hattie Mae let out a loud scream and fell to her knees. She burst into tears.

She picked up Baby Girl One's limp body and screamed out, "No, Baby Girl One, No."

Hattie Mae saw Mistress Mattie come into the room and sit on the bed rubbing Young Charles' blonde hair.

Mistress Mattie looked at Hattie Mae with the spirit of the devil in her eyes and said, "I had to save my boy. It was a small sacrifice to make."

For the first time Hattie Mae had saw Mistress Mattie for what she really was: an evil, self-righteous, entitled blue eyed devil.

Hattie Mae slowly said, "You sacrificed one child for the other one, Mistress Mattie. You satisfied death with the life of your daughter? Do you have any idea what you've done?"

Mistress Mattie coldly said, "Surely I do. Besides, Baby Girl One won't be missed. I never considered her my child. Besides Young Charles is going to grow up to accomplish great things as a white man in this world. Baby Girl One was just another mulatto child with no purpose."

Hattie Mae was furious. Before she knew it, she had her hands around Mistress Mattie's throat. Hattie Mae grabbed Mistress Mattie by her hair and dragged her to the top of the steps. Hattie Mae was about to toss her down the steps when she saw Baby Girl Two standing at the bottom with Robert Lee screaming for her not to kill Mistress Mattie. Hattie Mae turned to see Young Charles standing there looking at her. A sense of guilt came over Hattie Mae. She knew she couldn't kill Mistress Mattie, at least not in front of all these witnesses.

Hattie Mae flung Mistress Mattie like she was a rag-doll and threw her into the wall.

Hattie Mae looked at Mistress Mattie and said, "May your white Jesus see to it that you burn in hell for what you've done here tonight. Rest assured you will pay for this."

Mistress Mattie knew better to respond. She just put her head down.

Hattie Mae knew Mistress Mattie didn't have an ounce of remorse in her body for sacrificing Baby Girl One's life for Young Charles' life.

Hattie Mae picked Baby Girl One's lifeless body up and carried it down the stairs. When Hattie Mae got to the bottom, she handed the body to Robert Lee.

House of Fo'Rae

Hattie Mae stood in the middle of the floor. She lifted her hands and closed her eyes. Hattie Mae spoke in her native dialect. As Hattie Mae spoke, all the mirror coverings fell to the ground and you could hear the wind whipping through the corners of the house.

Hattie Mae looked at Mistress Mattie at the top of the steps.

She said, "From this day forth, I will never step foot in this house again. This House of Fo'Rae will never know true happiness again."

There was a loud thunder and the wind blew the French doors open and Hattie Mae walked out.

Robert Lee dug a grave for Baby Girl One's body and built her a casket. Robert Lee wasn't as upset as Hattie Mae was about Baby Girl One's death.

It was understandable even though she was his daughter. Robert Lee didn't know her. Hattie Mae refused to use the casket. She cremated Baby Girl One's body like they did where Hattie Mae was from. Then she had Robert Lee put the ashes in the casket and buried it.

Hattie Mae called Baby Girl Two to have a word with her.

Baby Girl Two looked a little upset, which was understandable. They had just said goodbye to her best friend.

Hattie Mae sat Baby Girl Two down. She said, "On the night Baby Girl One died, you said something that has me confused."

Baby Girl Two replied, "Mama Hattie Mae, where do you think Baby Girl One's spirit went? Do you think it tried to get in the mirrors? Is that why you uncovered them?"

Again Hattie Mae was confused. How could Baby Girl Two know about spirits leaving the body and covering mirrors so the spirits can't get in them? Hattie Mae had never spoken about any of those things around Baby Girl Two, or any of the children for that matter.

Hattie Mae responded, "Well, I'm not sure, but don't be sad. Baby Girl One's spirit will live on somewhere, but how do you know all these things?"

Baby Girl Two looked at Hattie Mae and said, "I don't know, I just know. Sometimes I hear things. Like voices, but I never see the people."

Hattie Mae knew Baby Girl Two had the gift. It was passed down through Savannah. It skipped Savannah and Baby Girl Two received it.

Hattie Mae said, "Baby Girl Two, are you scared when you hear these voices?"

Baby Girl Two climbed in Hattie Mae's lap. Hattie Mae rubbed her hair.

Baby Girl Two replied, "Nope, I'm not scared of nothing. Besides, the voices have always been with me."

Hattie Mae rocked Baby Girl Two in her arms. She sang her a song her Ouma used to sing to her. Hattie Mae remembered what Master Fo'Rae's brother said about naming the girls. Also about what he said about how Young Charles carrying his last name was his legacy.

Hattie Mae said, "Baby Girl Two, it's about time you got a real name. Would you like that?"

Baby Girl Two shook her head yes.

Hattie Mae said, "I'm going to name you Legacy."

Hattie Mae thought to herself. Although Baby Girl Two had Master Fo'Rae's white blood in her, she also had Hattie Mae's pure African blood running through her veins. Baby Girl Two was as much Hattie Mae's kinsfolk as she was the late Master Fo'Rae's.

Baby Girl Two replied, "Why Legacy, Mama Hattie Mae?"

Hattie Mae kissed her on the top of her head and said, "Because you're going to be my Legacy."

Chapter Four:
Haunted Mansion

H attie Mae was in her cabin clearing her belongings when she heard Young Charles calling her name. Hattie Mae was dreading this moment. As much as she loved Young Charles, because of Mistress Mattie's obsessive love for him, Baby Girl One was dead.

Young Charles stood next to Hattie Mae all dressed up like a southern gentlemen, with his little knicker boxer shorts and button down crisp white starched shirt. Mistress Mattie always put a dash of scented oil on him, so Young Charles always smelled good.

Young Charles was in between stages in his life so he still had his fat little chubby cheeks and, when he spoke, it sounded like he had a mouth full of cotton.

Young Charles said, "Mama Hattie Mae, do you hate me too? I know you hate Mama Mattie because she helped me get better and not Baby Girl One."

Hattie Mae didn't respond. She just continued packing her belongings. Hattie Mae knew that Young Charles was too young to understand exactly what happened. However, in time he would grow up to be just as self entitled as his mama, Mistress Mattie.

Young Charles grabbed Hattie Mae by the waist. He started crying.

Young Charles said, "Please don't hate me Mama Hattie Mae, I love you."

Young Charles handed Hattie Mae Baby Girl One's brush. He said, "Mama Mattie always says to hide our brushes from you because you might try to put some Voodoo on us."

Hattie Mae smiled to herself at the thought of Mistress Mattie lighting fire to her hair that was left in the brush. Hattie Mae remembered telling Mistress Mattie to always burn the left over strands of hair because you didn't want the birds to get it and build a nest; that would make you have an awful headache. Over the years, Mistress Mattie came to believe that Hattie Mae did Voodoo spells with the hair.

Young Charles looked up at Hattie Mae with those big blue eyes. He was such a handsome little rascal. As he grew older, he started looking like a white version of Robert Lee.

Young Charles said, "Well, maybe you could use Baby Girl One's hair to bring her back."

Then he looked down at the ground and said, "Or let death take me instead of her."

Hattie Mae stopped her packing. She picked Young Charles up and placed him on the table.

Hattie Mae said, "You know I brings you in this world?"

Young Charles replied, "Yes ma'am, Savannah told me all about it. Savannah told me that me and Baby Girl One was born at the same time and that Mama Mattie was both our Mama."

Hattie Mae wasn't shocked. Hattie Mae knew Young Charles knew Baby Girl One was his twin sister. She had overheard him telling Baby Girl Two. He told Baby Girl Two it was a big secret and that she couldn't tell nobody.

Hattie Mae said, "Well, if you knows that, what else do you know?"

Young Charles replied, "I know that Robert Lee is our father and I know I'm supposed to never tell anybody that I'm Negro."

Hattie Mae looked him in the eye and said, "It ain't fair baby, but it is better for you. Folks in this world hate Negro folks. I can't explain why, just is. You're better off being white."

Young Charles said, "But do you hate me Mama Hattie Mae?"

Hattie Mae hugged Young Charles and replied, "I could never hate you, baby. I loves you like you's my own child."

Young Charles put his arms around Hattie Mae and said, "Mama Hattie Mae, I'm going to love you forever. Please don't leave me here with Mama Mattie. She watches me day and night. She's always given me lesson on how to be a proper southern gentlemen, but Mama Hattie Mae I don't even know where the south is."

Young Charles looked at Hattie Mae and said, "Is the south as horrible as Savannah says? She says Negro people have to work for free and get beat with a whip. Mama Hattie Mae, have you ever been beat with a whip?"

Hattie Mae didn't want to talk about the United States. She quickly changed the story. Hattie Mae knew Young Charles was taking drawing lessons and he was quite good at it.

Hattie Mae said, "Have you been practicing your drawing?"

Young Charles' face lit up like a lighting bug when Hattie Mae said that.

He replied, "Why yes ma'am, I have. I made you a painting."

Then Young Charles took off to the mansion to get it. When he returned, he handed the painting to Hattie Mae.

Hattie Mae was saddened by the painting and a little confused. Young Charles had drawn a picture of the mansion, with Baby Girl One in the sky with angel wings and Legacy in the front yard playing with a little Negro boy. Hattie Mae assumed that the Negro lady sitting on the porch drinking lemonade was her.

Hattie Mae pointed to the little Negro boy in the picture and said, "Young Charles, who might this boy be?"

Young Charles replied, "That's me, Mama Hattie Mae."

Hattie Mae looked at the picture, turned it sideways and squinted her eyes.

Hattie Mae smiled and jokingly said, "Well, now that you's clarified that, it sho is you."

Hattie Mae and Young Charles laughed.

Hattie Mae said, "Why did you draw yourself so dark baby? Your skin is not dark. Although Robert Lee is your Papa, yo skin is white as snow like yo mammy."

Young Charles looked at Hattie Mae with tears in his eyes and said, "But I wanna be Negro like y'all: you, Legacy, Savannah, and everybody I love. All of you are Negro and so am I."

Hattie Mae explained to Young Charles that he had to pretend to be all white. Hattie Mae said it was for his own good. She told him he was going to go to all the finest schools and get to do all the things that white folks get to do.

Charles didn't seem to care about any of those things. So Hattie Mae told him after he was a grown man and finished with his schooling he could be whatever color he wanted to be.

Young Charles seemed to be satisfied with that. He ran off to find Robert Lee who was loading up the wagon with Hattie Mae's belongings.

Savannah refused to leave with Hattie Mae, but she allowed Hattie Mae to take Legacy. Savannah told Hattie Mae she would bring Young Charles to see her and Legacy as often as possible. Robert Lee also promised Hattie Mae he would make it his business that Young Charles stayed a part of her family.

As Robert Lee, Hattie Mae, and Legacy said their goodbyes, Hattie Mae cried when she saw Young Charles and Legacy saying goodbye.

Young Charles told Legacy he liked her new name and that he would always think about her. He hugged her tight and ran away.

Legacy cried. As they drove down the driveway Hattie Mae turned to see Mistress Mattie on the balcony watching them as they left.

Hattie Mae just turned her head. The very sight of Mistress Mattie sickened Hattie Mae.

Hattie Mae settled into Robert Lee's home comfortably. It was just an hour's horse ride away from the mansion. It wasn't as big and fine as the mansion, but it was home for now.

Hattie Mae wrote Master Fo'Rae's brother and told him all about what happened. He wrote her back and said that he couldn't believe her story, with all the spirit stuff and all. Nevertheless, he still wanted her to keep a close eye on Young Charles. So every other day Hattie Mae would ride to check on Young Charles, until he went away to France to boarding school. Master Fo'Rae said France had the best schools in the world. Master Fo'Rae's brother said that he would come there to investigate what Hattie Mae said Mistress Mattie had done. He said that if there were any truth to her story, he would see to it that Mistress Mattie paid dearly.

Legacy was pretty pissed off when she couldn't go away to school. Hattie Mae and some of the island people got together and taught the Island children themselves. Robert Lee even built them a little schoolhouse on his property.

Legacy grew up to be a beautiful dark chocolate young lady. When Legacy was younger, Hattie Mae was frightened that Legacy might be a little slow or foolish because she was a product of incest, but Hattie Mae was dead wrong. Legacy was sharp as a whip. She was gifted in every subject. Legacy excelled in everything Hattie Mae taught her.

Before long, Legacy was teaching her own school class. It was essential for Hattie Mae that the Island children had the best education she could provide. Hattie Mae wrote to Master Fo'Rae's brother often to request new textbooks and supplies. As per their agreement he did. Hattie Mae received letters from Young Charles and pictures he'd drawn. Young Charles was a great artist. However, his pictures were sometimes disturbing. He often drew pictures of Baby Girl One lingering in the background.

Savannah came to call one Sunday, she brought all her girls and Pierre Cordova who was still a little disappointed that he'd had five girls and no boy yet.

All Savannah's kids came in and hugged Hattie Mae. Then they went to play in the yard. Well, all of them except two; the lightest ones. Hattie Mae knew Savannah doted over them because they were light skinned.

Hattie Mae looked at the children and said, "Why come y'all ain't outside with the rest of the children?"

One of the girls looked at Hattie Mae and replied, "Because Mama said we can't play in the sun because we're special. Mama said the sun was going to make us dark and we was dark enough. It's not fair because the other kids get to play in the sun. All we can do is sit in the house and play dolls."

Hattie Mae was furious. She looked at Savannah and said, "Have you gone mad? Do you understand the damage you're doing to these here children? Making them believe they special cause they light skinned? In all my days I's never thought you would be so stupid."

Hattie Mae could tell Savannah wasn't in the mood to argue with her. Savannah just wrapped up the light-skinned children in scarfs to block the sun and sent them on their way.

Savannah looked at Legacy and said, "Girl, don't you speak to yo own mama no more? I been sitting here for more than half an hour and you haven't said one word to me."

Legacy looked at Savannah in disgust. Hattie Mae knew Legacy and Savannah had a bittersweet relationship. Savannah was only nice to Legacy when she wanted her to look after all her kids or something.

Hattie Mae looked at Savannah and said, "Don't go to picking with this baby. You ain't seen her in two months and you already trying to start a fight with her! Now state your business why you came calling today because I knows something's wrong, I can see it in your eyes."

Legacy stood up next to Hattie Mae and said, "It's okay, Mama Hattie Mae."

Then Legacy looked at Savannah and said, "Hello Savannah, how are you?"

Savannah was furious she replied, "How dare you address me as Savannah! You will refer to me as Mother. I demand you show me respect at all time or else."

Legacy leaned over the table and rudely said, "Or else what? I will show you not one drop of respect, and I will never refer to you as mother. You have never been a mother to me."

Hattie Mae knew this argument was going to heat up, so she stepped in between them and said, "Spit it out, Savannah, what is it you want?"

Savannah sat down in the chair and whispered, "I believe that Baby Girl One's spirit is haunting the Mansion."

Legacy stood back up and held her chest. Legacy said, "I believe you, I seen her spirit."

Savannah replied, "So have I. She's in the mirrors. Mistress Mattie had them all covered in thick black cloth, but that didn't stop the singing and the baby's crying from echoing through the hallways at night."

Savannah was shaking like a leaf. She looked at Hattie Mae and said, "Mama I'm scared to go in the mansion at night, hell I'm scared to go there period. It's a strange presence there and it follows you from room to room.

Mistress Mattie has confined herself to one room in the house and barricaded herself in the room at night. The night maids have refused to work until the spirit is removed from the home."

Hattie Mae smiled and said, "Well, that serves Mistress Mattie right. She should have thought about that before she did what she did. I say let Baby Girl One's spirit have free run of the mansion."

Savannah looked at Hattie Mae and said, "Now Mama you knows that ain't right. Baby Girl One's soul should be resting. It's been ten years since death came to claim Baby Girl One. Mama, I need you to show Baby Girl One the way to the light. Or work some of your Voodoo on her. Either way, I need her to go away. Mistress Mattie is going to worry the texture of my hair nappy."

Then Savannah looked at Legacy and said, "You got dark skin, but you got the prettiest hair I've ever seen."

Legacy said sarcastically, "I'm pretty sure you thought that was a compliment. I'll just add that to the list of ignorant things you've said to me."

Savannah warned Legacy to watch her mouth or she'd be sorry. Hattie Mae knew Legacy didn't fear Savannah at all. Legacy was a very powerful Voodoo Priestess. Although she was young, her gift was strong.

Hattie Mae took Legacy with her to Mistress Mattie's mansion. Hattie Mae had been on Mistress Mattie's property at least twice a week before Young Charles left for school. However, she'd never stepped a foot in Mistress Mattie's house in ten years. Neither had she spoken with Mistress Mattie.

Hattie Mae knew that Baby Girl's spirit was acting up because Young Charles had left for school. Hattie Mae could feel Baby Girl One's spirit when she walked in the door of the mansion. Hattie Mae found Mistress Mattie locked in the living room holding a shotgun.

Mistress Mattie ran to Hattie Mae, fell at her feet, and said, "Hattie Mae, please forgive me. I'm so sorry. I didn't know what I was doing. Please make them go away. They won't leave me alone. All day and night they torment me with the singing and crying. Hattie Mae please tell me you brung your herbs and potions to get rid of them."

Hattie Mae was confused. She said, "Them? Mistress Mattie you done gone mad. Why do you keep saying 'them'?" They ain't babies no more. Young

Charles is gone off to school, and you know what you did to Baby Girl One. I told you, you can't cheat death."

Legacy closed her eyes and raised her hands as if she was feeling the energy in the room. Legacy popped her eyes open and turned slowly towards Mistress Mattie.

Legacy said, "Tell Mama Hattie Mae about the other despicable things you've done and don't sugar coat it because I see it clear as day."

Hattie Mae looked at Mistress Mattie and said, "Please do, I can feel the spirit of two children in this house."

Hattie Mae froze. She looked up in the air and said, "Yes Baby Girl One, it's me, Hattie Mae."

All of a sudden all the doors started opening and shutting and Hattie Mae heard a baby crying. Mistress Mattie grabbed her gun and ran and hid in the corner.

Mistress Mattie was screaming hysterically, "I'm sorry, I'm sorry Hattie Mae, please make them go away."

Hattie Mae replied, "Mistress Mattie who is they? Why do you keep saying they?"

Mistress Mattie responded, "The baby! I had to get rid of it. I couldn't have another Negro baby."

Hattie Mae looked at Legacy and said, "What is she rambling about?"

Legacy replied, "After you begged Grandpa Robert Lee to be with Mistress Mattie for comfort, she conceived a son. Then she used a wire coat hanger to abort the baby. His spirit along with Baby Girl One's are roaming through this house trapped. They need us to set them free."

Legacy looked at Hattie Mae and said, "But Mama Hattie Mae, I believe you already knows about Baby Girl One's spirit. That's why you uncovered the mirrors the night Baby Girl One died. You was hoping that she would haunt Mistress Mattie."

Hattie Mae had to smile. Legacy was correct. Hattie Mae was secretly hoping Baby Girl One's spirit would drive Mistress Mattie mad. It would serve her ass right, for all the hateful stuff Mistress Mattie had done.

Hattie Mae felt Baby Girl One's spirit strong. It was like Baby Girl One's Spirit was tugging at Hattie Mae. All the shutters in the mansion were swinging open and shut, making a banging sound against the house. Every time the shutter hit the wall, Mistress Mattie would jump out of her skin and point her gun in the air.

Hattie Mae knew she was going to have to calm Mistress Mattie down and get that gun from her or Mistress Mattie was going to end up shooting all of them.

Hattie Mae poured Mistress Mattie a drink. Hattie Mae handed it to Mistress Mattie and had her sit in the chair. Hattie Mae grabbed the crystal candleholders and lit them.

Damn, Hattie Mae thought to herself. *The sun had gone down. That's when the spirits like to cut up the most, at night.*

Hattie Mae held up the crystal candlestick so she could clearly see Mistress Mattie. The drink she had given her seemed to be calming Mistress Mattie down. Hattie Mae sat the whole bottle next to Mistress Mattie and said, "So, you killed another baby? Why on earth would you do such a thing? This child killing business is so unlike you."

Hattie Mae lifted up Mistress Mattie's glass to refill it. Hattie Mae took a quick, sudden breath. Hattie Mae saw Baby Girl One's reflection in the glass. Baby Girl One held up her hand as if she was trying to show Hattie Mae something.

Hattie Mae didn't want to get Mistress Mattie all riled up again, so she just kept on talking to Mistress Mattie. Hattie Mae looked up at Legacy. Hattie

Mae tilted her head towards Mistress Mattie. Legacy walked over to Mistress Mattie and started talking to her.

Hattie Mae stayed with the reflection of Baby Girl One. Hattie Mae said quietly, "Show me, Baby Girl One, what's you wants me to see. Make it clear, Baby Girl One."

Hattie Mae was somewhat frightened herself. Although she'd always had the gift, Hattie Mae had never actually seen a spirit this clearly.

Hattie Mae held the glass up steady, so she could see Baby Girl One. Baby Girl One opened her hand wide open and held it up.

Hattie Mae could see a long cut on the inside of her hand. Then a strong wind blew through and rattled all the paper. One of Young Charles drawings landed at Hattie Mae's feet. Hattie Mae picked the drawing up and looked at it. In the drawing, Hattie Mae saw the usual people, but this time there was an extra person. Lucky for Hattie Mae, Young Charles had written everybody's name on this picture.

Hattie Mae read the names out loud. She said, "Mama Hattie Mae, Baby Girl One, Legacy, Mama Mattie and Robert Lee."

Hattie Mae smiled and said, "This boy always drawing himself Negro."

Hattie Mae noticed something odd. Young Charles never drew Robert Lee or Mistress Mattie in his paintings. However, this one he did and they both had their hands drawn on the opposite way. So you could see their palms.

Hattie Mae brought the picture closer to her eyes. Hattie Mae put her hand over her heart.

Hattie Mae said very slowly,

"Oh great spirits, no!"

Hattie Mae dropped the glass she was holding and the picture. She turned sharply towards Mistress Mattie. Hattie Mae grabbed Mistress Mattie's hand and opened it to reveal a scar. Hattie Mae stumbled back and fell into a chair. Hattie Mae slopped over as if she was remembering something.

Hattie Mae remembered seeing that same scar on Robert Lee's hand the day they cremated Baby Girl One's body. Hattie Mae remembered asking Robert Lee what happened and he told her he had hurt himself building Baby Girl One's casket. Then Hattie Mae reflected back on the day Baby Girl One died. She remembered Robert Lee trying his best to keep her busy. Hattie Mae obliged Robert Lee because she thought he was still pissed about her making him sleep with Mistress Mattie.

Hattie Mae grabbed Mistress Mattie by her throat and said, "You got five minutes to tell me what really happened the night Baby Girl One died or I'm going to leave this house and allow Baby Girl One and that little boy you killed to drive you mad."

Legacy got a little scared and said, "Mama Hattie Mae, whatcha talking about? We all knows what happened."

Hattie Mae replied, "No Legacy, we don't. There's a missing piece of the story and Mistress Mattie is fixing to spit it out or else!"

Mistress Mattie was screaming, "He made me do it! He said if I did it, we could be together as a family. He promised!"

Legacy looked at Mistress Mattie and said, "Who is he?"

Hattie Mae replied slowly, "He is Robert Lee."

Mistress Mattie just started sobbing uncontrollably and screaming, "Oh Hattie Mae, he lied to me. He let me kill my daughter to save him."

Mistress Mattie explained that when she left Hattie Mae's cabin the night after she begged Hattie Mae to help Young Charles, she ran into Robert Lee at the lake. Mistress Mattie said Robert Lee took her back to the house where they talked, and he told her all about Hattie Mae bargaining with him to sleep with her. Then she said there was a knock at the door and it was Hattie Mae's friend she practiced Voodoo with. Mistress Mattie said she begged the lady to help her get Young Charles better, but the Lady said Young Charles would be perfectly fine. The lady said death wasn't here for Young Charles, it was here for his daddy Robert Lee.

Mistress Mattie looked at Hattie Mae and said, "I loved him I couldn't let him die. The Lady said that the only thing that would satisfy death was a blood relative of Robert Lee's."

Mistress Mattie looked down at the floor and said, "He told me if I satisfied death with Baby Girl One instead of him, well, he said he'd stay with Young Charles and me. So I did it. I had your friend help me, and it was done. Baby Girl One was dead and Young Charles was better."

Hattie Mae was furious. She stood, took her hand and smacked Mistress Mattie across the face.

Hattie Mae said, "You are as dumb as you look. You are a pitiful excuse for a mother. How could you believe that a Negro runaway slave was going to be your night in shining armor? The world would never allow such a thing! A nigger with a white woman, have you gone mad?"

Mistress Mattie just lifted the brandy bottle up and drank it straight from the neck.

Mistress Mattie said, "I believed him, Hattie Mae, I believed him, but he lied. He took off with you and left me here to be haunted by Baby Girl One's spirit."

Mistress Mattie motioned for Legacy to hand her another bottle of brandy.

Mistress Mattie said, "I found out I was pregnant a few weeks later. Hell, y'all had left and I knew Robert Lee was never coming back, so I got rid of that thing inside me. I almost bled to death in the process. If it wasn't for Savannah stealing me some of your herbs, I'd be dead for sure."

Hattie Mae replied, "Savannah knew about this?"

Mistress Mattie said, "Just about me getting rid of the baby. She knows nothing about Robert Lee and Baby Girl One."

Mistress Mattie hung her head down and said, "My Lord Hattie Mae, I'm going straight to hell."

Hattie Mae sat in the chair for a while absorbing all that Mistress Mattie had just told her. Hattie Mae played back the night Baby Girl One died over and over in her mind. Nothing in Hattie Mae's spirit told her what was going on. That's the one thing Hattie Mae hated about the gift she and Legacy both had. The gift never worked the way Hattie Mae thought it should work. Hell, what was the use of having the gift of visions and sensing that something was going to happen if you couldn't do anything to prevent something from happening?

Hattie Mae was just at a lost for words. Mistress Mattie and Robert Lee had once again deceived her with their lies and secrets. Hattie Mae knew Mistress Mattie was a wicked person, but Robert Lee's behavior was extremely disturbing.

Hattie Mae thought to herself that she'd deal with Robert Lee and Savannah later. Right now she was going to get Mistress Mattie under control before the authorities come to lock her away in the insane asylum.

Hattie Mae stood up and said, "Mistress Mattie what did you do with the remains of the baby you snatched out of your womb? And don't you dare lie. Because I'll string you up by your toes myself."

Hattie Mae wiped the sweat from her forehead and said, "Mistress Mattie it's hot around my collar, and I ain't got time for your foolishness tonight. So spit it out. What did you do with it?"

Mistress Mattie pointed to the garden and said, "I put him in a jar and buried him under the tulips."

Hattie Mae simply walked to the garden and dug up the jar. Mistress Mattie, Hattie Mae, and Legacy took the baby boy's remains and burned them.

Hattie Mae swept out Mistress Mattie's house and lit some sage. She walked through every room chatting. Legacy followed behind her sprinkling some kind of herb on the floors. Hattie Mae lit a candle in every room and told Baby Girl One's spirit to go towards the light and not to be afraid, that she would see them again in the afterlife. Hattie Mae, Legacy and Mistress Mattie sat there until a strong wind blew the candles out.

Hattie Mae stood up and simply said, "Baby Girl One is with the ancestors now."

Legacy helped Mistress Mattie to get herself together. Mistress Mattie was in an awful way. Baby Girl One's spirit and the baby boy had scared the life out of Mistress Mattie. Although she was only years older than Hattie Mae Mistress Mattie looked to be one hundred and five. Hattie Mae didn't feel sorry for Mistress Mattie. Even though Hattie Mae believed that Robert Lee had sweet-talked Mistress Mattie into doing what she had done, Hattie Mae felt like Mistress Mattie should have never been that weak of a woman to trade her own daughter's life over some superstitious belief. For all Hattie Mae knew, Baby Girl One bled to death from the deep cut in her palm inflicted by Mistress Mattie. Hattie Mae knew that the Voodoo black magic believed that the cut was symbolic of the bloodline Robert Lee, Mistress Mattie and Baby Girl One shared. However, Mistress Mattie knew Hattie Mae had advised her against using dark magic.

Legacy got Mistress Mattie to finally go upstairs and get in her bed.

The next morning, Hattie Mae convinced all the servants that the spirits were gone. Hattie Mae eased their minds by giving them a root to keep in the bottom of their shoes at all times. Hattie Mae told them it would keep them safe from any evil spirits. Legacy laughed at the thought of the servants walking around with the root in their shoes. Besides, it wouldn't help them if Baby Girl One did come back because Baby Girl One wasn't evil.

Mistress Mattie came to speak with Hattie Mae and thank her for helping. Hattie Mae's contempt for Mistress Mattie was obvious. However, Mistress Mattie was continuing to act like she and Hattie Mae were the best of friends.

Hattie Mae warned Mistress Mattie that if she found out she told Robert Lee anything about their conversation that she would unleash Baby Girl One's soul. Mistress Mattie damn near fainted and promised never to go near Robert Lee again.

Mistress Mattie looked at Hattie Mae and said, "However, there's one more thing I haven't told you."

Legacy shook her head in disbelief and walked away.

Hattie Mae said, "Do tell!"

Mistress Mattie said, "Every other Thursday night, Robert Lee comes to call for a spell. After I'm satisfied, he leaves. That was the terms of our agreement to keep me from telling you about what we did to Baby Girl One. I'm so sorry."

Hattie Mae looked at Mistress Mattie and sarcastically replied, "Sure you are. Please continue with your every other Thursday night festivities until further notice. I'm sure it won't be hard for you to do."

As Hattie Mae and Legacy walked home, Hattie Mae told Legacy to keep what she knew to herself. Just tell everybody that Mistress Mattie had taken a leave of her mind for a spell, but she was all right now. Legacy agreed with no questions asked.

Hattie Mae and Legacy stopped at a field to pick wildflowers. Hattie Mae used the wildflowers for a number of things.

Hattie Mae and Legacy were picking wildflowers in the garden when Legacy looked at Hattie Mae and said, "Something's about to happen Mama Hattie Mae. I can feel it in my spirit. The voices are saying a strange name. One I've never heard before."

Hattie Mae had gotten used to Legacy's gift. It had gotten just as strong as Hattie Mae's. Hattie Mae remembered when she had to remind Legacy from time to time to stop telling the children at the schoolhouse things that were going to happen to them. Hattie Mae told Legacy that the gift was a secret that had to be kept between them.

Hattie Mae looked at Legacy and said, "What's the name you keep hearing, baby?"

Legacy replied, "The voices are saying Bactou is coming."

Hattie Mae tried to remain calm. She said, "Are you sure, baby?" Legacy replied, "As sure as I could be."

Hattie Mae and Legacy walked back to the house. Hattie Mae put away her herbs and started on dinner. She knew Robert Lee would be coming home shortly.

Chapter Five:
The Plan

As Hattie Mae stirred the gumbo she was cooking. She thought about what she was going to do about Robert Lee lying to her and convincing Mistress Mattie to go against her to use the dark magic. Hattie Mae always knew that Mistress Mattie was not that bright. She just assumed her friend she traded herbs with came up with the idea.

Then Hattie Mae remembered that Robert Lee had been with her for years. Although he never participated in Hattie Mae's Voodoo belief, he witnessed everything she did, and he had access to all her secret books Master Fo'Rae allowed her to have.

The question still remained. Why would Robert Lee be so devilish and trade Baby Girl One's life for his? He was willing to die for Hattie Mae and Savannah the night Hattie Mae hacked up Master Fo'Rae, and they aren't even blood related to him. So now why was he so willing to let his own child die? Something just wasn't adding up.

Hattie Mae went looking for Savannah. It was time for Savannah to answer for her part in helping Mistress Mattie get rid of the baby boy inside her. Hattie Mae found Savannah in the upstairs room where she kept all her diaries.

Hattie Mae had started keeping her own journals to pass down to her family from generation to generation. Hattie Mae figured, hell, she was keeping a diary for Young Charles, why not keep one for her family?

Hattie Mae sat next to Savannah and said, "Who told you to read my books? Did you ask me before you started rambling through my belongings? How rude child!"

Savannah replied, "How comes you writes so much about Legacy and so little about me? You loves her more than me, Mama?"

Hattie Mae knew Savannah was jealous because she thought Hattie Mae always loved Legacy more than her. Hell, Savannah always wanted all the attention at all times. Savannah was so selfish at times. Hattie Mae assumed she got that from Master Fo'Rae because she sure as hell didn't get it from her.

Hattie Mae slowly took her diary away from Savannah and said, "Hush child, that's nonsense. I loves you both the same. Both of you's my blood. I just writes more about Legacy because I spends more time with her. You always so busy with your girls and Pierre Cordova. That's all!"

Savannah frowned up her nose and smiled. Savannah laid her head on Hattie Mae's shoulder and replied, "Okay Mama, but remember I was here first. Even before Claude. So try your best to write more about me in your diaries."

Hattie Mae smiled and said, "Okay baby, I'll remember that."

Savannah replied, "Besides I don't know why you keep all these stories and goings on. Mistress Mattie gonna die and leave all her money to Young Charles and he ain't gonna have time to be reading no books of stuff he already lived through."

Hattie Mae rubbed Savannah's hair. She decided to take a different approach to get the truth about what Mistress Mattie had done out of Savannah.

Hattie Mae picked up a brush off the table. She brushed Savannah's hair.

Hattie Mae said, "You have such beautiful hair Lady Bug."

Savannah replied, "Just like white folks, huh Mama?"

Hattie Mae was never shocked by anything that came out of Savannah's mouth.

Even though Hattie Mae often wanted to smack the taste out of Savannah's mouth, this time she just grinned and bore Savannah's ignorance.

Hattie Mae bit her lip and replied, "No baby, even better than white folks' hair. Your hair is naturally golden brown like it's been kissed by the sun; you don't have to put all that hair color in your hair or even wash it every day like they do."

Hattie Mae braided Savannah's hair into two cornrows going straight back. Then she took the brush and laid some of her hair down on the side of her face. Hattie Mae tied two red ribbons on the ends of the braids.

She turned Savannah to the mirror and said, "Look how beautiful you are."

Savannah looked in the mirror and replied, "I look like a Creole Goddess. You can hardly tell I'm half Negro at all."

Hattie Mae knew she'd better get to the bottom of what she came in there to talk to Savannah about quick. Because if Savannah made one more ignorant comment like that, Hattie Mae knew she wasn't going to be able to keep herself from snatching Savannah bald.

Hattie Mae said, "Lady Bug tell me what you know about Mistress Mattie and the baby boy that she pulled from her womb."

Savannah's eyes got big ass marbles. She was floored by what Hattie Mae had just said.

Savannah replied, "All I know is she put it in a jar and buried it. Mistress Mattie said she had to do it. She wasn't married, and it wasn't right for her to be having more babies."

Hattie Mae said, "Did you help her pull it out of her womb?"

"No mama, I did no such thing. All I did was bring her some of your herbs to stop her from bleeding to death," was Savannah's response.

Hattie Mae replied, "Did Robert Lee, know about the baby?"

Savannah tilted her head to the side in confusion. She said, "Why would papa know anything about Mistress Mattie's business?"

Hattie Mae realized that Savannah didn't know what had been going on with Mistress Mattie and Robert Lee, or that Hattie Mae had convinced Robert Lee to have relations with Mistress Mattie the night before Baby Girl One died. Well, before Baby Girl One was murdered.

Hattie Mae said, "Have you seen Robert Lee around the mansion lately. I mean since Young Charles left?"

Savannah said, "Oh yeah, I see him every other Thursdays on his way to play cards and smoke cigars with gentlemen."

Hattie Mae replied, "Oh okay."

Then Hattie Mae had a thought. She said, "Lady Bug does Pierre Cordova go to these gatherings?"

Savannah responded, "Well, no. He went once, but he quickly came back. He said the games they were playing didn't appeal to him. Plus he didn't like cigar smoke. Which I found odd because he's always smoking cigars with Mistress Mattie's gentleman caller."

Hattie Mae was confused; she didn't know Mistress Mattie had a gentleman caller.

Hattie Mae looked at Savannah and said, "What have you been doing with your skin. It looks lighter as the days pass."

Savannah's face lit up with pride when Hattie Mae said she looked lighter. Savannah went on and on about how she kept her skin so light and smooth. Hattie Mae could have cared less, but she knew the more she implied that Savannah looked white, the more information Savannah was going to give up on Mistress Mattie.

Savannah told Hattie Mae all about Mistress Mattie and her gentleman caller. Savannah said Mistress Mattie had been courting him for weeks.

Savannah looked at Hattie Mae and said, "Mistress Mattie's gentleman caller said me and Mistress Mattie looked like we could be sisters. I told him that's because we be kinsfolk. Cause Mistress Mattie and I's cousins because her and Master Fo'Rae was cousins and, well he is my real Papa."

Hattie Mae got the urge to choke Savannah but decided against it. Hattie Mae had heard enough from Savannah today and simply said she had to go finish, preparing supper.

On the way out, Hattie Mae slipped over a camera box. Hattie Mae picked the box up and said, "This old thing always got on my nerves. I was so glad when Young Charles went off to school. I was so tired of taking photo pictures of him. Master Fo'Rae's brother insisted I capture every moment of his life."

Hattie Mae sat the picture box on the shelf and walked into the kitchen where she overheard Pierre Cordova complaining to Robert Lee that Savannah never has time for him because she's either pregnant or with the babies. Pierre Cordova told Robert Lee that Savannah didn't even try to satisfy him; it was almost like a chore she had to hurry up and get over with.

Hattie Mae wanted to hear the advice that Robert Lee was going to give Pierre Cordova because apparently, Robert Lee wasn't having an issue with his sex life. Hell, he had two women to please him.

All through dinner, Hattie Mae couldn't figure out what she was going to do about Robert Lee. She thought about killing his sorry ass but then changed her mind because Young Charles or Savannah would never forgive her. They loved Robert Lee so much it sickened Hattie Mae.

However, just because Hattie Mae wasn't going to kill Robert Lee, he was still going to pay for what he did. And payback was going to start today. Hattie Mae saw Robert Lee's facial expression. She knew the special herbs she put in his soup were settled in. Pretty soon he was going to have a terrible pain in his stomach.

Hattie Mae looked over at Savannah who was still rubbing her hair and telling her kids they had to stop talking like slaves. Savannah told them they are not slaves and had never been slaves. So from that moment on, if she heard slave talk from anyone of their mouths, all of them would be getting smacked. Savannah told them they, need to speak proper like white folks if they wanted to make it in the world.

Hattie Mae hated to agree with Savannah, but she was right this time.

Savannah excused herself from the table in the middle of her rant. Hattie Mae knew it was because the special soup she had made for Savannah was kicking in. Hattie Mae decided Savannah had worked her nerves earlier. With all that ridiculous talk about her looking white and having good white folk's hair. Hattie Mae decided Savannah needed to be taught a lesson. So she put the same herbs in Savannah's gumbo soup.

Hattie Mae watched Savannah make her way to the chamber pot. Hattie Mae laughed to herself at the thought of Savannah trying to take off all those damn clothes she had on. Everyday Savannah dressed up like a Southern Bell, which Hattie Mae found to be ridiculous.

Hattie Mae wrecked her mind all night trying to figure out what to do. Killing Robert Lee or Mistress Mattie was off limits at this point. Hattie Mae had a deal with Master Fo'Rae's brother to raise Young Charles properly.

A thought came to Hattie Mae's mind. Hattie Mae remembered what Master Fo'Rae's brother always said, "Knowledge is power and what's the sense of having power if you don't use it for profit." The only thing was, how Hattie Mae was going to use her evidence against Mistress Mattie when Master Fo'Rae's brother didn't believe in the spirits or ghost. He said it was just old slave talk. Master Fo'Rae's brother said the only thing that was real was power. And the only way to have power was to have money.

Hattie Mae was walking past the room she and Savannah were in earlier and remembered the picture box Master Fo'Rae's brother had sent her. Just then Hattie Mae thought of a plan. Hattie Mae figured she'd use her knowledge to make her family's lives better. Savannah was right; Young

Charles was going to inherit everything. And no matter how hard Pierre Cordova worked on those docks, he was never going to have enough money to live like rich white folks. Hell Mistress Mattie and Master Fo'Rae owned at least six dozen slaves in Louisiana. That worked all the cotton, tobacco, and sugarcane fields. Plus Mistress Mattie owned several homes and half a shipping company.

Hattie Mae knew she had to do what Master Fo'Rae Brother is always preaching to Young Charles, and that was to build family wealth. Hattie Mae decided that the price for what Mistress Mattie had done was going to cost her dearly. Hattie Mae was going to demand that she give her money to build a mansion of her own, plus buy Pierre Cordova a ship of his own so he could start his own shipping company.

Hattie Mae held up the picture box. She said, "I never did too much care for you, but you're about to come in handy."

Hattie Mae didn't like the picture box. She believed, just like the Indians did, that taking pictures took a piece of your soul away.

Hattie Mae knew that Mistress Mattie was very slick. Mistress Mattie played helpless; however, she was sharp as a whip when it came to conniving.

However, nobody was better at playing dumb like the slaves. Playing ignorant in front of white folks was their specialty. There's nothing more threatening to a white man than an intelligent Negro.

Hattie Mae also knew that Mistress Mattie wasn't about to just give up a small fortune just because Hattie Mae threatened to tell Master Fo'Rae's brother what Mistress Mattie had done. However, if Hattie Mae threatened to expose Mistress Mattie's trifling ways to the other island wives and Young Charles, Mistress Mattie would be horrified. Hattie Mae knew Mistress Mattie prided herself on being a grieving widowed Southern Bell. So how would she explain having sexual relations with a Negro? She'd never be able to deny it if Hattie Mae could capture the image on her picture box.

Hattie Mae knew she had to have a partner. The picture box required the proper lighting and made somewhat of a racket.

Hattie Mae ruled out the help of Legacy because of the compromising position Mistress Mattie and Robert Lee would be in. So Hattie Mae's last choice was Savannah, which Hattie Mae knew it was going to take some hell of convincing to get Savannah to help.

Hattie Mae pondered over her plan for a few weeks. Sure enough, every other Thursday Robert Lee said he was off to his card game. One Thursday night, he came home early. Hattie Mae was curious as to why, so she asked him.

Robert Lee said there was a change of plans and that he'd go back next Thursday.

The next morning, Hattie Mae got up early and headed to Mistress Mattie's mansion to inquire about what happened.

Hattie Mae had to make sure Savannah didn't slip and tell Mistress Mattie about Hattie Mae's plan. Hattie Mae knew that Savannah considered Mistress Mattie family. Plus Savannah talked too much.

Hattie Mae stopped at Savannah's house first. Hattie Mae walked in to find Savannah had hung a huge oil painting of white Jesus over the mantle. Hattie Mae just shook her head. Savannah was saying her morning prayers.

Hattie Mae looked at Savannah and said, "So you a Christian now?"

Savannah replied, "Catholic to be exact. Mama, you gotta believe in something."

Hattie Mae didn't have the time to debate over whether or not Savannah's Jesus was real or not. Besides, over the weeks, Jesus kept Savannah humble and busy. Hattie Mae hadn't heard about Savannah's good hair or light skin in weeks because Savannah was too busy praying and reading the Bible.

Hattie Mae thought this would be a good time to talk to Savannah about learning how to please her husband.

Hattie Mae said, "Lady Bug, I overheard Pierre Cordova and Robert Lee speaking about your private life. Pierre Cordova didn't seem to be pleased. Do you want to talk to me about it?"

Savannah replied, "I most certainly do not, Mother! My private life is exactly that, private! Besides, if my husband is not pleased, then he can take it upon himself to please himself."

Then Savannah smacked her lips and rolled her eyes. Which let Hattie Mae know that conversation was over.

Hattie Mae said, "Have you seen Mistress Mattie lately?"

Savannah replied angrily, "No I haven't, and I'm not particularly looking for Mistress Mattie either."

Hattie Mae sensed some hostility in Savanna's voice.

Hattie Mae replied, "Well, you sound a little upset with your cousin today. What happened?"

Hattie Mae referred to Mistress Mattie as Savannah's cousin trying to make Savannah feel better. However, that seemed to upset her even more.

"She ain't no cousin of mines. I heard her telling her gentleman caller that she's never going to let a nigger like me be in her wedding. Can you believe that mama?"

Hattie Mae was shocked. She said, "Wedding? What wedding? Who's getting married?"

Savannah said, "Mistress Mattie's gentleman caller asked her to marry him, and she said yes. They's just waiting on Master Fo'Rae's blessings to come from the states and some legal paperwork."

106

Hattie Mae felt ill. She knew once Mistress Mattie married her gentlemen friend, her plan of blackmailing Mistress Mattie wouldn't go as planned because after Mistress Mattie got married, her husband would be in charge of her finances. More importantly, Mistress Mattie wasn't out of the childbearing age yet. What if the Heffa got pregnant again and had a real white baby? She'd cut Young Charles off for certain.

Hattie Mae was going to have to get that photo picture of Mistress Mattie and Robert Lee soon.

Hattie Mae said, "Well, when did all this happen?"

Savannah replied, "Right after you and Legacy sent Baby Girl One to the light. Mistress Mattie came back to her senses and started acting normal. Her gentleman caller was so impressed with her. He asked her to be his wife."

Savannah looked around to see if anyone was listening and whispered, "He was impressed with her skills in the bedroom. The upstairs maid said she walked in on them supposedly praying. However, she said the way the man was screaming 'Oh God' she's sure God heard him."

Hattie Mae chuckled a little. She knew Mistress Mattie was a little whore in the bedroom. Hattie Mae just figured Mistress Mattie had way too much free time.

When Hattie Mae asked Savannah if she was still going to help her out with her plan, Savannah replied, "I'm afraid I can't mama. The lord our God doesn't condone wickedness."

Hattie Mae wanted to reach across the table and smack fire from Savannah. However, right now she had to devise another strategy because Savannah was too busy finding Jesus. Hattie Mae made a mental note of Savannah's sudden change in behavior. Hattie Mae reminded herself to set Savannah straight at a later date.

Hattie Mae made her way to the mansion where she found Mistress Mattie planning an extravagant wedding.

Mistress Mattie threw her arms around Hattie Mae when she saw her.

She seemed happy to see Hattie Mae.

Mistress Mattie said, "I knew my only friend on this entire planet wouldn't leave me alone on my wedding day. Oh, Hattie Mae you sure are a sight for sore eyes. I don't know the first thing about planning a party. Please tell me you've forgiven me and come to help me. I don't know what I'll do if you refuse me. We've been best friends for so long and I miss you."

Hattie Mae just stood there. She was at a loss for words. Hattie Mae figured she'd just say yes and then come up with a plan.

She replied, "Of course I came to help. You knows I wouldn't leave you alone on your big day."

She could have sworn she saw a tear run down Mistress Mattie's face. Hattie Mae couldn't believe Mistress Mattie was standing there going on and on about her being her best friend in the entire world, when every chance she got she had sex with Robert Lee. Hattie Mae figured there had to be more to this story. Either Mistress Mattie wanted something from Hattie Mae, or she was scared to death that Hattie Mae would unleash Baby Girl One's spirit.

Mistress Mattie told the maids to prepare her and Hattie Mae some lunch and pour them some strong drinks. Mistress Mattie said she and Hattie Mae had a lot of catching up to do.

Hattie Mae just sat there and listened to Mistress Mattie tell her all about her gentleman caller and how he loved her so. Then Mistress Mattie asked about Robert Lee. She told Hattie Mae that she'd ended their Thursday appointments.

Mistress Mattie looked at Hattie Mae and said, "Why Hattie Mae, I thought you would be delighted with that information? Now you have him all to yourself. The poor dear took it awfully hard though when I told him we'd had to end this romance. As much as we love each other, the world just will never accept what we have."

Hattie Mae just sat there dumbfounded. Mistress Mattie was more delusional as ever. Hell, she was blackmailing Robert Lee to sleep with her then pretending like they had some great love affair.

She decided to play along for a while until Mistress Mattie revealed what she truly wanted.

Hattie Mae figured she only had a short period to get her plan going. So she decided to test the waters with Mistress Mattie to see if she was really over Robert Lee.

Hattie Mae said, "Well, Mistress Mattie, I'm grateful for you sending Robert Lee home last night. The way he was all hot and bothered."

Hattie Mae pretended like she was embarrassed to say what she was going to say.

She said, "Robert Lee was like a wild man. He had me up until the wee hours of the morning. He was like a savage beast. I swear if I didn't get out of that house early, I would have been in bed all day trying to please him."

Hattie Mae could tell what she was saying about Robert Lee's sexual desire for her was making Mistress Mattie jealous.

Hattie Mae looked at Mistress Mattie and said, "We done been friends for quite some time now. So I feel like I can say certain things to you."

Mistress Mattie eagerly replied, "Why Hattie Mae, sure you can."

Hattie Mae said, "Well, I was just wondering about your gentleman caller, but I don't want to cross the line and be disrespectful."

Mistress Mattie replied, "Nonsense Hattie Mae, spit it out. What's your question?"

Hattie Mae responded, "Well, since I've only had two men in my life, one being Master with a very small penis..."

Hattie Mae stopped and turned her face around. Then she turned back around and said, "Well Master Fo'Rae had a very small penis compared to Robert Lee's. So I was wondering about your gentleman caller. Does he have a small penis too?"

Mistress Mattie giggled with excitement; she loved sex talk.

Mistress Mattie whispered, "Well, it's not quite as large as Robert Lee's, but nowhere near as small as Master Fo'Rae."

Mistress Mattie threw her hands up in the air, slapped her knee and giggled.

Mistress Mattie said, "Oh Hattie Mae, I do declare, now that I done had time to think on it, Master Fo'Rae's penis was like a little annoying bug. It made you just want to squeeze the life out of it."

Mistress Mattie laughed so hard talking about Master Fo'Rae's small penis that tears washed her face.
Mistress Mattie said, "Well, Hattie Mae, that's a memory we can both forget. Just lock that awful thought in the back of your mind. And thank God you have such a strong and well-endowed man such as Robert Lee. Hattie Mae God, is good."

Hattie Mae could tell thinking about Robert Lee made Mistress Mattie a little hot and bothered. Hattie Mae decided to turn up the heat.

Hattie Mae bit her lip and folded both her hands together. Hattie Mae looked around to see if anyone was listening. Hattie Mae knew how nosey Mistress Mattie was. Mistress Mattie begged Hattie Mae to tell her what had her so bothered.

Hattie Mae looked at Mistress Mattie and said shyly, "But I feel so silly asking you all these embarrassing questions."

Mistress Mattie replied, "Nonsense child. We are best friends, almost like sisters. There's nothing too embarrassing to ask me. Now spit it out, Hattie Mae."

Hattie Mae said quietly, "Well, last night when I was with Robert Lee, an overwhelming feeling of sensation came over my body. My entire body trembled from head to toe. It was like my body released a massive amount of energy.... "
Hattie Mae stopped talking and covered her face as if she was embarrassed. Hattie Mae peeked at Mistress Mattie through the tiny opening in her fingers. Mistress Mattie was so excited about Hattie Mae's story she almost jumped out of her chair.

Mistress Mattie blurted out, "What Hattie Mae? What happened?"

Hattie Mae knew she had Mistress Mattie just where she wanted her, about to die of a heart attack with curiosity.

Hattie Mae said, "The strangest feeling came through my vagina. I couldn't hardly breath. Why I thought I'd pass out for sure with pleasure."

Mistress Mattie jumped up and held her heart. She said, "Why I declare, Hattie Mae, you done gone and had an orgasm. You lucky little devil."

Hattie Mae laughed to herself. She could see the jealousy all over Mistress Mattie's face. Hattie Mae knew she'd just rekindled Mistress Mattie's desire for Robert Lee.

Hattie Mae told Mistress Mattie she had to be heading back home before it got dark.

Hattie Mae was getting ready to say her goodbyes to Savannah and her family when she heard a strange sound. It sounded like growling. Hattie Mae decided to skip Savannah's house and hurried home. Hattie Mae felt like something or somebody was following her. Hattie Mae stuck her hand in her pocket to feel for her protection stone and her hook knife.

When Hattie Mae made it home, she saw Robert Lee soaking his feet. Hattie Mae understood how hard Robert Lee worked. She felt sorry for him. Hell, they had escaped slavery only to come to St. Lucia to work harder. Although Robert Lee had his own shop and an undeniable set of skills, it was hard work, and no matter how hard they worked, they would never earn enough money to live like white folks.

Hattie Mae frowned her face and thought, "*Life just wasn't fair.*"

Hattie Mae then laughed and thought, "*Next time she saw Savannah, she was going to ask her to ask White Jesus what he was going to do about the awful treatment of colored folks.*"

Then Hattie Mae remembered that she needed a partner to carry out her plan to get that picture of Robert Lee and Mistress Mattie.

Hattie Mae decided that Robert Lee was going to be the one to help.

Shit, Hattie Mae thought to herself, *Robert Lee just otta help. Because of him Baby Girl One was dead, and he was still visiting with Mistress Mattie every other Thursday.*

Hattie Mae bent down and washed Robert Lee's feet. As she massaged them, she told Robert Lee what Mistress Mattie told her, about his part in Baby Girl One's death.

Robert Lee just shook his head and said, "All lies, I did nothing of the sorts. I would never hurt a child of mines. Mistress Mattie came to find me that night at the lake. I was still upset about you forcing me to have relations with Mistress Mattie earlier that evening. Mistress Mattie was holding one of your Voodoo spell books. She said that she'd found something that would save Young Charles. Mistress Mattie told me that it required my blood, so I allowed her to cut my hand and take some. Mistress Mattie also said that you refused to help her. She begged me to keep you occupied while someone else completed the spell."

Robert Lee looked at Hattie Mae and said, "Hattie Mae, you know me. You know I wouldn't hurt an innocent child."

Hattie Mae felt in her spirit Robert Lee was telling the truth. She said, "Then what happened?"

Robert Lee replied, "After Baby Girl One's funeral, I confronted Mistress Mattie about what she had done. She threatened me by saying I was still a runaway slave. She said she had insurance on me and that if I uttered a word of what happened to anyone, she would send a telegram to the states."

Robert Lee looked down at the ground. He grabbed Hattie Mae's hands and said, "But that's not all. Mistress Mattie had one more request."

Hattie Mae pretended like she didn't already know what he was about to say. She wanted him to tell her willingly. Robert Lee said, "Well, Hattie Mae, Mistress Mattie made me agree to come call on her every other Thursday night. I've been going for years now. Until yesterday when Mistress Mattie informed me she no longer needed my services."

Hattie Mae continued to wash Robert Lee's feet.

Hattie Mae slowly said, "Are you sorry for what you been doing? The lies and secrets?"

Robert Lee said, "Hattie Mae I been sorry since I was born. I was born into slavery, born to do what white folks tells me to do all my life. Then when I gets a taste of freedom, Mistress Mattie gets her hooks in me again. So yes I'm sorry."

Hattie Mae felt the pain in Robert Lee's words. She took a deep breath and said, "Life for colored folks in this world just ain't fair. You were born into slavery, and I was taken from my home, from my family to come and serve another family. I was raped, beaten, and abused. Made to give birth to two children. I had one snatched right out my arms. I've never known so much evil until I was brought to the United States."

Hattie Mae looked up to the sky and said, "The Great Spirits have given us another life here in St. Lucia. It's time to put the past behind us and build a better future for our kids."

Robert Lee looked at Hattie Mae and said, "I'll never have a real relationship with my son. He's too busy being white."

Hattie Mae was about to respond when she felt a presence close. She looked around, but she saw nothing. She stood up on the porch to get a better look. Still, she saw nothing, but she knew something or someone was watching.

Hattie Mae insisted that they go inside. Inside, she told Robert Lee all about her plan to blackmail Mistress Mattie.

Robert Lee thought Hattie Mae had gone mad. However, he agreed to help her. He said the thought of Mistress Mattie telegraphing the states terrified him.

Hattie Mae never believed that Mistress Mattie had the strength to ever make that telegraph. Mistress Mattie was obsessed with Robert Lee.

Robert Lee looked at Hattie Mae and said, "I would kill everybody in St. Lucia before I would allow them to take us back to the United States.

That night, Hattie Mae made her rounds through the house to make sure all the windows and doors were bolted tight.

As Hattie Mae blew out the last candle, she could have sworn she heard howling outside.

Chapter Six:
Puppet Master

After Hattie Mae confronted Robert Lee and finally got the truth out of him, it was time for her to get her plan in motion. Hattie Mae understood that she only had a short while before those papers from the states came. Once Mistress Mattie married her gentleman caller, she was going to cut off Robert Lee completely. Mistress Mattie's obsession with Robert Lee was coming to an end. Mistress Mattie enjoyed the thought of being a doting wife more than she did Robert Lee's penis.

Hattie Mae went to Mistress Mattie mansion while she was gone to church. Hattie Mae had to find the right spot in the room to get the correct lighting she would need for the picture.

As Hattie Mae searched around Mistress Mattie's master bedroom suite, she was amazed at the beauty of it. Hattie Mae had to admit that Mistress Mattie did have a talent for decorating. Mistress Mattie's room was fit for a queen. Everything was purple, the color of royalty, with crushed velvet and gold curtains, luxurious gold picture frames and gold satin sheets with crushed velvet covers.

Mistress Mattie's vanity set was lined with the finest perfumes and oils. Her jewelry box dripped over with diamonds and pearls.
Hattie Mae made her way to the closet that was big enough for her to sleep in. It, too, was filled to capacity with clothes, hats, and shoes.

Hattie Mae looked around and thought to herself, *this heffa is living lavish and never had to lift one finger in her life. All she did was be born white and marry Master Fo'Rae.* Hattie Mae thought about all the hard work the slaves do daily so that white folks could get rich and sleep on satin and velvet sheets.

Hattie Mae was trying to figure out how to position the camera to get a right shot when she heard Mistress Mattie screaming for all the maids to leave the mansion.

Mistress Mattie told the upstairs maid to stay, but do not disturb her, and to bring her dinner at six p.m. sharp.

Mistress Mattie entered the room too fast for Hattie Mae to leave. Hattie Mae hid in the closet behind the clothes and watched Mistress Mattie.

Mistress Mattie took off all her clothes down to her undergarments. She was whispering something over and over to herself. Hattie Mae couldn't make out what she was saying. By the look on Mistress Mattie's face, something had pissed her off. Mistress Mattie was five shades of red.

Mistress Mattie mumbled, "It's always about her! Hattie Mae this, Hattie Mae that! When is it going to be about me? How dare he ask me to invite Hattie Mae on our afternoon stroll so he could get to know her because he's heard so much about her? Like how beautiful she is and that she's a very powerful Voodoo Queen."

Mistress Mattie rolled her eyes and said, "Queen my ass! She's just a Nigger!"

Mistress Mattie pushed all the throw pillows on the floor and fell on the bed in tears. Mistress Mattie kicked her feet over the bed. She had a tantrum as a young child would.

Mistress Mattie started talking to herself again. She said, "Everybody thinks Hattie Mae's so exquisite. Her skin is so exotic. To hell with Hattie Mae and her cornrows and head scarves. I'm fabulous, too. My skin is lily white, and my lips are red and thin as sheets of paper. I have beautiful blue eyes and blonde hair."

Mistress Mattie grabbed her hand mirror and marveled at herself.

Mistress Mattie wiped the tears from her face. Then she sat at her vanity set. She fixed her makeup and reapplied the brightest red paint on her lips.

Mistress Mattie looked at herself in the mirror. She pointed at herself and said, "There, there now. You must get yourself together. You are the Mistress of this house. You are the beautiful one. No slave is ever going to steal your spot."

Mistress Mattie looked around the room as if she were looking for something. She walked over to the door and locked it. Then she reached under her bed and pulled out a beautifully decorated box. She pulled out two dolls. She held the first one up. It was a white porcelain doll. It had on the finest little clothes, and her hair was perfectly curled. The doll had the reddest lips just like Mistress Mattie's. Mistress Mattie sat the white doll in the bed. Then she picked up another doll. This doll was an old black rag doll. One of its eyes was missing, and it had on rags for clothes and a scarf tied around its head.

Mistress Mattie sat on the bed and played with the dolls as if she were a little girl again. She held the black doll up. Bucked her eyes out and said in her best imitation of a slave voice, "Oh my Mistress Mattie, I do believes you's getting more beautiful as the days goes by. Oh, how I wished I's white like you."

Then Mistress Mattie held up the white doll and said, "Hattie Mae you are nothing but a nigger slave with nappy hair. The only thing you were born to do was serve me."

Hattie Mae hid in the closet furious; she thought to herself, *Ain't that a bitch.*

Hattie Mae always knew Mistress Mattie wasn't wrapped too tight, but this was way crazier than she expected. Hattie Mae thought to herself that Mistress Mattie had finally lost it.

Mistress Mattie prompted the white doll up on a pillow. She placed the black Hattie Mae doll at the white doll's feet.

Mistress Mattie started crying, then she set the black doll next to the white one.

Mistress Mattie said, "Hattie Mae, please forgive me. You are my only friend in this world. We are best friends. I don't know what I would do without you. I didn't mean all those horrible things I said about you."

Mistress Mattie sobbed uncontrollably. She lay down on the pillow. Mistress Mattie grabbed the Hattie Mae doll and shook it violently.

Mistress Mattie said angrily, "Hattie Mae you are mines. You understand me? You will never be anyone else's."

Then Mistress Mattie flung the Hattie Mae doll into the wall.

Mistress Mattie ran over and sat beside the Hattie Mae doll. She said, "Master Fo'Rae gave you to me and me alone. You couldn't even speak English when I first got you. I taught you to speak. I took care of you like a big sister. I even made Master Fo'Rae give you Robert Lee. I picked him out personally for you. Then you stole the Master's love from me. That's how you repay my kindness? I kept you out of the fields, and you steal my husband."

Hattie Mae sat there and watched Mistress Mattie ramble on and on about how Hattie Mae stole all the attention.

Hattie Mae thought to herself that Mistress Mattie needed help because she was crazy. "*Hell!*" Hattie Mae said to herself. *Mistress Mattie only taught her English so she could work her harder. Besides, Master Fo'Rae had already taught her how to speak French. And the only reason she ever was with Master Fo'Rae was because he forced her to be. Shit*, Hattie Mae thought, *I was only an innocent child. Stolen from my home.*

Hattie Mae had a memory flash of Mistress Mattie and her hiding in the cellar one night when Master Fo'Rae had come home drunk. He was on one of his beating spells. Mistress Mattie and Hattie Mae hid in the cellar, until Master Fo'Rae decided to go calling on the slave girls. Hattie Mae remembered Mistress Mattie being somewhat nice to her. Nevertheless, Mistress Mattie was still in charge of her. Hattie Mae also remembered Mistress Mattie picking out Robert Lee for her, too, after Hattie Mae had Claude. However, Hattie Mae was starting to wonder if all along Robert Lee was really for Mistress Mattie's enjoyment.

Hattie Mae heard Mistress Mattie say, "What did you say?"

Hattie Mae looked around the room to see to whom Mistress Mattie was talking to. However, Hattie Mae didn't see anyone.

Then Mistress Mattie said in a man's voice, really hard and wicked, "I said Hattie Mae is mines. She always was. I never bought her for you. I was done with you years ago. You got too old."

Then Mistress Mattie opened the decorated box once again and took out a male doll.

Mistress Mattie looked at it and said, "How dare you speak to me like that. I'm your wife."

Hattie Mae put one hand over her mouth and the other one over her heart. Hattie Mae thought to herself, *Great Spirits, now I know that Mistress Mattie done went foolish.*

Mistress Mattie had a male doll of Master Fo'Rae and was having a full-blown conversation with all three dolls.

Mistress Mattie picked up the Hattie Mae doll and pretended to be hacking Master Fo'Rae up.

Hattie Mae heard a knock at the door, then the maid said, "Ma'am it's 6 p.m. sharp, and your supper is here."

Mistress Mattie composed herself. She put all the dolls back in the decorated box and put them back under the bed. She smoothed her hair down and threw on her robe. Mistress Mattie told the maid to leave the super by the door and she'd get it.

Hattie Mae waited until Mistress Mattie ate and had her shot of brandy. Just like clockwork, she was asleep. Hattie Mae eased out of the closet and sneaked out of the house unnoticed.

As Hattie Mae walked to Savannah's house, she realized it was too late for her to try and make it home. Although she was free in St. Lucia, bad things still happened to colored folks at night.

Hattie Mae decided to stay the night at Savannah's. Hattie Mae stopped to clear her mind of all that she just witnessed.

Mistress Mattie was really going crazy, Hattie Mae thought to herself.

Hattie Mae looked up to the sky to ask the Ancestors for help. Even though Mistress Mattie had done some dreadful things, Hattie Mae had a soft spot for her. Mistress Mattie had been Hattie Mae's only friend on the plantation. Everybody else was frightened of Hattie Mae and Hattie Mae learning how to cut animals up and being a butcher didn't make it no better.

Hattie Mae looked up to the sky and talked to the ancestors.

Hattie Mae said, "Great ones," then she stopped. Hattie Mae felt as if somebody was looking at her. She could feel another presence, yet she saw nothing.

Hattie Mae looked up to the sky. This time she caught a glimpse of the full moon. Hattie Mae felt drawn to it. It was almost like the moon was calling her. Hattie Mae ran towards the moon.

Hattie Mae stopped when she got a full view of it. There it was hanging in the sky in all its glory. shining brightly and lighting up the night. Hattie Mae felt compelled to remove all her clothes and bask in the power of the Moon. The moon seemed to be recharging Hattie Mae.

Hattie Mae felt a surge of energy. She closed her eyes and allowed her entire body to relax and absorb the power of the moon.

Hattie Mae spoke to her ancestors in her native tongue.

As Hattie Mae was absorbing the energy from the moon, she realized that she wasn't alone anymore. Hattie Mae could hear the ever so faint growl of an animal. Hattie Mae opened her eyes and slowly turned around. From all Hattie Mae's experience with animals, she knew quick movement was not acceptable.

121

Hattie Mae turned around still naked with her hands in the air. Hattie Mae's eyes widened with fear, and her heart almost stopped. Hattie Mae was frozen still.

Standing directly in front of her was a great wolf. He had the most beautiful fur of black along his top area and grey on his legs and feet. He had the sharpest teeth and his eyes were as blue as the ocean.

Hattie Mae said slowly, "It cannot be."

Hattie Mae's eyes closed and reopened and the animal was still there. Hattie Mae couldn't believe it.

Hattie Mae looked at the animal and said, "Well, Great one, you have to be the most magnificent creature I've ever seen. Oh my, you're a long way from home."

Hattie Mae remembered hearing tales from the island people that a British ambassador had brought two great wolves from Britain. However, the wolves got loose, then disappeared never to be seen again. Rumor was that on some nights, the island people heard them howling at the moon.

Hattie Mae looked at the wolf, then at the moon.

Hattie Mae said slowly, "Did you come to recharge your energy from the moon, too?"

Hattie Mae never moved a single muscle. She didn't want to seem like she was challenging the wolf.

Hattie Mae thought to herself; *if he's going to eat me, please let it be quick.*

Hattie Mae stood there in amazement until she heard a howl coming from the distance.

Hattie Mae said, "Great Spirits no, not another one."

The wolf looked at Hattie Mae and stretched his paw out. He ran it along the ground. Almost like he was telling Hattie Mae something.

The wolf slowly walked away. He turned back to look at Hattie Mae.

Hattie Mae turned to run the other way but stopped. Hattie Mae felt a strong urge to follow the wolf. Hattie Mae picked her dress up and quickly put it on.

The wolf seemed to be waiting patiently.

The wolf took a few steps and turned to look at Hattie Mae. Hattie Mae seemed to think he wanted her to follow him. So she did.

He led Hattie Mae to a cave where he stopped at the opening that was covered in tree branches.

The wolf turned to look at Hattie Mae then dragged one of the branches away to reveal a female wolf. After the wolf removed all the branches, he sat next to her and stared at Hattie Mae.

Hattie Mae was terrified, but thought to herself. *If the wolf wanted to eat her, he could have done that easily ten minutes ago. However he led her here to this female wolf, but why?*

Then Hattie Mae saw why.

The female wolf's leg was caught in a trap.

Hattie Mae looked over at the male wolf then back at the female wolf that was lying there helpless. Hattie Mae took baby steps towards the female wolf to get a better view of the situation. Sure enough, the female wolf's leg was caught in a trap.

Hattie Mae looked at the female wolf and said, "Great Queen, I want to help you, but I fear you might eat me alive."

Hattie Mae felt silly. Here she was in the midst of two of the most vicious animals on earth, and she was having a conversation with them, as if they understood.

Hattie Mae eased her way closer. She looked over at the male wolf for his permission to examine the female wolf.

The male wolf relaxed his body as if he was giving Hattie Mae permission to help.

Hattie Mae sat on the earth next to the female. The female wolf was almost as marvelous as her male counterpart. She was a black and grey mixture of fur, and you could see the strength in her body.

Hattie Mae understood that with one swift swipe of her paw, the female wolf could end Hattie Mae's life.

Yet the female wolf just lay there helpless. Hattie Mae rubbed her beautiful fur.

Hattie Mae said softly, "Fear me not beautiful Queen."

Then Hattie Mae struggled to release the female's leg from the trap.

After Hattie Mae got the female wolf's leg free, she examined it. Hattie Mae knew she was going to have to treat the leg. The only question was, was the female going to allow her to?

Hattie Mae stood up slowly and said out loud, "I have to go get medicine. I'll come back to help you."

Both wolves seemed unbothered by her statement.

Before Hattie Mae made any sudden movement, she remembered what she had learned about wild animals. That was to always show respect and remember that although the human is smarter, the animal is stronger.

Hattie Mae decided to try something she'd seen the animals in the wild do. She bowed down in a submissive position in front of the male wolf.

Then she slowly turned and walked away. When enough distance was between her and the wolves, she realized what has just happened. Fear came over her, and she took off running. Hattie Mae was all out of breath when she arrived at Savannah's house.

Hattie Mae could hear Pierre Cordova complaining about Savannah trying to feed his girls pork. Pierre Cordova told Savannah that she could worship any white God she wanted to, but he'd be damned if she was going to feed his girls swine.

Savannah seemed to be pissed about it, mainly because she had already prepared supper of smothered pork chops and gravy. Although Hattie Mae had never given Savannah pork when she was a child, Savannah seemed to enjoy it.

Hattie Mae told Savannah all about what had happened with Mistress Mattie and about her encounter with the wolves. Savannah didn't seem too interested in the story about Mistress Mattie. Savannah said that the maids always spoke of Mistress Mattie being crazy.

However, Savannah was intrigued with Hattie Mae's wolf tale. As Savannah wrung the neck of a chicken and chopped off its head, Savannah said, "Mama do you think they will come back and attack my girls?"

Hattie Mae wasn't sure, so she told Savannah to be on the safe side just keep those babies in the house at night.

Hattie Mae went to her old Voodoo shed she had on the property. It was exactly like she left it. Hattie Mae laughed to herself. She thought how silly everybody was. They were so afraid of the Voodoo religion that they'd let that shed sit untouched for years before they would dare go in it.

Hattie Mae quickly gathered up all her roots and herbs she needed to help heal the female wolf. Hattie Mae decided to wait until morning before she went back though. Hattie Mae figured that the wolves would have less strength in the morning.

Hattie Mae wanted to take a bath and wash her hair. She remembered her bathhouse that the late Master Fo'Rae had built for her. She smiled and thought that was the only thing she missed about the United States.

Hattie Mae made her way to the well to get her some bathe water. Although it was late, she still wanted to bath. She gathered up all her scented oils and sat them by the bathing tub.
As Hattie Mae was gathering her water, she heard a voice say, "There's power in the wolves' blood. If you would be so lucky to get a few drops, it could come in handy one day."

Hattie Mae turned around to see Legacy standing in front of her. Hattie Mae smiled and said, "Child yo gift never seems to amaze me. Now tell me how you know about my encounter." Legacy replied, "The spirits showed it to me in a dream. I walked here in the dark to check on you."

Hattie Mae reminded Legacy never to do that again. Hattie Mae said it wasn't safe for Legacy to be walking around the island by her self at night. Legacy assured Hattie Mae that she wasn't scared of nothing in the dark. However, whatever was in the dark should be afraid of her. Legacy smiled and held up her carving knife and special oils she had. Just in case an undesirable approached her. The oils Legacy was carrying could burn off your skin in a matter of seconds. It was a special potion Legacy had mixed up.

Hattie Mae and Legacy often mixed different herbs and oils together and sold them to the island people. Hattie Mae wrote down all her secret ingredients and passed them on to Legacy, who in return would pass them down to her children.

Thinking about Legacy having children made Hattie Mae a little sad. Hattie Mae knew that Young Charles often wrote Legacy. Also, every time Young Charles came home from boarding school to visit, he spent most of his time with Legacy. Hattie Mae could tell Young Charles was sweet on Legacy. However, Hattie Mae completely understood that Master Fo'Rae's brother and Mistress Mattie would never allow a relationship between Legacy and Young Charles to blossom. Not to mention Legacy's mama Savannah always telling them how they were cousins.

Hattie Mae begged Savannah to stop telling Legacy that she and Young Charles were cousins. Shit they were something like third cousins anyway.

Hattie Mae remembered her bath waiting. Hattie Mae boiled the water, then poured it into her tub.

Legacy sat on the floor while Hattie Mae soaked.

Legacy said, "Mama Hattie Mae, when you go to treat the wolf's leg I'm going with you. I want to see these beautiful creatures in real life. Not just in my visions."

Hattie Mae wanted to tell Legacy not a chance she was going with her, but Hattie Mae knew Legacy wasn't going to take no for an answer.

Legacy looked in her bag and pulled out a finely sharpened blade, which she had tied to a long broom handle. Legacy said, "Before we leave, I'll dip this into my potions. If anything goes wrong, well let's just say, the mighty wolf will not be so mighty any longer.

Hattie Mae tied a rope around one of the goats in Savannah's field and got some fresh water. Hattie Mae fed the goat a mixture of herbs and natural vitamins. The herbs and vitamins were intended for the wolves, but Hattie Mae knew the wolves wouldn't eat them. However, they would eat the goat and since goats are mindless and eat anything, Hattie Mae fed the goat the herbs and vitamins.

Hattie Mae smiled and looked at Legacy. she said, "This goat is another option for the wolves to eat instead of us."
Legacy replied, "Let's pray they also think that."

Hattie Mae went to the spot where she last left the wolves. The male wolf met her before she got anywhere near them.

127

Hattie Mae told Legacy to bow down low to the ground and not to say a word, not to even breathe too loud. Hattie Mae could see the fear in Legacy's eyes. Hattie Mae pushed the goat in front of them. Then she waited.

The male wolf swooped in the goat so fast and ripped his throat out. The poor little goat didn't even have a chance to run. Hattie Mae said very softly, "Great one I have come to help your mate. Please allow me to do so."

Legacy whispered, "Mama Hattie Mae, do you really think you can talk to him?" Hattie Mae replied, "I don't know, but we are going to find out."

After the wolf ate his portion of the goat, he picked it up and started dragging it to the female wolf.

The wolf turned and looked at Hattie Mae and Legacy as if he was giving them permission to proceed. Hattie Mae and Legacy treaded lightly behind him.

The female wolf was lying there almost lifeless. She appeared to be in a great deal of pain.

Hattie Mae looked over at the male wolf that was dozing off to sleep. The herbs she fed the goat were making him sleepy. Hattie Mae needed the wolves to relax so she could work on the female wolf's leg.

The female wolf refused to eat or drink anything. Hattie Mae had a feeling that the female could sense the herbs in the goat and water. After the male wolf fell off to sleep, Legacy relaxed and assisted Hattie Mae with helping the female wolf.

Hattie Mae eased by her and sat down. The female wolf was so weak. Legacy sat next to the female wolf and put the wolf's head in her lap. Legacy rubbed her fur.

Hattie Mae said, "Now, Great Queen, this is going to hurt a lot, but it has to be done. Your leg is infected, and I have to put this mixture on it."

Hattie Mae held up the mixture so that the female wolf could see it. Legacy said, "Mama Hattie Mae, I think she really understands!"

Hattie Mae replied, "Of course she does. Wolves are one of the smartest animals on the planet. They're just untamable. They're very loyal and they mate for life."

Hattie Mae looked up at Legacy who was in a sudden daydream. Hattie Mae figured after she said wolves mate for life, Legacy's mind went straight to a thought of Young Charles.

Hattie Mae snapped her fingers. She smiled at Legacy and said, "Look alive, child. We in the mist of the wolves' den and you daydreaming."

Hattie Mae slowly cleaned and applied the mixture to the female wolf's leg that was infected by the trap. It seemed to soothe the female wolf because she moved her paw onto Legacy's lap and relaxed her head. When Hattie Mae was finished dressing the wound, she said, "Now, Great Queen, you have to eat and drink to heal."

Before Hattie Mae offered the wolf food and drink, she reached in her pocket and pulled out a syringe.

Hattie Mae said, "Great Queen, I just need one thing from you. With your permission, I will fill up my small bottle with some of your blood. If this is not okay with you, I will not."

Hattie Mae held up the syringe so the female wolf could see it. Then Hattie Mae stuck the female with the needle and drew some of the female wolf's blood. The female wolf didn't seem to mind.

Legacy smiled and said, "I think she gave you her permission."

Hattie Mae and Legacy fed the female wolf and waited with her until she fell off to sleep. As the wolves slept, Hattie Mae tied a string around their necks with a tiny pouch that held a small protection stone inside of it.

Hattie Mae hugged both of the wolves really tight and rubbed their fur all over her body to capture their scent. Hattie Mae told Legacy that they had to make sure they got that sent on Savannah, Savannah's family, and Robert Lee.

Legacy replied, "Mama Hattie Mae, it's only right that Mistress Mattie have the scent too." Hattie Mae rolled her eyes.

Legacy smiled and replied, "Besides, you don't want the wolves to eat her before you get her photo image, do you?"

Hattie Mae wasn't shocked that Legacy knew about her plan. Legacy had a special gift of sight from the spirits. Hattie Mae really couldn't hide anything from Legacy.

When they got back to Savannah's house, all Savannah's daughters were all polished up and sitting on the porch. Each one off them had on bonnets to block the sun.

Hattie Mae just shook her head.

All Savannah's daughters were so happy to see their big sister Legacy.

Although Legacy and Savannah had a rocky relationship, Legacy and her little sisters had a beautiful relationship.

Hattie Mae hugged all the girls and rubbed the wolves' scent all over them. Although it was faint and couldn't be smelled off hand, the wolves could smell it. Hattie Mae was hoping the wolves would consider her family a part of their pack, now that she'd helped them.

Savannah came to the porch all dressed up in her finest clothes. She had on the biggest hat Hattie Mae had ever seen. Hattie Mae had to admit that Savannah did look beautiful, but Hattie Mae would never tell Savannah.

Savannah's ego was already as big as the entire island of St. Lucia.

Hattie Mae said to Savannah, "Where you going baby?" As she hugged her tight so she could get the scent in her.

Savannah looked at Hattie Mae like she knew Hattie Mae was up to something and replied, "Afternoon mass."

Then Savannah looked at Legacy and said, "Good afternoon, daughter. You look as lovely as ever. Hopefully, you can stay this evening for supper. I surely would be delighted with your company." Legacy was at a loss for words. She didn't know how to respond, she just said, "Sure, mama!"

Savannah smiled and said, "Excellent."

Savannah handed Legacy a bonnet and said, "My love, do wear it, and please stay out of the sun. My Lord, you're getting as dark as mama." Savannah reached for her smallest daughter's hand and looked at Hattie Mae and said, "No offense, mama, because you're a dark vision of loveliness."

Then Savannah leaned in close to Hattie Mae and said, "I smell them all over you. I know you wiped their scent all over me and my babies too."

Hattie Mae was taken aback for a second. Hattie Mae placed her hand on her heart and said to Savannah, "Whatever are you talking about child?"

Savannah looked at Hattie Mae and smiled, "You and Legacy ain't the only one blessed with the gift. I know y'all think y'all special, but guess what?"

Savannah laughed and said, "Y'all not." Savannah started walking to her horse buggy. Savannah pointed up to the hill a little ways away. She said, "I do believes you has company mama."

Hattie Mae looked up on the hill to see the female wolf and her mate resting under a tree watching them. As Savannah's buggy rode pass Legacy and Hattie Mae.

Savannah sarcastically said, "Mama, please be a darling and tell your new found friends to stay away from my precious babies."

131

Then Savannah blew Hattie Mae and Legacy a kiss and said, "Yall both do have lovely day and be blessed."

Legacy was a bit confused. She said, "What's gotten into my mother?"

Hattie Mae just stood there absorbing what Savannah has just told her about her gift. Then Hattie Mae laughed and said, "Jesus child, Yo mama done found Jesus. I'm not going to complain though. At least Jesus can humble her a bit."

Legacy told Hattie Mae that Savannah had always had the gift. It just wasn't as strong as theirs. Legacy also told Hattie Mae that Savannah's mind was so crowded with ridiculous thoughts of being half white. Legacy said until Savannah came to terms with being half white and raped by her white daddy that Savannah's gift would never shine through.

Hattie Mae was amazed at the maturity of Legacy. Legacy was only sixteen years old and had better sense than most adults. Hattie Mae took that opportunity to talk to Legacy about how she felt about what happened to her mom Savannah and her birth father also being her granddaddy.

Legacy explained to Hattie Mae that none of that ever bothered her. Legacy said it is what it is, and that while she was on this planet, she had to use all her positive energy for good. Legacy said she didn't have time to dwell on the past because the future was much more important.

As they spoke, Hattie Mae could tell something was troubling Legacy. Hattie Mae held Legacy's hand as they walked to Mistress Mattie's mansion. Hattie Mae was hoping that by holding Legacy's hand, the spirits would give her a glimpse of what was troubling Legacy. However, Hattie Mae had no such luck.

Legacy looked at Hattie Mae with the saddest face Hattie Mae had ever seen and said, "Mama Hattie Mae, a storm is coming."

As Hattie Mae and Legacy got closer to the mansion, they saw a man. It looked like he was dropping off a package. The man saw Hattie Mae. He looked as if he had seen the devil himself.

The man said very cowardly, "Madame Fo'Rae, I believe this package is for you. The note attached to it said it was urgent. However, you haven't left a forwarding address, so I continue to leave your packages at your daughter's house. And since this one said it was urgent, I decided to see if you were visiting with your best friend."

Hattie Mae looked puzzled, and replied, "No, I'm not Madame Fo'Rae. That would be the Mistress of this house, Mattie."

The man seemed as if he was scared to death of Hattie Mae. He wouldn't even look her in the eyes.

He responded, "No ma'am, I knows exactly who you are. You're Madame Fo'Rae the Voodoo Queen from Africa by way of New Orleans. Folks around the islands say you and your daughters have some of the strongest powers."

Legacy just stood there looking. Hattie Mae said, "Well, since you put it like that."

Then Hattie Mae reached out to get the package he was holding. The man just stood there.

Hattie Mae said, "Can I help you with something else?"
The man replied, "My mother has been suffering with dizzy spells lately.

She says they're so bad she can hardly stand. She's been to the doctor and yet she still suffers. People in town told me I should come see you and maybe you could heal her." Hattie Mae smirked her lips and said, "Folks in town sure have a lot to say about me. Seeing as half of them ain't never met me."

The man looked a little sad.

He said, "It's all good talk out of respect Madame Fo'Rae. Besides, folks are too scared to say anything against you, in fear you might put some kind of spell on them."

Hattie Mae smiled at the thought of her cursing folks.

She shook her hand back and forth and said, "Folks always scared of folks being different. And the herbs and potions I use are from the earth. A gift from The Spirits. Folks just need to learn how to properly mix them. So they can heal themselves."

The man put his head down and responded, "Yes, you're right, Madame Fo'Rae."

Hattie Mae felt sorry for him. She said, "Tell your mother to get an herb called feverfew. Mix it with some chamomile tea and rest for three days."

The man looked up at Hattie Mae and said, "Merci beaucoup, Madame Fo'Rae." Then he walked away.

Legacy looked at Hattie Mae and said, "I kind of like Madame Fo'Rae. It fits you. You should use it."

Hattie Mae waved her hands up in the air for Legacy to hush.

When the maids let Hattie Mae and Legacy in the house, Hattie Mae put her package down in her bag. Hattie Mae figured she'd open it later. Hattie Mae assumed it was from Master Fo'Rae's brother. He always sent her fabrics from around the world.

The maid led Hattie Mae and Legacy to the sitting room where they found Mistress Mattie laying across the sofa looking like she was pissed with the world. She had a letter in her hand.

When Mistress Mattie saw Hattie Mae and Legacy, she stood up and said, "Hattie Mae how could you allow this to happen?"

Then Mistress Mattie looked and Legacy and said, "It will never happen. My son is going to be a brilliant man. He's going to college. My son will fraternize with the elite people of this world. Young Charles is going to be a noble man."

Then Mistress Mattie paused. She held Legacy by her hand and said, "Oh Lord, don't take this personal child. It's nothing against you. It's just that you and Young Charles have grown in different directions. You're a great person. Just not the right woman for my son."

Hattie Mae picked the letter up and read it. It was from Young Charles. He had written to advise his mother, Mistress Mattie, that he intended on courting Legacy when he returned from boarding school. He also wrote that he wouldn't be attending college because he was going to be an artist and paint beautiful work from around the world.

Hattie Mae took a deep breath.

Hattie Mae looked at Mistress Mattie and said, "Watch how you speak to my granddaughter. Don't be so quick to voice your opinion."

Mistress Mattie backed away from Legacy. Hattie Mae could see the fear in Mistress Mattie's eyes.

Mistress Mattie said, "Please, Hattie Mae, don't judge me harsh. I didn't mean any harm. I just got so concerned when I received this letter from Young Charles."

Legacy looked at Mistress Mattie and from the expression on her face, Legacy was livid. She replied to Mistress Mattie, "Don't take what personal?

That you think your son, whom my grandmother all but raised, who's father is a runaway slave, and who's passing for white, is too good to marry the daughter of your late husband, my mother's father and my grandmother's Master?"

Mistress Mattie sat down in her chair and fanned herself.

135

Mistress Mattie responded, "Well, now let's just calm down. Let's just think about what's best for Young Charles."

Mistress Mattie looked at Legacy and said, "Surely you must know I love you, like you was my own child."

Legacy sarcastically responded, "Yes, but I've seen what you do to your own children. Remember Baby Girl One, my best friend?"

Hattie Mae stepped in and said, "Now ladies let's not argue. It's getting late and Legacy you promised your mother Savannah that you would have supper with her and your sisters. Mistress Mattie, you look exhausted. Why don't you get some sleep? Planning for your wedding is making you cranky, surely Legacy knows you love her."

Hattie Mae looked at Legacy and said, "You know Mistress Mattie loves you and only wants what's best for you. Don't you?"

Legacy looked at Hattie Mae and replied, "Yes ma'am I do."

Hattie Mae said, "Well then, let's just say our goodbyes and we'll postpone this conversation for another day."

Mistress Mattie responded, "Yes, I agree. We'll revisit this conversation when Master Fo'Rae's brother gets here. He's due to arrive sometime next week. He telegraphed and said he's personally delivering the papers I need for my wedding."

Hattie Mae and Legacy agreed to discuss the matter later. Hattie Mae insisted on Mistress Mattie giving her a hug goodbye. It was the only way she could get the wolves' scent on Mistress Mattie. However, after Mistress Mattie had insulted Legacy, Hattie Mae was reluctant to do it, but she needed her in one piece so she could get that photo image.

When Legacy and Hattie Mae left, Legacy said, "Quite a show you put on, Madame Fo'Rae. The nerve of Mistress Mattie."

Hattie Mae looked at Legacy and said, "Wait until your mother Savannah hears the news that Young Charles intends on courting you. All hell is going to break loose."

Legacy smiled and replied, "I'm used to her foolishness, Mama Hattie Mae, but what about you? How do you feel about me courting Young Charles?"

Hattie Mae sighed and replied, "I only want what's best for you baby.

However, your mother is going to point out that Young Charles is your kinsman."

Legacy replied, "Partially, although his hateful mother is my crazy mother's second cousin, so that makes him what my third or fourth? Anyway, it doesn't matter." Legacy stopped talking as they entered Savannah's house.

Hattie Mae was always amazed by how clean Savannah's house stayed and how disciplined Savannah's daughters were.

Savannah had prepared a feast: baked chicken and dressing, collard greens, sweet potatoes, cornbread, fruit, and coconut-banana pie for dessert.

Legacy looked at Hattie Mae and whispered, "It's a set up."

Both ladies laughed.

Hattie Mae excused herself to go outside for a second. Hattie Mae saw the deliveryman still lingering around the property. He was talking to one of the maids. Hattie Mae pulled him to the side and told him, that if he ran and fetched Robert Lee and told him to bring her camera box, she would personally go to his mother and heal her of her headaches. Hattie Mae told the deliveryman to make sure to tell Robert Lee it was imperative that he bring her photo box.

Hattie Mae decided that she needed to get that photo image as soon as possible. Master Fo'Rae's brother was on his way. Hattie Mae remembered what Legacy said, "A storm was coming."

Chapter Seven:
Say Cheese

A s Hattie Mae walked back in Savannah's house for supper, she heard Savannah say, "So Young Charles wrote me a very interesting letter."

Hattie Mae said, "Savannah, Mistress Mattie and Legacy done already agreed to discuss this matter at a later date."

Savannah replied, "Well, that's fine for Mistress Mattie and Legacy.

However, Legacy is my child, and, as her Mother, I say we're going to discuss it tonight."

Legacy looked at her mother Savannah and said sarcastically, "What's there to discuss? You've never shown any interest in anything I've ever done. You gave me to Mama Hattie, for her to raise me and the only thing you ever tell me when you see me is how dark I'm getting."

Hattie Mae looked over at Savannah, who was visibly upset.

Savannah cleared her throat and replied, "Mind your manners, young lady. How dare you disrespect me in my own house!"

Legacy responded rudely, "A house I've never slept one night in. I didn't ask to come here, you invited me here, remember?"

Savannah stood up and walked slowly towards Legacy. Savannah got in Legacy's face and said, "The Bible teaches that a disrespectful child doesn't live his days out."

Legacy replied by rolling her eyes and rudely saying, "Lucky for me I don't believe in your white Jesus or your Bible. Furthermore, I've never considered you my parent; therefore, if I choose to court Young Charles, your opinion really doesn't matter to me."

Hattie Mae stepped in between Legacy and Savannah.

Hattie Mae said, "No, Legacy, don't talk to your mother like that, child."

Legacy responded, "Like I said, she ain't no mother of mines."

Savannah was so furious she stepped around Hattie Mae and got back in Legacy's face.

Savannah pointed her finger in Legacy's face and said, "In my teenage womb, I carried your frail body for nine months. Your life began when through my thighs your head pushed out and you took your first breath. I nursed you from my breast, stayed with you at night when you was sick and I raised you as I was supposed to. So don't you ever in your life use that tone with me? I brought you in this world and, rest assured, I'll take you out of it. I'm your natural God-given mother, and you will respect me as such. Now on the matter of you courting and marrying Young Charles, I forbid it. The house of Cordova will not allow it."

Legacy replied hatefully, "Oh, but mother, did you forget, I'm not from the house of Cordova remember? I'm a Fo'Rae."

Savannah looked like the top of her head was going to blow off. She held on to the table, and everything in the room shook a tiny bit.

Hattie Mae and Legacy could both feel Savannah's energy. It appeared her gift was getting stronger. Apparently, Savannah was learning how to control it. As Savannah calmed down, so did the shaking in the room.

Savannah slowly looked up at Hattie Mae and Legacy. The look in her eyes was almost scary. Then Savannah slowly lifted up two fingers and pointed them towards the door. Savannah swiped her fingers at the door, and it flung open with a bang.

Hattie Mae's and Legacy's eyes were bulging out in disbelief. Savannah looked at them both and coldly said, "Legacy, I'm your mother and, contrary to your belief, I love you the same as I love all my daughters. My mother gave me the option of killing you and myself before you were born.

I chose to save us. That should be proof enough. Now on the matter of Young Charles, who despite what you believe, he's your kinsman. Being with him would be incest, and this generation will not have that blemishing its name any further. You do not have my blessing. However, you are free to make your own choice. Now I have spoken, it's time for my nightly prayers, and I have to get ready for Carnival tomorrow. So if y'all could kindly show yourselves out of my home, I'd appreciate it. Thank you and goodnight."

As Hattie Mae and Legacy were walking out of the door, Savannah snidely said, "Yes mother, I've embraced my gift."

Hattie Mae had to smile at that. Hattie Mae had always thought the gift had skipped Savannah. Savannah had never shown a sign that she had the gift.

When they got to Hattie Mae's voodoo shed, where they were forced to spend the night, they talked about the problem at hand. Hattie Mae told Legacy she had her support and blessing. If she was in love with Young Charles, then so be it.

Hattie Mae still felt like Legacy was keeping something from her. However, Hattie Mae had to get her plan in motion.

Robert Lee showed up with the camera box and they planned out exactly how they were going to get the picture. Tomorrow had to be the day, which would work out perfect because it was Carnival Day on St. Lucia and the flash from the camera and sound could be passed off as light from the fireworks.

Hattie Mae mixed up some of her herbs for Robert Lee to slip into Mistress Mattie's drink tomorrow. The herbs would intensify Mistress Mattie's desire for Robert Lee. Hattie Mae also got her bag ready to pay a visit to the deliveryman's mama in town early tomorrow morning. Hattie Mae rarely went into town. The folks there always acted strangely around Hattie Mae.

Early the next morning before dawn, Hattie Mae and Legacy made their way to town. Hattie Mae grabbed her cutting utensils before she left, even though she wasn't going to be butchering any animals. Something in her spirit told her she would need those utensils and some other herbs. She quickly stuffed them in her bag.

When she arrived at the home of the deliveryman, all the towns' people scattered about. None of them made eye contact with Hattie Mae or Legacy.

Hattie Mae and Legacy didn't mind. They were used to people shying away from them. Half of the folks didn't understand the gifts they had, and the other half figured the gifts were from the devil. Hattie Mae always considered them such small-minded hypocrites. They could believe in and worship a God they could not see, but wouldn't believe what they saw with their own eyes. The thought of Hattie Mae being evil was ludicrous. Hattie Mae believed in The Spirits and the Ancestors. She understood that there was a divine being with unquestionable power. Just because she didn't believe in the Bible all of a sudden she was the devil.

Hattie Mae laughed to herself as she entered the home of the deliveryman. Just like Savannah, they had a huge painting of Jesus and a cross in the entryway.

Hattie Mae set her bag down. Legacy quickly picked up on the energy in the home.

Legacy said, "This home is full of love and respect for their Lord and Savior. Let's try not to disturb that Mama Hattie Mae."

Hattie Mae walked to the bed where the sick woman was lying.

Hattie Mae lifted the lady's weak hand and held it in hers. Hattie Mae could feel the lady's pain. Hattie Mae stumbled back in a rocking motion.

She swiftly released the lady's hand.

Hattie Mae gave the lady a quick examination She put both her hands around the lady's head and squeezed.

Hattie Mae had a disturbing look on her face.

Hattie Mae looked at the deliveryman and calmly said, "Did you give her the tea like I instructed you?"

The delivery man replied, "Yes ma'am, Madame Fo'Rae, but it doesn't seem to be working as of yet."

Hattie Mae said, "Make her some more and put this mixture in it. Boil a pot of water and bring me lots of clean linens."

The Deliveryman did as he was told.

Legacy helped hold up the lady's head as she drank down all the tea mixture. The lady fell into a deep sleep after she drank the tea.

Hattie Mae set the deliveryman down and patiently but firmly said, "Your mother is very sick, near death. It's imperative that I cut into her scalp to get to the problem. It's going to be very bloody, however, it's going to look worse than it is. I have to do it very quickly. So I don't have time to explain the process. I just need your permission. Now if you don't allow me to do this, rest assured your mother is going to meet her Jesus in the next few hours. Now do I have your permission?"

The deliveryman, with tears in his eyes, nodded his head yes.

Hattie Mae said, "Now sit down and watch. Don't be afraid, be brave for your mother."

Hattie Mae laid the lady's head flat down on the table. Hattie Mae pulled a small sharp scalpel out and cut the crown of the lady's head scalp off. The deliveryman just sat there crying. After Hattie Mae cut the crown of the lady's scalp off, she motioned for the deliveryman to come to her. Hattie Mae pointed into the hole she had carved out.

Hattie Mae said, "Look, do you see that?" as she pointed to some worms crawling around in his mother's head. "That's the cause of your mother's pain. They got in her head one of two ways: Either they entered through her ears or through her mouth in something she ate."

The Delivery Man almost threw up.

Hattie Mae pulled out seven worms and she placed them in a bowl. Then she took a mixture and cleaned the lady's head. Hattie Mae simply stitched back on the lady's scalp and bandaged her up. Hattie Mae told the deliveryman to watch her closely for the next few days. She said she should feel better as soon as she opened her eyes.

Hattie Mae set the worms in the bowl on fire and told the deliveryman to tell his mom never to eat pork again.

Legacy said, "How did you know she had parasites in her head?"

Hattie Mae replied, "When I was on the plantation, one of my many skills was carving meat. Sometimes the animals would eat parasites and they would travel to their brains. Mostly, you find them in pigs and goats because they eat anything."

As they were leaving, Hattie Mae saw the town's people preparing for the Carnival.

Hattie Mae laughed and said, "For people who are supposed to be so religious, they sure do a lot of partying and drinking. Every week they're celebrating something." Hattie Mae had to admit they did have the most beautiful costumes she'd ever seen and the music was beautiful.

Legacy and Hattie Mae stuck around for a while listening to the music and shopping at the flea market. Hattie Mae purchased some beautiful seashells, stones and cloth.

Legacy purchased some writing material and some little what-nots.

When they arrived back at Savannah's, they saw Pierre Cordova packing up the horse and buggy. Savannah seemed to be in a more pleasant mood. She even invited them to Carnival. Legacy agreed to go to help with her sisters.

Hattie Mae declined. She had business with Mistress Mattie and Robert Lee.

Hattie Mae asked Savannah at what time the fireworks would be going off. She told Savannah that she and Mistress Mattie were going to watch them from the upstairs porch of the mansion.

Savannah went on and on about how beautiful they were going to be this year. Savannah said the show started at dusk.

Hattie Mae hurried to get the photo box and Robert Lee in place. Hattie Mae told Robert Lee to get Mistress Mattie out of the mansion by asking her to take a walk with him to the lake. Hattie Mae had to get the picture box in the house and upstairs in position. All the maids were off for carnival, so the house was empty.

It didn't take long for Robert Lee to get Mistress Mattie out of the mansion. Hattie Mae saw Mistress Mattie drinking her refreshment. Hattie Mae had about an hour before the side effects of the herbs kicked in and Mistress Mattie would have the sudden urge to be intimate.

Hattie Mae set up the picture box and waited in the closet. Sure enough, she heard Mistress Mattie and Robert Lee getting it on. Robert Lee told Mistress Mattie to leave the patio doors open so they could hear the music from town and see the fireworks. Mistress Mattie, with her freaky self, agreed.

Mistress Mattie said, "That's really risky, but the thrill of somebody catching us is so exciting."

Hattie Mae just shook her head in disgust.

Robert Lee positioned Mistress Mattie facing the patio doors away from the closet. As soon as the first fireworks went off, Hattie snapped a picture.

Mistress Mattie was so into Robert Lee she never even saw the flash. Hattie Mae decided to take another. This time Mistress Mattie caught a glimpse of the flash.

Hattie Mae grabbed her picture box and tried to hide.

Mistress Mattie jumped up stark naked and screamed "What in the world is going on? Robert Lee I just saw a flash coming from my closet."

Robert Lee convinced Mistress Mattie it was a reflection from the fireworks outside.

Mistress Mattie calmed down and fell asleep. Hattie Mae made her way out of the closet with her photo image in hand. She gathered up the photo box and she and Robert Lee made their way to the door.

They heard Mistress Mattie softly say, "Does someone want to explain to me why Hattie Mae is creeping around in the closet?"

Robert Lee and Hattie Mae froze in their tracks.

Mistress Mattie stormed over to Robert Lee and said, "Did you know this whole time Hattie Mae was lurking around in the closet spying on me?"

Mistress Mattie looked at Hattie Mae and said, "Hattie Mae, I do believe this is the sickest thing you've ever done. It's strange even for you. Why would you be watching Robert Lee and I in our most intimate moments?

Sick, just sick I tell you."

Then Mistress Mattie saw the camera box. She turned red she said, "And just what are you doing with that thing? Did you photograph me? How dare you, Hattie Mae. Shameful!"

Mistress Mattie reached for the camera box, but Hattie Mae smacked her hand away.

Hattie Mae said, "Don't you dare touch it. I surely did photograph you on your knees doing unspeakable things with Robert Lee. For years, you have been taking advantage of him. But it ends tonight."

Mistress Mattie composed herself. She didn't want to upset Hattie Mae further.

Mistress Mattie said, "And just what do you plan on doing with that photo image, Hattie Mae?"

Hattie Mae looked at Mistress Mattie and smirked. She said, "Wouldn't you like to know. Maybe I'll send it to Master Fo'Rae's brother, maybe I'll show it to all the maids, or, better yet, maybe I'll send it to your gentleman caller."

Mistress Mattie was furious. She said, "Why, Hattie Mae, you wouldn't dare!"

Hattie Mae replied, "Oh, but I would! You have used and abused my family way too many times. You've gotten away with murder, and yet you continue to be selfish. You lied to me about Robert Lee helping you murder Baby Girl One, when all along you were threatening to report him to the slave trackers. You have a gentleman caller who wants to marry you, yet you still want to have Robert Lee. You say we are best friends, even sisters, but you still continue to be wicked. So yes, yes I will expose you to all these island folks. So they can see the real you."

Hattie Mae waved the photo image up and said, "If a picture speaks a thousand words, Oh my, then this one speaks a million. Yes a million, that's what this picture are gonna cost you, Mistress Mattie. I have a list of things I would like."

Mistress Mattie was about to respond when they heard a knock on the double doors and Mistress Mattie's gentleman caller saying, "Hello?"

Hattie Mae and Robert Lee were standing at the edge of the staircase.

Hattie Mae said, "Well, do we have a deal or not?"

Then Hattie Mae proceeded to the door.

Hattie Mae looked back, to the top of the stairs where Mistress Mattie was standing in her robe.

Hattie Mae smiled and said, "Let's see how the photo image came out. I'm sure they're beautiful. Maybe I'll get your gentleman caller's opinion."

Hattie Mae reached for the door handle when Mistress Mattie yelled, "We will finish this discussion in the morning! Please, Hattie Mae, don't do this!"

Hattie Mae and Robert Lee turned and exited the back door. Hattie Mae never stuck around to see if Mistress Mattie let her gentleman caller in the mansion.

Robert Lee wasn't saying much. Hattie Mae knew he was pissed. Hattie Mae felt bad. Poor Robert Lee had been through enough. Hell, what he was going through with Mistress Mattie was the same thing Hattie Mae had gone through with Master Fo'Rae.

Hattie Mae and Robert Lee made their way back to their house. Hattie Mae figured Mistress Mattie would show up bright and early the next morning. Hattie Mae had her list of demands ready. Hattie Mae was confident Mistress Mattie wouldn't deny her anything.

Hattie Mae remembered the package the deliveryman had given her yesterday. She retrieved it from her bag.

Robert Lee washed up and went to sleep. He hadn't said a word since Mistress Mattie's mansion.

Hattie Mae brewed her some tea and sat down to open her package. She was right about it being from Master Fo'Rae's brother, but it was not fabric as she suspected. It was something wrapped in cloth. As Hattie Mae unwrapped the cloth, she saw a painting in a beautiful picture frame.

Hattie Mae set the painting on the table. She grabbed her heart. The man in the painting was caramel colored brown skin, heavy eyebrows, defined cheekbones, with a strong chin line, with thick juicy full lips and almond-shaped eyes. He was the most handsome man she'd ever seen. It looked like he was holding a piece of rolled-up paper. The engravement on the painting read, "Doctor Claude Jean Fo'Rae. Rush Medical College in Chicago year of 1853."

Hattie Mae damn near fainted. Tears flowed down her cheeks. She stared at the painting for hours. The only mystery was why would Master Fo'Rae's brother send her this painting of her son? And why did he have to come all the way to the Island to deliver the papers Mistress Mattie needed.

Hattie Mae remembered Legacy's words, "A storm is coming!"

Hattie Mae was starting to think that this storm Legacy was speaking of was turning into a hurricane.

Chapter Eight:
Here Comes the Messiah

The next morning, Hattie Mae got up at dawn. She wanted to go pray to the ancestors for guidance. Also for strength, Hattie Mae knew Mistress Mattie would be coming to call soon. Hattie Mae had to get mentally prepared to deal with Mistress Mattie's carrying on: especially after Legacy tells her she intends on accepting Young Charles' courting.

Also, Hattie Mae had to enlighten the ancestors on Savannah and her gift. Hattie Mae could feel trouble coming with Savannah's gift.

Robert Lee was sleeping soundly as Hattie Mae walked out of the door. Hattie Mae turned around and walked over to Robert Lee. She put her finger under his nose to see if he was still breathing; he was.

Hattie Mae was getting a bit concerned about Robert Lee. He hadn't said a word since the incident at Mistress Mattie's mansion. Hattie Mae decided to let him sleep peacefully.

Hattie Mae opened the door to see the two great wolves lying at her doorstep. She had to admit she was frightened at first. Then a sense of calm came over her. She felt somewhat protected. Here she was walking around outside, and the sun hadn't even risen.

Hattie Mae stepped down off the porch. She bowed down and said, "Good morning, beautiful ones."

The wolves both rose up as if they were waiting for her next move. Hattie Mae simply walked right past them. Both wolves followed. Still, Hattie Mae didn't feel fear.

Hattie Mae talked to them as they walked to the top of the hill where Hattie Mae prayed to her ancestors.

Hattie Mae said, "So, I guess y'all saw what happened with Mistress Mattie yesterday. It had to be done; she's been taking advantage of Robert Lee for years."

Hattie Mae turned around to see the wolves attentively listening.

Hattie Mae looked at the female wolf and said, "Yes, Great Queen, I know, both of them were disloyal to me. But you must understand Robert Lee was born a slave. He has always taken orders and done what he was told to do.

He's never known freedom like us, until now. Robert Lee is so scared to have that freedom taken away. Well, he'd do anything, including pleasuring Mistress Mattie."

The female wolf walked alongside Hattie Mae as if she were truly listening.

Hattie Mae looked at the male wolf that wasn't paying a bit of attention to either one of them.

Hattie Mae looked at the female wolf and said, "Just like a man, right?"

Hattie Mae laughed at herself for carrying a conversation with the wolves.

Hattie Mae stopped, she bent down and looked directly into the female wolf's eyes and said, "I love Robert Lee and I know he loves me. Mistress Mattie and I have a dysfunctional love-hate relationship. It's a long story, too long for me to tell you today anyway. But we all we got, so please don't judge them for the secrets they kept."

The female stopped as if she heard something. Both she and her mate stood at attention, in attack mode. Hattie Mae grabbed a long branch she saw laying on the ground.

Hattie Mae saw a black snake come slithering quickly across the path. The snake was too fast for the wolves to catch. As a matter of fact, they never moved an inch to try to get the snake. Hattie Mae took that as a sign that the snake was poisonous.

Hattie Mae decided to keep the big branch she had. As they reached the top of the hill, Hattie Mae wrapped her head with a scarf. She bent down to her knees and prayed to her Ancestors. Hattie Mae stayed at the top of the hill long after the sun had risen. Hattie Mae continued to pray and ask for guidance from her Ancestors. The wolves stood on both sides of the hill as if they were standing guard.

Hattie Mae said a prayer in her native tongue and headed back to the house. Hattie Mae figured that Mistress Mattie would be making her way there by now trying to find those photo images. Hattie Mae laughed to herself. She thought about how she'd covered them and buried them in Baby Girl One's mock grave: a place that Mistress Mattie would never go.

The pictures didn't come out perfect, but you could clearly see Robert Lee and Mistress Mattie lying together naked.

As Hattie Mae and the wolves got closer to the house, the wolves walked in front of Hattie Mae. Hattie Mae was still carrying her big tree branch, and she still had her headscarf on.

Hattie Mae saw people up ahead. Then she saw a line of people. Hattie Mae had rarely seen so many people traveling on this road. She was curious. For a second Hattie Mae forgot the wolves were with her. However, the people didn't seem to mind. They seemed more interested in Hattie Mae.

Hattie Mae noticed all the people seemed to be lining up for something. Hattie Mae saw people with livestock, clothes and stones. For a second Hattie Mae felt like she'd walked into the flea market.

As she got closer to her property, she saw all the people lined up at her door.

Hattie Mae heard the people calling her name. They were saying, "Madame Fo'Rae." Then all the people bowed down to the ground and chanted Madame Fo'Rae, the Voodoo Queen."

Hattie Mae saw Legacy trying to talk to the people.

Then Hattie Mae saw Mistress Mattie handing out pieces of paper with numbers on them.

Hattie Mae looked at Legacy and said, "Please tell me what's going on?"

Before Legacy could say anything, Hattie Mae heard Savannah say sarcastically, "Well, if it ain't the people's Messiah, herself. And I see you've brung your two new friends with you."

The two wolves sat down at Hattie Mae's feet.

Savannah said, "I see they've taken a liking to you, mother. That was a nice show you just put on. The only thing missing was you riding in on a donkey. Mother, you've got all these people worked up. As if you can cure them of all their illnesses. Why did you perform surgery on that woman?

You are not a doctor. Good Lord, now you got the entire Island at your doorstep, and mine. All these folks followed me here this morning. They showed up at the mansion."

Hattie Mae was about to say something when Robert Lee stormed to the front of the house. He walked right up to Hattie Mae and said, "Woman, you have turned our home into a circus. You got wolves, Voodoo, and all these sick folks standing on my property waiting for a cure."

Then he looked over at Savannah who was holding her rosary, praying, and said, "And now we got St. Savannah praying for the people."

Savannah looked up from her prayers and replied sarcastically, "Wolves don't perform in the circus. They can't be tamed. However, yes I'm praying because this situation needs all the saints."

Robert Lee looked over at Hattie Mae and said, "Hattie Mae, my patience is wearing thin with you. If you don't do something with all these folks, I swear I'm going to start acting a fool."

Savannah said under her breath, "Start acting a fool. Huh seems like that started already."

Robert Lee looked over at Savannah and said, "What did you say?"

Savannah replied, "Who me? I didn't say anything."

Hattie Mae assured Robert Lee she would have those people cleared out of there before he returned from his shop.

Robert Lee just frowned and left.

Hattie Mae noticed that Robert Lee wasn't moving about at his usual pace. Seemed like he was dragging his leg.

Hattie Mae wanted to ask him if he was feeling okay but decided she'd talk to him later. Right now she had to get these people out of there.

Mistress Mattie walked over to Hattie Mae and said sarcastically, "Good Lord, Hattie Mae, what have you started, aside from being a photographer?

I see you're a healer now. What in heaven's name were you thinking performing surgery on that women? I've given them all a number in which they arrived here. However, I don't know how much good that's going to do. Seeing that there are so many people with so many afflictions. I'll help out any way I can."

Hattie Mae just looked at Mistress Mattie in disbelief. Then Hattie Mae remembered that Mistress Mattie wasn't wrapped too tight.

Hattie Mae said, "Why don't you say what you're really here for? You want that picture!"

Mistress Mattie turned red at the thought of the picture.

Then she said, "Well, that is a matter of great importance, and yes we must discuss that immediately. However, seeing how big this crowd is growing, I think we better attend to them first. Wouldn't you agree Hattie Mae?"

Hattie Mae was about to say something when she felt pain in her eyes.

Hattie Mae doubled over in agony.

Mistress Mattie grabbed Hattie Mae before she fell.

Mistress Mattie screamed, "Hattie Mae dear what ever is the problem?"

Hattie Mae looked up to see a teenage boy lying in his father's lap. Hattie Mae was drawn to him.

Mistress Mattie helped Hattie Mae over to the teenage boy.

Hattie Mae said to his father, "What's wrong with this young man?"

The boy's father told Hattie Mae that the boy had been playing outside. He was running and ran into a tree. He fell down and hit his head. He was fine at first, then a couple of hours later, his vision blurred, he was throwing up, and he had a sharp pain in his head.

Hattie Mae could barely stand. For some reason she was feeling his pain. It was so intense she could hardly speak. She instructed the father to carry him into her house and lay him in one of the rooms.

When the teenager was away from Hattie Mae, the pain left her. Mistress Mattie continued to hold her up.

Mistress Mattie said, "Hattie Mae, what are we going to do?"

Hattie Mae stood up straight and said, "I have to relieve his pain. It's more than he can stand."

Hattie Mae begged for strength from The Spirits. Then she gathered up all the supplies she needed.

Savannah, Legacy and Mistress Mattie waited for orders from Hattie Mae. Savannah said a quick prayer over the boy and tried to comfort the boy's father.

Hattie Mae walked over to the teenager and said, "You are in a lot of pain because you have fluid on your brain. When you fell and hit your head, you caused your spinal cord fluid to build up. I have to relieve the pressure from your spine. It's going to be very painful, but it's going to save your life and your eyesight."

The teenager looked scared.

Hattie Mae said, "Now you have to sit up, grab your knees, and don't move!"

Hattie Mae looked at the teenage boy and said, "If you move, you're going to be crippled and blind for the rest of your life, which will be short and miserable because you'll still be in tremendous pain until you finally pass out and die."

The teenage boy looked at Hattie Mae and said, "I understand, Madame Fo'Rae."

The teenage boy did exactly what Hattie Mae told him. Hattie Mae then stuck a long, sharp needle in his back between his spinal cord blocks.

The pain had to be unbearable, but the boy never flinched.

Hattie Mae stuck a long tube in his back and fluid started to flow through the tube. After Hattie Mae drained his spinal cord, she told the teenage boy to lie down until she allowed him to get up. She put a blindfold over his eyes and told him not to move a muscle. Hattie Mae rubbed some cream on his back and left him and his father alone in the room in her house.

Hattie Mae then walked out to the crowd that was still gathered outside her house.

Hattie Mae said, "I'm sorry, but you people are confused. I have no magical powers of healing. I do have the gift of sight sometimes. However, I can't control it. I do have herbs and natural ingredients that could possibly cure some of your illnesses."

All the people just kept begging and pleading for Hattie Mae's attention.

One lady in the back of the line said she wasn't leaving until Hattie Mae cured her of her illness.

Hattie Mae could feel the determination in their energy. These people believed down in their hearts that Hattie Mae had a cure for what they needed.

Savannah was going down the line saying a prayer for everybody.

Hattie Mae decided to see if there was something she could do.

Legacy brought Hattie Mae's herb bag and, as Savannah prayed for the people, Hattie Mae assessed their condition. The majority of them just needed simple things. Most of them were just too poor to see a real doctor.

So Hattie Mae's herbs were the next best things. Some people traded goods with Hattie Mae for the herbs they needed.

After hours of seeing people, Hattie Mae had to get back to the teenage boy.

When Hattie Mae entered the room where he was lying, the teenager was as stiff as a board. Hattie Mae removed the bandage from his eyes.

Hattie Mae said, "Tell me what you see child."

The teenage boy replied, "I see a beautiful angel sent from heaven. Madame Fo'Rae, you brought my sight back. You truly are the Voodoo Queen."

Hattie Mae smiled and said, "Well child, I don't know about all that."

Hattie Mae helped him down and told him to take it easy for a few days and be more careful.

Savannah, Legacy and Hattie Mae escorted the teenage boy to the door.

Mistress Mattie was just standing there looking.

As the teenage boy and his father walked down the road, all the people started clapping and chanting, "Madame Fo'Rae has done it again."

Savannah looked at Hattie Mae and said, "Well, I guess you'll be walking on water by the end of the week."

Hattie Mae just rolled her eyes at Savannah and replied sarcastically, "Maybe child, you never know."

Savannah was appalled and responded, "Blasphemy, mother. Stop giving this people false hope. Instead of praising you, they should be praising God himself."

Legacy looked at Savannah and said, "If there is a God. I'm pretty sure he's a woman."

Hattie Mae and Mistress Mattie had to laugh at that because the expression on Savannah's face was priceless.

Savannah turned sharply and grabbed her sun hat. As she put it on, she looked at Hattie Mae and said, "Messiah, I'll be back in the morning to help you with this crowd. I'm sure after your latest miracle, it will be bigger by tomorrow."

Hattie Mae remembered what Robert Lee said about having all these folks away by the time he returned.

Savannah suggested that Hattie Mae have them line up by the school tomorrow. Savannah told Hattie Mae that she needed to give those people a good talk and a warning to stop coming to her property.

As Savannah was walking to the door, she caught a glimpse of the portrait Master Fo'Rae had sent Hattie Mae.

Savannah said, "Good Lord mama, it can't be. And he's a doctor no less."

Savannah stared at the portrait of Claude. She seemed to be taken with it; a sense of pride filled Savannah's face.

Savannah laughed and said, "Well, I'm not surprised he's a doctor, his mammy is the Messiah."

Hattie Mae smiled and replied, "Life sure is amazing. Here I am practicing the skills I learned from my grandmother, and my son, whom I haven't seen since birth is practicing medicine."

Mistress Mattie looked at the portrait and said, "He sure is a handsome rascal. He looks just like Savannah only more Negro. He's kind of dark like you Hattie Mae, but not as dark."

Savannah replied, "Yes, he is on the darker side. Nevertheless, he is a handsome gentleman."

Hattie Mae just looked at Mistress Mattie and Savannah. Hattie Mae figured Mistress Mattie was just trying to appeal to Savannah's color struck side so that Savannah could continue to agree with Mistress Mattie on the matter of Legacy not courting Young Charles.

Hattie Mae rolled her eyes and replied, "Well, maybe it's just the paint the painter used. He may be just as light as Savannah if not lighter."

Savannah just frowned and walked out. She gathered up all her girls and made them come and look at the portrait of their Uncle Claude. Savannah explained to her girls that he lived in a part of the states where black people were free.

When Savannah said the word *free*, Legacy gripped the side of the table as if she were going to fall. Legacy appeared to be in a daze for a second. When Legacy regained her composure, she told them she was just tired from the long day.

However, Hattie Mae could tell by the look in Legacy's eyes that she'd had a vision and by the way Legacy was looking, and the vision was bad.

Legacy walked Savannah out and went to the schoolhouse to check on the crowd.

Mistress Mattie sat quietly in the corner and said, "Okay Hattie Mae, what do you want in exchange for the picture? You're a very clever woman, so I know you've thought it out thoroughly. I must say this has been the most sinister thing you've ever done. Well, besides hacking up my husband."

Hattie Mae decided not to respond to that. Hattie Mae said, "Well, for starters, I want you to give Robert Lee papers with the Fo'Rae seal saying he's free."

Mistress Mattie replied, "Whatever, for he's been free in St. Lucia for going on sixteen years."

Hattie Mae looked at Mistress Mattie and responded, "Just do it!"

Mistress Mattie shook her head yes.

Hattie Mae said, "And the ship Pierre Cordova works on- sign it over to him. He wants to start a fishing company. Away from Fo'Rae shipping fleet."

Mistress Mattie replied, "Done!"

Hattie Mae sat back in her chair and put her feet up.

Hattie Mae said, "I want to expand my house. Why should you be the only one who gets to live in a big house? I would like the construction to start immediately. We can go to town tomorrow, and you can write a check for it."

Mistress Mattie turned five shades of red.

Mistress Mattie replied, "And how would I explain to my bankers that I'm giving you a small fortune?"

Hattie Mae smirked and said, "Well, you can tell them whatever you want to tell them. Or I could just show them your photo image. Oh, and by the way, the fortune won't be small because I'm not done with my demands."

Hattie Mae handed Mistress Mattie a paper with a number on it.

Mistress Mattie grabbed her chest and said, "Hattie Mae, however do you expect me to come up with this amount of money?"

Hattie Mae poured her a cup of tea. She sat down and slowly stirred in her sugar.

Hattie Mae replied, "Your husband, Master Fo'Rae, was an evil person in every way imaginable. He was greedy and cruel. I watched him day in and day out for sixteen years use and abuse Negro folks. He only did one good thing for me in his life. He taught me how to add and subtract numbers and read business papers. So you see, I don't really value money as your people do, but I know the value of it, and the Fo'Rae estate has a lot of it; way more than the number that I've written on that paper. So, yes, I will accept nothing less than that."

Mistress Mattie smiled and said, "You sure are a sharp one, Hattie Mae. However, if you're not careful you may very well turn into one of my people."

Hattie Mae poured Mistress Mattie a cup of tea.

Mistress Mattie just looked at the cup, as if she were afraid to drink the tea.

Hattie Mae smiled and said, "If I wanted to kill you, Mistress Mattie, I would have done so a long time ago. Besides, you know my specialty is hacking not poison."

Mistress Mattie looked at Hattie Mae. She picked up the cup and drank from it.

Mistress Mattie said, "Well, since you put it like that."

Mistress Mattie agreed to Hattie Mae's terms. She told Hattie Mae that she'd have it done by the end of the week.

Hattie Mae warned her that if she didn't, she'd have the photo image printed in every paper on the island.

Hattie Mae looked at Mistress Mattie, who had that stupid look on her face. The look that let Hattie Mae know Mistress Mattie was more concerned with something else besides those pictures.

Hattie Mae said, "If you want to discuss Young Charles and Legacy, I'm afraid you will have to talk to her mother about that. I've already given her my blessing and Young Charles' real father, Robert Lee, has too. So talking to me is a waste of time."

Mistress Mattie looked at Hattie Mae and said, "Oh Hattie Mae, why do you encourage this behavior from them? My God, they're cousins."

Hattie Mae replied, "They are only cousins when it suits you. You know damn well you don't think of them as cousins."

Hattie Mae looked at Mistress Mattie, who for some reason was daydreaming about something.

Hattie Mae snapped her fingers in Mistress Mattie's face and said, "Hello, and just what are you scamming up?"

Mistress Mattie looked at Hattie Mae and started carrying on about how they were best friends, and Hattie Mae was like a sister to her. Mistress Mattie told Hattie Mae she trusted her with her life.

Hattie Mae just rolled her eyes and said, "Spit it out, Mistress Mattie. Every time you go to plotting and scheming you get yourself in a world of trouble."

Mistress Mattie waited a couple of seconds.

Then she said, "Hattie Mae, this is a very sensitive situation. I would like to think that this conversation would stay between you and me."

Hattie Mae frowned and replied, "Child, everything we discuss is always between you and me. Hell if I tell anyone, folks will start to think I'm just as crazy as you."

Mistress Mattie poked out her lips and said, "Now, Hattie Mae, that wasn't very nice."

Hattie Mae replied, "Just tell me what you've done now!"

Mistress Mattie squinted her eyes and said, "Yes, but just listen, don't judge."

Hattie Mae poured her another cup of tea. She knew whatever Mistress Mattie was getting ready to tell her was going to be good.

Mistress Mattie stood up. She peeked out through the window and looked around to see if anybody was around to hear.

Then Mistress Mattie said, "Well, you know my gentleman caller and I haven't been all the way intimate as of yet. However, we've had some encounters."

Mistress Mattie looked at Hattie Mae and said, "You know what I mean! Just some rubbing, kissing, and well."

Hattie Mae was hanging on to Mistress Mattie's every word.

Hattie Mae replied, "And well, what?"

Mistress Mattie said, "Well, let's just say I've been close up and personal with his manhood and while size doesn't really matter to me. However, my past relations may cause a problem."

Hattie Mae responded, "Come again, Mistress Mattie. I don't believe I heard you correctly. Did you say you were concerned with the size of your gentleman caller's private area?"

Hattie Mae cracked a smile and fanned herself.

Hattie Mae said, "Well, child, now I can see how that may cause a problem.

Child, I'll tell you a small problem like that could end a relationship."

Mistress Mattie had to laugh. She gently slapped Hattie Mae's hand and said, "Hattie Mae, we should not be discussing such things. It's just not lady like."

Mistress Mattie bit her lip and said, "Oh but, Hattie Mae, do help me out. I know you have something in your Voodoo bag that can fix the problem."

Mistress Mattie begged and pleaded with Hattie Mae to help her.

Hattie Mae replied jokingly, "Oh, child, you out of luck. In all my days, I've never enlarged a penis. I don't believe it could be done. Mistress Mattie, my love, you're going to have to just work with the hand you was dealt."

Mistress Mattie was almost in tears. She said, "Oh, Hattie Mae, why do you torment me so? You know very well what I need. Please tell me what to do."

Hattie Mae continued to laugh. Then, she told Mistress Mattie that she had to research her herb books. Hattie Mae said she'd never had anyone request such a thing. She told Mistress Mattie that she would give her what she needed after Mistress Mattie had completed her list of demands.

Mistress Mattie looked at Hattie Mae and said, "You know I've never had a real sister, friend, or a mother to discuss such personal matters with. My mother died when I was a child and my father, well, you already know he gave me to his kinsfolk in exchange for land and money. You are the closest family or friend I have."

Then Mistress Mattie walked out of the door to her buggy.

Hattie Mae almost felt sorry for Mistress Mattie until she remembered that Mistress Mattie had wicked ways and couldn't be trusted. Although, Mistress Mattie and Hattie Mae had something in common: both their mothers died when they were children. Hattie Mae grew up with her grandmother and well who knows with whom Mistress Mattie grew up.

Chapter Nine:
Love Hurts

Over the following weeks, Mistress Mattie kept up her end of the bargain. Mistress Mattie met all Hattie Mae's demands. Hattie Mae purchased the surrounding lands around Robert Lee's small house. Construction began on Hattie Mae's mansion. The town's people continued to come to Hattie Mae's house every day at sunrise hoping she'd cure them of their illnesses. They'd leave every day at sunset. Hattie Mae figured the people knew Robert Lee was headed home about sundown and they didn't want to run into him.

Robert Lee had no tolerance for Hattie Mae's believers.

Hattie Mae smiled to herself at the thought of Robert Lee acting a fool if he came home to find one believer on his property.

It was getting closer to the day for Master Fo'Rae's brother to arrive, also closer to Mistress Mattie's wedding date. Mistress Mattie scheduled the wedding date without speaking to Master Fo'Rae's brother. Mistress Mattie told Hattie Mae that Master Fo'Rae's brother was so dramatic about everything. Mistress Mattie said Master Fo'Rae's brother probably only needed her signature on a few legal documents.

Mistress Mattie appeared to be excited about her nuptials. Except for the constant begging for Hattie Mae to bring Mistress Mattie's vagina back to virgin status. Mistress Mattie had been too busy even to demand the nude pictures of her and Robert Lee. Besides, Hattie Mae refused to give them to Mistress Mattie until everything on her list was complete. The matter of her signing over one of her ships to Pierre Cordova was still in negotiations because Mistress Mattie and Master Fo'Rae's brother owned that company together. Mistress Mattie needed to purchase the ship from him first.

Hattie Mae was confident that Mistress Mattie could pull it off. Although Master Fo'Rae's brother was a wealthy man, Mistress Mattie was pretty wealthy, also. Mistress Mattie had inherited Master Fo'Rae's holding, and all the property her father owned when he died. Apparently, Mistress Mattie was an only child her father cared for.

As usual, Hattie Mae had Robert Lee's supper on the table when he arrived home. Hattie Mae was still a bit worried about Robert Lee. He always looked tired and drained of energy. Robert Lee said he looked tired and felt tired because he worked all day. Hattie Mae believed it to be more. Hell, Robert Lee was an ex-slave, he was used to hard work.

After supper, Hattie Mae heard horses outside. Hattie Mae walked out to see Mistress Mattie's driver sitting on the buggy afraid to get down because the two wolves were blocking his path. The wolves stood in attack mode; Hattie Mae only saw them act like that when there was a threat. Hattie Mae never liked Mistress Mattie's driver anyway. Besides the fact that he looked like a fool, he always dressed up in some horrific outfit of crushed velvet. He was always lurking around and listening for something to report back to Master Fo'Rae's brother.

Hattie Mae looked at him and said sarcastically, "What brings you to this neck of the woods at such a late hour?"

Hattie Mae opened the carriage door to see no one was inside.

The driver responded rudely as if he were too good to be in Hattie Mae's presence, "Good evening, Madame Fo'Rae. Mistress Mattie's brother in law, Collin Fo'Rae will be arriving tomorrow morning. Mistress Mattie would like for you and your husband Robert Lee to come to the mansion at noon to discuss an important matter."

Hattie Mae had never heard anyone refer to Master Fo'Rae's brother by his name. It was always "Master Fo'Rae."

Hattie Mae did pick up on the fact that Master Fo'Rae's brother didn't like to be called Master. He always told them to call him Mr. Fo'Rae, however, no one did.

Hattie Mae looked at the driver and said, "Run along back to your Mistress.

Kindly remind her that I am no longer one of her slaves. She cannot summon me on demand. If I so desire to meet her tomorrow at noon, I will, but tell her never to summon me again."

Hattie Mae rubbed the female wolf's fur to calm her down and said, "Yes, Great Queen he is annoying, but I'm sure he tastes almost as awful as he looks. So, biting him wouldn't be a good idea."

Then Hattie Mae looked up at the driver.

The driver looked down at Hattie Mae and said, "Oh my, how our attitude has changed since we've come into money! Your healing business must be soaring. However, word around town is that you, Madame Fo'Rae, came into a great deal of money. On the very same day that Mistress Mattie withdrew a large amount of cash."

Hattie Mae responded calmly, "Well, you know how simple folks like to talk."

Hattie Mae leaned in close to the carriage and whispered, "Have you ever heard the saying dead men tell no tales?"

Mistress Mattie's driver seemed somewhat frightened of Hattie Mae.

He looked at Hattie Mae and said, "No, but have you heard the saying; don't kill the messenger?"

Then he drove off into the night.

Hattie Mae was certain it was Mistress Mattie's driver who kept Master Fo'Rae's brother informed and always two steps ahead of her.

Hattie Mae didn't want the driver to get to Master Fo'Rae's brother and tell what he thought he knew. Hattie Mae decided to increase his fear of her.

Hattie Mae sewed up a little fat rag doll to resemble the driver. Then she stitched his eyes out and stuck a knife in his back. Hattie Mae rode her horse through the night with the wolves following her to Mistress Mattie's driver's house. Hattie Mae placed the rag doll on the driver's porch and waited until morning for him to come outside. Hattie Mae hid out of sight when she saw the door open. The driver's wife screamed to the top of her lungs when she saw the doll.

Hattie Mae laughed to herself. That simple little doll struck fear into the hearts of adults.

Hattie Mae dropped in to visit with Savannah before she went to Mistress Mattie's house. Hattie Mae wanted to tell Savannah that she had taken Legacy's side on the matter of Young Charles. Hattie Mae never considered Young Charles and Legacy cousins. And neither did Mistress Mattie until Young Charles verbally expressed his love for Legacy.

Legacy was sitting on Savannah's porch sewing a dress when Hattie Mae arrived. Legacy was so deep in her thoughts she didn't even hear Hattie Mae walk up behind her and sit on the porch.

Hattie Mae had been watching Legacy for weeks; She had been acting very strange. However, Hattie Mae never asked her what was bothering her.

Hattie Mae was waiting for Legacy to tell her freely.

Hattie Mae tapped Legacy on the shoulder and said, "What a beautiful dress you're making. Is that for Mistress Mattie's wedding?"

Legacy smiled when she saw Hattie Mae and replied, "No ma'am, I fear I won't make it to Mistress Mattie's wedding."

Hattie Mae just assumed Legacy said that because Mistress Mattie would be fit to be tied after Young Charles starts courting Legacy.

Hattie Mae was about to ask her why when she heard Savannah screaming, "Well, I be damned!"

Hattie Mae and Legacy rushed into Savannah's house to see what happened. They saw Savannah standing up reading the Bible with her jaw dropped to the floor.

Hattie Mae said, "Savannah, what is? what happened?"

Savannah sat down in her chair. She could barely speak. Savannah handed Hattie Mae the Bible and said, "Read that to me please."

Savannah pointed to a scripture in the Bible.

Hattie Mae read, "His head and his hairs were white like wool, as white as snow; and his eyes were as a flame of fire; and his feet like unto fine brass, as if they burned in a furnace; and his voice as the sound of many waters."

Hattie Mae looked at Savannah in confusion and said, "And why does that have you all worked up?"

Savannah looked at Hattie Mae and whispered as if she couldn't believe what she was saying, "Don't you understand? Jesus is Negro, like us."

Hattie Mae just stood there looking at Savannah.

Legacy frowned her face up and said, "Negro like us? When did you become Negro? I thought you were a creole princess?"

Legacy rolled her eyes and went back to the porch to finish her dress.

Hattie Mae didn't even respond to what Savannah said.

Hattie Mae said, "Savannah, have you seen Master Fo'Rae's brother yet? He's here on the island."

Savannah was just reading about Jesus' hair and feet over and over and looking at her hair and feet.

Savannah mumbled, "Yes, Uncle Collin came by this morning. I'm supposed to meet him and Mistress Mattie's mansion at noon."

Hattie Mae was taken aback by Savannah referring to Master Fo'Rae's brother as Uncle Collin.

Hattie Mae said, "So, when did you start calling him Uncle Collin?"

Savannah never looked up from the Bible. She said, "Since this morning when he asked me to. He also told all the girls to call him Uncle Collin too. He bought each of them beautiful dresses from the state. They're trying them on as we speak."

Then Savannah called for all of her girls to come in the room. Hattie Mae had to admit that the dresses were beautiful. Savannah showed Hattie Mae boxes of clothes and shoes Master Fo'Rae's brother had bought for the girls.

He even bought Savannah a fancy dress and petticoat.

One of Savannah's daughters didn't seem too impressed with the dresses.

Savannah's daughter sat down and rubbed her legs. Hattie Mae walked over to her and sat beside her.

Savannah's daughter said, "Hey Madame Fo'Rae," and smiled.

Hattie Mae smiled. She had never heard one of her granddaughters call her Madame Fo'Rae before. Only the island folks called her that.

Hattie Mae said, "So, I'm not Mama Hattie Mae anymore?"

Savannah's daughter replied, "No, not today, Madame Fo'Rae sounds much better than Mama Hattie Mae. Madame Fo'Rae sounds important and exciting. Mama Hattie Mae sounds like an old slave name!"

Hattie Mae had to smile at that.

Hattie Mae replied, "Child, you might be right about that! But who told you that? You've never been a slave."

Savannah's daughter told Hattie Mae that Savannah told them all about being a slave in America. And that they should never go to America ever.

Savannah's daughter also said Savannah showed them the Fo'Rae name that

172

Master Fo'Rae branded on all his slaves.

Savannah's daughter kept rubbing her legs.

Hattie Mae rubbed Savanna's daughter's legs and said, "What's wrong, baby? Are those old weather legs bothering you again?"

Savannah's daughter replied, "Yes, Madame Fo'Rae, every time it's going to rain, they just ache."

Hattie Mae rubbed her grandbaby's legs and told her later she would bring her some cream to apply to them.

Hattie Mae and Savannah walked up to the mansion to meet with Mistress Mattie, Robert Lee, and Master Fo'Rae's brother.

When they arrived, Mistress Mattie was sitting in the living room. She didn't look too pleased. Hattie Mae looked around to see that Mistress Mattie had created a feast.

Hattie Mae assumed all the hospitality was to butter her up to agree with Mistress Mattie.

Mistress Mattie looked at Savannah and Hattie Mae and said, "Well, hello ladies."

Then she looked at Hattie Mae and said, "I'm so glad you made it here. I would have sent my driver to get you. However, for some mysterious reason he and his family just up and left this morning. Hattie Mae, you wouldn't know anything about that, would you?"

Hattie Mae gave a smile, smirked and replied, "Now, why would I know why your driver suddenly left?"

Mistress Mattie said, "Well, maybe because he left a message for you. He says, please forgive him he was only doing what he was instructed to do.

Please have mercy on him and his family."

173

Mistress Mattie looked at Master Fo'Rae's brother and back at Hattie Mae and said, "Can you explain that?"

Hattie Mae replied, "I'm not even going to try and make sense of that. Why don't we just get to the business at hand? The real reason why you've summoned all of us to your mansion."

Master Fo'Rae's brother interrupted. He smiled and said, "Now, now Madame Fo'Rae. Let us not be uncivilized in front of company."

Then he pointed to a man sitting in a chair in the corner. Hattie Mae hadn't seen the man yet.

Master Fo'Rae said, "Allow me to introduce him. He's a lawyer from the States."

Hattie Mae remembered the man's face. She had seen him a few times in New Orleans with Master Fo'Rae. He always looked uncomfortable at the plantation.

Mistress Mattie looked at the lawyer and frowned. His presence seemed to irritate Mistress Mattie.

Master Fo'Rae's brother said, "Before we discuss the situation with my great niece Legacy and my nephew Young Charles, we have more important family business to discuss. That's why I had Mistress Mattie gather you all here today."

Hattie Mae was floored. She thought to herself, *"Did he just refer to Legacy as his great niece and to all of them as family?" Hattie Mae had a feeling this meeting was getting ready to turn into a disaster."*

Hattie Mae said, "If you're discussing family business, why would you invite me and my daughter and Robert Lee? Shouldn't you and Mistress Mattie be discussing family business in private?"

Mistress Mattie said, "I agree, Hattie Mae."

Master Fo'Rae's brother smiled and sat in his chair. He gathered some papers from his briefcase and he handed them to the lawyer.

He looked at all of them and said, "This meeting is to discuss the terms laid out in the late Claude Fo'Rae's last will and testament."

Hattie Mae slowly said, "My boy died?"

Master Fo'Rae's brother replied, "Why no, Hattie Mae, not your boy, We're speaking of my brother Claude Fo'Rae Sr."

Hattie Mae was a bit confused. She never knew Master Fo'Rae's first name. Everybody always called him Master Fo'Rae.

Hattie Mae just sat in her chair confused.

Mistress Mattie seemed a bit annoyed and said, "My late husband had no will and testament. Whatever are you talking about?"

The lawyer replied, "To the contrary Mistress Mattie, your husband did indeed have a will, and he was adamant on me following every aspect of it down to the smallest detail. I've tried over a dozen times to reach you before and after you left the states. As a result, I had to reach out to your husband's younger brother, Collin Fo'Rae, to find you. Luckily, on my last visit to the plantation, in an attempt to find you, I ran into him. And well, now we're here."

The lawyer continued. He said, "Your husband had very specific instructions. I might add that they were sort of tricky also because they involved one slave and a free mulatto male. The mulatto, whose name is also Claude Fo'Rae, well, I've been in contact with him and we've settled our business."

Mistress Mattie was pissed; she screamed out, "And what business was that?"

The lawyer simply replied, "Quite frankly, ma'am, that's none of your business. If you would allow me to finish. I'm getting to your business."

Mistress Mattie was turning red; she was furious. She said, "Anything involving my late husband is most certainly my business. I demand you tell me at once what is going on."

The lawyer looked at Master Fo'Rae's brother and said, "Please can you ask her to stop interrupting me?"

Collin Fo'Rae looked at Mistress Mattie and said, "Please allow him to finish. He will soon answer all of your questions."

Mistress Mattie sat back down in her chair, looked at the lawyer, and said, "Proceed!"

The lawyer continued; he said, "As you know, Claude Fo'Rae was losing his eyesight to glaucoma."

Savannah was shocked and said, "No, we didn't know that!"

The lawyer looked over at Collin Fo'Rae and said bitterly, "Shall these outbursts continue all evening?"

Master Fo'Rae's brother Collin walked over to Savannah and said, "My dear, please do contain your questions until after our guest has conducted his business. But to answer your question, yes, your father was losing his eyesight."

Hattie Mae rolled her eyes and said, "Her father, well that's a different way to describe him. I don't think I've ever heard anyone refer to Master as Savannah's father."

Mistress Mattie took a sip of her tea and sarcastically said, "Surely I never have, and I was married to the bastard."

Collin Fo'Rae was getting annoyed and said, "Let us all keep our remarks to ourselves."

Collin Fo'Rae looked at the lawyer and said, "Please continue."

The lawyer replied, "Like I was saying, Claude Fo'Rae commissioned this will to be read after his death. He wanted it written and sealed directly after he read it with his own eyes. This is what he wanted."

The lawyer picked up a paper and showed everyone the seal from the great state of Louisiana and the two witness' signatures. To everyone's surprise, the signatures were Collin Fo'Rae's and Mistress Mattie's.

Hattie Mae looked at Mistress Mattie with a disgusted look and said, "I thought you knew nothing of this last will and testament?"

Mistress Mattie never responded.

The lawyer said, "Claude Fo'Rae's wishes read as such;

I Claude Fo'Rae being of sound mind and body, leave all my possessions to be divided equally amongst my two blood born children: Savannah Michelle Fo'Rae and Claude Fo'Rae, and my wife Mattie Fo'Rae. Upon my death, Savannah and Hattie Mae Fo'Rae shall be set free and relocated to my mansion in St. Lucia."

Mistress Mattie looked down to the ground as if she had never heard anything.

Savannah was livid. She looked at Mistress Mattie and said, "You knew this all along and you said nothing?"

Hattie Mae felt the table vibrate and looked over to see Savannah's temple throbbing as if it were going to burst out of her forehead.

Hattie Mae also looked out of the glass doors to see the wolves watching from the hill. It appeared that Savannah's anger agitated the female wolf; she was pacing back and forth.

Hattie Mae walked over to Savannah and calmed her down. Hattie Mae said, "Let's just hear the lawyer out."

Savannah stood there listening. Hattie Mae looked over at Master Fo'Rae's brother Collin, who was sitting with his legs crossed, smoking a cigar and smirking. He appeared to be getting a thrill out of the reading of the will.

The Lawyer continued and said, "Mr. Fo'Rae had unmasked a fortune. He had holdings in several large companies, he owned property and land in three countries and two territories. He also had artwork, jewels and a list of other possessions. Before he died, he liquidated most of his assets into cash value. He sold the majority of his shares of the shipping company to his brother Collin Fo'Rae, and he deeded his properties as follows:

My mansion in St. Lucia, and all the surrounding land, goes to Savannah Michelle Fo'Rae. The plantation in Louisiana, and all the surrounding land, goes to my wife Mistress Mattie. My home in New York and all my holdings such as artwork, statues, and others go to Claude Fo'Rae. In closing, all my books, journals, and writings go to my slave girl, Hattie Mae along, with my house in Paris France."

Hattie Mae and Savannah stood there with their jaws dropped.

Savannah was just staring at Mistress Mattie, who was making a fuss about Young Charles being left out of the will.

The lawyer simply said that Young Charles was not born at the time the will was written and that the will was legal and binding. He said that if Mistress Mattie had a problem with it, she could take it up with the courts in the United States.

Master Fo'Rae asked the lawyer if the will included the property that Mistress Mattie inherited from her father when he died. The lawyer told Collin Fo'Rae that it wasn't, however, any of the mentioned recipients in the will could bring it up in a court of law. The lawyer said that the property was considered a marital asset since Mistress Mattie acquired it while they were married. All the other assets belonged to Master Fo'Rae before he married Mistress Mattie.

Mistress Mattie was fit to be tied. She looked at Collin Fo'Rae and said,

"How dare you! You want to assist these people in robbing me of my inheritance. Haven't I suffered enough at your brother's hands? I will contest this will. This is foolishness. I will never allow slaves to be superior to me."

The lawyer stepped in and said, "About contesting your late husband's will; your husband left a clause that if anyone contested anything written, then everything he had would go to his brother Collin Fo'Rae."

Collin Fo'Rae winked his eye at Hattie Mae and said, "Oh my, what a situation we have."

The lawyer said he had legal document for all of them to sign, and after that, he would personally see to it that everything promised in the will would come to pass.

Hattie Mae asked the lawyer about what he meant when he said he'd settled his business with her son Claude Fo'Rae. The lawyer said, "Claude signed his papers years ago, graduated from medical school, and used the property willed to him to open up a private practice for colored folks." The lawyer told Hattie Mae that she should be proud of her boy. Then he left.

Savannah was still just sitting on the chair taking in and trying to make sense of what just happened.

Master Fo'Rae's brother, Collin, said, "Well, since we are all here. Let's discuss the situation between Young Charles and Legacy. This entire ordeal is out of control."

He looked at Savannah who appeared to be in deep thought.

Collin Fo'Rae said, "I understand your daughter, my niece, his cousin, thinks she loves him. And he probably does love her. However, Young Charles is destined for greatness. He may very well be a senator or a congressman. Hell who knows he may very well be a famous artist one day.

We both know he can't do any of those things with a colored Voodoo-practicing wife."

Mistress Mattie stepped in to give her two cents. She said, "Now let's be reasonable, Savannah. They are cousins for heavens sake. Plus, Legacy as bright as she is, is no match for my son. He was educated in all the finest schools in France."

Hattie Mae was still processing what just happened. What she didn't understand was, what did Master Fo'Rae's brother Collin get out of the deal?

Then it hit Hattie Mae. If Mistress Mattie contested the will, she would get nothing. However, Mistress Mattie had an inheritance already from her father. It wasn't as much as Master Fo'Rae's estate, but it would allow Mistress Mattie to live comfortably. Hattie Mae believed Master Fo'Rae's brother Collin was banking on Mistress Mattie loving Young Charles obsessively and hating the idea of him marrying a Negro more.

That was ridiculous because Young Charles was half Negro and Mistress Mattie had been in love with Robert Lee for years.

Hattie Mae remembered that Mistress Mattie wasn't working with a full deck of cards. So whatever Mistress Mattie did or said never made sense.

Mistress Mattie was too busy explaining to Savannah how much better than Legacy Young Charles was to notice that the room was slightly trembling from Savannah's anger.

Mistress Mattie stood up and pointed her finger in Savannah's face and said very rudely and extremely sharp, "The bottom line is, my son will never marry and have children with a nigger! I will not allow it, not even over my dead cold body. Like I said before, Young Charles is destined for greatness.

He will not have his entire future tarnished by some nappy-headed plantation baby and her Mammy. Now I've tried to appeal to your softer side. I've even gone as far as to referring to you and your children as my cousins."

Mistress Mattie took a deep breath as if referring to Savannah and her children as her cousins diminished her self-value in some way.

Mistress Mattie continued, "Master Fo'Rae's brother even found my late husbands old will and testament that names you as his daughter and as an inheritant. And, yet, you still refuse to put an end to this foolishness of your daughter courting my son. Well, I'll tell you what. If you don't put an end to this madness, I will contest everything in that will, which will leave you and your family with nothing. Which would serve you right! Whoever heard of such madness, a Master leaving his slaves freedom and land.

Master Fo'Rae must not have only been going blind, but he had to be going foolish as well!"

Hattie Mae looked over at Master Fo'Rae's brother Collin, who was hanging on to Mistress Mattie's every word.

Savannah turned her back sharply on Mistress Mattie and bent down like she was in pain.

Savannah quickly spun around and stared directly into Mistress Mattie eyes. Savannah raised her hand in the air and sharply swiveled her fingers to make a tight fist.

The room started trembling; things started flying off the walls and all the windows in the mansion- started cracking.

Savannah said softly and slowly, with authority, "How dare you insult me and my family! You stand there and mock me as if you are so much better than me. Well, let me tell you about yourself. You are nothing! Your daddy sold you to his nephew for land and cattle. You were nothing to your so-called husband Master Fo'Rae, but a piece of property. Better yet, a concubine until you got too old for him and he replaced you with what he really desired, a young slave girl, my mother. For years you've taken advantage of Robert Lee, turning him into your personal sex slave. You've lied, cheated, and killed your own daughter to protect your son, who has Negro blood flowing through his veins. Yet you disrespect my daughter Legacy, who, by the way is a product of rape and incest, committed by your very own husband!"

Savannah walked closer to Mistress Mattie and whispered, "Yes, your husband, who's also your first cousin."

Mistress Mattie backed away from Savannah and held one hand on the mantle and another over her heart. Mistress Mattie's face was red as fire and flushed with sweat.

Savannah looked over at Collin Fo'Rae who was now holding on to his chair.

The house was still slightly trembling and glass from the windows was everywhere.

Hattie Mae paid close attention to Collin Fo'Rae. Hattie Mae was certain he knew the reason the house was shaking and all the windows cracking were caused by Savannah's energy. However, he never flinched. Savannah's gift never appeared to frighten him.

Hattie Mae thought she'd add her two cents to the show Savannah was already putting on.

Hattie Mae whistled for the wolves standing on the hill to come to her.

The wolves charged down the hill for the house and stood at attention waiting on Hattie Mae to give the order to strike. They scratched and howled and paced back and forth.

Mistress Mattie started screaming "Lord, Jesus, what in the world is going on? Hattie Mae, please end this at once."

Hattie Mae looked at Mistress Mattie and coldly replied, "I will do no such thing. It appears you need a dose of your own medicine."

Then Hattie Mae looked over at the huge gold-framed mirror. Hattie Mae closed her eyes and stretched out her arms. She twirled her fingers around and said, "Come to me Baby Girl One, come to Mama Hattie Mae from the beyond."

They all heard a baby crying. Mistress Mattie almost jumped out of her skin at the sound of the baby crying.

Mistress Mattie's eyes grew larger than gold coins.

Mistress Mattie screamed out, "Oh God, Lord Jesus, no!"

Savannah looked at Mistress Mattie, smirked and said; "Now why in the world would you call on Jesus? Don't you know he's a nigger, just like me?"

Then Savannah quoted the Bible word for word and described Jesus.

Savannah said, "Only a nigger would have feet of brass and hair like lambs wool."

Savannah tilted her head to the side, looked at Mistress Mattie and said, "Wouldn't you agree, ma'am?"

Savannah's energy shook the house. Savannah shouted out, "I will shake this house to its very foundation. A foundation that my slave ancestors built, I might add. Don't ever disrespect my daughter or my family again. I will never choose to put anybody's happiness before my own child's. I was on your side about them not courting because they were cousins, until you showed your true colors and how you really felt about us niggers!"

Hattie Mae looked at the mirror and said, "Come to me, Baby Girl One!"

All of a sudden Baby Girl One appeared in the mirror.

Baby Girl One looked at Mistress Mattie and said, "Hello, Mother!"

Mistress Mattie's face turned white as a ghost and she fainted on the floor.

Master Fo'Rae's brother Collin stood up when he saw the spirit of Baby Girl One in the mirror. He uttered the words, "Well, I be damned!"

Collin Fo'Rae never took his eyes off the spirit of Baby Girl One, not even when the male wolf walked over and stood beside him.

Hattie Mae found it odd that the male wolf never perceived Collin Fo'Rae as a threat. As a matter of fact, neither did the female wolf. It was as if the wolves had adopted Collin Fo'Rae as one of the pack, but Hattie Mae couldn't understand why; she had never given Collin the wolves' scent and Collin hadn't been around the wolves.

Collin and the male wolf just stood there gazing at Baby Girl One's spirit.

Mistress Mattie woke up screaming and carrying on. Mistress Mattie was so scared of Baby Girl One's spirit that she crawled inside the oversized marble fireplace and curled up in the fetal position, screaming for Hattie Mae to send Baby Girl One's spirit back to the beyond.

Hattie Mae refused to send Baby Girl One's spirit back.

Hattie Mae said, "Mistress Mattie, you are indeed a wicked woman. You've done too many wicked deeds to number. I freed you from this spirit once before and this is how you repay me? By talking to my daughter as if she were scum beneath your feet. Mistress Mattie, you lie, manipulate, and deceive everyone you come in contact with."

Mistress Mattie placed her hands over her ears so she couldn't hear the baby spirit crying.

Mistress Mattie was screaming, "I'm sorry, Hattie Mae, I'm sorry!"

Hattie Mae raised her hand up as if she were signaling for silence. The baby's crying stopped.

Mistress Mattie uncovered her eyes. She peeked out of the fireplace only to see Baby Girl One's spirit still hovering in the mirror.

Hattie Mae walked over to Mistress Mattie, who was still inside the fireplace shaking like a leaf. Between Savannah's energy trembling the house, the wolves howling and scratching, and Hattie Mae calling on the spirits, well Mistress Mattie looked like she was a true believer.

Hattie Mae looked at Mistress Mattie and said, "Every dog has his day, and this is your day. Baby Girl One's spirit will follow you throughout your days. You honestly deserve worse."

Hattie Mae was about to say something when she saw Legacy standing there.

Legacy walked over to Hattie Mae and held her hand. Legacy said, "No more, Madame Fo'Rae. This is not what these gifts were given to us for. We do not inflict harm on people."

Legacy looked over at Mistress Mattie and said, "Even if they deserve it."

Legacy walked over to her mother Savannah and said, "Enough Mama, I know you're just defending me."

Collin Fo'Rae sat in his chair and dusted his pants off. He called for Mistress Mattie to come from out of the fireplace.

He said, "Why, Mistress Mattie, if you don't crawl your behind from out of that fire pit. You never have to fear the dead; it's the living you should fear!"

Savannah rolled her eyes and said, "That pit fits her well. She may as well get used to being there. Because in a pit of fire, in hell, is where she'll end up."

Savannah shook her finger at Mistress Mattie and said, "I surely hope none of your evil ancestors' blood doesn't ruin me. Surely I have more of my mother's African blood in me."

Legacy helped Mistress Mattie, who was still somewhat distraught, off the floor.

Legacy said, "Now, now, Mistress Mattie pull yourself together. I've got something to tell you."

Mistress Mattie was still screaming for Hattie Mae to make Baby Girl One's spirits go away.

Legacy sat Mistress Mattie down on the sofa. Then she walked to the mirror where the spirit of Baby Girl One was.

Legacy looked at Baby Girl One, she smiled and said, "I surely do miss you, my dear friend. All these years without you, I've never forgotten about you.

However, you know you're not supposed to be here. All sins are forgiven in the afterlife. Go rest peacefully until it is time for us to meet again."

Baby Girl One's spirit seemed to smile. Then Baby Girl One lifted up her finger. She pointed to Master Fo'Rae's brother Collin and shook her head.

Everybody turned to look at Collin. He was sitting there with his legs crossed smirking. The wolves were relaxed at his feet.

Then Baby Girl One's spirit was gone away.

Mistress Mattie cried out, "Oh thank God, Legacy, you are a lifesaver."

Legacy looked over at Mistress Mattie and said, "A lifesaver, yet not good enough for your son!"

Mistress Mattie started to reply when Legacy fell to the floor.

Hattie Mae rushed to her side. Collin Fo'Rae picked her up off the floor and sat her on the sofa.

Legacy mumbled, "You've won. I won't accept Young Charles' courting."

Mistress Mattie glanced over at Hattie Mae who was daring her to say one word in response to what Legacy just said.

Hattie Mae rolled her eyes and looked over at the mirror. Mistress Mattie didn't say a word. She just grabbed a bottle of Kentucky whiskey and a cup.

Savannah said, "Now child, is that your final decision? Nobody in this room can force you to do anything. You are free to do whatever you desire."

Then Savannah looked around the room.

Mistress Mattie didn't even bother to look up from her Kentucky Whisky. She just kept on drinking it straight from the bottle and holding her shotgun, which Hattie Mae found comical because spirits were already dead. No gun was going to protect Mistress Mattie from them.

Legacy responded, "Yes, that's my decision."

Collin Fo'Rae stood up and said, "Well, that's that! Legacy darling, don't worry about a thing. I'll make all the arrangements. Where ever you decide to go, you'll go in style. My ship is stocked with the finest of everything."

Savannah replied, "Wait, who said anything about Legacy leaving St. Lucia? This is her home. She's never been off this island. Her entire family is here. No, I won't allow it. She's already given up Young Charles, now you want her to give up her home? No, no sir, it's not going to happen!"

Collin Fo'Rae looked at Hattie Mae whose heart was breaking at the thought of Legacy leaving the Island. He said, "Hattie Mae please help me out. You and I know very well that Young Charles won't take no for an answer. He won't just walk away from Legacy. She has to be far away from here."

Legacy responded, "Uncle Collin is right. Young Charles will tear this island apart searching for me. I have to leave."

Collin Fo'Rae took a deep sigh of relief. He said, "And I have the perfect get away for you. I have a château in the south of France. My father bought it for my mother before I was born. Nobody knows its location. The only people there are the groundskeeper and his family, and my childhood nanny. I'll make all the arrangements."

Collin Fo'Rae looked at Hattie Mae standing there with tears rolling down her cheeks. The thought of Legacy leaving tore Hattie Mae apart.

Collin Fo'Rae seemed to have compassion for Hattie Mae, he said, "Awe don't weep, Hattie Mae, it's only for a short while. Just until."

Then Collin abruptly stopped as if he had over spoken.

Savannah said, "Just until when?"

Collin Fo'Rae walked out of the room to make arrangements and ignored Savannah's question.

Hattie Mae heard Mistress Mattie mumble, "I wish he'd died in childbirth with his Mammy!"

Then Mistress Mattie rolled her eyes as Collin Fo'Rae left the room.

Hattie Mae found that statement odd. She could have sworn she read in Master Fo'Rae journals that his mother died of a heart attack.

Hattie Mae decided to investigate that later. Right now she had to get some more important questions answered. Like what was going on with Legacy.

The look on Legacy's face told Hattie Mae that Legacy had a vision.

Savannah stormed out of the room behind Collin Fo'Rae shouting something about Legacy not going nowhere without her.

Mistress Mattie was searching for another bottle of whiskey, and the wolves had returned to their post on the hilltop.

Hattie Mae asked Legacy to take a walk with her.

As they strolled through the gardens, Hattie Mae turned to Legacy and said, "I know you saw something child. Now, why don't you share whatcha seen with your old grandmother?"

Hattie Mae winked at Legacy and gave a smile.

Legacy replied, "Freedom, Mama Hattie Mae, freedom."

Hattie Mae was confused. She looked at Legacy and said, "Well, surely you ain't talking about yourself child, cause you was born free. And everybody on this island is free. So tell me who's this freedom for."

Legacy replied, "Freedom in the United States! I seen all the slaves free!"

Chapter Ten:
Love Still Hurts

The matter of Legacy and Young Charles had been settled. The plan was that Legacy would leave Saint Lucia going to France in the following days. However, she wouldn't be traveling alone.

Savannah's husband Pierre Cordova insisted on sailing her on his new ship.

With all that had happened the day the last will and testament was read, Mistress Mattie forgot that Hattie Mae had that photo image of her.

Mistress Mattie soon came back to her senses and closed the deal with Hattie Mae. Hattie Mae held on to the picture for safekeeping. Mistress Mattie did her usual begging and pleading for Hattie Mae's friendship.

However, after the show Mistress Mattie put on at the reading of the will, Hattie Mae was finished dealing with Mistress Mattie.

Mistress Mattie showed up at Savannah's house where Legacy, Savannah and Hattie Mae were having lunch and discussing Legacy's trip to France.

Mistress Mattie just walked up on the porch as if nothing had ever happened. She handed Legacy some newly purchased dresses and said, "You're just going to love France. I went there once with my late husband, your grandfather, or should I say your daddy. I just fell in love with the place."

Savannah looked at Mistress Mattie and said, "You're not welcome here, and we most certainly don't want your dresses."

Savannah smirked and said, "With my new inheritance, I can buy whatever my child needs."

Mistress Mattie looked at Savannah and said, "Well, that's true."

Mistress Mattie stomped her foot and pouted and said, "Oh y'all please don't treat me like this. Y'all are all the family I have. Surely you can't still be cross at me. I admit I should have never used that awful word nigger. I promise I'll never say it again."

191

Mistress Mattie looked and Hattie Mae and said, "It was just a family argument. Families argue all the time. Hattie Mae, you are my best friend. The thought of you never speaking to me again, well, it's frightening. I tell you, just downright frightening."

Nobody said anything; they just continued to look at Mistress Mattie carry on.

Mistress Mattie looked at Savannah and said, "I swear on your colored Jesus, I knew nothing about the will! Hell, it's written in French! You know perfectly well I can't read French. Hell, I can barely read at all. The lawyer always had papers for me to sign. I just signed them and went on with my day."

Hattie Mae grew tired of Mistress Mattie rambling and said, "I don't forgive you, but Legacy will accept your dresses."

Hattie Mae thought to herself that Mistress Mattie was going to have her hands tied in the following weeks with her wedding, and Young Charles was going to raise hell when he comes home to find Legacy gone. Somehow that gave Hattie Mae comfort and took her mind off the fact that her oldest granddaughter was going across the ocean to a country she never knew existed.

Collin Fo'Rae showed up at Savannah's house.

Hattie Mae said, "Well, it's just one big family reunion."

Collin Fo'Rae had a serious look on his face. He said he wanted to talk to Legacy about how to conduct herself in Paris. He told Legacy although Paris was a free country and pretty liberal, prejudice ignorant people lived everywhere. Collin Fo'Rae told Legacy never to wander around alone, and never to be too friendly with white folks. He told her to stay with her kind, but always let them know her last name was Fo'Rae. Never let them forget it.

Hattie Mae heard Mistress Mattie mumble, "He's always so proud of his father's last name."

Hattie Mae had started to get a little curious about why Mistress Mattie was always making snide remarks about Collin Fo'Rae's parents. Hell, after all Collin was her cousin slash brother in law.

Hattie Mae just shook her head with disgust thinking about the sick twisted Fo'Rae family.

It still surprised Hattie Mae to this day how normal and adjusted Legacy was. Even after learning that her father was also her grandfather. Legacy just accepted it. She never once questioned her existence.

Hattie Mae smiled and thought, *That's the African blood in Legacy that made her so strong.*

Hattie Mae glanced over at Savannah and thought *Savannah sure did have a lot of white family characteristics in her.*

Savannah went off to pray. Mistress Mattie insisted on Legacy trying on every dress she'd bought her. When Legacy was finished, Mistress Mattie decided that Legacy needed bonnets and shoes to match. So they headed up to the market place to see what they could find.

Collin Fo'Rae stayed behind. He wanted to make sure Hattie Mae was going to keep her end of their bargain and not tell Young Charles where Legacy had ran off to.

Collin Fo'Rae made sure nobody else knew where Legacy was going either.

Hattie Mae looked over to see Collin Fo'Rae's servant just staring at her.

His glare made Hattie Mae a little uneasy. Hattie Mae remembered him from the plantation in New Orleans.

Hattie Mae thought it odd that Collin Fo'Rae always brought about three slaves with him from New Orleans, however, he never took them back when he left.

The slaves he brought never said a word. They just worked the fields during the day and went to their quarters at night. The funny thing was, they never tried to escape or leave the island. Not even after Collin Fo'Rae left. They just kept up their routine.

If Hattie Mae didn't know anybody better, it was like they were all keeping secrets. Even Savannah's husband Pierre Cordova seemed to be in on it.

Pierre Cordova and Collin Fo'Rae always had their heads together whispering. Then they would make their way down to the docks and unload an entire ship full of valuables Collin Fo'Rae would bring from the United States. They would remove it from one ship and put it on another ship, then send that ship on to Paris.

Hattie Mae really never questioned Collin FoRae bringing over item from the United States. Although the Fo'Rae's had a few houses in the United States,
Collin Fo'Rae always insisted his family home was in Paris.

Hattie Mae found it odd that he would move all his most valuable possessions to Paris though.

Hattie Mae spotted Pierre Cordova talking to one of the ladies that had come over with Collin Fo'Rae. Hattie Mae wondered why Mistress Mattie didn't give this lady a job as a maid or field hand.

The lady didn't really look like a slave. She was well dressed, well kept, and appeared to be well studied. She was medium height, medium build, and light brown, so Hattie Mae knew somewhere down the line, somebody's Master had been tipping in the slave quarters.

The lady had a gentle spirit about her, but she seemed to be a little nervous at the same time. The lady spent most of her time in the mansion in a room Mistress Mattie assigned to her.

For some reason or another, Mistress Mattie didn't seem to care for the lady. Hattie Mae just chalked that up to Mistress Mattie thinking she was superior to all women.

After Pierre Cordova's conversation with the lady, Hattie Mae went to have a talk with Pierre Cordova about Legacy's trip.

On the day Legacy left, Hattie Mae couldn't bring herself to leave the docks. Hattie Mae just stood there and watched the ship until it disappeared in the horizon.

Hattie Mae felt like a piece of her heart left with Legacy. In the following weeks, everything around the Fo'Rae Manor was in an uproar.

Mistress Mattie was preparing for her wedding and it was like a madhouse.

Collin Fo'Rae convinced Hattie Mae to step in and help Mistress Mattie. He said that doing something would take Hattie Mae's mind off Legacy.

Savannah hadn't been around much. She was spending most of her time praying to her Jesus and taking care of her girls.

Hattie Mae's house was under construction, so Hattie Mae was staying at the mansion with Mistress Mattie, who was working Hattie Mae's last nerve about her issue with her oversized vagina.

Hattie Mae continually told Mistress Mattie that there was nothing she could do to fix her vagina. There was no herb or potion for oversized vaginas!

Hattie Mae looked at Mistress Mattie, sitting there looking like the life had been sucked out of her.

Hattie Mae smiled and said, "Child, cheer up, you're getting married in a few days. Besides, there's really nothing I can do to fix your vagina. It's unheard of.

Only a good tight stitching can fix you, and since that's not possible, nothing short of a miracle from your white Jesus will fix you. You're just going to have to deal with it, sister girl."

195

Then Hattie Mae laughed uncontrollably. The thought of Mistress Mattie explaining her loose vagina to her new husband bought Hattie Mae a small piece of happiness.

Hattie Mae looked over at Mistress Mattie who appeared to be in deep thought.

Hattie Mae walked over to Mistress Mattie, bumped her with her hip slightly and said, "Whatcha thinking, child? You got that, 'I'm about to do something real stupid look!' So tell me the foolishness you thinking about."

Mistress Mattie made that stupid face she always made when she knew what she was about to do was wrong, but she was going to do it anyway!

Mistress Mattie said, "Hattie Mae, do you remember that time when one of Savannah's girls fell off the porch and split her lip open?"

Hattie Mae reluctantly replied, "Yes, why?"

Mistress Mae said, "Do you recall what you stitched her up with?"

Hattie Mae stood there and looked at Mistress Mattie. Hattie Mae knew this line of questioning was leading to a place more ridiculous than ever.

Mistress Mattie's mind just came up with the craziest things. Hattie Mae never knew what to expect to come out of Mistress Mattie's mouth.

Mistress Mattie walked out to the sun porch and stared at the ocean.

Mistress Mattie said, "And, Hattie Mae, remember when Savannah had her last girl. Why her head was huge, it split Savannah wide open. Do you remember what you stitched her up with?"

Hattie Mae just shook her head back and forth and said with disgust, "Yes, I sure do. I used seaweed!"

Mistress Mattie smiled as if she'd just struck oil in her fields.

Mistress Mattie said, "Hattie Mae, remember what you said? You said you used seaweed because it had natural healing powers and would dissolve on its own. You said it would help the healing process and give the body aide at the same time!"

Hattie Mae looked at Mistress Mattie and said, "I swear you've finally lost it, child. Whatever you're thinking, the answer is no!"

Mistress Mattie turned around swiftly and batted those big blue eyes and pouted.

Mistress Mattie said, "Oh please, Hattie Mae! Please help me. You're my only friend. I'd do anything for you."

Hattie Mae replied, "Well, I can tell you right now batting your eyes and pouting your little paper thin lips ain't gonna work with me. However, tell me exactly what it is you want me to help you with?"

Mistress Mattie whispered, "I want you to stitch me up with the seaweed. Just like you did Savanna after she had her baby."

Hattie Mae took a deep breath and sat down on the edge of the bed. Hattie Mae gathered up her thoughts.

Hattie Mae looked at Mistress Mattie and said, "Please tell me you heard how ridiculously crazy you sound! Let me get this straight. You want me to stitch up your vagina?"

Hattie Mae grinned and said, "Girl I got the right mind to drag your narrow ass down to the nearest asylum and tell them to throw away the key.

In all my years on this planet, and in all my years working with herbs and healing folks, I've never had such a request. I swear white folks are the strangest folks I've ever known. Nothing but a bunch of killers, thieves, and rapist."

Hattie Mae looked over at Mistress Mattie who was standing there plotting the entire procedure in her mind.

Hattie Mae said, "And, in your case, sick in the head. Where do you get these ideas? What in your right mind allows you to think such nonsense?"

Mistress Mattie replied calmly, "Not all white people are rapist!"

Then Mistress Mattie laughed.

She swung around the bedpost.

Mistress Mattie said, "It's the absolute greatest idea I've ever had Hattie Mae. Just think about it. You give me a few stitches of seaweed. On my wedding night, my husband will penetrate through them thinking I'm extremely tight down there because I haven't been with a man since my late husband."

Mistress Mattie jumped up with her eyes stretched out as big as bow dollars.

She said, "I'm going to add blood on the bed when we're finished! You know just for special effect."

Hattie Mae was utterly disgusted with Mistress Mattie!

Hattie Mae said, "You are truly sick!"

Mistress Mattie replied, "Not sick Hattie Mae, just a women in love trying to please her husband!"

Hattie Mae mumbled, "Right, I wonder was you worried about pleasing your husband when you was sleeping with mines?"

Mistress Mattie looked at Hattie Mae and said, "You know what Hattie Mae? I was wrong for blackmailing Robert Lee into pleasuring me. And since we are best friends, I'm going to make that up to you. So you if want

House of Fo'Rae

to you can please yourself with my new husband anytime you feel the urge. That way we'll be even."

Hattie Mae just hung her head down. She had no response for Mistress Mattie's foolishness. She just chalked it up as Mistress Mattie's craziness was finally getting the best of her.

After hours of Mistress Mattie begging and pleading with Hattie Mae to stitch up her vagina, Hattie Mae grew tired of Mistress Mattie's voice and agreed to stitch her up a few days before the wedding.

Hattie Mae was in the garden showing the maids which flowers to pick for the flower arrangements for Mistress Mattie's wedding.

When she heard a familiar voice say, "Well, if it isn't one of my favorite girls in the whole world a beautiful sight for sore eyes you are, Mama Hattie Mae."

Hattie Mae turned to see Young Charles standing there as handsome as he wanted to be. He had grown at least six inches since she'd seen him last.

He was tall, thin framed, and had the biggest bluest eyes just like Mistress Mattie.

Hattie Mae was always amazed how Young Charles and Baby Girl One were twins, but never looked anything alike. If Hattie Mae hadn't delivered them herself, she'd never believe it.

Young Charles didn't look like he had a drop of Negro blood in his body.

But Hattie Mae knew it was that Negro blood that gave him the height, strong body frame, and breath-taking smile.

When Young Charles smiled, he looked just like his daddy Robert Lee.

Young Charles hugged Hattie Mae so tight. He said, "Oh, how I've missed y'all so. Now tell me Mama Hattie Mae, where is my darling mother and my beautiful Legacy. I have something for you all!"

199

Hattie Mae stood there speechless. She surely didn't want to be the one to tell Young Charles that Legacy had gone away. Hell, she hadn't heard any word from Legacy or Pierre Cordova. They both promised as soon as they could they'd send a telegram saying they made it safely there.

Hattie Mae was relieved when she saw Mistress Mattie running towards her and Young Charles.

Mistress Mattie threw her arms around Young Charles and held on to him.

Mistress Mattie was out of breath with happiness over seeing Young Charles.

As wicked as Mistress Mattie was, she adored her son and would do anything for him. Well, almost anything.

Mistress Mattie insisted on Young Charles coming into the house for lunch to discuss him walking her down the aisle for her wedding.

During lunch, Master Fo'Rae's brother Collin showed up with Savannah.

Hattie Mae was confused as to why they were there together. However, by the look on Savannah's face, Hattie Mae figured she was getting ready to find out.

Young Charles said his hellos and repeatedly asked for Legacy.

Master Fo'Rae looked at Savannah and said, "We have to tell him!"

Then Savannah looked at Young Charles and said, "I hate to be the one to tell you this but Legacy was taken away. She was down on the docks with Pierre Cordova, helping him with some work on one of the ships. Pierre Cordova left to take the rest of the girls home, leaving Savannah behind to finish up some paperwork. Some locals said they saw two white men drag her to a ship headed to the states."

Savannah stopped her story and burst into tears.

Young Charles was outraged. He stood up from the table and said, "What the hell is going on here? How could y'all allow such a thing to happen and why would some strange white men take Legacy?"

Master Fo'Rae's brother said, "The townsfolks seemed to think they were slave trackers looking to make some money. They said a few locals came up missing a few weeks ago around the same time."

Hattie Mae just hung her head low. After all the lies the Fo'Rae's had told, this was the best one they could come up with to explain Legacy's disappearance. Hattie Mae decided she was going to let this one just ride out. From Young Charles expression and body language, Hattie May could tell Young Charles wasn't buying the story either.

Young Charles calmed down. He smiled and said, "Come now uncle and Savannah, you guys are just kidding me right? Such a cruel joke!"

Young Charles laughed, but no one laughed with him. They all just stood there.

Young Charles replied, "Would somebody tell me what's going on?"

Young Charles started running through the house screaming for Legacy.

There was no reply.

Young Charles stood in the hallway looking defeated and lost. Tears washed down his face.

Collin Fo'Rae walked over and put his hand on Young Charles' shoulder.

Collin Fo'Rae said, "I'll do everything in my power to find her nephew."

Young Charles slowly replied, "Will you, uncle? That's odd because for the longest you've been trying to discourage me from loving her. You pulled out all the stops. 'She's a Negro, she's my cousin, and we're too close it will never work.' Now you want to find her."

Collin Fo'Rae said, "All that is still true. She's not right for you. I strongly believe that. However, Legacy is family. I love her just as I love you."

Young Charles wasn't buying the story he was being sold. However, Young Charles had great respect for his Uncle Collin Fo'Rae, so he directed his anger towards the one person he had the most resentment for: his mother.

Young Charles looked at Mistress Mattie and screamed, "Wicked woman, I know this was your doing. Nobody could think of such a devious story but the devil herself: you! You've gone too far this time, mother. I love her. I will search the ends of the earth until I find her."

Young Charles walked closer to his mother, Mistress Mattie.

Young Charles said, "Do you have so much bitterness in your heart that you would allow this to happen? You'd see me suffer just to serve your sick twisted immoral believes. You hated the idea of having a Negro daughter-in- law and Negro grandchildren."

Robert Lee walked in on the conversation. His presence fueled the rage in Young Charles.

Young Charles, who was only eighteen decided, he needed a drink to calm his nerves.

Everyone was just standing there looking puzzled.

Hattie Mae had made up her mind that she wasn't touching that conversation with a ten-foot pole. If Young Charles wanted to put all the blame on Mistress Mattie, then so be it.

Hattie Mae thought she'd add an extra touch. She walked over to Young Charles and held his hand just like she did when he was a little boy.

Hattie Mae said, "Now, now everything will work itself out son."

Young Charles took a moment of comfort from Hattie Mae's touch. Then he focused his anger on Robert Lee.

Young Charles looked at Robert Lee with utter disgust and sarcastically said, "Speaking of sons; is this how you protect your son, father?"

Mistress Mattie gasped for breath. She turned red as a beet. She put her hand over her heart.

Mistress Mattie said, "Now, Charles, I think you've said quite enough for one day. You must be exhausted from your trip home from school, and the news about Legacy has drained you. Get some rest, and we will discuss this matter in the morning."

Young Charles poured himself another drink. He said, "What matter would that be Mother? The matter of how you've betrayed me my entire life, the matter of how you got rid of Legacy to God only knows where."

Young Charles looked over at Robert Lee and tilted his glass at him.

Young Charles said, "Or should we discuss our most top secrets."

Young Charles threw his glass into the wall.

He screamed, "Y'all disgust me: the whole lot of y'all, such a sick twisted bunch. Y'all deserve each other."

Then he stormed out of the room only, to return a few minutes later with a huge hammer and nails.

Young Charles began pounding the wall. After he got the nail on the wall, he ran to retrieve a mirror. He hung the mirror on the nail.

Mistress Mattie, Hattie Mae, Robert Lee, Collin Fo'Rae, and Savannah didn't know what to say. The room was totally silent.

Young Charles said, "Mother, what do think of the mirror? It's beautiful isn't it?"

Hattie Mae had to laugh to herself. For years Mistress Mattie had banned mirrors in the mansion. And the ones that were there were covered with black cloth and only used on occasion. Mistress Mattie was still terrified of mirrors. And although Hattie Mae was sure that Young Charles didn't know the entire story of why, he did know that his mother had an issue with mirrors.

Young Charles said, "So many secrets in this family. Once upon a time, I had a sister that I truly loved. Mysteriously she was taken away from me just like Legacy was."

Young Charles looked at himself in the mirror and said, "Your whole life is a lie. And you have all the people who claim to love you to thank for."

Young Charles stormed out of the mansion.

Collin Fo'Rae stood up and said, "Well, he's really upset."

Robert Lee just turned and walked away. He appeared to have had enough of all of them. Although Robert Lee and Young Charles didn't have the best relationship, they had an understanding.

Hattie Mae knew that seeing Young Charles in all that pain broke Robert Lee's heart.

Hattie Mae looked for Young Charles for hours. He was nowhere to be found. Hattie Mae decided to try one more place, Baby Girl One's gave.

There she found Young Charles slumped over crying.

Hattie Mae walked over to Young Charles. She said, "All things work for better. In time your heart will heal. You'll move on and find yourself someone else. Your love for Legacy will be a faded memory."

Young Charles looked up and said, "Is your love for Africa a faded memory? Do you never long to go home? Have you found a new love with this place?"

Hattie Mae was at a loss for words.

Young Charles said, "No. Exactly, Mama Hattie Mae. The Fo'Rae's stole you from your homeland, took you to America, and treated you horribly. They've done the same thing to me. My Mother, the great selfish bitch Mistress Mattie, stole me from my real father Robert Lee, made me pretend I was a white man, and then she robbed me of happiness by sending Legacy away."

Hattie Mae replied, "Son, sometimes in life, we all have to adjust. This is one of your adjustments. You'll adjust to this in time."

Young Charles was livid. He looked at Hattie Mae and opened his hands. He was holding Hattie Mae's blackmail picture of his mother Mistress Mattie and his birth father, Robert Lee.

When Hattie Mae buried it there, she never thought anyone would find it.

He said, "Tell me how you adjusted to this? I came here to sit with my sister. I don't know why. Something in my spirit just pulled me here to this spot to dig. Look what treasure I found."

Then he laid the picture at Hattie Mae's feet and walked off.

Hattie Mae said out loud, "Well, Baby Girl One, I see you just couldn't rest until you got the last word."

Hattie Mae felt the wind blow strong and the air blew the picture up to Hattie Mae's hands.

Hattie Mae held the picture and shook her head back and forth.

Chapter Eleven:
Paintings say a Thousand Words

Young Charles was doing all he could to find out where Legacy had disappeared. He telegraphed a few contacts he'd made at boarding school, however, they all came to a dead end.

Collin Fo'Rae had hidden Legacy away safely. There was no word yet from Pierre Cordova or Legacy. Hattie Mae wasn't worried though; she knew Pierre Cordova would take good care of Legacy.

However, Savannah seemed to be going crazy with worry over Legacy and Pierre Cordova. Hattie Mae realized that after a trip to the beach with Savannah's girls. Hattie Mae had braided all Savannah's girls' hair and put seashells in them for decorations. Hattie Mae thought surely Savannah would flip out and tell them how they all looked like little Jigga-boo babies. However, Savannah didn't even seem to notice.

The night before the wedding, Mistress Mattie called Hattie Mae to the mansion.

Mistress Mattie was upstairs in her quarters.

Hattie Mae spotted Young Charles in the parlor drinking. It seems like Young Charles had made drinking Kentucky whiskey his favorite pastime.

Young Charles slushed passed Hattie Mae and mumbled something about how he hated the whole lot of them and how he wished they'd all just jump off a cliff.

Hattie Mae found her way to Mistress Mattie's room where she saw Mistress Mattie setting up what looked like a hospital scene.

Mistress Mattie had put white sheets on the bed. She was wearing a white gown and she had a table full of operating equipment.

Hattie Mae dared not ask where Mistress Mattie got all that stuff.

Hattie Mae looked over to see a bowl of fresh seaweed and a needle.

Hattie Mae rolled her eyes, took a deep breath, and said, "You truly intend on going through with this nonsense of stitching your vagina closed."

Mistress Mattie looked at Hattie Mae with those big marble blue eyes and pouting her bottom lip, replied, "As surely as the sun will shine tomorrow I do!"

Mistress Mattie jumped up on the bed and spread her legs wide open and said, "Now, Hattie Mae, let's get on with this show. And don't act like you're all offended by seeing my vagina. You've seen it before when I had the twins. Hell, you stuck your arm elbow deep in it. Now stop standing around and let's do this!"

The foolishness of Mistress Mattie never seemed to amaze Hattie Mae.

Hattie Mae said, "You do realize this will be painful. I can numb you a little with this Aloe Vera leaf cream and this Arnica root, but you still will feel it."

Mistress Mattie grabbed her bottle of Kentucky whiskey, took a swig, and opened her legs wider.

Mistress Mattie said, "So be it, child!"

Hattie Mae threaded her needle with the seaweed, all the while trying to talk Mistress Mattie out of this foolishness. However, she was unsuccessful.

Hattie Mae ran the needle through the flames of the candlelight to kill any germs it may have.

Hattie Mae said, "If you are damaged for life, you'll only have yourself to blame. I've never done such a thing before."

Mistress Mattie just looked at Hattie Mae squinted her eyes real low and said, "I'll take those chances, now enough talking! Sew it up already."

Hattie Mae washed her hands and began the procedure. First, Hattie Mae asked Mistress Mattie if she had cleaned her vagina with the vinegar and soaked in hot water liked she'd told her. Mistress Mattie said yes she did all that.

Hattie Mae then proceeded to line Mistress Mattie's vagina's insides with herbs. Hattie Mae said that they would help the healing, tighten the walls, and would dissolve in a matter of hours.

Then Hattie Mae simply stitched the entrance to Mistress Mattie vagina up with the seaweed stitches.

Mistress Mattie was so tipsy from the Kentucky whiskey she was drinking she hardly flinched.

Hattie Mae told Mistress Mattie not to take a bath the next morning, just have the servants wash her up and to spot-wipe her vagina.

Hattie Mae walked to her room. She was exhausted from preparing for Mistress Mattie's wedding, and she was missing her granddaughter Legacy.

Hattie Mae thought to herself, *This must be how father and grandfather felt the day she came up missing from her village.* Thoughts of her village sent Hattie Mae into a depression. Tears started running down Hattie Mae's face. She was crying uncontrollably. She thought of her village, all she had gone through, and the terrible things she had done.

Mistress Mattie tiptoed over to where Hattie Mae was doubled over in tears. Mistress Mattie handed Hattie Mae the bottle of Kentucky whiskey.

Mistress Mattie said, "Drink up, child, I promise this will kill anything you're feeling. Trust me, I know!"

Mistress Mattie was standing there squeezing a hot towel between her legs.

Mistress Mattie pointed to the towel and said, "My pain reliever!"

Hattie Mae just shook her head and smiled.

Hattie Mae took a drink of Mistress Mattie's Kentucky whiskey. It was the most disgusting thing she'd ever tasted.

However, after a few swigs, the taste went away and her happy feeling kicked in.

Mistress Mattie and Hattie Mae sat upstairs in the hallway of the mansion drinking and talking for hours.

When Mistress Mattie was drunk, her guard was down. Although Hattie Mae was drinking, she thought she'd take the opportunity to learn more about Collin Fo'Rae and why Mistress Mattie seemed to know something about him she wasn't saying.

Hattie Mae said, "Lord, on days like this, I too wish I died just like Collin's mama."

Mistress Mattie laughed and said, "Child, you mean Collin's Mammie! And he has the nerve to judge me about my Young Charles."

Hattie Mae knew she was going to have to ease into getting more information out of Mistress Mattie.

Hattie Mae said, "I would have liked to have met that devil who gave birth to such an evil spirit as Master Fo'Rae and Collin."

Mistress Mattie replied, "Well, to hell with both of those bitches! They both birthed two horrible individuals."

Then Mistress Mattie must have known she'd said the wrong thing because she put her hand over her mouth and looked like she'd just over-spoken.

Mistress Mattie tried to clean it up by saying, "I mean the bitch!" but it was too late. Hattie Mae had already caught on. When Hattie Mae tried to question Mistress Mattie about what she'd just said, Mistress Mattie simply tiptoed away holding one hand on the wall, and one hand holding the towel on her vagina. She said, "Hattie Mae some things are better left alone. Child, I warn you, leave this one alone."

Hattie Mae was going to follow her when she heard the maid whispering to Young Charles in the hallway.

The maid told Young Charles that she heard a telegram had been delivered to the mansion earlier with Legacy's whereabouts. However, she doesn't know who received it.

Hattie Mae interrupted that conversation.

Hattie Mae walked up to the maid and said, "Don't you have some rooms to clean, food to cook or something to do?"

The maid just walked off.

Young Charles kicked the wall and stormed out of the mansion.

Hattie Mae figured that the telegram went to Master Fo'Rae's brother, Collin.

Hattie Mae hurried off to his room upstairs. When she knocked at his door, she got no answer. The maid walked past and told Hattie Mae he had gone to bed early in the day.

Hattie Mae insisted that the maid unlock Collin Fo'Rae's bedroom door and go away. The maid did as she was told, but not before she told Hattie Mae that she wasn't taking the blame for it.

Hattie Mae walked into the room and quietly shut and locked the door behind her.

Hattie Mae figured Collin would just lie about the telegram and, since he was asleep, she'd just look through his things and find it herself.

Hattie Mae went to check to see if Collin Fo'Rae was sleeping soundly. To her surprise, he wasn't in bed. Hattie Mae tipped over to the bathroom, but Collin wasn't in there either. As a matter of fact he was nowhere in the room. Hattie Mae started searching the room when she heard a noise coming from what she thought was the closet. Hattie Mae got closer to check it out. The sound turned into moans of passion.

Hattie Mae was confused; she thought why would Collin be in the closet doing whatever it was he was doing.

Hattie Mae crept closer to the closet. She heard Collin say, "I've always loved you, my love."

Hattie Mae's curiosity got the better of her. She had to know who Collin was in that closet with.

Hattie Mae eased the closet door open only to find out that it wasn't a closet at all. It was a door connecting the room next door to Collins Fo'Rae's room.

Hattie Mae's eyes bolted out at what she saw.

She stood there for a second spying on the both of them.

Collin Fo'Rae was in a compromising position with his mulatto servant he'd brought from the states. Apparently, from the pillow talk going on, they were in love. They never saw Hattie Mae.

Hattie Mae saw Collin Fo'Rae's pants on the floor and a telegram slip hanging out of his pocket.

"Damn," Hattie Mae thought. She needed to get her hands on the telegram.

Hattie Mae thought to herself. If Collin Fo'Rae is anything like the average man, he's going to fall asleep after he's completed his business. And just like the average man, Collin Fo'Rae was knocked out sleeping within five minutes after reaching his peak.

Hattie Mae thought about waiting for the servant to fall asleep, but then decided she didn't give a damn if both the servant and Collin Fo'Rae knew she saw the telegram. All she needed to do was get it in her hands and read it first.

Hattie Mae simply opened the door and walked over and grabbed the telegram.

Hattie Mae assumed the servant would start screaming or at least wake up Collin Fo'Rae, but to her surprise, the servant just covered her body and laid there looking at Hattie Mae.

The telegram read, "Made it to Paris safely. Legacy hasn't said much. It's beautiful here. However, Legacy has discovered your secret. Leaving back for home in a week.
Pierre Cordova"

Hattie Mae felt a small piece of comfort knowing that Legacy was safe.

Hattie Mae put the telegram back and walked out.

Hattie Mae never even gave the servant a second thought. Hattie Mae understood why the servant never screamed. Half the island was afraid of Hattie Mae. The fear of the Voodoo power they believed Hattie Mae had scared the shit out of them.

The morning of the wedding, the house was all in an uproar. People were everywhere. Flowers, canopies, food, centerpieces, you name it- it was there. Master Fo'Rae's brother spared no expense for Mistress Mattie.

Hattie Mae figured it was just a thank you for going along with him to get rid of Legacy. The funny thing is, Hattie Mae knew in her heart that nothing was going to keep Young Charles and Legacy apart. Hattie Mae knew that Legacy was aware of it too. That's why she agreed to go away.

Hattie Mae was a little concerned about the vision Legacy had. That vision was key in Legacy deciding to leave.

Hattie Mae put all that foolishness out of her mind. She decided to enjoy this extravagant wedding. Hattie Mae had a feeling that this wedding was going to be one to remember.

Hattie Mae saw Young Charles all dressed up and carrying a huge painting. He had it all covered up. He said it was a special gift just for his mother on her special day. Hattie Mae wanted to breathe a sigh of relief, but her spirit wouldn't let her. Young Charles put his bulldog next to the painting. He told the bulldog to watch it and let no one touch it. Hattie Mae just continued with her day. She figured that was just the leftover alcohol in Young Charles speaking. Hell, he hadn't been sober since he'd gotten the bad news about Legacy.

Hattie Mae heard Mistress Mattie hollering for her from her room. When Hattie Mae got to Mistress Mattie, she was a wreck. Mistress Mattie was shaking like a leaf.

Mistress Mattie told Hattie Mae she was scared to death.

Hattie Mae assured Mistress Mattie it was just her nerves and that everything would be alright. Mistress Mattie insisted on having a shot of her Kentucky whiskey.

After it was all said and done, the servants got Mistress Mattie together.

Hattie Mae had to admit that Mistress Mattie was beautiful.

Mistress Mattie gently held Hattie Mae's hand and whispered, "After all we've been through, the ugliness of it all, all the wicked things we've both done, let us not think of those things today. Let us not think of what we've lost, but let us think of what we've gained. Hattie Mae, you've gained your freedom back, a beautiful family, and a not-so-bad life. And I've gained a husband who truly loves me."

A tear rolled down Mistress Mattie's cheek.

Mistress Mattie looked at Hattie Mae and said, "So on this day, we will enjoy life. Let us have this day to celebrate love and kindness."

Hattie Mae hugged Mistress Mattie and whispered, "Then shall it be a beautiful day."

Hattie Mae stood back and looked at Mistress Mattie. For a split second, Hattie Mae caught a glimpse of the woman Mistress Mattie might have turned out to be if Master Fo'Rae hadn't ruined her years ago.

Hattie Mae smiled and went to her room. She decided to get all fancied up too. Hattie Mae put on her best dress of gold and red silk. The beaded detail in it alone took Legacy days to complete. The wrap around dress fitted Hattie Mae like a glove. Hattie Mae wrapped her finest head wrap around her head. She even put some of the painted oils on her lips. Hattie Mae looked like a vision.

For a minute, Hattie Mae thought that this day might just end well.

That was until she caught the look on Young Charles' face as he stood in the hallway ordering the servants to uncover all the mirrors in the house and to place any mirrors they could find around the house, too.

If Young Charles was uncovering mirrors, that could only mean one thing.

Young Charles was expecting a visit from beyond.

Hattie Mae ran down the steps and stood in front of Young Charles and whispered, "Just what the hell do you think you're doing? You know how frightened of mirrors your mother is. Why are you doing this, today out of all days? Your mother is marrying a man that truly loves her. Behave yourself, if not for your mother than for me. I surely don't have the energy to take on you and your family today."

Young Charles replied, "My family? Well, that's odd. I thought we were family!"

Hattie Mae pointed her finger in Young Charles' face and said, "Boy, I got the right mind to smack the taste out of your mouth. Don't sass me. After all the years I took care of you and your sister Baby Girl One."

Hattie Mae tried to calm herself down.

That was until Young Charles replied, "Oh, so you do remember my sister Baby Girl One."

Hattie Mae was about to let Young Charles have it good, but what she thought she saw in the mirror distracted her.

Hattie Mae froze still and stared at the mirror.

Young Charles smiled that devilish grin. He looked just like his Mama, Mistress Mattie, at that moment.

Young Charles whispered, "She's here, isn't she? Baby Girl One. I knew she would come."

Young Charles walked over to the mirror and started talking to the mirror as if someone was in the mirror.

Hattie Mae was standing there trying to compose herself. What she thought she saw riled her up a bit. Hattie Mae swore she saw an image of a familiar man.

Hattie Mae moved closer toward the mirror. Young Charles was standing there like a kid in a candy store. He begged Hattie Mae to call for Baby Girl One. Young Charles jokingly said it would be the greatest gift he could give his mother for her wedding.

Hattie Mae, turned slowly, looked at Young Charles and simply said, "Go away!"

Young Charles knew that when Hattie Mae spoke like that, he she meant serious business.

Hattie Mae said, "Take your foolishness in another room."

Young Charles went off looking for more mirrors. He said if Hattie Mae wouldn't help him then he'd find Baby Girl One himself.

Hattie Mae stood in front of the mirror and said, "Show yourself and come to me."

Hattie Mae stood there, but nothing happened. The man never reappeared in the mirror.

Hattie Mae was shaken a bit. The image of the familiar face had come and disappeared so quickly, Hattie Mae couldn't help but wonder if it was just her imagination playing tricks on her. Nevertheless, the familiar image of the man sent Hattie Mae into an emotional moment.

Hattie Mae tried to gather her thoughts. As soon as she saw Young Charles spying on her from the corner, she knew the day was going to be long.

Young Charles slowly walked over to Hattie Mae and said, "Tell me, Mama Hattie Mae, what did you see? Did you see her? Did you see my sister? Oh, how I've longed for her to come to me. I swear sometimes I can hear her voice laughing and singing. I loved my sister. Even though I was made to keep her a secret from the world. She was always in my heart."

Hattie Mae held Young Charles' hand. She said, "It's okay, baby!"

Young Charles sadly said, "Mama Hattie Mae, I've heard all the stories about how it's my fault that Baby Girl One is gone. People on the island say my Mama begged the dark Magic to take Baby Girl One instead of me. I don't remember what happened. All I know is I was sick one day and then the next thing I remember, Baby Girl One was gone and I was better."

Young Charles opened his hand to reveal a scar on his palms.

Young Charles said, "I have no clue how I got this scar. It was there when I woke up all those years ago. Please tell me the truth. What happened?"

Hattie Mae simply said, "Let the past stay in the past, baby! Right now let's look forward to the future. Speaking of which, your mama is getting married in a few minutes. Let's focus on that."

Young Charles looked at Hattie Mae with those piercing blue eyes. At that moment he looked just like his deceitful mama.

Young Charles replied, "Yes, let's focus on mother!"

Hattie Mae's gut feeling told her Young Charles was a little too focused on Mistress Mattie, and it wasn't for good either.

The mansion soon filled up with guests.

Mistress Mattie was beautiful in all white.

Hattie Mae had to smile because of the way Mistress Mattie was tipping slowly down the aisle because of those seaweed stitches she insisted on having. The ceremony was beautiful. Everybody seemed to be having a great time.

Young Charles was over drinking, and Collin Fo'Rae was spending all his time peering at his love: his Negro servant. The funny thing was, as free as all the Negros were in St Lucia, some things were still forbidden, and that was white folks socially interacting with niggers. It was clear to see that only Negros in the room were working, except for Hattie Mae and Savannah.

Hattie Mae laughed to herself as she thought about the Fo'Rae family's obsession with Negros.

All the guests were in the garden when Young Charles decided he wanted to make a toast. He motioned his hand for one of the servants to bring his painting, which he sat upon a platform for all to see. Mistress Mattie was so proud of Young Charles. He was her pride and joy. However, Hattie Mae's gift told her this wasn't going to end well.

Young Charles straightened up his tie and cleared his throat. He smoothed his hair down and raised his glass.

Young Charles said, "I just want to give a toast to my beautiful mother and her charming new husband."

Mistress Mattie's eyes lit up with pride.

Young Charles continued, "Speaking of charming, why my mother the great and all powerful Mistress Mattie is quite the charmer herself, yes, but more like a snake charmer."

Mistress Mattie gasped and clutched her pearls.

She nodded her head at her guests and smiled. She said, "Oh my, Charles, I think you've said quite enough already."

Young Charles replied, "Oh no, mother, I've just gotten started."

He lifted his glass and said, "Yes, Mistress Mattie is a beautiful specimen for the eye to behold. Yet true beauty is only skin deep. Her southern charm sucks you in, but you have no idea of the demons that live inside her cold black heart. Full of ugliness."

All of the guests were frozen still with all eyes focused on Young Charles. Mistress Mattie's face was blood red. Collin Fo'Rae' was making his way towards Young Charles.

Young Charles looked at Collin Fo'Rae and said, "My, my, Uncle Collin, did you come to interrupt my speech?"

Young Charles shook his Index finger back and forth in the air and said, "No! No! I think not. Besides, you have your own secrets to keep, don't you?"

Then Young Charles looked over at Collin Fo'Rae's servant who was standing there looking.

Collin Fo'Rae replied, "Son, I know you're upset, but this is not the time and the place. It's your mother's wedding. Even your dead father, God rest his soul, would want you to respect that."

Collin Fo'Rae's remarks about Young Charles dead father infuriated Young Charles.

Young Charles screamed, "My dead father? That's a joke."

Young Charles looked over at Mistress Mattie then at Robert Lee who was working the bar.

Young Charles said, "All-powerful Mistress of the Manor, Mistress Mattie, is my father really dead?"

Mistress Mattie stumbled back in her seat a bit.

Young Charles gave an evil grin and looked at Robert Lee.

Young Charles put his hand over his mouth and said, "Oops, did I say that?"

Hattie Mae had, had enough. She walked over to Young Charles and said, "I think you've had too much to drink. Come with me. I'll help you to your room where you can rest. Let's allow the rest of your mother's guest enjoy this beautiful occasion."

Young Charles snatched his hand away from Hattie Mae and said, "Good old Hattie Mae always to the rescue. You know, Mama Hattie Mae, you've always been good to me. Better than my own mama. Hell, you taught me everything I know. You taught me how to be a good person, how to be responsible, how to study hard and earn good grades, and most importantly how to believe."

Young Charles tapped his champagne glass with his fork.

Young Charles said, "We're here to celebrate my mother Mistress Mattie, but I ask you, who's the real Mistress of the house? Well, I've always known who the real Mistress of the house was."

Young Charles walked over to his painting.

He said, In honor of The Mistress of the house, I painted this special painting."

Young Charles swiftly lifted the cloth from the painting to reveal a portrait of a naked Mistress Mattie lying with a naked Robert Lee, with Hattie Mae dressed as the Mistress of the house, wearing all white with a halo crown of diamonds.

Young Charles said, "I call it, 'All Hail the Voodoo Queen: Madame Fo'Rae and Her Subjects.'"

With that said, all of the guest gasped for breath. Mistress Mattie fainted, Collin Fo'Rae took a shot of vodka, and Hattie Mae just stood there.

Mistress Mattie's new husband quickly covered the painting and carried Mistress Mattie off to another room.

Hattie Mae instructed all of the servants to make sure all the guest had plenty of champagne and food.

Hattie Mae grabbed Young Charles by the ear and dragged him to the hallway.

Hattie Mae said, "Have you lost your damn mind, child? Do you know what you've done?"

Hattie Mae was pacing back and forth.

Hattie Mae said, "You just as simple as they come. I thought I taught you better than that. Why would you do such a thing?"

Robert Lee had made his way to the hallway.

Robert got right in Young Charles' face and stared him down.

Robert Lee said, "You feel like a man now, son? Did humiliating your mother in public make you feel better? Did that give you a sense of pride? "

Robert Lee stood there hovering over Young Charles as if he wished he would answer back so that he could slap the shit out of him.

Young Charles put his head down.

Robert Lee said, "Look at me, boy. Yes, I said boy! Yes, I know all these years of pretending to be white has filled your mind with a false sense of entitlement, but guess what? Let me be the first one to tell you. You're just another nigger!"

Hattie Mae stepped in. She said, "Robert Lee, maybe you're being too hard on the boy."

Robert Lee gave Hattie Mae that look that meant he wasn't playing. Hattie Mae stepped back.

Robert Lee looked at Young Charles and said, "Look at me, son. I know all your life your mama made you pretend you were white. I know she shipped you off to boarding school and then she took the love of your life away. However, that gives you no right to be disrespectful to your mother. Son, you are a man put on this earth to protect women not to attack them. Now that was a cowardly act you just done."

Young Charles started crying. He said, "You don't understand how I feel; but what about my pain?"

Robert Lee replied in anger, "Your pain? Damn your pain! That's right; to hell with your pain. What about the millions of slaves back in the states? What about the humiliation of black men daily: forced to work from sun up to sun down, forced to watch their women and daughters being raped by white masters? Always having to say, yes sir. Watching their families ripped apart and sold off to the next white devil. Your pain can't even begin to compare. How dare you tell me I don't understand how you feel! I had my only son just snatched from me never to acknowledge me as his father, pretending to be a dead white man's son. Boy, I got mind enough to slap the taste out of your mouth. Not to mention Hattie Mae's pain of being snatched from her homeland and don't even get me started on your mother's cruelty towards me."

Young Charles fell on the floor in tears. He just kept saying over and over, "But Legacy was mine. I loved her; I would have given everything away for her."

Hattie Mae felt compassion in her heart for Young Charles; hell, she had raised him from a baby.

Robert Lee sat on the floor with Young Charles. Young Charles put his head in Robert Lee's lap and cried like an infant baby.

Robert Lee said, "Its okay, son. Let it out. You can cry today, but tomorrow you have to be strong. We have to survive. This is our life, we either survive or perish."

Robert Lee cleaned up Young Charles and insisted that he must go and apologize to his mother, Mistress Mattie.

Young Charles apologized and he, Mistress Mattie, and Mistress Mattie's new husband rejoined the guest.

Collin Fo'Rae saved the day by telling the guest that Young Charles suffered a head injury as a child and sometimes he went off into these spells. He said it would wear off and Young Charles would be fine.

Collin Fo'Rae even made a joke about auctioning Young Charles' painting off at the flea market.

Mistress Mattie's new husband joined in by making a joke saying, "Over My cold dead body. I would never allow such a thing to happen." He said he was definitely hanging the portrait over the mantelpiece. Besides, he said it was a gift from his stepson.

All of the guest laughed and enjoyed the rest of the night.

Sure enough, the painting disappeared. Mistress Mattie and her new husband retired to their quarters, and Collin Fo'Rae vanished along with his servant.

Hattie Mae sat on the steps in the hallway for the rest of the night waiting for the image to reappear. It never happened.

Chapter Twelve:
Revenge

After what happened at the wedding fiasco, Hattie Mae spent a lot of time with the ancestors praying for direction. Legacy hadn't sent a telegram in weeks. Young Charles was still pissed and threatening to join the north in the war that was brewing in the United States.

Master Fo'Rae's brother was still lingering around acting like they were really a family, and his creepy servants he brought with him didn't make it any better. Besides, the vibe Hattie Mae got from them didn't settle right in her spirit. Hattie Mae couldn't put her finger on it, but she knew they weren't right.

Hattie Mae figured she couldn't connect well with the ancestors because of all the drama that was going on. She also assumed it was all the chaos going on that she couldn't clearly see Master Fo'Rae's brother's servants for what they were.

The only pleasure Hattie Mae seemed to get lately was healing the sick folks.

Hattie Mae had healed so many people the last week that she just stayed in town. Hattie Mae decided to go to her own house. She needed a good night's rest and a hot bath, and she wanted to enjoy the company of Robert Lee.

Hattie Mae decided to walk instead of taking her carriage. She figured the fresh air would do her good and clear her mind.

As Hattie Mae set out to her house, her two wolf companions followed on both sides.

Hattie Mae had walked that path to her house a million times it seemed like, but today something was different. Hattie Mae looked up to see the storm clouds coming in. Hattie Mae hurried along. She surely didn't want to get caught out in the rain.

As they were walking, Hattie Mae sang an old tribal song to herself.

It had begun to sprinkle. Hattie Mae looked down in a small puddle of raindrops that had gathered on the ground. She stopped dead in her tracks.

Hattie Mae gasped and grabbed her heart.

Hattie Mae saw the reflection of Baby Girl One in the water puddle. Hattie Mae wasn't frightened of Baby Girl One; it was the sudden appearance of Baby Girl One that startled Hattie Mae.

Just then, Hattie Mae looked over to see both wolves in attack mode and growling at the bushes. Hattie Mae had felt like somebody was following her but her senses had been a little off all week.

Hattie Mae looked down into the puddle at Baby Girl One. Hattie Mae put her finger to her lip to signal for Baby Girl One to be silent.

Hattie Mae held a tight grip on her walking stick.

Hattie Mae said, "Who's over there? Please show yourself. If you need healing, you will have to wait a few more days. I'm off to rest now. Please come out of the dark so I can see you."

Hattie Mae saw a large figure emerge from the bushes. As he stepped closer, she saw it was one of Master Fo'Rae's brother's servant. He was pointing a gun at Hattie Mae.

He said, "You don't even know who I am, do you, Voodoo Lady?"

Hattie Mae remained calm and replied, "Well, I can't say I rightly do, but you appear to be upset. However, pointing the gun at me isn't going to solve your problem. Now if I can be of any service to you, I may be able to help you. First, I would kindly ask you to put away your weapon."

Hattie Mae heard Baby Girl One whisper, "No Mama Hattie Mae, he's here to hurt you."

When the man heard that, he panicked.

He looked around and said, "Who's here with you? It's some of your Voodoo magic, but I'm not afraid I have this."

Then he held up a necklace around his neck with a stone that Voodoo charlatans sold to scared people. They told them that the magic from the stone protected them. When, in fact, it was just a lavender stone; all it did was keep them calm.

Hattie Mae smiled and said, "You don't need protection from me."

Then she pointed to the two wolves standing in attack mode and said, "But you might need protection from them."

The man pointed the gun at the wolves and said, "Keep your devil dogs back! Or I'll shoot them and you."

Hattie Mae replied, "Well, from what I know about guns, you only have one shot. So you must be a really excellent shooter or have speed record reloading time, because the way I see it, you can only shoot one of us. I'd make my choice wisely. Look at it like this. If you shoot either one of them."

Hattie Mae pointed to the wolves.

She said, "The other one is going to rip you to shreds. They're soul mates, meaning they mate for life. So you'd more than likely be better off shooting me. That way, the blast from the gun might scare them and they run off. Either way, it's your choice."

The female wolf eased next to Hattie Mae.

Hattie Mae looked down at the wolf and said, "Yes, Great Queen, we have a terrible situation."

Hattie Mae looked at the man and said, "Before you shoot me, do you mind telling me what your quarrel with me is about? Maybe it's all just a misunderstanding."

Hattie Mae had a quick memory flash of when she gave all Master Fo'Rae's mulatto children the poisoned drink.

Hattie Mae heard Baby Girl One whisper, "He was in love with one of the plantation babies. He planned on marrying her."

The man said, "Yes, whatever ghostly creature you are speaking to is right. You killed the only woman in this world who loved me. You took her from me trying to get revenge on Master Fo'Rae. Yet you let your own child live. Now that doesn't seem right to me."

Hattie Mae felt bad. She knew she was wrong for killing all of those mulattos, but she couldn't take the chance of another male child born in Master Fo'Rae's family. What if one of them had the same evil spirit as him? Hell, Hattie Mae had fixed it so that Savannah or any of her girls wouldn't produce a male child.

Hattie Mae said, "I'm so sorry. Understand it had to be done. There can never be another male Fo'Rae child allowed to walk this earth."

The man said, "Only yours right? Everybody knows that your son was sent up north and set free on Master Fo'Rae's brother's demand."

Hattie Mae was a little confused. She'd never heard that before.

Hattie Mae replied, "Well, I just learned something new."

The Man aimed his gun right at Hattie Mae's head. He was about to pull the trigger when all of a sudden, Hattie Mae heard a loud rumbling coming towards them.

They looked up to see Mistress Mattie's carriage coming towards them at full speed.

Savanna was driving so fast the carriage was rolling on two wheels and tilted to the side.

Mistress Mattie was wielding her gun and screaming various obscenities such as "You son of a bitch. I'll send your ass straight to hell."

The carriage came to an abrupt stop, and Savannah fell out.

Mistress Mattie was still standing on the carriage pointing her gun at the man.

It started raining a bit harder and the water puddle got bigger.

Suddenly Baby Girls One's image was bigger and visible for all to see.

Baby Girl One looked at Mistress Mattie and said, "Hello Mother, it's nice to see you again."

Mistress Mattie was a little startled, but she never took her focus off of the man holding the pistol at Hattie Mae.

She replied, "Hello daughter, I know you're here to torture me, by scaring the living shit out of me. However, I'm a little busy saving your precious Mama Hattie Mae's life at the moment. If you could be so kind as to focus your demonic intentions towards this gentleman who is pointing the pistol at Hattie Mae well, I would greatly appreciate it."

Mistress Mattie's reaction to Baby Girl One's reflection infuriated the man. He said, "Stop it right now, all this nonsense and spirits appearing out of nowhere. It's all of the devil."

Just then, Savannah rose up and stretched her hands out towards him, causing the ground to shake, and he fell to the ground dropping his gun.

The male wolf pounced on him within seconds.

Hattie Mae screamed, "No Great king!"

The male wolf was about to rip the man apart. He stopped and looked up at Hattie Mae, all while still pinning the man to the ground.

Hattie Mae said, "No Great King, you don't want to taste human blood, you don't want the venom in your system. Blood is the soul, the key to life. Once you've tasted it, you'll crave it."

Hattie Mae waved her arms for the wolf to come and stand next to her.

The male wolf slowly lifted his paw off the man. He walked over and stood next to Hattie Mae.

Savannah grabbed his gun.

Hattie Mae held up her hands for everybody to be silent, especially Baby Girl One who was promising Mistress Mattie that she would pay dearly for ending her life.

Hattie Mae said to the man, "I'm deeply sorry for the pain and the agony that I have caused you. I was wrong for what I did. I had no authority to take those lives, and for that, the Ancestors will deal with me. Nevertheless, I would like to think I did them a favor. They were slaves living an unbearable life. I'd rather be dead than be a slave."

The man was furious. He said, "How dare you! You took several lives! You will burn in hell for sure. The Lord will see to it."

Hattie Mae responded, "I'm not concerned with your God. I'm just trying to express my apologies to you."

Hattie Mae looked down in the puddle at Baby Girl One.

Hattie Mae looked over at the man. She said, "What was your lover's name?"

The man told Hattie Mae the girl's name and Hattie Mae summoned her at the water puddle. Even though the spirits normally only appeared in the mirrors, Hattie Mae figured if Baby Girl One's reflection came through the puddle so would the man's lover.

Hattie Mae had never summoned any other spirit except Baby Girl One's.

230

She didn't know if it would work, but she tried it anyway. She called for his lover to come to her. Sure enough after a couple of callings there she was. The girl's reflection was in the puddle next to Baby Girl One.

The man gasped for breath when he saw his lover. He said, "What kind of wickedness is this. This has got to be of the devil."

Hattie Mae looked at the man and said, "This gift I have is not of the devil. I know nothing of the devil you keep referring to. Nevertheless, I do have this gift. Now I've brought your love to you. You can say your goodbyes. Either you want this chance to speak to her, or you don't. The choice is yours."

Mistress Mattie was still standing there holding her gun to the man and trying not to flip out about seeing not only Baby Girl One's spirit, but also the spirit of the man's love.

Savannah was fixing her clothes from the fall she had taken, and the wolves were still standing in attack mode next to Hattie Mae.

Hattie Mae motioned her arm for the man to come closer to the rain puddle to see his lover's reflection. It was still raining a little, so the puddle was getting bigger.

Baby Girl One's spirit had moved to another rain puddle closer to Mistress Mattie. Baby Girl One had also brought her brother's spirit with her. As usual, the baby's spirit was crying. Hattie Mae knew Baby Girl One only wanted to scare Mistress Mattie. It seemed that Baby Girl One's spirit got a kick out of seeing Mistress Mattie scared.

The man walked over to the rain puddle and looked down at his lover's reflection. He said, "Is that really you?"

The reflection spoke and said, "Yes, don't be afraid. I'm not here to hurt you. I'm here to give you comfort. Death for me was the greatest thing that ever happened to me. Slavery is a wicked thing."

Hattie Mae was listening to the man and the reflection speak, when she was distracted by something.

Hattie Mae gasped for breath as she walked towards a smaller rain puddle. Hattie Mae hesitated for a second. She felt her knees give way and she fell to the ground. She closed her eyes and whispered, "Oh great spirits, please don't deceive my eyes. Please don't let this be a cruel illusion."

Hattie Mae opened her eyes and looked into the puddle. She saw a man's face staring back at her, smiling.

Hattie Mae looked over at the man who was talking to his lover's reflection.

Everyone was so busy watching them that they hadn't noticed Hattie Mae and the situation she had going on.

Hattie Mae just stared at the man's face in the puddle. She whispered, "Father, is that you?"

At that point, Savannah had made her way over to Hattie Mae.

Savannah never said a word. She and Hattie Mae both just looked at the man's face in the puddle. He was dressed in African burial attire.

Hattie Mae said, "I've longed to see your face, father. I've cried for my old life in our village. So many years have passed. I've often wondered if you had moved on to be with the ancestors."

Hattie Mae put her head down and said; "Now I have my answers. I'm so sorry, father, I never should have left the village. It's my fault the white man got me."

Hattie Mae's father's reflection never said a word. He just smiled at Hattie Mae with delight.

Hattie Mae heard Mistress Mattie screaming, "No! No! No!"

The man talking to his lover's reflection had picked up the gun Savannah had laid down when she walked over to Hattie Mae and shot himself.

Before he shot himself, he said he'd rather be dead with his lover than living in this evil world.

When his body hit the ground, his lover's reflection disappeared.

Mistress Mattie said, "Well, he surely went to hell. Everybody knows killing yourself is a sin."

Hattie Mae just stood there still looking at her father's reflection.

Hattie Mae turned to look at Mistress Mattie when she heard Baby Girl One speaking.

Baby Girl One said, "Do my ears deceive me mother or are you still quoting the Bible? You should be the last person to speak on someone's afterlife experience."

Baby Girl One's reflection rose up with the raindrops. It was like she was hovering in the air above them.

Baby Girl One looked down at Mistress Mattie and said, "I've never seen this hell you speak of, but I will tell you this. I've never seen one of your kind where I'm at."

Mistress Mattie screamed, "Enough child, I've had enough of you. I'm not scared of you anymore."

She looked at Hattie Mae and back over at Baby Girl One, still hovering in the raindrops above them.

Mistress Mattie was soaking wet standing there looking like a little rat.

She lowered her tone and said to Baby Girl One, "If I've learned nothing from Hattie Mae, I've learned that I don't have to fear the dead. It's the living I should fear. Now as for what I did to you, over the years it has haunted my soul."

She put her head down and said, "It's something I've regretted deeply. It was the most sinister thing I've ever done. You were my flesh and blood. Please forgive me."

Hattie Mae had heard Mistress Mattie apologize for a countless number of things over the years. All of which she was never really sorry for, just sorry she got caught, but this time Hattie Mae could feel the sincerity in Mistress Mattie's voice.

Mistress Mattie said, "I did you wrong, child. I favored your brother Charles over you. I hated you because you were a colored. Every time I looked at you, I hated myself for loving your father, Robert Lee."

Mistress Mattie looked over at Hattie Mae and said, "Please forgive me, Hattie Mae. I've wronged you too. I'm a wicked person."

Hattie Mae just looked at Mistress Mattie and thought *this heffa done went way too far.* Although Mistress Mattie may have been sorry for killing Baby Girl One, she sure as hell wasn't sorry for carrying on with Robert Lee. Hattie Mae knew that Mistress Mattie didn't give a rat's ass about Robert Lee being her husband. Mistress Mattie felt like Robert Lee was her property and she could do whatever she wanted to him.

Mistress Mattie looked at Baby Girl One and said, "I never gave you a name. It's not proper for a child not to have a name. If I could do it all over, I would name you Sara, which was my mother's name. She died when I was a child."

Hattie Mae had never heard Mistress Mattie speak of her childhood or her mother.

After Mistress Mattie said that, Baby Girl One's reflection disappeared, and so did the reflection of Hattie Mae's father.

Mistress Mattie said, "Well, I don't know what everybody is standing around for. Hell, we got a body to bury."

Hattie Mae was still shaken by her father's image in the water.

Savannah walked over and said, "Okay, just so we're clear, we both saw the man, right?"

Hattie Mae shook her head yes.

Savannah replied, "By the way you reacted, I'm assuming he's very important to us?"

Hattie Mae responded, "Extremely, he was my father."

Hattie Mae fell to the ground in tears.

Mistress Mattie eased over to Hattie Mae and said, "Well, I don't want to be rude or unsympathetic to your pain, however, at the moment, we have a more serious situation going on."

Mistress Mattie pointed to the dead body and said, "Yes, I think this trumps your emotional breakdown."

Hattie Mae wiped her tears and said, "No one cares, he's just another dead nigger!"

Mistress Mattie looked over at the body and said, "Well, at least we could give him a proper burial Hattie Mae. My God, it's the proper thing to do."

Hattie Mae was going to respond when she heard a voice calling her name.

She heard a voice say, "Hattie Mae, get the children. Savannah's babies."

Hattie Mae jumped to her feet and screamed out, "Who said that?"

Savannah and Mistress Mattie stood there looking around.

Mistress Mattie said, "Hattie Mae, what in the dickens are you talking about? Better yet, whom are you talking to?"

Hattie Mae heard the voice again.

It said, "Hurry, get to the babies."

Hattie Mae took off running back towards Savannah's house.

Savannah and Mistress Mattie followed.

When Hattie Mae finally got to Savannah's house, she was out of breath and screaming for the children.

The children were nowhere to be found.

Hattie Mae was panicking. She started screaming, "Children, please come to me!"

Savannah and Mistress Mattie were calling for them as well, but the children never answered.

Savannah was having a nervous breakdown, and her anger shook the ground.

Hattie Mae told her that if she didn't calm down, she was going to surely kill them all.

Hattie Mae looked into the mirror to summon Baby Girl One, now known as Sara, but she never appeared in the mirror.

All the servants said the last time they saw the girls, they were playing in the yard having a tea party.

The tea table was still set, and it looked like the girls just walked off and left the party. Hattie Mae was livid.

Hattie Mae was screaming at the servants, "How can five little girls just disappear and nobody saw them?"

Hattie Mae asked one of the servants if there were any new servants on the property that came with Collin Fo'Rae from the states.

The servant held his head down and said, "Well, there was one young lady who snuck on Master Fo'Rae's ship. She's been hiding on the island. She said she had unfinished business with you."

Hattie Mae's heart sunk to the bottom of her feet.

Hattie Mae held her heart and replied, "Did she say what kind of unfinished business?"

The servant replied, "All she said was you took something from her. Now she was going to take something from you."

Savannah stretched out her arm towards the servant in anger. The energy from Savannah's hand sent the servant in pain to his knees.

Savannah pulled her arm back, and her energy pulled the servant to Savannah's feet.

Savannah looked down at the servant and said, "You knew this and didn't feel the need to tell my mother?"

Savannah tightened her fingers and made a fist. The tighter Savannah's fist squeezed, the more pain the servant seemed to be in.

Hattie Mae said, "Enough, Savannah!"

Savannah placed both her hands together and lifted them in the air.

Savannah's energy pulled the servant off the ground and suspended him in mid-air.

Savannah said, "If one eyelash on even one of my girls is hurt, I promise you will be going to meet your Lord and Savior today!"

Mistress Mattie was just standing there in amazement and praying to her Jesus.

Mistress Mattie whispered, "This can't be happening, how is she doing this? Hattie Mae, this Voodoo has to stop. It's just not natural."

Hattie Mae remembered that when she heard the voice tell her to go and get the babies, she could have sworn it was Collin Fo'Rae's voice.

Hattie Mae looked up to see a horse running with the speed of lighting coming directly towards them.

As the horse got closer, Hattie Mae could see Collin Fo'Rae riding.

Collin Fo'Rae was sitting up on the horse like he was a racing jockey. He was hitting the horse with the reigns and shouting "Come on now, faster!"

Hattie Mae's eyes stretched out big as coins. She couldn't believe what she was witnessing. Collin Fo'Rae was riding the horse so fast it looked like he was flying. The odd thing was Hattie Mae could have sworn she saw another man on the horse with Collin Fo'Rae. However, it was no ordinary man. It was a faceless warrior, dressed in warrior attire from Hattie Mae's village. Hattie Mae closed her eyes; surely she was imagining this, however when she opened them she saw the same thing. As Collin Fo'Rae got closer, Hattie Mae saw the faceless warrior and Collin Fo'Rae merge together. It was like they were one.

All of a sudden, Collin Fo'Rae pulled his walking cane from his side and emerged from the horse in mid-air. He seemed to be moving in slow motion towards the ground. He put his walking stick out to brace his fall. Collin Fo'Rae made a clean land on one knee.

Hattie Mae saw the faceless warrior once again as Collin Fo'Rae stood up. The faceless warrior once again merged with Collin Fo'Rae's body.

Hattie Mae turned to see if she was the only one witnessing this incredible sight.

Apparently, not everyone could see the faceless warrior, but Hattie Mae and Savannah could.

Savanna's energy lifted the servant higher then slammed him to the ground.

Collin ran over to the man and grabbed him by the throat. With anger and authority in his voice, Collin Fo'Rae said, "Mister, I'm only going to ask you this question one time. Depending on your response, that's going to be the defining decision if I'm going to allow you one more second of life. Now think clearly before you answer this question."

The man was scared to death. He shook his head up and down yes! Collin Fo'Rae's voice cracked as if he was going to cry. He put his head down and straightened his self up.

He said, "Where are my nieces?" The man responded, "I swear, Mr. Fo'Rae, I have no idea. Like I was telling your family. When last I saw them, they were having a tea party. Then just like that, they were gone.

Collin Fo'Rae composed himself. He stood up straight. He was shaking with fear. He tried to muster up some words.

He uttered the words, "Girls, it's me Uncle Collin. You can come out now."

Hattie Mae was confused, she said, "What are you talking about? Better yet who are you talking to?"

Collin Fo'Rae wiped the sweat from his forehead and tears formed in his eyes. He walked closer to Savannah's house.

He said, "Girls, please come out. It's me, Uncle Collin. I'm here."

Mistress Mattie said, "Collin, it's no one in the house, we checked it thoroughly."

Collin Fo'Rae said, "Girls, you don't have to hide anymore Uncle Collin is here."

All of them just stood there looking, but no one said a word and the girls were nowhere to be found.

Collin Fo'Rae burst into tears. Just then they heard laughing and saw all Savannah's daughters come running from the house.

All the girls piled up on Collin Fo'Rae and said, "Uncle, you lose! We stayed quiet as church mice just like you said. You spoke first, so you owe us candy."

Collin Fo'Rae held on to Savannah's girls like they were his very own.

Mistress Mattie threw up her hands in the air and said, "Would somebody tell me what the hell is going on?"

One of Savannah's girls said, "Uncle Collin told us to hide and don't say a word until he came. Not even if we heard or saw other people. He said if we did he'd give us candy."

Savannah's girls ran off to Mistress Mattie's house with Mistress Mattie to get candy.

Collin Fo'Rae told Hattie Mae that his crew told him he had a stowaway on his ship. He said they found some items that lead him to believe she wanted to hurt Savannah's girls.

Collin Fo'Rae said he caught her in the marketplace, but she told him she had a partner and that he would take care of Hattie Mae and the girls.

Hattie Mae asked him what happened to the lady and Collin Fo'Rae replied, "Let's just say her stay in St Lucia has been canceled permanently."

Savannah went off to retrieve her girls. Collin Fo'Rae buried the man that killed himself.

Hattie Mae was standing in the field thinking. She couldn't understand how Collin Fo'Rae had told Savannah's girls to hide, when he was all the way across town at the docks. What puzzled her most was how could she hear Collin Fo'Rae's voice in her head telling her to go and get the babies.

Hattie Mae looked up to see Collin Fo'Rae's servant slash lover standing there looking at her.

The lady walked over to her and said, "Collin Fo'Rae is special. Very special. I know you have your doubts about him, but you don't know him like I do."

Hattie Mae said, "That's an odd thing for a slave to say about her master, but I understand. You do what you have to do to survive."

The lady replied, "Slavery is a nasty business. My mama was a slave, her mama was a slave, and her mama was a slave. I was born into slavery. The first twenty years of my life was a living hell."

The lady looked at Hattie Mae and pointed to her skin.

The lady said, "This light skin didn't make it no better either. In fact, it made it worse. I was passed around to so many men I lost count."

The lady sat down in the field. She said, "My mama was called to the big house every night I could remember until I was sold."

Hattie Mae felt a little sad. She knew the feeling of being violated.

Hattie Mae said, "How did you end up with Collin Fo'Rae?"

The lady replied, "Collin Fo'Rae is the best thing that ever happened to me or any other slave, including you."

Hattie Mae responded, "Me? How do you figure that?"

The lady smiled and said, "Look at you, Madame Fo'Rae The Great Voodoo Queen."

The lady said, "Collin Fo'Rae won me in a card game. My previous master had a nasty habit of drinking too much and gambling. One night he couldn't pay his debt, so he offered me up. Collin Fo'Rae took me to his ranch in Texas, and the rest is history. He's like no other master I've ever had. The slaves on his ranch are treated with respect, like human beings, not cattle. Collin Fo'Rae never laid a finger on me. I lived on that ranch for years. Collin Fo'Rae always said, "Never leave off those ranch grounds! On the ranch, he could protect the slaves. Keep them out of harm. He always

241

said when we had visitors act the part of slaves. Never let anyone know the freedom we had there."

Hattie Mae was confused. She said, "What freedom? Y'all was slaves."

The lady just smiled and said, "On paper only. Collin Fo'Rae always said, "A man's basic right is to be free!"

Hattie Mae laughed and said, "Well he stole that saying from Thomas Jefferson! That's for sure, and Thomas Jefferson himself owned slaves."

The lady said, "Yes, Collin Fo'Rae read a lot of books written by Jefferson."

Hattie Mae said, "So let me get this straight, all the Negros on Collin Fo'Rae's ranch are free to do what they want?"

The lady responded, "As free as they can be, they work a honest days work, and they get food and shelter. Some even worked enough to buy their freedom. I was there on that ranch for years, and no one was whipped, hanged or treated cruelly. No slave ever tried to run away either. When we came from Texas to Louisiana, when Collin Fo'Rae took over for his brother, no slave was whipped again. The overseer was replaced, and the same rules of the ranch applied there."

The lady stopped and looked at Hattie Mae.

The lady said, "Oh yeah, and if you're wondering if any of those slaves you help escape made it to New York. Well, six of them did. A few got caught and brung back. However, Collin Fo'Rae didn't beat them. He simply isolated them for weeks then put them back to work."

The lady smiled and said, "There isn't a cruel bone in Collin Fo'Rae's body. He's the smartest man I know. Oh yeah, those bodies Pierre Cordova buried under the mansion floated out when the storms came."

The lady laughed and said, "Dead bodies floating around the plantation. It was a mess!"

Hattie Mae could hear in the lady's voice her love for Collin Fo'Rae. Yet Hattie Mae could sense she was still hiding something.

Hattie Mae said, "You say Collin Fo'Rae is special. In what way is he special?"

The Lady replied, "It's all in the books he gave you to read. He said you loved to read that's why he gave you all Master Fo'Rae's old journals. If you read them, the truth is between the lines. All you have to do is read."

The lady got up to walk away.

Hattie Mae had a thought. If the lady and Collin Fo'Rae had been lovers all those years, where were their children?

Hattie Mae said, "Why come y'all never had any children?"

That question seemed to make the lady sad; it brought tears to her eyes.

She replied, "I'm sure that's all in the books, too! Besides our baby would only be just another nigger in the world. Who wants to subject a child to that kind of cruelty?"

Hattie Mae could tell she'd touched a soft spot with that question.

Hattie Mae was eager to get home to the journals Collin Fo'Rae had given her years ago. It had to be fifteen years ago, at least. Hell, they had been on the island for twenty-one years.

First, Hattie Mae had to make a stop at Savannah's house; she was going to get to the bottom of how Collin Fo'Rae was able to tell those girls to hide.

Hattie Mae kept going over how she heard Collin Fo'Rae's voice in her head. She thought she'd try something.

Hattie Mae stood in front of Savannah's house and in her mind she called for the girls.

In her mind, without moving her lips, she said, "Girls, come to mama Hattie Mae."

Hattie Mae stood there for a second. No one came. Hattie Mae felt a little foolish. Hell, maybe she just thought she heard Collin Fo'Rae's voice.

Hattie Mae tried it again. She said, "Girls, come to mama Hattie Mae, I'm outside."

Hattie Mae heard the door open and one of Savannah's daughters was standing in the door. It was the youngest one who always complained her legs hurt.

She said, "Yes, Mama Hattie Mae. Do you need anything?"

Hattie Mae was speechless. She couldn't believe it.

Hattie Mae said, "You heard me calling you baby?"

The little girl said, "Yes ma'am."

Hattie Mae sat on the porch and called her granddaughter to come and sit with her.

Hattie Mae held her granddaughter in her lap and said, "Is it only you that can hear me or can your sisters hear me too?"

Hattie Mae's granddaughter replied, "It's only me, Mama Hattie Mae. I can hear everybody all the time. Sometimes I get scared."

Hattie Mae said, "What do you mean you can hear everybody?"

Hattie Mae's granddaughter replied, "I can hear your brain, Mama Hattie Mae. I can hear what everybody is thinking. Even the people that are dead."

Hattie Mae took a deep breath and said, "Child, you been blessed with the gift."

Hattie Mae's granddaughter responded, "Well, whoever gave it to me should have asked me what I wanted because I would have asked for a different gift, like maybe some new dolls. Besides the voices scare me sometimes, Especially the ones who don't sleep at night. They keep me up all night asking me to tell people stuff."

Hattie Mae smiled and said, "Child you never have to fear the dead. Tell the voices to go to light!"

Hattie Mae's granddaughter said, "Okay, Mama Hattie Mae, but one of them I can't understand what he's saying. He's always beating a drum and singing to me. Then he talks in some language I don't understand."

The hairs on the back of Hattie Mae's neck stood up when her granddaughter said that. Then Hattie Mae remembered the image of her father she saw in the rain puddle.

Hattie Mae said, "Are you saying you can see people too? What does this man look like?"

He granddaughter said, "Yes, I can see the spirits. He's big."

Then she held her hands way up in the air.

Hattie Mae said, "Oh, he's tall?"

Her granddaughter responded, "Yes, and his skin is very dark and Mama Hattie Mae, he has paint all over his face and body."

Hattie Mae's granddaughter looked at Hattie Mae and said, "Oh yeah, he has eyes just like you, Mama Hattie Mae."

Hattie Mae closed her eyes to keep the tears from falling.

Hattie Mae made a rhythm of beats with her hand on the steps. Then Hattie Mae sang a song to her grandbaby. Hattie Mae sang it in her native language.

Hattie Mae's granddaughter laid her head on Hattie Mae's breast.

Hattie Mae's granddaughter said, "Mama Hattie Mae, that's the song he sings to me. How do you know that song?"

Tears ran down Hattie Mae's cheeks. She responded, "My daddy use to sing it to me when I was your age."

Hattie Mae's granddaughter said, "So is he my grandfather? That's why he never lets the other spirits come to me at night. He sings until I fall asleep and in the morning he leaves."

Hattie Mae wiped her tears and said, "Did you tell anyone else this?"

Her Granddaughter said, "Only Uncle Collin, but he said not to tell anybody. He said all the kids would think I'm a Voodoo Queen like you, Mama Hattie Mae. Uncle Collin said the gifts we have are special. That they were passed down to us by the ancestors."

Hattie Mae was confused. She said, "When you say us, you mean me, you, your sister Legacy, and your mom Savannah, right?"

Her granddaughter said, "Yes, and my other sisters; they have gifts too, they just don't know it yet."

Then she looked at Hattie Mae and said that it wasn't fair because one of her big sisters was going to be able to move things just like her mom.

Her granddaughter said, "Oh yeah and Uncle Collin. He's just like me."

Hattie Mae stood up. She said, "What do you mean he's just like you?"

Her Granddaughter said, "Uncle Collin can hear the voices too, and he can talk to me without moving his lips. I just hear him. Like today I heard him tell me to go to the roof and hide. He said we were in danger and not to tell my sisters. He said just hide on the roof until I heard his voice. So that's what we did."

Chapter Thirteen:
Blast from the Past

H attie Mae hurried home to find the journals Collin Fo'Rae had given her years ago.

After Hattie Mae started keeping her own journals, she forgot all about the ones Collin had given her.

Hattie Mae wrote all her journals in English, unlike Master Fo'Rae, who wrote all his in French. Hattie Mae wanted to make sure generations of her family could read them.

Hattie Mae sat down with the journals. She remembered that Collin's lover had told her to read between the lines. Hattie Mae read for hours about Collin Fo'Rae and Master Fo'Rae's childhood. It was pretty boring until she got to the trips they took to Africa. However, Collin had already told Hattie Mae the story of how he met her family.

Hattie Mae read all about how they visited her village and how Collin loved it there, but for some reason, Master Fo'Rae hated it. Hattie Mae remembered that Collin stressed that his grandfather took him on these trips.

Hattie Mae read for hours. Master Fo'Rae had documented every horrible thing he'd ever done to the slaves. He hated Negro people, especially the Negro man.

Hattie Mae's eyes were getting tired, but she had to get to the bottom of the situation. Then Hattie Mae thought about how Mistress Mattie told her that Collin's mammy died in childbirth. Hattie Mae found it odd that Mistress Mattie would refer to Collin's mother as mammy. Mammy was a term used to refer to Negro females that took care of children.

Hattie Mae dug deeper in the box to find an old journal. The handwriting was different and it appeared to be written by Collin's father. The dates were way before Hattie Mae's time.

Hattie Mae came across an interesting page that read,

"My Lord I think I've stumbled upon God herself. She has feet of bronze and hair of wool. She is the most beautiful creature I have ever laid eyes on."

Hattie Mae read down to another date, and it read,

"I finally spoke to her today. She speaks French and a number of different languages. My son is not too fond of her. However, he hasn't been the same since his mother died of a heart attack."

Hattie Mae sat up. She said to herself, (*"That son was Master Fo'Rae, but where is Collin and why is he surprised that she speaks French if he's in France."*)

Hattie Mae continued reading. She came across a page that read,

"My son is not doing well with this African heat. He misses home and seems to be suffering from depression. Our trip is almost at an end. I must say I'm not looking forward to going back to France. She won't be there and I'll miss her terribly. Our nights together are magical. She sneaks out of the village to see me. We almost got caught by her witch doctor mama."

Hattie Mae gasped for breath and reread that to make sure she was reading it right. Hattie Mae said aloud, "No, it can't be!"

Hattie Mae continued reading. The next entry said,

"She came to me today. She cried on my shoulders. I don't know what to do. We were as careful as can be. She said her grandmother knows and tried to take it from her body. She said she ran to me. I hid her aboard my ship. Her brother, who is a fearless warrior, (might I add that he scares the living shit out of me also.), he came to me and said I had dishonored his sister. He said she was soiled and no man in that village or the entire continent of Africa would have her after defiling herself with a white man."

Hattie Mae put her hands over her mouth and gasped.

Hattie Mae continued to read,

249

"Lord, what do I do? I love her, I don't care about the color of her skin. True love is what we have. However, the world will never accept it. Her brother came back. He said he had a plan. The plan is for me to take her back to France and pass her off as my servant. He said with the money and power I had, nobody would question it. He said never bring her back to the coast again. To the village and her family, she was dead. The demonic life growing inside her was a disgrace to their entire race. Although he said all those things about her, he wept like a baby as he said goodbye to her."

Tears rolled down Hattie Mae's cheek as she read on.

"The journey across the sea was rough for her. Her stomach grows bigger every day. My son has figured out she's having a baby. He hates her. He refers to her as "My Nigger Queen!" He says I love her more than him and, although he's only ten years old he is the most racist person I've ever met. I don't know where he gets that. My family has never owned slaves, we don't own any slave ships and we believe that all men have the right to freedom. My family even cut off ties with the southern Americans because of their slave trade. My family is not the most honest family in the world, but we do have some standards and morals."

Hattie Mae said, "Little rotten bastard!"

She continued to read:

"We've finally made it here. I purchased a house in the Paris countryside. There is no one around for miles. I brought some of her things from her homeland. She says she's fine, but I know she misses her homeland. She's getting bigger every day. She's settling in. She and my son don't get along too well. They keep their distance."

Hattie Mae was putting all the pieces to the puzzle together as she continued to read. She read the next entry. Which read:

"My lord, she went into labor. All the servants are gone because it's Christmas Eve. My son is pissed because he wanted to go into town to see the Christmas trees. He said my Nigger Queen spoils everything. She's in a lot of pain, and it's storming something awful outside. I told my son to run

to the farm down the road. It's a few miles, but I know they're having a Christmas party there. There will be lots of people around to come help. She's screaming something awful I hope he comes back soon. The baby came. It's a boy. He's strong and healthy. His lungs seem to be well developed because his screaming to the top of his lungs. She's bleeding a lot and my son still hasn't come back."

Hattie Mae kept reading. The next, and final entry read:

"The good Lord took my love away from me. She bled to death. I tried with all my power to stop the bleeding. My heart is heavy with grief. My world is at a standstill. Both my sons have no mother. My first love died of a heart attack and the new love I found died in childbirth. To top that off, my oldest son never went to get help. I found him asleep in the laundry room. When I asked him why he never went to get help, he said the coldest thing I ever heard from a child. He said, "Nobody cares about your whore! She's a nigger! Niggers die every day. My God I slapped him clean across the floor. I told him I pray his new brother, whom I've named Collin, never grows up to be like him. He's such a hateful child. I fear him. I know he's just a child, but he is evil. I'm not sure what he's capable of."

Hattie Mae flipped the page to find a newspaper clipping that read:

"Father dies in a house fire. His two sons survive him; One infant who was saved by nanny and one older son who was playing outside when the fire started. Candles that fell over caused the fire. Children have been sent to live with their grandfather Claude Fo'Rae, who happens to be one of the wealthiest men in France."

Hattie Mae just sat there holding the journals staring at them. She couldn't believe it! According to these journals, Collin Fo'Rae was half African and half French, however, he looked like a white man. Hattie Mae wasn't surprised. Hell Young Charles was a white as the pure driven snow. And his twin was dark as coal.

Hattie Mae thought to herself that those journals explained a lot about Collin Fo'Rae that seemed to be a mystery. Like how he was obsessed with Young Charles, how he knew so much about Hattie Mae and her gifts, why he wasn't afraid of Hattie Mae, and, most of all why he was in love with his Negro servant. Hell, he was a Negro. Collin Fo'Rae tried to tell Hattie Mae years ago when he gave her those journals. Hattie Mae never read through all of them because of the disgusting things Master Fo'Rae wrote. She never got to the older ones.

Hattie Mae made herself some tea. She knew she was going to be up all night reading these journals. Hell, she just found out Collin Fo'Rae was her cousin. His father had fallen in love with her auntie. Her father sent her away to be with Collin's father and then she died in childbirth.

Collin Fo'Rae had told Hattie Mae years ago that Master Fo'Rae stole her from her father because he was mad at him for not allowing them to do business in his village. Hattie Mae was starting to think it was more to the story. Plus she was suspicious about the fire that killed The Fo'Rae brothers' father. Hell, the clip said that the baby was rescued, but the older son was in the yard playing when the fire started. From how the father had described Master Fo'Rae', shit, he was a little devil. He could have very well set that fire.

Hattie Mae dug deeper into the box and pulled out another journal. This time it was the Grandfather's writing

Hattie Mae read the first entry:

"Well, the boys are settling in. The grief I feel over the loss of my son is still unbearable after two years. My wife is taking it hard as well. The two boys bring us some sense of peace. The younger one is still showing no signs of his African heritage, which may be a good thing later on in his life. The oldest one is problematic. He always seems to be in trouble. I've read my son's journals about how his oldest son never went to get help for his pregnant companion. Also, I have to watch him around the younger one because he seems to want to hurt him too. I've put him in therapy, however, it doesn't seem to be working. I promised my wife that I would take the younger one to meet his African family, even though they want nothing to do with him. We leave tomorrow for Africa.

Hattie Mae continued to read:

"We finally made it here. I sent word to the Voodoo Priestess that her grandson was here. I'm not sure if she'll show up. I dare not take the child off the ship. I'm not sure what they'll do to him. I left two crewmembers ashore with a boat just in case they come. I'll wait for one week then we will leave. I sent word two years ago that the daughter died in childbirth.

Hattie Mae read on:

"Well, it's been two days and no sign of them. I've visited with some associates of mine that are here. I wait patiently for them. My oldest grandson, who's twelve now, is fascinated with slaves. He made a comment that maybe I should sell Collin to the slave ship headed to America. I damn near took his head off. I told him if I ever hear him speaking of owning another human life I would beat the devil out of him.

(Day three) And still, no show. Time is slipping away; the ship is pulling out in four days. I've almost given up hope.

Hattie Mae felt sorry for Collin. She continued to read.

"Late in the night on day five and we have visitors. The warrior and his Voodoo mother came to see the child. They seemed to love him. The warrior cried as he held him. Odd thing though, his Voodoo grandmother insisted on doing some Voodoo ritual over him. She said he was blessed with special gifts that she had to give thanks to the ancestors for. How was I supposed to deny her that? I allowed it even though I didn't believe it. My oldest grandson was jealous of all the attention the two-year-old was getting. My oldest grandson said the only gift Collin had was the gift of being annoying. The Voodoo grandmother did her ritual. As she walked out, she said, "You must bring him to me once a year." I asked why, she simply said, "Because I love him."

Hattie Mae read through the journals for hours. Over the years Collin's grandfather brought him back once a year.

Hattie Mae continued reading:

"My, how the years have passed; it's been ten years since my son's death. The boys are getting up in age. My oldest grandson just turned twenty years old and he's still a troublemaker. He's still trying to convince me to take my shipping company to another level. By another level, he means turning my ships into slave ships. I've refused I want no parts in the slave trade. Although, I'm not a saint, I want no parts in the slave trade. I've made some unethical dealings when doing business, but I will never own, sell or trade human lives. It's just that simple for me. Over my lifetime, I've made more money than I could ever spend. I made it all with my head held high. I will not compromise my beliefs for money. Besides, my very own grandson is half African. Speaking of which, Collin is now ten years old. He's such an intelligent boy. He has a heart of pure gold. Over the years, he's traveled back to see his African side of the family. However, he doesn't know that they are family. He just thinks they're just some more of my business associates. His Voodoo grandmother has become extremely attached to him. His uncle, the great warrior, just had a baby girl. Collin has taken a liking to her. His Voodoo grandmother insisted the new little girl and Collin have a special Voodoo gift. I've yet to witness anything special about Collin other than he seems to know what everybody is thinking before they say it."

Hattie Mae gasped for breath. She said, "That little girl is me. My God, Collin Fo'Rae knew me when I was a child. The grandfather didn't realize that knowing things before people said them was Collin's gift."

Hattie Mae continued reading:

"I got sick on this last trip. The locals took me to a Voodoo Priestess to heal me. Of course, I had to pretend as if I didn't know her. All her visits with Collin had been in secret. My overzealous older grandson got into an argument with the great warrior, who was now the leader of the village. The village has a diamond mine sitting right smack dap in the middle of it. As a matter of fact, all the natural resources you can think of are sitting just behind the village. Warriors have always protected the village; no white man has ever been allowed to enter. These warriors are not just equipped

with fighting skills and spears, no, they have guns, cannons and grenades. They took over one of the slave ships and captured all the artillery. They hung the slave traders' heads on poles as a warning to other potential slave traders seeking to enter their village. My business here is strictly shipping and receiving. I buy what the elders want to sell. Although I must admit at one point, I did have a certain shipment of weapons I wanted to unload quickly. My knucklehead oldest grandson was under the impression that his white skin gave him all authority over the village. He quickly learned it did not. I do believe after I leave this earth, this village will cut ties with my oldest grandson. However, my youngest grandson will always be welcome on shore."

Hattie Mae thought back to the conversation she had with Collin Fo'Rae years ago about how Master Fo'Rae stole her from her village.

Hattie Mae now knew the real reason. If only she'd read those books years ago when Collin gave them to her.

Now Hattie Mae knew why Collin was obsessed with Young Charles.

Collin Fo'Rae saw himself in Young Charles. He felt obligated to guide him.

Hattie Mae continued reading!

She read:

"Well, today all hell broke loose. My oldest grandson, with his spiteful ass, told my youngest grandson that he was a nigger. He told him all about how his black Mammy died in childbirth and how that's why we traveled to Africa so often. You would think at the age of twenty-five that he'd be an adult now, but he is not. My youngest grandson took it quite well though. I think somewhere in his heart he always knew. The odd thing is, he never questioned me about it, even as my health continues to fade. Collin is always here by my side. I know my oldest grandson fears I'll die and leave my fortune to Collin. I have the right mind to do so, but fair is fair, and although Collin is my favorite, they are both my grandsons. I know Collin will continue to build my legacy. At fifteen, he has the business mind of an

Oxford graduate. He has his heart set on going to Oxford University to study business. On the other hand, I know as soon as I leave this earth, there will be no one here to control my oldest grandson, and I do fear he will make horrible business decisions that will leave him broke. Nevertheless, everything I possess will be split equally between them. Except for the house in the countryside of Paris where Collin was born. I had it rebuilt after the fire, and it alone will go to Collin in memory of his mother."

Hattie Mae said out loud, "That's where Collin Fo'Rae sent Legacy. Legacy must know all of this. That's the secret Pierre Cordova was speaking of in the telegram."

Hattie Mae couldn't seem to put down the journals. She continued reading:

"My oldest grandson has been in America for some time now. He writes back often about the wealth in the south from the slave trade. He's purchased an extravagant plantation, which puzzles me because he knows nothing about farming. However, he knows a great deal about shipping and receiving. He says his plantation is a sugarcane and cotton plantation. The drawings he sent of it are so grand. It looks like it's fit for a king. This plantation purchase has put an even greater strain on our relationship. However, I've stopped voicing my opinion on my oldest grandson's business because at one point he insinuated that if I tried to stop him, he would be forced to tell our family secrets, such as the biggest one of all, my youngest grandson's true identity. My grandson Collin has yet to visit the United States, but he has taken an interest in their college system. I fear him ever entering the United States. His older brother is not to be trusted, and God only knew what he'd do to him. However, Collin always assured me that he had discovered quite a few of my oldest grandson's secrets. So they both had secrets they didn't want to get out."

Hattie Mae was very curious to know what other devilish deeds Master Fo'Rae had done.

Hattie Mae had always wondered why, since Master Fo'Rae didn't trust or even like Americans, why did he choose to live in the United States?

Hattie Mae knew that Collin Fo'Rae had that answer and she was going to get to the bottom of all this madness. Hell, Collin Fo'Rae was her blood cousin. All these years he knew and he allowed Master Fo'Rae to steal her away from her homeland.

The bigger question was how Collin Fo'Rae was involved with Hattie Mae's son Claude Fo'Rae, Sr?

Hattie Mae now knew Master Fo'Rae had named her son after his grandfather, Claude Fo'Rae Senior.

Hattie Mae discovered the death certificate of Mr. Claude Fo'Rae folded up in between the pages of the journal. He died the same year Master Fo'Rae stole her from Africa.

Hattie Mae got her thoughts together. Armed with her knowledge of the past, she set out to find Collin Fo'Rae. He had some serious explaining to do. All these years he has known the truth and he didn't tell her. He allowed his sick and twisted older brother Master Fo'Rae to rape her and steal her son from her. He could have saved her from that life if he just spoke up.

Hattie Mae was furious. Hell, all these years Collin Fo'Rae had been living as a wealthy, white, respected businessman when he was really just another mulatto. Born under the same sick desire white men had for black women. He was still a secret nobody wanted to discuss.

Hattie Mae thought she'd better be careful around Collin Fo'Rae. She didn't really know what he was capable of. Although his black companion talked about him like he was the salt of the earth, Hattie Mae was still suspicious of him.

Hattie Mae thought she'd try to see if she could get some information from Baby Girl One, now known as Sara.

Hattie Mae went to the mirror and called for her, however, Baby Girl One/Sara, never showed up. As a matter of fact, she never came back after

Mistress Mattie's apology.

Hattie Mae turned to get her wrap. When she turned back to cover the mirror, she froze in her tracks.

Hattie Mae stared at the mirror. She was afraid to say anything.

She slowly whispered, "Father!"

Hattie Mae gazed at the mirror while she inched her way closer. Tears rolled down her cheeks.

Hattie Mae said, "Oh how I've prayed to the ancestors for this day."

The image of Hattie Mae's father was as clear as water. He was standing there smiling. He was dressed in his war clothes. Hattie Mae assumed he'd died in battle.

Hattie Mae said, "Father, I know you died a glorious death."

Hattie Mae's father finally spoke. He said, "Be at peace, my fearless little princess. Through it all, you have been the true warrior. Be at peace knowing I watch with the ancestors over you. Know that we love you and nothing has been held against you."

Hattie Mae allowed the tears to roll down her face. She never lifted a hand to wipe them in fear that if she moved a muscle, the image of her father would disappear.

Hattie Mae replied, "Yes father!"

Then Hattie Mae remembered Bactou, the great warrior who was captured with her but escaped to the sea. Hattie Mae assumed he drowned to death.

Hattie Mae said, "Father, does not Bactou, the great warrior, watch over me with you and the ancestors?"

The image of Hattie Mae's father smiled.

He replied, "So many questions, Princess. The ancestors move in mysterious ways. Few are given the gifts that you and your daughters have. Some questions you already have the answers to. Believe in your heart what you feel."

With that said, the image of her father disappeared as quickly as he had come.

Hattie Mae sat on the floor and cried. Then she pulled herself together.

She remembered her father's words, "Believe what you feel!"

Hattie Mae sat quietly like a church mouse on the floor. She had to horn in on her gifts. She knew all the answers she needed were already in her mind. She just had to clear her thoughts.

Hattie Mae lit some candles and made some tea. She put off going to find Collin Fo'Rae for another day.

The visit from her father put Hattie Mae's mind and heart at ease.

As Hattie Mae sipped her tea, she hummed an old tribal tune.

Hattie Mae left the mirror uncovered. She was hoping her father would revisit.

As Hattie Mae hummed her song, she felt the wind blow, and she felt energy rest on her leg. She looked down to see nothing, but when she looked over in the mirror, she saw Baby Girl One, now known as Sara lying at her feet with her head in her lap listening to Hattie Mae sing.

Hattie Mae looked in the mirror and placed her hands on Baby Girl One's hair.

As she stroked her hair, Hattie Mae said, "Rest child, rest. Mama Hattie Mae is always here."

Chapter Fourteen:
War is coming

S ome time had passed, and Hattie Mae pondered over the information she had learned. She went over it in her mind and reread the journals for hours over the weeks. Young Charles had left to the states to attend college and he came back every so often. He was still pissed about Legacy, but he did love Mistress Mattie. Young Charles was dating a girl from his school.

Word had it that her daddy was some high profile politician, which pleased Collin Fo'Rae to no ends. Collin Fo'Rae was always encouraging Young Charles to get closer to the family. Status was everything to Collin Fo'Rae. He was obsessed with nobility and social standing.

Collin Fo'Rae was still busy shipping things to France. Whenever Hattie Mae ran into Collin Fo'Rae, she just pretended everything was normal. However, Hattie Mae remembered that Collin Fo'Rae could sometimes hear thoughts.

So as a bonus, just to mess with him, whenever she had to be around him, she just thought about the encounter she witnessed with Collin Fo'Rae' and his servant. Hattie Mae wasn't sure if Collin Fo'Rae picked up on it, but he never stayed near Hattie Mae long.

One thing the Fo'Rae family did well was document their history. The Fo'Rae family had millions from their different business adventures. A major chunk of the wealth came from their shipping business.

Master Fo'Rae made a small fortune off the plantations he purchased. The plantation in Louisiana and the one in St. Lucia turned a huge profit every year. Master Fo'Rae' was a wicked man, but obviously, he had business smarts that he learned from his father. However, Master Fo'Rae seemed to be getting sued often. Every lawsuit was settled out of court though.

After the death of Claude Fo'Rae, Master Fo'Rae never returned to France.

Collin Fo'Rae apparently ended up going to college in the United States and studying business. Collin Fo'Rae earned a Ph.D. in business.

Over the years, it seemed like he made his home in Texas for some odd reason. However, for his first years in the United States, he spent them in New York.

Hattie Mae heard a knock at the door. She looked out through the window to see Mistress Mattie standing there looking like the life had been sucked out of her.

Hattie Mae was not in the mood for Mistress Mattie's bullshit. Whatever Mistress Mattie was all up in arms about was going to have to wait.

Hattie Mae decided she was going to tell Mistress Mattie she knew all about Collin Fo'Rae's little secret.

Mistress Mattie didn't blink an eye when Hattie Mae told her all what she knew.

Mistress Mattie's only reply was, "Hattie Mae that's a fascinating story. One day we must have tea and discuss it properly. However, we have more pressing business to discuss."

Mistress Mattie pounced out of her seat and clutched her pearl necklace as if what she was about to say was detrimental to her existence.

Hattie Mae just sat there looking at Mistress Mattie. Hattie Mae thought Mistress Mattie was so dramatic. Everything for Mistress Mattie always had a sense of urgency.

Hattie Mae just waited for Mistress Mattie to tell her what life-defining altercation was currently keeping her woke at night and had her at Hattie Mae's door at the wee hours in the morning.

Hattie Mae was expecting something petty.

Mistress Mattie blurted out, "There are talks of war in the United States. Lincoln is pushing to free the slaves. The south says they won't have it. It's going to be a bloodbath."

Hattie Mae was taken aback by that news. It seems like this Lincoln fellow just popped up on the scene. However, what went on in the United States had very little impact on what happened in the small island of St. Lucia.

Hattie Mae kept listening to Mistress Mattie ramble on about how she wished Lincoln would just go away.

Mistress Mattie had a newspaper with an image of Lincoln.

She handed Hattie Mae the newspaper.

Mistress Mattie said, "Look how ridiculous he looks. Standing there with that damn big ass top hat on. Just looks foolish, like he's about to go dance."

Mistress Mattie rambled on. She said, "And there are talks that his wife is as crazy as they come."

Hattie Mae smiled and said, "Well, Mistress Mattie, you should know because I declare, I've never met anyone as crazy as you."

Mistress Mattie frowned up her face and pouted her thin little lips.

Mistress Mattie replied, "Hattie Mae, this is no time for jokes. This is serious."

Hattie Mae responded, "How does this Lincoln person affect you."

Hattie Mae lifted up the paper to read the article.

Hattie Mae looked at the picture of Lincoln.

Hattie Mae sat back in her chair. Something about the picture of Lincoln drew Hattie Mae to it. Hattie Mae looked closer. For a split second Hattie Mae thought about Young Charles and Collin Fo'Rae masquerading as white men. If Hattie Mae didn't know any better, she'd put good money on it, so was this Lincoln fellow.

Mistress Mattie said, "For one thing, Hattie Mae, his name is President Lincoln! And he is currently recruiting for his army."

Hattie Mae looked over at Mistress Mattie. Hattie Mae was still puzzled with what that had to do with her.

Hattie Mae said, "Well, unless you plan on signing up to fight, which you can't because you're a woman, how on earth does that affect you?"

Mistress Mattie was livid.

Mistress Mattie replied, "No! The question is, how does that affect us?"

Mistress Mattie squinted her big blue eyes together really tight and said, "My husband is planning on signing up to fight for the North and my God, Young Charles said he would fight to the death for the North. Young Charles is in the yard right now with Collin Fo'Rae having target practice. My God, Hattie Mae, why would Collin Fo'Rae condone such a wicked thing? Young Charles knows nothing of fighting in a war."

Hattie Mae stood up. A flash of Robert Lee came across her mind. Robert Lee was standing there wearing a blue uniform.

Hattie Mae said, "How does Young Charles know about this war anyway."

Mistress Mattie replied, "Its posted all over town. The North offered any runaway slaves freedom if they fight for them. Young Charles said he was going for his people."

Mistress Mattie kicked the door.

She yelled, "His fucking people? He knows nothing about being a Negro! All his life I've tried to protect him from that cold, harsh reality. Now he wants to fight and most likely die in a war for some slaves. My Lord!"

Hattie Mae softly said, "He wants to fight because he has great character, self-respect, a sense of honor, and, unlike you his mother, he has compassion."

264

Mistress Mattie said, "I have compassion, Hattie Mae! Didn't I help you and Savannah escape the South to freedom? Didn't I give you freedom papers?"

Mistress Mattie composed herself. She said, "Would you want your precious son, who's now a doctor, fighting in this war?"

Hattie Mae sat down. She hadn't thought about that. Besides she didn't even know her son Claude Fo'Rae. For years, she thought he was on a plantation working, only to find out he was in New York practicing medicine in an all colored community. Hattie Mae never wrote to him. The picture she had of him she put it in the closet out of sight. She didn't want to look at it.

Hattie Mae said, "Well, Mistress Mattie, as much as I love both my children, even Claude Fo'Rae whom I don't even know, the thought of something bad happening to them haunts me. However, the thought of all my people being free is well worth dying for. So, to answer your question, I would feel honored if my son went to war for something worth fighting for. It's not about honor or bravery. It's simply the right thing to do."

Hattie Mae looked at Mistress Mattie and said, "But since you were born white and privileged, you don't understand that!"

Mistress Mattie was furious, she rolled her eyes and said, "My dear, Hattie Mae, my skin may be white, but I was not born privileged by no means. My mother Sara died because my father didn't have money to buy medicine. My no good father sold me to his nephew, Master Fo'Rae when I was just a teenager. Hattie Mae, he was my cousin for God's sake."

Hattie Mae thought about it. She'd read all the Fo'Rae journals and not once did they ever mention that the senior Fo'Rae had a brother.

Hattie Mae said, "What was the relationship with your father and Master Fo'Rae's father?"

"They were brothers." Replied Mistress Mattie.

"But there's no mention of your father in the journals Collin Fo'Rae gave me. Why is that?" asked Hattie Mae.

Mistress Mattie replied, "Why must you drudge up things from the past? Let it go! Let those old Fo'Raes be dead. It makes no sense to discuss past events. What we should be discussing is the future of generations of Fo'Raes to come."

Hattie Mae looked at Mistress Mattie and coldly responded, "Well now, let's discuss that, but is Young Charles truly a Fo'Rae? Besides, I don't understand what the big deal about being a Fo'Rae is!"

Mistress Mattie replied, "How dare you, Hattie Mae. As surely as I'm standing here breathing, my son Young Charles is a Fo'Rae. It's his birthright. By all means, he's as much a Fo'Rae as your precious Savannah and Claude. My Fo'Rae blood flows through his veins."

Hattie Mae knew she'd ruffled Mistress Mattie's feathers with that question.

Hattie Mae said, "What do you want me to do?"

Mistress Mattie smiled and said, "Oh please ,Hattie Mae, talk to Young Charles and make him see how dangerous this is. He's only doing this to punish me. He's still cross at me about Legacy."

Hattie Mae replied, "Tell him where Legacy is! It's the only way to stop him. He'll leave at once to find her. Problem solved."

Mistress Mattie said, "Regrettably, I cannot do that!"

Hattie Mae responded, "Well, think about it like this. What's worse, having Negro grandbabies or a dead son?"

Mistress Mattie wrapped the blanket around her that was on the chair. She laid her head back on the chair and looked at Hattie Mae.

Mistress Mattie said, "Hattie Mae, they are cousins. Even though we've never acknowledged it, they are blood cousins. Legacy's father, as awful as she was conceived, was her grandfather who raped his daughter."

Mistress Mattie closed her eyes.

She said, "Such a cruel thing for a child to endure. No matter what color her skin is. The same man was my husband also my first cousin."

Mistress Mattie's eyes filled with tears.

She said, "My father wasn't as bright as his brother. He couldn't make savvy business deals and charm a room full of people. He was just a simple man. He came to the United States and met my mother Sara, who was a plantation owner's daughter. His family didn't believe in slavery and when he married my mother and got into the slavery business, well, they disowned him. When my grandfather died, my father became the master. He knew nothing of running a plantation, and soon he lost the plantation by taking out loans he couldn't repay. My father's nephew, Master Fo'Rae, was still wealthy from his inheritance. He made a deal with my father to bail him out of debt in exchange for me."

Mistress Mattie just sat there staring at Hattie Mae.

Mistress Mattie said, "I was just a child Hattie Mae. So the same cruelty you suffered, I also endured that cruelty for years before you got there."

Mistress Mattie let the tears fall from her eyes.

She continued, "The sad thing about it was, at first, I was happy because my torment was over. Then in some sick twisted way, I was jealous of you because you had all the attention."

Mistress Mattie looked up.

She said, "You know I read a book at the doctor's office that they have these doctors that can cure you of all your demons. They call them psychiatrists!"

Hattie Mae smiled and replied, "Child, if you take your crazy self to this psychiatrist, he's probably going to need one himself."

Hattie Mae and Mistress Mattie laughed.

Mistress Mattie said, "Well, Hattie Mae, through it all at least we've got each other."

Mistress Mattie got up and wiped her face. She looked at Hattie Mae and said, "My Lord, Hattie Mae, how dark could these Negro grandbabies we gonna be having get?"

Then Mistress Mattie walked out.

Robert Lee walked in shortly after Mistress Mattie left.

Robert Lee looked at Hattie Mae and said, "I guess she told you about Young Charles."

Hattie Mae replied, "Yes, she did. She's trying to stop him by telling him where Legacy is hiding."

Robert Lee responded, "Well, she'll be wasting her time. He already knows where Legacy is. I told him. He said nothing was going to stop him from doing the right thing. He said as much as he loved Legacy, the right thing to do was help his people. Besides, I think this girl from the states has given him something he never got from Legacy. So at this point, he's in love. Plus, he wants to help his people. I can't do nothing but respect that. It's an honorable thing to do."

Hattie Mae looked at Robert Lee standing there with such pride in his eyes for his son Young Charles. Although they kept their relationship secret all these years, Hattie Mae always knew that Robert Lee loved Young Charles. Hattie Mae dared not ask what it was that this girl had given Young Charles that Legacy hadn't. The very thought of her granddaughter being sexually active made Hattie Mae blush.

Hattie Mae said, "Oh my, Mistress Mattie is going to have a nervous breakdown."

Hattie Mae poured Robert Lee a cup of tea.

Hattie Mae looked at Robert Lee and said softly, "Tell me how Young Charles going off to war makes you feel?"

Robert Lee said, "I'm scared, but I won't try to stop him. He's a man now Hattie Mae."

Robert Lee looked at Hattie Mae and said, "I heard talks that this Lincoln character might even allow Negros to fight in this war."

Hattie Mae remembered her vision of Robert Lee in a blue uniform.

Hattie Mae looked at Robert Lee and said, "And?"

Robert Lee replied, "And? Well, if this is true, he can sign me up. I'd love to kill a whole bunch of red necks with my bare hands. Besides, if this is true, how can I hide out like a coward on this island? Living lavish when my people are suffering every day. If this is true, I have an opportunity to help them. I'm taking it."

Well, if Hattie Mae believed in her visions, then the ancestors have already spoken. It appeared that Robert Lee, Young Charles and Mistress Mattie's husband would be going to war soon.

As the weeks wore on, the possibility of the war was becoming a reality. Eleven states left the Union and formed the Confederate States. Hattie Mae knew without a doubt that Louisiana would be one. Hattie Mae hated Louisiana.

Collin Fo'Rae finally made his way to talk to Hattie Mae.

Collin Fo'Rae told Hattie Mae that the war was happening.

Collin said that the Fo'Raes' stay on St. Lucia was coming to an end. He told Hattie Mae there was no way in hell he could protect them on that island. Collin Fo'Rae said that the safest place for them to be was in France.

Hattie Mae looked at Collin Fo'Rae and said, "What gives you the authority to come in my home and issue out orders? I'm not your property any longer."

Collin Fo'Rae simply replied, "I've never thought of you as property. I've always thought of you as family. Cousin!"

Hattie Mae was furious. She shouted, "Liar! If you thought that why did you allow your sick and twisted brother to steal me from my homeland, take me to America, and treat me with such disrespect? You never spoke up. You could have sent me home, back to a place where I was loved. You're nothing but a fake, a phony, and a wannabe. You love pretending to be white so much you've even convinced Young Charles he's white. If there was a devil folks talk about, I'd put good money on it the devil was you!"

Collin Fo'Rae sat there quiet. He didn't say a word.

Then he said, "Yes, my whole life has been pretending I was a white man. However, in my defense, I never knew I was a Negro until my older brother told me when I was a teenager."

Collin Fo'Rae smiled and said, "I guess you could say I'm sorta like Moses in the Bible. He never knew he was Hebrew until later in his life."

Hattie Mae just shook her head. She knew nothing she said was going to rattle Collin Fo'Rae; he had mastered showing no emotions.

Hattie Mae laughed and replied, "If Savannah heard you say that, she'd have your head. She's a Bible-quoting fool. Always spreading the word."

Collin Fo'Rae said, "Well, some people have to believe in something."

Hattie Mae replied, "You tried to tell me about all this years ago, didn't you?"

Collin Fo'Rae responded, "Yes, I did. It always puzzled me why you never said anything. I assumed you hadn't read the journals."

Hattie Mae said, "After I read one of Master Fo'Rae's entries, I was so disgusted that I couldn't bring myself to read on."

Collin Fo'Rae replied, "Hattie Mae, let's let that awful time be done. The present is now, and right now I have to protect you and our family."

Collin Fo'Rae smiled and said, "All my girls. I love y'all so much."

Collin Fo'Rae looked at Hattie Mae and said, "I remember you as a tiny baby. You looked like a little black teddy bear. Just as cute as you wanted to be. Please know if there was anything I could do to save you, I would have."

Hattie Mae was furious, and replied, "You could have taken me back."

Collin Fo'Rae replied, "Sadly, I couldn't. I didn't even know you were on the ship until days after we had left. Plus, Hattie Mae, the repercussions for my older brother were too great. He would have been killed on sight. So my love for him, as wicked as he was, stood greater at the time than my love for you. Besides, the family would have never taken you back because they would have sworn you were spoiled. Meaning you were no good for any brave warrior."

Hattie Mae sat down. The words brave warrior made her think of Bactou.

Hattie Mae said, "Perhaps you're right. Besides, after the death of Bactou, I doubt if there was another who could have taken his place."

Hattie Mae looked at Collin Fo'Rae and said, "Why did they take him if Master just wanted to punish my father. Taking me alone would have broken his heart."

Collin Fo'Rae said, "Well, from my understanding, the men only captured him with you. They made him accompany them to the ships. When the ship sailed, they released him. It was said that, somehow, he made his way back aboard the vessel to save you."

Collin Fo'Rae put his head down. He continued, "Well, you know the rest."

Hattie Mae felt her eyes filling with water. The thought of Bactou made her very sad. Hattie Mae never liked to think about home or Bactou. Besides, her home was now on this Island.

Hattie Mae said, "He probably died a terrible death!"

Collin Fo'Rae replied, "Hattie Mae that was a lifetime ago. But I would say he died an honorable death. He was trying to save the girl he loved. He was a brave warrior."

Hattie Mae had a sharp pain in her head. She bent over a bit. Just then she had a flash.

In the flash, Hattie Mae saw a man kissing her hand. But she couldn't see his face because he was kneeling before her. She saw the American flag and a fireplace.

Hattie Mae said, "This war is going to be bloody, isn't it?"

Collin Fo'Rae said, "War is always bloody, Hattie Mae. However, there is no way around it. Men have been fighting for years. It's like second nature."

Hattie Mae said, "So I guess you're not going to try to talk Young Charles out of this foolishness?"

Collin Fo'Rae replied, "Why of course not. I'm encouraging him to go. It's the right thing to do. If I was a young man, I'd be right beside him."

Hattie Mae smiled and said, "You old goat, I don't know how old you are, but you look as young as the day I met you."

Collin Fo'Rae smiled and replied, "Well, thank you, Hattie Mae, you don't look so bad yourself. It must be in the blood."

Then he tipped his hat at Hattie Mae and smiled.

Collin Fo'Rae said, "Hattie Mae, you, your girls, Savannah, and Mistress Mattie will be leaving for France at once. I will not take no for an answer. If I have to drag you to that boat kicking and screaming, you're going. It's for the safety of this family."

Hattie Mae knew Collin Fo'Rae wasn't going to take no for an answer, plus Hattie Mae hadn't seen Legacy in years. She missed her grandbaby.

Hattie Mae said, "But what about my property and all my possessions here?"

Collin Fo'Rae laughed and said, "Well, just because you're not physically here doesn't mean you don't still own them. You can leave someone to manage your houses and other property while you're gone."

Collin Fo'Rae laughed and said, "Hattie Mae my dear, if you're going to be a businesswoman, you're gonna have to learn how business works."

Hattie Mae smiled and said, "Well, so be it."

Hattie Mae thought about something. She was curious why Master Fo'Rae allowed Claude to leave the plantation and not Savannah.

Hattie Mae said, "I'll go to France peacefully if you answer one question honestly."

Collin Fo'Rae replied, "Okay, what is your question."

Hattie Mae said, "Tell me why Claude was allowed to leave the plantation and not Savannah? And don't say it was to preserve the family name because I don't believe that. It's more to the story, and I want to know. You owe me that. I have a son in this world that I've never met and know nothing about. Only that he's a doctor and lives in New York. Now I know you had something to do with that. And I wanna know the entire story now!"

Collin Fo'Rae said, "You're right, Hattie Mae. It wasn't to preserve the family name. It was because I blackmailed him to give Claude a better life."

Hattie Mae simply replied, "How did you do that?"

Collin Fo'Rae said, "Well, Hattie Mae, as you know, my brother had a thing for young girls. He also felt as if he were entitled to have anyone he wanted.

In New Orleans, the richest plantation owners and aristocrats would have periods where they partied for days. They had elaborate celebrations. They would travel from the plantations to the French quarters to party. My brother owned an apartment there. He was well respected by most folks. He talked a good game.

Well, one evening he went to call on a young lady, and when he got there, he found out she had a younger sister, just barely a teen."

Collin Fo'Rae looked at Hattie Mae and said, "Needless to say he took advantage of her. The girl ended up taking her life. He thought he got away with it. Only the girl left a letter before she took her life explaining what happened."

Hattie Mae was intrigued and replied, "So why wasn't he hanged?"

Collin Fo'Rae replied, "Well, no one ever got the letter. The slave that worked in that house had witnessed the entire ordeal. She assumed the letter was going to expose Master Fo'Rae, so she stole the letter."

Hattie Mae said, "Why would she give a rat's ass about Master Fo'Rae?"

Collin Fo'Rae replied, "She didn't, she gave a rat's ass about me."

Hattie Mae smiled and said, "Why, you old tom cat! How many women have you had?"

Master Fo'Rae laughed and said, "Nope, it wasn't like that. The slave lady had a young daughter and son. I helped them escape into Mexico years before this happened. She felt obligated to me. So she brought me the letter."

Hattie Mae stood up and said, "Oh my, you were a part of the Underground Railroad?"

Collin Fo'Rae replied, "I guess you could say that, Hattie Mae. I bought property in Texas because at the time they weren't a part of the United States. They had the closest border to Mexico and the least slaves. Plus, it was a beautiful place. Slaves often escaped to Mexico. It was an easier trip than trying to get to the north."

Hattie Mae said, "Why didn't the lady go with her kids?"

Collin Fo'Rae responded, "She was too old. Plus her kids could pass for white and she couldn't. So in Mexico, they would just be poor white people looking for work."

Hattie Mae said, "What did you do with the suicide letter?"

Collin Fo'Rae said, "I tried to blackmail my brother with it. But he had one thing on me that would top that letter: I was half Negro. He threatened to expose me. I convinced him that I didn't care and by the time people in the states would find out, I'd be on a ship back to France. I threatened that if he didn't release his newborn child to me, I'd give that letter to the girl's redneck father, who I'm quite sure, would have taken the law into his own hands and taken my brother out that very night."

Collin Fo'Rae continued, "I tried to get you, and Savannah, but Mistress Mattie wouldn't have it. She said you were her only companion and I felt sorry for her. So my brother gave me Claude Fo'Rae and I took him to New York City, a place where lots of free Negros lived. Over the years, I checked in on him. He never knew I was his uncle. I wanted to see if I could pass him off as a white man, but he was too dark. I provided for him over the years until I lost contact with him."

Hattie Mae said, "And the part about Master Fo'Rae's last will and testament?"

Collin Fo'Rae replied, "Well, that was sort of complicated. My foolish brother never made a last will and testament. Luckily, I knew some people that knew some people who could get me what I needed."

Collin Fo'Rae looked at Hattie Mae and winked his eye.

He said, "You follow my meaning? I thought it only right that Savannah and her younger brother Claude received their proper portion of their father's estate."

Hattie Mae replied," You made the entire thing up?"

Collin Fo'Rae smiled and said, "Yes, it's what my grandfather would have wanted. My grandfather adored family. It didn't matter what color your skin was. Blood is red. His blood flows through your children's veins, and your blood flows through mine. So you see, Hattie Mae, we are family whether you like it or not. I will always protect you."

Hattie Mae said, "Thank you!"

Collin Fo'Rae said, "Hattie Mae, I need you to be packed and ready by the end of the week."

Over the next few days, Hattie Mae packed up all her personal belongings and got her house in order.

Collin Fo'Rae took care of all the legal business concerning the properties and such.

Mistress Mattie, as always, was being overly dramatic about everything. Hattie Mae could have sworn she heard Mistress Mattie say that all the men she loved were going off to war. Hattie Mae assumed Mistress Mattie was talking about Robert Lee, also.

That day two ships sailed off: one ship to America holding Mistress Mattie's husband, Young Charles and Robert Lee: the other ship to France holding Collin Fo'Rae, Mistress Mattie, Savannah and her girls, Hattie Mae and Pierre Cordova.

Pierre Cordova wasn't allowed to sign up for the war. Something about him being born in Mexico kept the United States from allowing him to join the army.

Mistress Mattie carried on something terrible as the ships left.

Young Charles gave Hattie Mae a letter to give to Legacy.

Hattie Mae looked at St Lucia as the ship sailed away.

St Lucia was such a beautiful place.

Hattie Mae was thinking about how her grandchildren had never encountered slavery. They had faced racism, but never on the level Hattie Mae had experienced.

Hattie Mae blessed the island of St Lucia as it faded away in the distance.

Although Hattie Mae wished that ship was sailing to Africa, the place she called home. Hattie Mae braced herself for a new adventure in France.

Chapter Fifteen:
The Old World

During the months, sailing the sea to get to France, Hattie Mae spent the majority of her time writing in her journals and working on her potions.

Hattie Mae tried to stay as busy as possible.

Savannah's girls suffered from seasickness for a while.

Mistress Mattie was busy all day worrying about Young Charles and her new husband. She spent three weeks in her quarters pouting and crying.

Hattie Mae was concerned about Robert Lee, also.
The hardest thing about the trip was not knowing. They had no way of knowing where the men where: if they had made it to the United States or not; they knew nothing.

Hattie Mae just continued to pray to the ancestors daily.

Hattie Mae had never been happier to see a shore in all her life. When they saw the shores of France, Savannah's girls jumped up and down and shouted.

Everybody was sick of sailing.

Hattie Mae had a strange feeling about France. The overwhelming presence of the dead was alarming.

The wolves were pacing back and forth in their cage. It seemed like they could feel they were close to their homeland.

Hattie Mae paid close attention to the female wolf. It was almost like her eyes were telling Hattie Mae to be careful in this strange land.

Collin Fo'Rae packed all the ladies in a carriage and sent them directly to the estate.

Collin Fo'Rae said he had some business to attend to and that he would meet them in a few days.

Mistress Mattie was livid. She couldn't believe that Collin Fo'Rae was letting them ride through a strange country alone.

Collin Fo'Rae reminded Mistress Mattie that Pierre Cordova was with them and that Pierre Cordova had been in France before and knew exactly where he was going. He also asserted that Hattie Mae and Savannah could handle themselves.

Collin Fo'Rae looked at Hattie Mae and said, "Always be aware of your surroundings. Everything and everyone is not always what it seems to be."

Then Collin Fo'Rae looked over at a couple that was standing next to the docks.

The couple was unusually pale, and the vibe Hattie Mae got from them was very uncomfortable. Even the wolves felt it. The wolves were standing absolutely still and watching the couple's every move.

After the couple made eye contact with Hattie Mae, they moved on.

Collin Fo'Rae looked at Hattie Mae and said, "Strange things happen in one of the oldest countries in the world."

Hattie Mae looked over at her wolf companions then back at Collin Fo'Rae and said, "We recognize strange things, and we're always ready."

Hattie Mae took a deep breath. She'd never had that feeling before. But, everything in her told her that the couple was very different from anything she'd ever witnessed.

Savannah and the girls weren't saying much. They were too busy taking in the magnificence of France. Hattie Mae had never quite seen anything like it. France was something to be seen.
The grandness of France stood out to them the most.

Hattie Mae saw giant statues of people she'd read about in books. Hattie

Mae thought to herself that the French were obsessed with gold, marble, and demonic looking statues.

Hattie Mae had to admit that the countryside was beautiful. The views alone were breathtaking.

Mistress Mattie seemed to be enjoying the views also, in between her crying spells.

When they arrived at the house, Hattie Mae gasped for breath. Everybody just stirred in silence.

Mistress Mattie said, "My Lord, is this a house or a city?"

Hattie Mae just stood there marveling at what she saw.

Hattie Mae couldn't understand what the French's obsession with statues was about. She thought they were sort of scary.

Hattie Mae looked in the back of the carriage and uncovered the wolves' cage.

Hattie Mae said, "Check out your new home," as they rolled through the gates.

Hattie Mae was so excited to see Legacy.

Legacy ran to the carriage and threw her arms around Hattie Mae and said, "Mama Hattie Mae, I've missed you terribly."

Hattie Mae stood back and looked at Legacy.

Hattie Mae said, "What a beautiful women you have become."

Legacy smiled and said, "Thanks, Mama Hattie Mae."

Legacy hugged all her sisters and her mother, Savannah.

Legacy seemed very happy to see them all.

After they had settled in what Legacy was calling "Fo'Rae Manor," they all met in the living room.

Hattie Mae saw a life-size painting of a beautiful African woman hanging over the fireplace.

Legacy looked at Hattie Mae and said, "That's Uncle Collin's mother, your auntie."

Hattie Mae just stood there looking at the portrait.

As Hattie Mae looked closer, she could see that the lady was with child.

Legacy said, "Collin's father ordered this painting commissioned while she was pregnant with Uncle Collin."

Legacy continued, "She was beautiful. I think she looked like you, Mama Hattie Mae."

Hattie Mae was about to say something when she heard her wolves growling and scratching at the floor.

Hattie Mae saw one of the maids walk into the living room to announce that dinner would soon be ready.

The maid caught Hattie Mae's attention because of the paleness of her skin. The maid had the whitest skin Hattie Mae had ever seen.

Hattie Mae's wolves were in an uproar. Hattie Mae had never seen her wolves act like that. Normally, they were relaxed and calm. They only growled when something was wrong.

Legacy walked over to the maid and said, "Thanks, we will adjourn to the dining room."

Legacy walked over to Hattie Mae and they both watched the maid walk away.

Legacy whispered to Hattie Mae, "Yes, she's an odd one. I can't pick up on her energy, but my gifts tell me to keep my eye on her."

Legacy looked at Hattie Mae and said, "One day, when she handed me a cup of tea, I accidentally touched her hand and it was as cold as ice. It was like touching a corpse. After that day, she started wearing white gloves. Folks around here talk of the walking dead. Soul-less beings. I can't say that I believe them, but I can't say that I don't believe them either. I've taken the locals' advice and set up certain precautions."

Hattie Mae replied, "What type of precautions?"

Legacy told Hattie Mae that the locals said to protect yourself from the soul-less beings, you have to eat garlic and keep holy water on you and have something silver at all times.

Hattie Mae found that odd. However, given the gifts that she and her girls had, anything was possible.

Hattie Mae said, "Well, we should get all those things together for the girls at once."

Legacy smiled and replied, "It is already done. Everything cooked in this kitchen is prepared with a pinch of garlic."

Then Legacy rang a little bell.

A servant came with a tray of tiny jewelry boxes.

Legacy opened one of the boxes and placed a silver necklace with a family crest around Hattie Mae's neck.

Legacy said, "Everyone has one. It's a gift from Uncle Collin. It symbolizes family unity. We must wear them at all times."

Hattie Mae looked at Legacy with a side eye and said, "Collin Fo'Rae is such an interesting man."

Legacy looked at Hattie Mae and smiled. Legacy replied, "Extremely, Mama Hattie Mae."

Hattie Mae looked at Pierre Cordova. She noticed Legacy never gave him a box. When the maid walked out carrying a tray of hors d'oeuvres, Hattie Mae saw Pierre Cordova rubbing something around his neck. Pierre Cordova had a silver chain already.

Hattie Mae assumed he'd gotten it from the previous trip.

Hattie Mae noticed that Mistress Mattie never said a mumbling word about wearing her silver chain. Usually, Mistress Mattie bitched about everything. However, this time, she just put her chain on and went about her business.

Hattie Mae calmed down her wolves. She released them from the cage and let them roam the property.

Legacy told Hattie Mae that the Fo'Rae property was surrounded by a huge gate and that they were safe.

Hattie Mae could sense that her wolves were pleased to be back on their side of the world.

After dinner, Hattie Mae made it her business to let the ice-cold maid know that whatever she was, she wasn't afraid of her.

Hattie Mae tried to use her mind to speak with her.

Hattie Mae said, "Whatever you are and whatever you do is no business of mine. We mean you no harm. However, I will protect my family at all cost. So as long as we understand each other, there shouldn't be any problems."

Hattie Mae wasn't sure if she got through to her at first, until after dinner. The maid said to Hattie Mae, "Madame Fo'Rae, your reputation precedes you. You're more beautiful than your image has been described."

284

Hattie Mae replied, "Why thank you, but may I ask, what is this reputation you speak of?"

The maid smiled and said, "Everyone speaks highly of Madame Fo'Rae, the Voodoo Queen."

Hattie Mae smiled and said, "You can't believe everything you hear, child."

The maid looked at Hattie Mae and replied, "Even if you hear it directly from the source itself?"

Then the maid gave Hattie Mae a wink of her eye and whispered, "I heard you loud and clear, Madame Fo'Rae. Rest assured, me and my people mean you and your family no harm."

Hattie Mae replied, "I see. Well then, carry on about your business."

Legacy gave Hattie Mae and the girls a tour of the Manor.

Mistress Mattie had no interest in touring the manor. All Mistress Mattie wanted to do was get back to town in the morning to send a telegram.

The next morning, Collin Fo'Rae arrived. He seemed exhausted from the trip.

Collin Fo'Rae told Hattie Mae that he just needed to rest a spell.

Legacy took Hattie Mae, Mistress Mattie, and the girls on a tour of France.

The maid from last night insisted on going. She said she'd help watch the girls and keep them out of mischief.

For some reason, Hattie Mae took a liking to the maid and allowed her to accompany them. For some strange reason, it was almost like she had taken the wolves' place as a keeper over the girls.

As much as Hattie Mae wanted to take her wolves, Hattie Mae understood that she couldn't be walking through France with two huge wolves, although she got away with it on the small island of St. Lucia. Hattie Mae knew it was unacceptable in France.

Over the months, everybody seemed to be settling into his or her new lives.

The war in the States was bloodier than ever. Every day there was news of soldiers dying or being sent home without legs and arms. Savannah's girls had a tutor that would come to the house every day for hours for their school lessons. Also, they had a lady that would come in to teach them proper etiquette. Hattie Mae, Legacy, and Savannah were becoming even closer.

Mistress Mattie was losing her mind with worry, until one day Collin Fo'Rae got a letter saying Mistress Mattie's husband had been killed in battle. Mistress Mattie went into a state of depression. For months, she wore only black with a black veil covering her face.

Hattie Mae felt bad for Mistress Mattie. The death of Mistress Mattie's husband seemed to suck the life right out of her. Instead of being her normal over- dramatic, annoying self. Mistress Mattie was very quiet and sad all the time. The only joy that Mistress Mattie seemed to have was getting a letter from Young Charles, and the letters were few and far in between.

The one thing that slightly cheered up Mistress Mattie was an invitation to Balmoral Castle from The Queen herself.

The Queen had invited the entire House of Fo'Rae to her dinner party.

Hattie Mae didn't understand why, but she realized it was a big deal.

Hattie Mae laughed at the girls when they went on and on about The Queen living in a big castle. Hell, the estate they lived on was huge.

Collin Fo'Rae had a seamstress come in and make all of them new dresses.

Hattie Mae was amazed at how formal the Europeans seemed to be. Everything they did had to be done in exact order. The Europeans had an obsession with tradition. However, Hattie was impressed with the difference in how the Europeans treated the African population there. It was entirely different from being in the states. These Africans were free and had been for years. However, there was still a clear line of who was who.

The Africans stayed on their side and the Europeans on their side.

Just like Americans, the Europeans were obsessed with wealth and social standing. It was becoming clear to Hattie Mae why Collin Fo'Rae put so much emphasis on being a Fo'Rae.

Hattie Mae quickly learned that the Fo'Rae name opened a lot of doors for her family, the Queen's dinner party included.

Everyone got all dressed up for the event. Although Collin Fo'Rae was acting like it was no big deal, Hattie Mae could tell he was excited as well.

As the carriages arrived to pick them up, the maid that Hattie Mae had been watching asked to speak with Hattie Mae alone.

Hattie Mae laughed at herself when she thought of the nickname she had given her.

Hattie Mae and Legacy had started calling the maid, Icy, on the account of Legacy saying how cold her hands were when she touched her.

The maid said, "Madame Fo'Rae, a word of caution from me to you. In my experience, anytime one gets invited to The Queen's Castle, well, in my opinion, it's always because The Queen wants something from that person."

Hattie Mae replied, "What could this Queen want from Collin Fo'Rae?"

The maid responded, "No, the question is, what does the Queen want from Madame Fo'Rae? Word has spread all over France that you are here. Some people just want to meet you, some people want to be you, and most people want something from you. The gift that you and your daughters possess is unlike anything this country has seen. Sure, they have their healers and what not. However, no one as gifted as you and your daughters."

Hattie Mae replied, "I only have one daughter. The rest are my granddaughters."

Hattie Mae thought for a second, then she said, "You say this country and they, as if you weren't a part of this country. Why is that?"

The maid smiled and said, "Simply because I'm not from France. I was born in Romania, but that's an entirely different story. Right now, I'm giving you clear warning of how these people work."

Hattie Mae replied, "Alright, I hear you. Thanks for the warning. Someday I would love to hear all about how you came here from your country. I'm sure it's very interesting."

The maid responded, "Very!"

Colin Fo'Rae rushed everyone into the carriages, and they were off. He said it was a long ride to the castle.

Collin Fo'Rae looked at Hattie Mae and said, "So, what were you and Icy talking about?"

Hattie Mae couldn't help but laugh when Collin Fo'Rae referred to the maid as Icy!

Collin Fo'Rae smiled and said, "Yes, I hear everything. Including the nickname you've given my maid."

Hattie Mae responded, "Don't you find her a little odd?"

Collin Fo'Rae smiled and replied; "I've known her since I was a child. Yes, she's a little odd, but she's always been loyal to my father and me."

Hattie Mae smiled and then she thought, *wait a minute. How could Collin*

Fo'Rae have known Icy since he was a child? Icy didn't look any older than her late twenty's.

Hattie Mae replied, "How can that be she's years younger than you?"

Collin Fo'Rae responded, "I've always asked myself that same question, however, I've never had the courage to ask Icy. Maybe it's out of fear of what she might say."

Hattie Mae slowly replied, "Or fear of what she might do."

Collin Fo'Rae winked his eye at Hattie Mae and said, "Luckily I'm always ten steps ahead. However, I don't fear her. Her loyalty to my father is unquestionable. It was said that my father's house was always a safe haven for misfits. My Grandfather told me my father took her in when I was a baby. It seems she was running from something."

Hattie Mae just nodded her head.

Hattie Mae had got a glimpse of the Palace.
Hattie Mae thought to herself that if the size of this place indicated how much drama was going to happen tonight, than it was going to be plenty.

The Queen's reaction to Hattie Mae was unexpected. She seemed to be smitten with Hattie Mae. All night she just stared at Hattie Mae.

Hattie Mae just figured the Queen had never been that close to an African before.

Hattie Mae found one thing a little peculiar. The Queen never referred to Hattie Mae and her girls as Collin Fo'Rae's servants. Most folks just assumed that they were. The Queen, however, referred to them as Collin Fo'Rae's family.

It seemed that this dinner party was a private dinner party just for the Fo'Rae's. That let Hattie Mae know what Icy said was true. Hattie Mae enjoyed the grand festivities. Hattie Mae waited patiently for the Queen to make her request. She knew whatever it was she wasn't going to be able to refuse The Queen. Collin Fo'Rae had made that quite clear in the carriage.

The dinner party went smoothly. Everything was so formal.

The Queen insisted that they would stay the night as her guest.

Then the time came as they got ready for bed. The Queen's adviser handed Hattie Mae a note to meet them in the east wing of The Castle and to bring Legacy and Savannah with her.

Mistress Mattie had drunk wine until she passed out asleep, holding her dead husband's picture.

Hattie Mae just shook her head when she looked over at Mistress Mattie all sprawled out on the bed still wearing her all black ballroom dress and black veil. Hattie Mae just sighed and said, "How long is Mistress Mattie going to mourn? It's been months!"

Legacy and Savannah never responded. It seemed they grew tired of Mistress Mattie's shenanigans as well.

Hattie Mae told Legacy and Savannah whatever The Queen wanted, they would try their best to oblige her.

As they stood in the east wing of the castle waiting, they didn't know what to expect.

Savannah complained of how cold and damp it was in the castle. Legacy said it was creepy.

Finally, two guards showed up and escorted them to The Queen's chambers.

The Queen was lying in a bed that seemed as if it was built for an entire family. You had to go up steps just to get close to it.

The Queen looked different. She was just plain. No jewels, no crown, just a plump lady in a nightgown.

The Queen's adviser placed three chairs beside the bed.

The Queen pointed to the chairs and said, "Sit, please."

Legacy, Hattie Mae and Savannah sat before the Queen.

Hattie Mae said, "How can I be of service to you, Your Majesty?"

Hattie Mae smiled at herself. She'd heard everyone referring to the Queen as Your Majesty all night. Hattie Mae felt it was the proper thing to do.

The Queen said, "Madame Fo'Rae, I've heard lots of stories about this power you seem to possess. Tell me, is there any truth to these stories?"

Hattie Mae replied, "Well, Your Majesty, people tend to embellish often. So, the answer is, there could be some truth to these stories. It all depends on what power you seek."

The Queen smiled and replied, "Such a beautiful Nubian Queen you are. I hear your father was a brave warrior, and your grandmother was into healing, so to be perfectly honest, I'm looking for healing powers, my dear."

The Queen looked at Hattie Mae and her girls and said, "You can have all the riches in the world and buy all the material possessions you want, but do you know what the one thing is you can't buy?"

Legacy replied, "Love?"

The Queen smiled and said, "Sadly, no my dear. Love is bought and sold to the highest bidder daily. There is no use for love. Love blinds your judgment and fills your heart with emotions that your mind can't process. I say to hell with love."

Hattie Mae noticed that one of The Queen's African advisors left the room when The Queen said that. It seemed to strike a nerve with him.

Hattie Mae slowly said, "Money can not buy good health."

291

The Queen looked at Hattie Mae and smiled.

The Queen said, "Have you ever read the Bible, my child?"

Hattie Mae replied, "I'm not a religious person, nor do I believe in your God either, but yes I have read the Bible. I find it to be a fascinating story."

The Queen replied, "I've never known one of your kind that did believe in my God, but that's quite alright my child. The Lord is with all, believers and non-believers. So let me tell my tale. There's a story about a woman in the Bible. Her only wish is to get to Jesus. However, she suffers from a blood condition. She's too weak to get to him. So as he passes her, she simply touches the hem of his garment. Jesus feels energy drained from his body. She's automatically healed because of her faith. I too suffer from a blood disease."

The Queen stopped, then she said, "I tried this with God's representative on earth; His Holiness the Pope. Needless to say, it didn't work.

Hattie Mae held out her hands and said, "Do you believe me to have those same powers? If so feel free to touch me."

The Queen smiled and replied, "No my dear, I don't believe you to have those same powers as Jesus, but you have the next best thing."

Hattie Mae said, "And what would that be?"

The Queen responded, "The skills and know-how to create herbs to make a cure for my disease."

Hattie Mae looked at The Queen and said, "Your Majesty, you do understand that I'm not a healer. I have no formal education on medicines. Just the skills that my grandmother taught me, and what I've learned studying on my own. It's all trial and error. I have no for sure cure for whatever your case may be. I cannot promise you anything."

The Queen raised up a bit she said, "My dear, what is it you're bargaining for? I have anything you need. What I don't have I'd make it available for you."

Hattie Mae responded, "With all due respect Your Majesty, if that is the case, then you have an entire world of doctors and scientist at your disposal. Why not call on them? Why call on my daughters and me?"

The Queen said, "My father has sought a cure for this for years. I've sent my people to the ends of the earth to find a cure. However, I was unsuccessful. Until it was brought to my attention that a most powerful Voodoo Queen landed on the shores of France."

The Queen looked at Hattie Mae and smiled.

The Queen said, "From one Queen to another, allow me to speak freely. This is a job we both did not ask for. It was in our genes. A privilege bestowed upon us at birth. In my case, a gift that was likely never to be, but circumstances have it that I sit on the throne."

The Queen looked over at her crown then back at Hattie Mae.

The Queen said, "In your case, you were born into a respectable family of brave warriors and what we Britain's call Witch Doctors. No offense my dear, it just is what it is. However, those skills that your grandmother and your Ancestors gave you are very powerful."

The Queen looked at Legacy and said, "My sources said amongst the many things you can do, you can see into the future."

Then she looked at Savannah and said, "Is it true that you can manipulate objects at your will?"

The Queen smiled, looked at Hattie Mae and said, "And you, Madame Fo'Rae the Voodoo Queen. Well, you're the icing on the cake. Not only can you mix different herbs to potions, I heard you could speak to the dead and countless other skills. Please say you'll help me. I beg of you."

Hattie Mae looked at The Queen and replied, "Alright, I will see what I can do."

The Queen responded, "That's all I ask!"

Hattie Mae noticed that the Queen had a rosary tied around her hands the entire night, even as they ate dinner. Also, they had crucifixes almost on every wall and angels with wings painted everywhere.

Hattie Mae also noticed the pearls the Queen wore around her neck were set in silver. Also, Hattie Mae remembered The Queen touching her hands when they first said hello, which Hattie Mae was shocked by because Collin Fo'Rae had previously told Hattie Mae never to touch The Queen!

Hattie Mae said, "I'll be getting you a list of items I will need to work with."

The Queen replied, "Whatever you need. I also would like for you to have a space to work a little closer to me. I'll arrange something for you. Is there anything else you need?"

Hattie Mae said, "That will be all for now, but I would like to ask you about the silver you wear and why you have so many crucifixes around. Are you afraid of something or maybe someone?"

The Queen gave a devilish grin and slowly replied, "My dear, one could never be too close to The Lord, ergo, the rosary and crucifixes. As for the silver, I don't know what my fascination with it is. I just know I always feel safe with it on."

The Queen looked at Hattie Mae with the look all mothers give their children when they're trying to tell them to behave in public without actually saying it.

Hattie Mae replied, "Oh, I see."

The Queen looked at Hattie Mae and said, "Well, my dear, I'm growing tired. I shall rest now."

As Hattie Mae and the girls left The Queen's chamber, The Queen said,

"Madame Fo'Rae, please be a dear and remain in your quarters until sunrise. This castle is awfully big and old. I would hate for you to stumble upon something you're not familiar with."

As the door opened, Hattie Mae could have sworn she saw a shadow of something swoop past her.

Hattie Mae replied, "Sure thing, Your Majesty."

Hattie Mae looked around to see if she could see the shadow again that swooped past her.

It was nowhere to be found. The only thing that Hattie Mae did see was the African Advisor reentering The Queen's quarters.

Legacy looked at Hattie Mae and smiled.

Legacy said, "He's The Queens lover, and she loves him."

Hattie Mae, Legacy and Savannah held hands as they walked back to their suite.

Legacy looked up and said, "The Spirits speak loud and clear in this place. There is so much death and deceit in this place. Its history dates back hundreds of years."

Savannah wasn't saying much, she was too busy praying as usual. Over the years, Savannah's religious beliefs grew stronger. Her knowledge of the Catholic history was incredible. Hell, Savannah knew more about Roman Catholics than she did her own African history.

Hattie Mae was a little concerned about that at times. Then Hattie Mae decided that Savannah could believe whatever she wanted. Besides, God seemed to keep Savannah in line. Anything that Savannah deemed wouldn't please God, she wasn't involved in. If Savannah felt she'd offended God, she'd repent for hours or days. She'd lock herself away and say all her prayers.

Legacy was more like Hattie Mae; she believed in the ancestors and the Gods of Africa. Savannah's daughters didn't have a choice in the matter. They did what they were told.

Over the days, The Queen's people set up a workroom for Hattie Mae in a little town close to the Queen.

Savannah, Legacy, Mistress Mattie and the girls all stayed with Hattie Mae.

Hattie Mae laughed and said to herself, "This family sticking together stuff is beginning to be exhausting."

Collin Fo'Rae and Pierre Cordova were back off to Fo'Rae Manor. Neither one of them liked the idea of them being so far away. Since they seemed to be protected by The Queen, it was okay.

Collin Fo'Rae's maid Icy just showed up one day. She said she was there to help with Savannah's girls and housekeeping.

Icy smiled and said, "Collin Fo'Rae told me to tell you that whatever you're working on, you need to do it with the speed of angels because as much as he loves your wolves, he's terrified of what they might do if you stay away much longer."

Hattie Mae smiled and said, "Well, lucky for him I'm just about finished."

Icy assured Hattie Mae that her two wolves were fine. They had enough food and water to last for weeks, and they had enough land to roam around for months.

When Icy walked to her chambers, Legacy said, "Icy is hoping you can help her with her situation also."

Hattie Mae smiled and said, "Child, I can do a lot of things, but I highly doubt it if I could bring life back."

Savannah walked in praying as usual.

Savannah just frowned and said, "It's just ungodly for such things to exist. I'm sure it's of the devil!"

Hattie Mae smiled and sarcastically said, "What things?"

Since none of them could quite put their finger on exactly what was going on with Icy, none of them said a word.

All of a sudden, Hattie Mae felt a chill run through her entire body. The hairs on the back of her neck stood up.

Icy came back into the room; she moved as fast as the speed of lightning. It was almost as if Icy were flying. Icy stood right in front of Hattie Mae as if she was protecting her. The odd thing was, Hattie Mae could have sworn she heard Icy growling like one of her wolves.

Hattie Mae's workshop bell rang.

Icy shouted out, "Whatever you do, do not invite them in! Understand?"

Hattie Mae was about to say she was leaving for the day when the door opened, and in the doorway stood the odd couple Hattie Mae saw on the docks of France when she first arrived. Behind them stood another man.

The Man looked at Icy and said sarcastically, "Well, if it isn't little misfit Nivea, I see you've found a new owner. Do you really think it's wise to be fraternizing with witches? Are you really so desperate that you believe Madame Fo'Rae, the Voodoo Queen from American, can cure you of your so called disease?"

Icy backed up a bit and stretched her arm out against Hattie Mae as if she was telling Hattie Mae to step back.

The man walked closer but never entered the shop. He said, "Poor little girl, who was given the gift of eternal life. Yet, she still wants to die!"

He spat on the floor and yelled, "You should be ashamed of yourself! You're ungrateful and a disgrace to your kind!"

Hattie Mae slowly moved Icy's arm down and stepped closer to the door.

Hattie Mae looked him up and down and said softly, "And what kind might that be mister?"

The man's appearance slightly changed and his eyes flickered colors like sparks of fire.

Hattie Mae could feel the energy of danger exuding from him. Yet, she wasn't afraid.

Hattie Mae said, "I don't know exactly what's going on or what you want, but be assured that you don't frighten my girls or me. I've never quite seen your kind before. Nevertheless, we fear nothing.

The lady that was with him walked towards Hattie Mae, and, suddenly, Savannah used her gift to block her path by sliding the table in her way.

Although it seemed there was no need to block her path because she too stopped at the door.

Legacy moved in closer to Hattie Mae with her hatchet.

Just then, the man standing behind the couple said, "Enough!"

The couple stopped in their tracks as if they were pets giving a command by their owner.

The couple backed up and stood behind the man.

The man said, "Madame Fo'Rae the Voodoo Queen from America, by way of Africa and the Caribbean, it's a pleasure to meet you and your lovely daughters. If only you would invite me into your space so I could greet you properly."

Hattie Mae got a good look at him. He was very handsome, slender built, with a full goatee, with the darkest hair and eyes for such pale skin, and extremely charming.

When he smiled, it took Hattie Mae's breath away. It was almost like he hypnotized Hattie Mae.

Hattie Mae had to smile because the man standing in front of her looked similar to the picture of Jesus Savannah had hanging in her house. Except he had brown eyes, not blue.

Hattie Mae said, "I'm afraid you have me at a disadvantage because, although you know my name, I don't know yours."

He smiled and bowed his head.

He said, "Allow me to introduce myself, I'm DeMarco Lagos from the House of Lagos and these are my companions."

Then he looked at Icy and said, "And I see you've already met my sister Nivea!"

Icy looked at DeMarco and blurted out, "Half-sister, asshole."

DeMarco smiled and replied, "Oh little sister such language is very unbecoming, even for a concubine's daughter."

Icy frowned her face and said, "What is it you want?"

DeMarco replied, "Your love and devotion to me as your older brother is what I desire. However, for now, I would just like to meet your new acquaintance."

Everything in Hattie Mae's spirit
told her that everything about him was dangerous. However, something about him drew her to him.

Icy replied, "Then you shall have it as soon as hell freezes over."

DeMarco smiled and replied, "Well, luckily we'll both still be around to see

299

that happen. Now back to your beautiful new friends."

DeMarco turned and looked at Hattie Mae.

DeMarco said, "I've heard so much about you since you've come to these shores. I only wanted to meet you."

Something inside Hattie Mae had to get to know him.

Hattie Mae slowly said, "You and only you may come in."

Icy gasped for breath as if Hattie Mae had unleashed hounds from hell.

DeMarco looked at his sister Icy and said, "I truly only want to meet her. I mean her no harm."

Hattie Mae stuck her hand out and said, "Well, in that case, it's nice to meet you, Mister DeMarco Lagos."

DeMarco raised Hattie Mae's hand and kissed it.

Hattie Mae said, "Now if you don't mind, Mister DeMarco, I'd like to be about my business. My shop is closed and I'm powerfully tired."

DeMarco was still holding Hattie Mae's hand when he noticed the silver necklace around her neck. He stepped closer to her.

DeMarco said, "Such a beautiful piece of jewelry, sterling silver, and rare precious stone."

DeMarco stared at the necklace. Then he sniffed as if he smelled something.

He looked at Hattie Mae and said, "And you smell as delicious as you look."

Hattie Mae stepped back. She was a little frightened.

DeMarco let go of Hattie Mae's hand and said, "I've rarely witnessed such beauty as yours. You are black as night, yet radiant as the moonlight, and your beauty shines as bright as all the stars in the sky. Are all the women in your country this beautiful?"

DeMarco stood there gazing at Hattie Mae.

Icy stepped in and said sarcastically, "Is that the best you can do? That has got to be the most dreadfully tacky thing I've ever heard. How many harlots have you used that on?"

DeMarco cracked a smile.

Hattie Mae replied, "Thanks for the compliment. However, I couldn't tell you much about my homeland. My memory fades, as I grow older. I've been away from my homeland so long, I'm not sure if what I remember is real or something I've made up."

DeMarco seemed to be saddened by what Hattie Mae said.

DeMarco replied, "Sadly I must say that in all my travels, I've never been to your homeland."

DeMarco looked at Hattie Mae and said, "I prefer the cold weather."

Hattie Mae smiled and said, "I see!"

DeMarco replied, "Maybe I can clear your memory up just a bit. I seem to be good at helping people remember things."

Then DeMarco looked over at his half-sister Icy and said, "Remembering things like where they came from."

Hattie Mae responded, "And just how can you help me remember a place you've never seen?"

DeMarco replied, "The gifts you and your lovely daughters have, which you believe were passed down by your ancestors, well, I believe my ancestors gave me gifts too. Some of them good and, well, some of them, depending on how you look at them, bad."

DeMarco held his hands out to Hattie Mae and said, "Please oblige me for a minute."

Hattie Mae allowed him to hold her hands.

DeMarco said, "Now, close your eyes and think of your homeland. Remember everything you can."

Hattie Mae closed her eyes and remembered a time when her family had a celebration. All her family members were dancing and singing. The memory wasn't as clear as it had once been. It was just bits and pieces, but it made Hattie Mae smile.

As DeMarco held Hattie Mae's hand, her memory became clearer. It was like she was standing in the middle of her village. Hattie Mae could clearly hear her grandmother singing and the ladies dancing. Hattie Mae could smell the food from her homeland cooking. It was almost like she could taste it. Tears rolled down Hattie Mae's cheeks.

Hattie Mae clearly saw and felt her grandmother kiss her on the cheek and say, "I love you, my child."

Before Hattie Mae knew it, she screamed out, "No, please don't leave me," Icy snatched DeMarco's hands from Hattie Mae.

Hattie Mae fell to the floor in tears.

Icy demanded that DeMarco leave at once.

Icy said, "And don't come back. Nobody wants your help. Just go away."

And just like that DeMarco was gone.

Hattie Mae had never experienced a memory that vivid. The pain and grief she felt for her country were overwhelming.

And even more overwhelming was the thought of DeMarco and what he was.

Hattie Mae had never seen anything like his kind.

Hattie Mae spent the next day in the bed. She was exhausted from her experience with DeMarco. Plus she had that horrible feeling she got when she knew something was going to happen.

Hattie Mae knew whatever was going to happen, she couldn't stop it. All she could do was wait to see what happened and deal with it.

As the days went on, Hattie Mae felt the feeling get stronger. Hattie Mae just went on about her business.

Finally, she was ready to give The Queen her tonics she'd made up for her to drink daily. Hattie Mae wrote down exactly how to make them so that The Queen's people could prepare them for her.

Hattie Mae strongly disliked the winter weather in France. It was always cold and rainy.

The night she went to drop off the tonics to The Queen, Icy accompanied Hattie Mae.

As they stood in the rain waiting for the guards to allow them entry, Hattie Mae felt like somebody was watching them.

However, no one was around.

The guard came back and said disrespectfully, "Madame Fo'Rae may enter!"

Then he looked at Icy and said, "But, you, you could never enter this place!"

He took his sword and put it to her throat.

He said, "Now step back. This is holy ground you're standing on. No devils

303

have ever entered through these gates and never will."

Then he took his foot and kicked her to the ground.

Icy gave him a look that sent chills down Hattie Mae's spine.

Hattie Mae bent down to help Icy up. Icy's eyes flickered colors just like the couple's eyes did who came to Hattie Mae's little shop. But what Hattie Mae saw next scared her. Icy's teeth seemed to sharpen almost like dog's front teeth. They were sharp as knives.

Icy raised her hands up and put her head down in shame.

Icy said, "Give me a minute, Madame Fo'Rae. I'm okay."

Seeing Icy lying there in the rain soaking wet and ashamed of whatever she was infuriated Hattie Mae.

Hattie Mae turned to the guard and said, "You go tell your Queen that Madame Fo'Rae the great Voodoo Queen refuses her invitation of entry to this palace unless my assistant is granted entry. Furthermore, if my assistant is not allowed entry, I will leave this place and take my cure with me."

Hattie Mae stood up tall with all authority and said, "Do you understand?"

The guard replied, "How dare you! No one speaks to the Queen with such disrespect. You'll be lucky if you survive through the night."

He slammed the gate and left them standing in the rain.

Hattie Mae helped Icy to her feet.

Icy said, "Don't you think we should be running?"

Hattie Mae cracked a smile and said, "Child, no! The Queen wants what I have. She's a very wise woman! You'll see!"

Hattie Mae looked up to see DeMarco and his two companions watching from the alleyway. They were just standing there in the rain watching, dressed in all black.

Hattie Mae looked at Icy and said, "Appears your brother is here."

Icy replied coldly, "He's always around."

Hattie Mae smiled and said, "Can I ask you a question? Why does he always wear black? It's not very flattering to his complexion."

Icy laughed and replied, "I guess for dramatic effect!"

Hattie Mae and Icy laughed, then they heard the gate open.

The guard looked at them both in utter disgust.

He said, "By the Queen's order, you both may enter."

Hattie Mae looked over at DeMarco who was staring in amazement. He tipped his hat at Hattie Mae.

Icy's eyes bulged out. Icy looked at Hattie Mae and said, "Never in history has this happened. I guess she really wants whatever it is you have."

Hattie Mae's meeting with The Queen was brief. Hattie Mae gave the Queen all she needed to live a long healthy life.

As Hattie Mae left, she saw all the guards bent over on their knees in prayer, as if whom they referred to as the devil had entered the gates himself.

They slowly walked passed DeMarco, who still seemed to be a little pissed at the guard who was so disrespectful to his sister.

DeMarco walked next to Hattie Mae and said, "Please allow me to walk with you."

Hattie Mae replied, "Of course, be my guest."

Hattie Mae smiled and said, "I guess you witnessed what happened. That was totally uncalled for. Sometimes the people here can be so rude!"

DeMarco looked like he was getting even more pissed.

DeMarco replied, "The nerve of them acting like civilized citizens. Wasn't that long ago they were crawling around in a cave on their hands and knees. Self-righteous cave dwellers."

Hattie Mae had a feeling that DeMarco wasn't just figuratively speaking. She sensed DeMarco had been on this earth to witness many things.

Hattie Mae replied, "I bet that was a sight to be seen."

DeMarco smiled and replied, "Oh, you're a sharp one, Madame Fo'Rae. You're hoping that my answer will give you the answer you seek on how old I might be."

Hattie Mae smiled and replied, "Well, by appearance, if I had to guess I'd say you were about thirty, give or take a few years."

Icy rolled her eyes and replied, "Yeah, give that number about a few hundred years and you might be on to something."

DeMarco gripped his heart and said, "Ouch, dear sister, your hatred of me grows stronger with the years."

DeMarco looked at Hattie Mae and said, "Madame Fo'Rae, sometimes not knowing something is better."

Hattie Mae looked at DeMarco. He had such pain and anguish in his eyes. Although he looked young, his eyes told a different story.

Hattie Mae replied, "Maybe you're right. Besides, only the here and now is what really matters."

DeMarco smiled and gave a nod. He bid Hattie Mae a goodnight and disappeared into the night.

The next day, Hattie Mae heard the people mumbling something about the palace guard being attacked by a wild animal. The people said that he had his throat ripped out. The people were awfully hushed about it though. It was like they just wanted the situation to go away.

It may have had something to do with the young lover that was lying next to the guard at the time of his death. However, he swears he saw nothing. Then suddenly he left the city.

Hattie Mae had a feeling DeMarco had something to do with that. She dared not ask him, though. Because like he said, "Something's are better left alone.

The Queen sent her messengers with gifts for Hattie Mae and the girls. The Queen said Hattie Mae could keep the little shop, but now she'd have to pay rent on the space.

Chapter Sixteen:
Broken Hearted

Thee was still no word from Robert Lee, and Hattie Mae was worried.

Over the months, DeMarco often came to call on Hattie Mae.

Hattie Mae had to admit she loved his company. He always had such fascinating tales to tell.

Mistress Mattie always reminded Hattie Mae that she was a married woman and maybe she should think twice about indulging in such scandalous affairs.

Hattie Mae told Mistress Mattie it was nothing scandalous about her relationship with DeMarco. They were just friends, nothing more and nothing less.

Mistress Mattie raised her eyebrow and replied, "Well, I've never known you to have a male friend and such a handsome one, I might add. Hattie Mae, I warn you to stay away from him. He's trouble, and we both know he desires to be more than just your friend."

Hattie Mae was about to respond when she got a glimpse of Mistress Mattie's outfit. Again she was dressed in all black from head to toe and wearing that black veil.

Hattie Mae was so sick of looking at that damn black dress. Hattie Mae hated to admit this, but she missed the southern bell Mistress Mattie, the one who was always dressed for tea.

Hattie Mae said, "Mistress Mattie, I know you can't understand the concept of men and women being friends. However, it does happen."

Mistress Mattie replied sarcastically, "Sure it does, until one day when you find yourself bent over a chair with your undergarments around your ankles and DeMarco ravaging your unmentionables."

Mistress Mattie looked at Hattie Mae. She lifted up her veil and stared at

Hattie Mae with those piercing blue eyes.

Mistress Mattie said, "Hattie Mae, if I don't know nothing in this world, I know men! Believe me when I say all they want to do is eat and have sex. Period point blank."

Hattie Mae just carried on about her business and made her way to her shop.

That night, Collin Fo'Rae showed up at the shop. The odd thing was, he brought Savannah and Legacy with him.

Collin Fo'Rae looked like he had been crying, and so did the girls.

Hattie Mae's heart dropped to her feet when she saw the letter in Collin Fo'Rae's hand.

Tears welled up in Hattie Mae's eyes.

Hattie Mae said slowly, "I see there's news from America."

Collin Fo'Rae could barely speak, he said, "Hattie Mae I swear I hate to be the one to tell you this. My heart aches over what I'm about to say."

A tear slowly ran down Hattie Mae's face.

Hattie Mae mumbled, "Tell me please."

Colin Fo'Rae wiped tears from his eyes; he was overcome with emotion and couldn't speak.

Savannah walked over to Hattie Mae and said, "Mama, maybe you should sit down for this."

Legacy poured Hattie Mae a cup of water.

Savannah said, "Mama a letter came to Uncle Collin today. The letter said it regrettably had to report that Robert Lee Fo'Rae had been killed in battle."

Hattie Mae felt her head slump over in her lap. It was like she was numb. She closed her eyes and prayed to the ancestors that this was just a nightmare. Tears washed over Hattie Mae's face. The room was dead silent for a second.

Savannah slowly said, "Mama, are you alright?"

Hattie Mae didn't have the words to describe how she felt. She felt as if she couldn't breath, like something heavy was weighing on her chest. Like, in that instant, her world, as dysfunctional as it was, had come to an end.

Collin Fo'Rae walked over to Hattie Mae and said, "Oh my dear, I'm so sorry."

Collin Fo'Rae abruptly headed to the door. His face was full of tears.

Hattie Mae couldn't accept the fact that Robert Lee was gone. All those years he had been her only companion. They'd been through so much. He was her strength. Hattie Mae couldn't imagine life without Robert Lee.

Hattie Mae fell to her knees and let out a blood-curdling scream. She shouted, "Please no, what will I do without you?"

Hattie Mae doubled over on the floor, curled up in a fetal position and cried.

Savannah and Legacy tried to comfort her, but she was inconsolable.

Hattie Mae lay on the floor for hours crying.

Nobody said anything; they just sat there watching her.

Hattie Mae saw Mistress Mattie enter the shop.

Mistress Mattie walked over and sat on the floor next to Hattie Mae.

Mistress Mattie placed Hattie Mae's head in her lap and rubbed her hair.

Mistress Mattie said, "Now, now child. That's right, cry and let it all out. I truly understand how you feel. I'm here for you in your time of need. You cry as much as you need too."

With that said, Hattie Mae cried until she had no more tears. At that point, she just lay there. Hattie Mae couldn't pull herself together.

Collin Fo'Rae picked Hattie Mae up off the floor and carried her to his carriage.

On the way to the carriage, Hattie Mae caught I glimpse of DeMarco saying something to Mistress Mattie.

Hattie Mae heard Mistress Mattie say this is not a good time. The family is grieving a great loss.

Hattie Mae spent days in her room alone. She didn't want to talk or see anyone.

Finally, Mistress Mattie came in the room. She had the maids bring the tub and all Hattie Mae's oils and lotions.

Mistress Mattie hung a black dress and a black veil on the back of the door. Then she laid out Hattie Mae's underclothes and shoes.

Mistress Mattie sat on the bed. Slowly she said, "My love it's time for you to pull yourself together. No one knows better than me how you feel. I've lost two husbands. One I despised and one I loved with every breath in my body. I'd give anything to bring him back. However, he is not coming back, and neither is Robert Lee. Sadly, my dear, we are both widows. And life goes on."

Hattie Mae couldn't say anything. She could only cry. The odd thing was, Hattie Mae never thought Mistress Mattie would be the one comforting her. And to top it all off, Mistress Mattie was being sincere.

Mistress Mattie said, "Come now, you must bathe and get dressed."

Mistress Mattie wiped Hattie Mae's tears. "She said, "Enough, no more crying. You're the strongest person I know. Leave the crying and the crazy for me. I need you to be Hattie Mae, the fearless Voodoo Queen."

Hattie Mae cracked a half of smile and said, "Yes, you are crazy!"

Mistress Mattie smiled and replied, "Hattie Mae, if you ever tell anybody I said this, I'll deny it to the end. However, everybody knows you are the backbone of this Fo'Rae family. Without you, we'd all be up shit's creek without a paddle."

Mistress Mattie extended her hand to Hattie Mae and led her to the bathtub.

Mistress Mattie said, "Now I've laid out your things. My Lord, Hattie Mae, please don't tell me I have to bathe you, too?"

Mistress Mattie smiled and said, "Yes, everything is black. It's only proper that a grieving widow wear black for at least a year."

Hattie Mae didn't have the strength to argue with Mistress Mattie.

As Mistress Mattie was leaving, she pointed to flowers in a vase on the dresser.

Mistress Mattie said, "Your friend DeMarco bought these. He's outside on the porch. He's been here every day this week."

Hattie Mae said, "Don't invite him in!"

Mistress Mattie replied, "Funny thing you say that because Icy says the same thing. I never invited him in. What should I tell him? My God Hattie Mae, he's lingering around like a lost puppy."

Hattie Mae relaxed in the bathtub. She got dressed in the all black clothes Mistress Mattie had laid out for her. Hattie Mae frowned her face when she

Marsha Bullock

saw the veil. However, she decided to wear it. She thought at least it would hide the sour look on her face.

Hattie Mae went outside to find DeMarco sitting on the porch.

DeMarco looked at Hattie Mae and said, "I'm very sorry for your loss. You have my deepest sympathy."

Hattie Mae replied, "That's very kind of you."

Hattie Mae felt faint. She felt as if she was losing her balance.

DeMarco grabbed her and walked her to the patio table that was on the porch. He sat her down in the chair.

He said, "It seems that the news from the states has taken a toll on your health."

Hattie Mae just sat there. She was trying to shake the empty feeling she had.

DeMarco sat next to her. He stared at her as if he couldn't believe she was actually real.

DeMarco caught himself staring and said, "Please forgive me. I know my timing is terribly off, but your beauty is remarkable. Even through all this drab black you've chosen to wear, you radiate beauty. Your energy is magnetic."

Hattie Mae tried to smile, but her heart was broken. The loss of Robert Lee was weighing heavy on her heart. She felt the tears scrolling down her face.

DeMarco said, "War is such an ugly thing. I've witnessed and fought in many battles. Man has waged war over some of the most ridiculous things. However, in the case of this particular war, I believe that a man's freedom is worth fighting for."

DeMarco looked at Hattie Mae and said, "I have walked this earth a

314

number of years, and I'm here to tell you that slavery is nothing new. However, the cruel and inhuman treatment of slaves is. If the Americans treat their slaves how I've heard, then this is deplorable."

Hattie Mae and DeMarco had a long discussion about slavery in America.

Then DeMarco asked Hattie Mae the most difficult question. Hattie Mae wasn't sure how to respond. It was a question she'd asked herself for quite some time now.
DeMarco said, "Hattie Mae, with all the ships you have at your disposal, why is it that you have never gone back to your homeland?"

Hattie Mae didn't really know what to say. She hesitated for a while. Hattie Mae had strong emotional feelings about where she called home.

Hattie Mae replied as if she didn't really want to say it, "I'm ashamed to go back to my homeland of Africa. I'm ashamed of what I've been through."

DeMarco simply replied, "It's understandable, I know you come from a strong line of people. However, being ashamed of how your life turned out is utterly ridiculous. You, as were many others of your kind, were stolen from your homeland and taken as slaves. You were treated cruelly and abused by your captors. You were powerless. What could you have done? Nothing, you could have done nothing."

Hattie Mae just looked at DeMarco; she really didn't have anything to say. She knew he was right.

DeMarco said, "Hattie Mae, in all my years, I've never met anyone I wanted to know more than you. I'd help you go home. I'd lead you to your people. I'd be your protection from anyone trying to harm you. Please allow me to do this for you. Let me take you home to your people. People you were stolen from."

Hattie Mae's heart felt as if it would burst with so many emotions she was feeling. The thought of seeing her homeland shores raced through her mind, as well as the thought of having DeMarco there to protect her from anything that might be waiting to harm her."

DeMarco said, "Although, I must tell you this. You might not like what you find."

Hattie Mae sat there for a while. She thought long and hard.

Hattie Mae said, "Home is a place where I always felt safe."

Hattie Mae smiled as she remembered her village.

Hattie Mae said, "I can still remember my father's voice calling my name."

Hattie Mae looked at DeMarco and said, "Yes, I would like to go home now. I need to lay eyes on my country."

DeMarco smiled and replied, "So, it shall be Madame Fo'Rae. Home to your country, I shall take you."

Hattie Mae looked up to see Icy looking at them through the window.

The look on Icy's face was of pure disgust.

Hattie Mae smiled and said, "Your sister seems to strongly dislike you! Why is that?"

DeMarco replied, "She does seem to loathe me, doesn't she?"

Hattie Mae had to laugh because Icy's hatred for DeMarco seemed to conflict with the love Icy felt for him. It was like she loved him, she just didn't want him around.

DeMarco looked at Hattie Mae and said, "If we are going to be traveling companions, there are a few things I must tell you. Some things you will just have to accept. Some things might frighten you. If what I tell you frightens you and you decide you no longer want to travel with me, I'll understand."

Hattie Mae looked at DeMarco and said, "First, you must tell me why Icy loathes you."

DeMarco replied, "It's basically one in the same. Long years ago, way before your time, in the year of fourteen hundred and twenty-seven, I had just returned home from a bloody battle."

Hattie Mae lifted up her veil and replied, "Come again, I'm afraid I've misunderstood you. Did you say the year was fourteen hundred and twenty-seven?"

DeMarco responded, "Yes, January of fourteen hundred and twenty-seven, to be exact. Snow had just begun to cover the ground. I was in an awful way. I'd been shot in my leg. The bullet went clean through. When I arrived in my city, all I saw was smoke and burning wood. I smelled the awful smell of flesh burning. The city was basically empty. The people that were there had their faces covered with cloth. You could only see their eyes. One woman told me that warriors had come through and destroyed and killed everyone."

DeMarco looked at Hattie Mae and said, "I ran to my house to find my wife and son dead. After I wrapped them up and placed the two coins over their eyes, I burned their bodies."

Hattie Mae said, "Why did you cover their eyes with coins?"

DeMarco smiled and said, "In my country, they believed the two coins were entry fee into the afterlife."

Hattie Mae replied, "Oh!"

DeMarco continued, "After I sent them into the afterlife, I left to check on my parents. Although I was still furious with my father for his monstrous behavior previously, yet I still loved him.

Hattie Mae said, "What did your father do that made you so angry?"

DeMarco seemed to be very troubled by that question. He just replied, "That's a story for another day."

317

Then he continued on with his story.

He said, "Unfortunately, I was too late. My father and mother both were dead. I looked all over for my father's concubine and her daughter. One of the ladies told me she saw them running for the woods."

DeMarco looked at Hattie Mae and said, "My mother hated my father's lover and his daughter, my half-sister. However, she could do nothing about it. She was a woman. She could only pretend it wasn't happening. The sad thing is, my father didn't even like his whore, but he loved his daughter, my half-sister who you've named Icy."

DeMarco laughed and said, "Icy, that is a clever name and fits her well. Her heart is cold as ice."

Hattie Mae said eagerly, "Finish your story!"

DeMarco replied, "Okay, as you wish. Well, I headed into the woods to find them. I assumed they hadn't gotten far. My sister was just a child. I was overwhelmed with the death of my wife and son. I prayed for death to take me."

DeMarco looked at Hattie Mae and slowly said, "Then death came."

Hattie Mae stood up.

DeMarco said, "What happened next has remained a mystery to me for hundreds of years. Until this day, I cannot tell you who or what it was that attacked me in those woods. All I remember is being attacked and bitten by something. I lay on that cold hard ground gasping for air and struggling for life."

Hattie Mae replied, "I thought you wanted to die?"

DeMarco said, "I thought I did, but man's basic instinct is to survive. So that's just what I did. I crawled my way through those woods. It took me days. I passed out and woke up in a strange town. Some ladies found me and carried me to safety. They nursed me back to health."

DeMarco stopped. He looked at Hattie Mae and said, "Remember I told you, you might not like some things I have to say."

Hattie Mae replied, "Go on and finish, what happened?"

DeMarco replied, "Well, when I woke from my slumber, I remembered having awful nightmares about a woman."

DeMarco was silent for a second.

Then he said, "I had an awful thirst for something I'd never smelled before. The aroma was tantalizing. It was like the aroma was calling for me."

Hattie Mae said, "What was it?"

DeMarco looked down at the ground and replied, "Blood, Hattie Mae. It was blood."

Hattie Mae backed up. She had to admit that frightened her a bit.

DeMarco looked at Hattie Mae and said, "Are you sure you want me to continue?"

Hattie Mae had to hear the end of the story. She shook her head yes.

DeMarco said, "In my thirst for blood, I killed everybody in the house. After I'd drained them, I felt awful. I feared I'd gone mad. I was like a rabid dog. I balled up in the corner. I was so confused I didn't know what to do. In all my life, I'd never thought I'd do such a thing. I cried like an infant child until I heard a familiar voice. It was my father's whore. I made my way to the door. When she saw me standing there covered in blood, she didn't scream or run. She simply helped me out of the house, and we left."

Hattie Mae was confused. She said, "And why would she do that? Why would she help you?"

DeMarco replied, "I have no idea, but if it had not been for her, I don't know where I would be. She nursed me back to health. She quenched my thirst for blood with raw animal meat. When I was stronger, she told me a story her mother used to tell her about the soulless beings walking the earth. She said I'd been attacked by one and she didn't know how I survived the attack."

She allowed me to stay with her and her daughter, my sister. Over the years, I remained youthful while everyone grew old. We went from town to town, so no one figured it out. Over the years, I met two others like me. You've met my two companions. I also learned how to control my thirst."

Hattie Mae said, "Until you got thirsty enough to eat your sister!"

DeMarco smiled and replied, "No, Madame Fo'Rae, I did no such thing."

Hattie Mae said, "Well Icy seems to be just like you, so something happened to her."

DeMarco replied, "Yes something happened to her. As the years went on, her mother grew older. Icy's mother was a whore. It was the only thing she knew how to do. She was concerned that Icy would grow up to be one, too. In the meantime, Icy fell in love with a young man who she could never fully have because of her social standing. Icy's mother knew Icy would end up being his mistress. On Icy's twenty-first birthday, her mother came to me and begged me to make Icy like me."

Hattie Mae said, "How could you?"

DeMarco replied, "Her mother pled a very convincing case. She insisted that the world especially men, would use and abuse Icy. She feared after her death Icy wouldn't be able to protect herself. She said they'd been given a terrible life and I was a way to fix it. The strength that came along with being like me would protect Icy from the savage men that lived in that time."

DeMarco looked at Hattie Mae and said, "However, it didn't take much convincing. She was my sister and since my entire family was gone, I feared traveling through this life alone without any kin. So one night, while she lay asleep, I bit her. I wasn't totally sure what would happen. However, her mother was, and just like she said, after that, my sister was just like me. However, she was furious. She said I ruined her chance with her young man."

Hattie Mae was speechless and a little scared. All this talk about thirsting for blood and biting folks was a bit much. Hell, Hattie Mae had the gift, but she'd never heard of humans living hundreds of years and drinking blood. If ever there was a devil, Hattie Mae thought this was surely his doing.

Hattie Mae said, "Well, what happened to her young man?"

DeMarco said, "Sadly, Madame Fo'Rae, her young man wasn't what she thought him to be. In fact, it wasn't her he lusted for at all. It turned out he was a sodomite."

Hattie Mae just looked at DeMarco.

DeMarco said, "One thing about who we are is that all your senses seem to take on a life of their own. My sister swore she could smell his lover all over him, especially his anus. He denied it to the end until she followed him one day. She caught them lying together and professing their love for one another. Her anger got the better of her, and she ripped them both to pieces."

Hattie Mae was just listening. She never said a word.

DeMarco said, "Needless to say, we had to leave that place."

Hattie Mae said, "And you came here to France?"

DeMarco smiled and said, "Hattie Mae, I've been to so many places I can't begin to count them all. But, to answer your question, no, we traveled from place to place. Along those places, we ran into some extremely interesting people. A few like us, but far in between. My dear sister has lived many lives and been many people. However, it was something about this place, this town that drew her here. Once she came here, she never wanted to leave."

Hattie Mae replied sarcastically, "I couldn't imagine what it could be. Nothing about this place is exciting. It's cold, it rains too much, and it's dreary."

DeMarco smiled and replied, "Just how someone like me would like."

Hattie Mae had to laugh.

Icy came outside and sat next to Hattie Mae.

Icy said sarcastically, "My brother spins such a fascinating tale. However, he left out a few details."

DeMarco looked at his sister and frowned.

DeMarco said, "Which I'm sure you'll be more than happy to fill Madame Fo'Rae in on. Please be kind my dear sister, I'm afraid I've already frightened Madame Fo'Rae to death. The look on her face is proof."

Hattie Mae had to admit she was a little scared, but still interested.

Icy replied, "Dear half-brother, I'll just clear up some things. Starting with my mother; who wasn't a whore. My mother was a seamstress in Romania, until your Neanderthal father convinced her to leave her country and go with him. Only after she got away from him did she start selling her body."

DeMarco interrupted and said, "Our Neanderthal father. And I beg to differ, my father was a nobleman."

Icy frowned her face and replied, "In whose eyes? Certainly not in mine or my mother's. He treated my mother like trash once he used her up and stole her youth. When he grew tired of her, he replaced her with another."

Hattie Mae smiled. She was enjoying the bickering between DeMarco and Icy. It took her mind off her cruel life.
Icy said "And not to mention how my mother cried every night and had

nightmares about ships and murderers."

DeMarco looked upset when Icy mentioned her mother's nightmares and a ship. Hattie Mae could tell DeMarco didn't want to talk about that.

Hattie Mae said, "Sounds like all the men I've come across, even the ones in my country. When the milk dries up, they simply get a new goat."

DeMarco laughed and replied, "Come now, men aren't all that bad."

Icy looked at DeMarco then back at Hattie Mae.

Icy said, "All men, Madame Fo'Rae, are pigs. Especially the ones pretending to be noblemen. They're the worst."
Icy looked back at DeMarco and said, "My dear half-brother, how many women might you say you've had over the years? How many innocent hearts have you crushed with your promises of love and a happily ever after? I certainly can recall at least one, and that would be your wife."

DeMarco gave a little smirk and replied, "Why, sister, do you have such a low opinion of me? I must say it's truly heartbreaking. However, in my defense, I really did love them all. Especially my dear wife."

Icy rolled her eyes and looked at Hattie Mae.

Icy said, "Beware of wolves who come in sheep's clothing."

DeMarco responded, "Speaking of wolves, Madame Hattie Mae, I think yours may require your attention."

Then DeMarco pointed to Hattie Mae's wolf that was approaching.

Icy hurried back to the house. It seemed her conversation with DeMarco sparked bitterness in her.

Hattie Mae stood up as the male wolf approached. The male wolf looked at DeMarco and growled. Hattie Mae didn't know what to expect. Normally the wolves weren't around people, just Hattie Mae's family whom the wolves apparently considered a part of their pack.

DeMarco didn't appear to be afraid. He simply bowed down and extended his arm in submission.

DeMarco looked up at Hattie Mae and said, "Respect is always given to the more dominant creature."

DeMarco's act of respect seemed to please the male wolf.

The male wolf turned his back and then looked back at Hattie Mae as if he wanted her to follow him.

Hattie Mae heard the female wolf howling. It sounded like she was in a great deal of pain.

Hattie Mae followed the male wolf to where the female wolf was. It appeared she was in labor.

Hattie Mae said, "Well, I be damned. In all the years I spent with them, they've never had babies."

DeMarco replied, "Perhaps because they weren't in their natural habitat."

Hattie Mae bowed down to the female wolf as she approached her.

Hattie Mae looked at the wolf, held her hands up slowly and said, "My Queen, with your permission I can help you."

The female wolf seemed to welcome Hattie Mae. She allowed Hattie Mae to help her deliver four pups.

When it was all said and done, all the wolves rested comfortably in the den they had created.

As DeMarco and Hattie Mae walked back to the house, Hattie Mae said, "Well, Mr. DeMarco, you can't be all that bad. A soulless creature you may be, however, my wolves seem to like you. If you posed any danger to me, they would have ripped you to shreds."

DeMarco smiled and bid Hattie Mae a goodnight.

As he walked away, he said, "Madame Fo'Rae such exciting adventures I'm sure we will have on our journey to your homeland. I look forward to your company."

Hattie Mae looked up to see Mistress Mattie in the doorway.

Mistress Mattie snidely said, "My Lord Hattie Mae, I was just on my way to find you. I thought for sure you'd jumped off one of these cliffs in grief. Only I find you cozying up with this DeMarco character. I must say, Madame Fo'Rae, you do have some of the strangest acquaintances I've ever known."

As Hattie Mae walked through the door, she heard Icy add her two cents in by saying, "I'd agree with you, Mistress Mattie. Strange indeed."

Hattie Mae rolled her eyes at both of them.

Icy said, "Hattie Mae, I warn you. Stay away from Mr. Smooth Talker, DeMarco. Although he is pleasant to the eye and his words fall softly on the ears, he is not what he appears. He's a cold-hearted, self-centered, egotistical tyrant, who always gets what he wants, no matter what the cost."

Mistress Mattie couldn't resist adding in her say.

Mistress Mattie stood behind Hattie Mae and whispered, "Seems to me he wants some black coffee to go with his sweet talk."

Icy replied, "He's had every flavor of coffee imaginable, yet he seems to be fixated on this black cup."

Hattie Mae said, "Excuse me. I can hear y'all. And if you don't mind, please stop referring to me as black coffee. DeMarco and I are just friends."

Hattie Mae put her head down. Then she said, "And now we're going to be traveling companions."

Mistress Mattie blurted out, "What in heavens does that mean? Where might you two be traveling to?"

Hattie Mae replied, "Home?"

Mistress Mattie sat down on the sofa.

Mistress Mattie said, "Well, please count me in. I'd love to go back home to St. Lucia. I'm so sick of this cold weather. If I never see snow and rain again, it will be too soon. Why, Hattie Mae, I think that's the best idea you've have all year. I'll have the staff start packing at once."

Icy wasn't saying anything. She was just standing there looking at Hattie Mae.

Hattie Mae replied, "No, Mistress Mattie, not St. Lucia!"

Mistress Mattie stood up and walked over to Hattie Mae.

Mistress Mattie said, "My dear Hattie Mae, you must be awfully tired. Maybe you should go lay down, because if you're talking about going home, meaning back to Louisiana, surely you've taken ill!"

Hattie Mae said, "Mistress Mattie, I'm not talking about St. Lucia or Louisiana. I've never considered either one of those places home. I'm talking about going back to Africa, my real home."

All the life seemed to be sucked out of Mistress Mattie's face. Mistress Mattie sat back down, and straightened out her dress. She seemed to be at a loss for words.

Mistress Mattie finally said, "Oh, I see. And whose idea was this? Was it yours or your new friend Mr. Good- looking? Hattie Mae, surely you don't plan on running off with this stranger and leaving me?"

Mistress Mattie caught herself and she stopped talking for a second.

Then Mistress Mattie said, "I mean leaving us, your family, behind."

Hattie Mae didn't have the energy to fight with Mistress Mattie.

Hattie Mae simply replied, "I've spoken. I said what I had to say."

Mistress Mattie mumbled under her breath, "Hmm, we'll see about that."

Mistress Mattie jumped up and ran off to find Collin Fo'Rae.

Icy walked over and sat down next to Hattie Mae.

Icy said, "Madame Fo'Rae, I support you going to your homeland. However, I must warn you again, my brother is a force to be reckoned with. Although I'm sure you can take care of yourself, he's set on having you. I don't know what it is about you that has him so intrigued. I've never seen him act like this over a woman. Just be very careful. He could turn on the flip of a coin. He's lived several lifetimes and has seen and done more than you can possibly imagine."

Hattie Mae took a deep breath. Although she knew Icy was only looking out for her best interest, Hattie Mae did not fear DeMarco. And the truth is, she was just intrigued with him as he was with her.

Over the months following, Hattie Mae prepared for the trip back to her homeland. Mistress Mattie was still pissed and was still trying to convince Hattie Mae it was a bad idea. Hattie Mae's girls were fine with it, and Legacy intended on joining Hattie Mae on her journey. Savannah wasn't thrilled with Hattie Mae leaving, but she accepted it. Savannah had a life with Pierre Cordova and her girls. To Hattie Mae's surprise, Savannah was expecting another child in the spring. Hattie Mae often joked with Savannah saying that Savannah was like a breeding plantation. Collin Fo'Rae was enjoying life with his companion and seemed to be getting all his affairs in order. He sold most of his ships and properties. Collin Fo'Rae was spending more time with his white Fo'Rae relatives in France. There was little news from Young Charles about the war in the states, except it was bloody and men were dying daily. Hattie Mae spent the majority of her time with DeMarco. DeMarco had the most interesting stories.

A couple of days before Hattie Mae and DeMarco were set to leave, a letter came from the United States.

Collin Fo'Rae sent for Hattie Mae. He said he had important news to discuss with her and Mistress Mattie.

Hattie Mae feared the worst.

Mistress Mattie, Hattie Mae, Savannah, Legacy, Pierre Cordova, and all Savannah's girls gathered in the living room.

Collin Fo'Rae had Icy bring out a bottle of champagne and glasses.

Hattie Mae figured if Collin Fo'Rae handed out drinks, then there must be good news from America.

Collin Fo'Rae said, "I have some wonderful news. President Lincoln has freed all the slaves."

Hattie Mae looked over at Legacy who had predicted this years ago.

Mistress Mattie said, "Why that's wonderful news. So the war is over and we can all go back to St Lucia. I can finally see my son again."

Collin Fo'Rae smiled and said, "Yes Mistress Mattie, you are right about that. We all can go home."

Then Collin Fo'Rae looked at Hattie Mae and said, "All of us who want to go!"

Hattie Mae said, "The news from the States is truly wonderful. However, I plan to continue my journey back to my own home."

Hattie Mae looked at Mistress Mattie and said, "I wish you well my friend, but this is where we part ways."

Savannah wasn't saying much. It didn't seem like she cared if the war was over or not.

Savannah said, "Well, as for me and my girls, we will remain here. Until after I have the baby, then we will be going back to our home in St. Lucia. My girls and I will never step one foot on America soil as long as there is breath in my body."

Collin Fo'Rae looked at Savannah and said, "I understand, but I fear that this trip will be my last. I'm getting old, and my body is tired. All this traveling is taking a toll on me."

Collin Fo'Rae looked at Hattie Mae and said, "I have more good news."

Then Collin Fo'Rae looked at Legacy.

Collin Fo'Rae put his head down. Then he said, "Seems Young Charles has taken a bride and they're expecting a baby."

Mistress Mattie was furious. She tightened up her lips and said, "How dare he, and without even telling me. This is unheard of."

Hattie Mae looked over at Legacy. Hattie Mae's heart broke for Legacy. Once again Legacy was heartbroken over Young Charles. Hattie Mae knew that Legacy loved Young Charles and believed that eventually, they'd be together. But after hearing this news about the marriage and the baby, Hattie Mae had her doubts.

Legacy walked off to her room.

Savannah, Pierre Cordova and the girls left.

Mistress Mattie was rumbling on about how disrespectful Young Charles was.

Collin Fo'Rae handed Hattie Mae a letter. It appeared to be from Young Charles.

It read:

My dearest Mama Hattie Mae, I do hope this letter finds you in the best of health and spirits. I must say I miss you all terribly. I'm hoping to rectify that soon. Please extend my love to Legacy and tell her getting married was the hardest decision I ever had to make. However, it was the right thing to do seeing that the young lady was carrying my child. My love for Legacy I still carry in my soul. She is the only one who holds my heart.

Now on the matter of this baby that's coming. You and I both know that this could be a sticky situation although, my wife knows much about me. My deepest secrets remain just that, my secrets. I fear at the time of birth things could get complicated. Mama Hattie, I implore you to come to New York and be my wife's midwife.
I fear I'll need your strength and wisdom if things should go wrong. Please find it in your heart to oblige me.

With great love and respect

Your dearest
Charles Fo'Rae,

P.S

Hattie Mae, I have a wonderful surprise for you.

Hattie Mae looked at Collin Fo'Rae and said, "Did you write this?"

Collin Fo'Rae responded, "No, I did not!"

Hattie Mae replied, "Did you read this?"

Collin Fo'Rae responded, "I'm afraid I'll have to admit that I did!"

Hattie Mae said, "I'm sure you agree with Young Charles."

Collin Fo'Rae replied, "I do!"

Collin Fo'Rae looked at Hattie Mae and said, "Hattie Mae, you know how this could turn out. There's a fifty-fifty chance that baby could come out colored. My Lord, can you imagine what would happen? Young Charles has married one of the most top ranking army officials in America's daughter, under the pretense of being a white man. This baby could make or break Young Charles. If he goes on to have a white baby and happy marriage, his career in the military can soar. Hell, he could go on to be a congressman or senator. However, if this baby comes out."

Collin Fo'Rae stopped and looked at Hattie Mae.

Collin Fo'Rae said, "Hattie Mae, if this baby comes out as anything other than white, all hell is going to break loose."

Hattie Mae set down and took a deep breath.

Hattie Mae said, "How is that my problem?"

Collin Fo'Rae said, "Because you love that boy more than life. You practically raised him."

Icy was standing in the doorway.

Collin Fo'Rae walked off to his room.

Icy said, "And this is the part where you get to see the monster in DeMarco."

Hattie Mae replied, "What are you talking about?"

Icy responded, "We both know you're going to New York to deliver that baby. We both know Young Charles is like your very own child. You would never choose DeMarco over one of your own children. As bad as you want to go to your homeland, we both know you're going to put the needs of your own children in front of yours. And Young Charles is just as much your son as he is Mistress Mattie and Robert Lee's."

Icy got in Hattie Mae's face and said, "Now, correct me if I'm wrong or send me away if I've overstepped my boundaries."

Hattie Mae hated to admit that Icy was right. There was no way Hattie Mae could let Young Charles go through this alone.

Hattie Mae walked off to find Legacy. She found Legacy in her room still packing.

Hattie Mae said, "How are you, child?"

Legacy replied with tears in her eyes, "I'm fine."

Hattie Mae responded, "You don't have to be strong for me. I know you love him still."

Legacy allowed the tears to fall from her eyes. She laid her head on Hattie Mae's shoulder.

Hattie Mae said, "He sends his love. He told me to tell you he's never loved another as he's loved you. He wants me to come to New York to deliver the baby."

Legacy didn't say a word. It was complete silence for a minute then Legacy said, "Mama Hattie Mae, my visions have never been wrong. However, I never envisioned this!"

Hattie Mae said, "Tell me what you saw child."

Legacy replied, "I saw I glimpse of Charles and I living in a big house next to an ocean, holding a baby. We were very happy. There were other children playing in the yard and lots of little shacks in the backyard."

When Legacy said little shacks in the backyard, it sparked a memory in Hattie Mae's mind.

Hattie Mae said, "Can you describe this house to me?"

Legacy said, "Well, the house was huge like the mansion in St. Lucia, except it wasn't the mansion in St. Lucia. The house had a roll of beautiful trees that lined the walkway and a huge balcony that wrapped around the entire second floor. In the center of the yard was a huge fountain dripping with water."

Legacy stopped. It seemed like whatever she was going to say, something made her change her mind. Whatever it was, Hattie Mae could tell it touched Legacy's heart.

Hattie Mae closed her eyes. She knew Legacy was describing The Fo'Rae plantation in Louisiana. Hattie Mae hated that place. It was beautiful on the outside, but so many ugly things had happened there.

Hattie Mae said, "Tell me child, did you see any slaves in this vision?"

Legacy replied, "No ma'am. Not one."

Hattie Mae said, "Is that all you saw?"

Legacy hesitated then said, "Yes, ma'am."

Hattie Mae felt like Legacy was holding a piece of that vision back. Whatever Legacy saw she didn't want to tell Hattie Mae.

Right now Hattie Mae wasn't too concerned with it.

However, she was concerned about how she was going to break the news of her leaving for America to DeMarco.

Legacy said, "It's going to break DeMarco's heart. Mama Hattie Mae, you have to know he's in love with you."

Hattie Mae sighed and laid her head on the pillow.

Hattie Mae said, "I know you plan on coming with me to America. The only question is. Can you handle it?"

Legacy replied, "I can handle it. Like you always say Mama Hattie Mae, my visions are never wrong. So I'll look at this as just one step closer to happiness."

It was settled; Mistress Mattie, Hattie Mae, Legacy and Collin Fo'Rae were going to New York.

Savannah, her girls and Pierre Cordova were staying in France.

Icy agreed to stay and help Savannah and take care of Hattie Mae's wolves.

DeMarco was furious when Hattie Mae told him she'd be canceling their journey. He got so angry he flipped over all the tables in Hattie Mae's shop and knocked everything to the floor. He had a full-blown tantrum and wept on the floor like a child.

After his tantrum, he composed himself, apologized for his outrages behavior and left.

Icy told Hattie Mae that DeMarco had locked himself in his house and refused to have visitors. Icy said she'd never seen him act like that. She said his behavior was worse than all the nightmares he always had.

Hattie Mae felt bad, so, she created him a bracelet with a protection spell on it to keep the nightmares away.

In the weeks it took to prepare for the trip to America, Hattie Mae didn't hear from DeMarco.

The night before she was scheduled to leave, Hattie Mae went to DeMarco's house, but he never came to the door.

Hattie Mae said her goodbyes through the door. She laid the bracelet she made for him on the doorstep.

She was sure DeMarco heard her. As she walked off, Hattie Mae heard glass shattering.

Hattie Mae said her goodbyes to her wolf companions.

That morning, all Savannah's children came to say goodbye to Hattie Mae.

Hattie Mae went to Savannah's room to say her goodbyes. Hattie Mae heard Pierre Cordova wishing for a boy. He said with all those girls he had no one to carry on his last name. Hattie Mae felt sorry for him. She knew she was responsible for him not having a son.

As Hattie Mae said her goodbyes to Savannah, she rubbed Savannah's stomach and said, "May the ancestors bless you with a strong, healthy baby boy."

In that instance, Hattie Mae felt the energy of the ancestors flow through her fingertips into Savannah's stomach. Hattie Mae was sure Savannah felt it too because Savannah looked at Hattie Mae and said, "Thank you, mama."

Hattie Mae looked at Savannah; she was as beautiful as ever. Hattie Mae's soul told her it would be a long time before she laid eyes on Savannah again. However, Hattie Mae's soul was at peace. She knew Savannah was in the right place with the right people.

Hattie Mae saw DeMarco in the yard talking to Legacy.

Hattie Mae ran down the stairs and out of the door to talk to him. But when she got there, he was gone.

Legacy told Hattie Mae that DeMarco wished her well and that he couldn't bear to see her.

Hattie Mae felt pain in her heart. Hattie Mae loved DeMarco, but The States called out to her. She knew America was where she was supposed to be.

Legacy looked at Hattie Mae and said, "Love, it's an odd thing. Folks say it's supposed to make you feel good, but I beg to differ. It seems to only cause pain!"

Hattie Mae never said a word. She was struggling with her feelings. Robert Lee was dead, she felt something in her heart for DeMarco, but clearly this was the wrong time for it, and then something in the states was calling her spirit."

Hattie Mae sat in the carriage and hung the curtains back so that she could see out of the window. She was disappointed that she didn't get to say her goodbyes to DeMarco.

Legacy sat on top of the carriage with Collin Fo'Rae and the driver.

Mistress Mattie sat in the carriage across from Hattie Mae.

As Hattie Mae looked out of the window, she saw the male wolf running fast up on the hill. Hattie could have sworn she saw a man on a horse alongside her wolf.

Hattie Mae set up to get a closer look.

Sure enough, she saw DeMarco riding a black horse really fast trying to catch up with the carriage.

Mistress Mattie leaned over and said, "Hattie Mae, must your friend be so dramatic? I mean, does he really have to make such a scene? He could have simply opened the damn door last night when you went to his house."

Mistress Mattie signaled the carriage to stop.

Hattie Mae pushed the door open and stood there.

DeMarco jumped off his horse and ran to Hattie Mae. He scooped her up in his arms.

Mistress Mattie rolled her eyes and said, "Lord, why?"

DeMarco couldn't help himself. He kissed Hattie Mae on her lips.

Hattie Mae held DeMarco in her arms.

DeMarco said, "Please forgive me Madame Fo'Rae, I could no longer control myself. I do apologize if I've offended you in any way. I was a fool for ignoring you these past weeks. My love for you cannot allow you to leave without laying eyes on you one more time."

Hattie Mae replied, "You say that as if you'll never see me again."

DeMarco looked up at the carriage at Legacy then down at his arm. He was wearing the bracelet Hattie Mae made for him to keep the nightmares away.

Then he looked back at Hattie Mae.

DeMarco said, "My love, when souls truly connect, it's forever. However, sometimes the timing is off. Lucky for us, I have all the time in the world. Madame Fo'Rae, I promise I will love you for a thousand lifetimes and I will have you, if not in this lifetime, then in the next. Your body may die, but your spirit never will. The best thing about love, it knows no time or color."

Hattie Mae felt DeMarco's words touch her heart. She knew that this lifetime wasn't for them, but this moment was one she'd remember for the rest of her life.

As the boat pulled off from the harbor, Hattie Mae took a good look at France. She soaked in all the sounds and smells of France. She stored all her memories of DeMarco away in a pocket in her mind. The love she had for him would never die, but for now, it would have to wait. Something in America was pulling at her soul.

Chapter Seventeen:
New York City

Mistress Mattie, Collin Fo'Rae, Legacy and Hattie Mae finally arrived in New York. They were exhausted from traveling. The boat ride seemed to be taking a toll on Mistress Mattie.

Mistress Mattie was very quiet as they traveled to the house where Young Charles and his new bride lived.

Hattie Mae found that to be odd. She thought Mistress Mattie would be bursting with joy. Mistress Mattie hadn't seen Young Charles in at least two years. Hattie Mae figured that Mistress Mattie was still a little pissed because Young Charles didn't tell her that he was getting married.

New York was different from the places Hattie Mae had been before. The roads were crowded with people selling what seemed to be everything.

As they arrived at Young Charles' residence, a woman telling them that Young Charles and his wife had a prior dinner engagement and would be meeting them after dinner, greeted them. She showed them to their rooms and told them anything they needed, they should just ask. Everybody freshened up and waited for Young Charles and his bride.

After Hattie Mae put her things away, she went to check on Legacy. She wanted to talk with her before Young Charles arrived.

Hattie Mae found Legacy in the garden sitting in the grass. It appeared she was meditating.

Hattie Mae sat in the grass next to her.

Hattie Mae said, "You feel it too, don't you?"

Legacy replied, "Yes, the spirits here are so strong. They won't let me rest."

Hattie Mae looked at Legacy and said, "She's here."

Legacy responded, "I know, and so does Mistress Mattie. I believe she saw her on the ship. That's why she's been so quiet. However, I don't believe

Sara, whom I prefer to call Baby Girl One, came to frighten Mistress Mattie."

Hattie Mae replied, "Well, maybe not, but I do believe Sara; whom I also like to call Baby Girl One, gets a big kick out of doing so. However, what do you think she wants?"

Legacy replied, "Freedom, just like the slaves. Her life was taken from her too soon. She never had a chance at life. Her soul cannot rest with the ancestors. Whatever her purpose in life was, she did not fulfill it, yet. So she lingers on. Waiting for another opportunity to come back."

Hattie Mae stood up. She turned around to see Young Charles and his pregnant bride walking towards them.

Hattie Mae looked at the pregnant bride's stomach and said, "Looks like Baby Girl One found a way back."

Legacy looked up at Hattie Mae and replied, "Maybe!"

Young Charles ran to Hattie Mae like a little child. He was so happy to see her.

Young Charles was even more handsome than Hattie Mae had remembered. It seemed that the army had toughened him up and aged him a little. He no longer looked like a cute little boy. He was a full-grown man. He had gotten a few inches taller and put on a few pounds of muscle and, although he was not raised in The South, all those years of Mistress Mattie training him to be a proper southern gentleman had paid off. Young Charles was dazzling.

Young Charles looked at Legacy. He just stared at her. Hattie Mae almost felt like she'd have to intervene if Young Charles didn't take his eyes off her. Young Charles seemed to be at a loss for words at the sight of Legacy. He just stood there looking at her.

Until his bride said, "You must be Mama Hattie Mae. Charles has told me all about you. He loves you so."

At the sound of his wife's voice, Young Charles seemed to snap back.

Young Charles smiled and said, "Yes, this is the one and only Mama Hattie Mae, also known as Madame Fo'Rae the Voodoo Queen of St. Lucia."

Hattie Mae got a strong sense of deceitful energy from Young Charles's wife. Something about her didn't sit well in Hattie Mae's spirit.

Then Young Charles looked over at Legacy and said, "And this is her granddaughter Legacy."

Young Charles' wife looked Legacy up and down; she walked towards Legacy and hugged her.

Hattie Mae could have sworn Young Charles's wife whispered something in Legacy's ear and the expression on Legacy's face confirmed it.

Young Charles' wife stepped back to get a better look at Legacy.

Young Charles wife said sarcastically, "So, this is your best friend Legacy from St. Lucia. In all your wonderful stories of her, my love, you never seemed to mention how beautiful she was."

Young Charles looked at Legacy and back at his wife.

Young Charles said, "Yes she is beautiful inside and out. She's also very smart and a gifted healer.

Young Charles grabbed Hattie Mae's hand and said, "Come, Mama Hattie Mae, we have so much to catch up on."

Hattie Mae said, "Have you seen your mother yet?"

Young Charles replied, "Why of course I have. She's as lovely as ever. Full of questions and judgment as usual."

Young Charles pulled on to Hattie Mae's dress and said, "Please save me from her Mama Hattie Mae. You know she could be overwhelming at times. And my poor wife, Mama Hattie Mae, you know she is no match for my mother's sharp tongue and wicked ways. You should have seen the cold way my mother greeted her, as if she were scum beneath her feet."

Hattie Mae smiled and said, "I see the wicked witch is feeling better."

Hattie Mae promised Young Charles she would talk to Mistress Mattie about her attitude towards Young Charles's wife. However, Hattie Mae feared it wouldn't do any good. Mistress Mattie had been obsessed with Young Charles since his birth, and nothing or nobody was going to change that. In Mistress Mattie's mind, she was the center of Young Charles' world and that was that.

Collin Fo'Rae seemed to be impressed with Young Charles. The look of pride on Collin Fo'Rae's face was priceless. It was as if Young Charles was his very own son instead of his nephew.

Hattie Mae spoke with Mistress Mattie about her behavior. Of course, Mistress Mattie pretended she didn't have a clue as to what Hattie Mae was speaking about. Nevertheless, Mistress Mattie promised to behave.

Hattie Mae finally got around to asking Legacy what Young Charles' wife whispered in her ear.

Legacy said, "She whispered, 'He's mine.'"

Hattie Mae stepped back in disbelief.

Hattie Mae replied, "Well, that hateful little heffa."

Legacy smiled and responded, "Don't worry. I can handle her. Besides, she'll be too busy defending herself against Mistress Mattie to be concerned with me."

Hattie Mae and Legacy both laughed because they knew Mistress Mattie was going to be a handful.

The next day, Young Charles had his servants prepare a feast. He said he was celebrating the return of his family and the new addition to the family. Young Charles kept looking at Hattie Mae.

Before dinner, they all gathered in the living room. Everyone looked so beautiful, especially Legacy. She had on the prettiest yellow dress and gold jewelry Hattie Mae had ever seen. Legacy had twisted her hair into braids and added beautiful seashells.

Hattie Mae smiled. She figured Legacy added an extra touch just to make Young Charles wife a little more jealous than she already was.

Legacy said the dress and the jewelry were gifts from Young Charles. He had them delivered to the house earlier. Young Charles said he had dresses for Hattie Mae and Mistress Mattie also, however, since they were still grieving, he'd wait for a later time to give it to them.

Mistress Mattie and Hattie Mae stood next to the fireplace dressed in all black and, once again, wearing those ridiculous veils.

Hattie Mae was glad Mistress Mattie had hers on because the dreadful look she was giving Young Charles' wife was awful.

Hattie Mae looked at Mistress Mattie and said, "Please try to behave yourself. Your son has invited us into his home. Please try to respect that."

Mistress Mattie replied, "Well, I'll do my best. But can my son behave himself?"

Then Mistress Mattie looked over at Young Charles who was standing in the corner staring at Legacy.

Mistress Mattie said, "Lust, it's a powerful tonic. Hattie Mae, I'm terribly frightened that this visit will not end well."

Hattie Mae said, "Well, you just pray to your Jesus that your precious son can maintain his lust until after we leave."

343

Mistress Mattie replied, "Hmm, we shall see Hattie Mae!"

Young Charles picked up a little bell and rang it. He said, "Please, may I have your attention. I have an announcement to make."

Everyone turned to see what was going on.

Hattie Mae looked at Mistress Mattie and said, "I see Young Charles has developed your love for theatrics."

Young Charles walked over to Hattie Mae. He held up his glass.

Young Charles said, "Madame Fo'Rae, I could never repay you for all the things you've done for me. You've always been there for me. I cannot remember a time when I have not loved you and counted on you. To me, you are family, even though your blood doesn't run through my body. I would give my very life for you. As a boy, you taught me how to love and respect others and myself regardless of their skin color. You taught me how to survive in a hateful world and remain positive of the future. You've loved me unconditionally even when I acted out like a spoiled rotten child. Well, Madame Fo'Rae, I've grown into a man now, but I still hold that place in my heart for you. I still love you as if I were that little boy in St. Lucia, waiting on the road for you to come visit. There is no way I can ever repay you."

Hattie Mae felt a sense of pride in her heart. Although Young Charles wasn't her son, he was Robert Lee's and Hattie Mae loved him.

Hattie Mae didn't know what to say.

Young Charles smiled and said, "You taught me that family is everything."

Young Charles leaned over and kissed his mother, Mistress Mattie. Then he kissed Hattie Mae.

Young Charles looked at his pregnant wife and said, "As I eagerly wait for the gift of life to bless my home, I have I gift for you, Madame Fo'Rae, a gift of life that was stolen from you long years ago. The good Lord has blessed this house tonight with a special person."

Hattie Mae was confused. She didn't know what the hell was going on.

Young Charles said, "On the battlefield I met some amazing people. And, sadly, I lost some amazing people. One of those people I lost was an amazing man named Robert Lee."

Hattie Mae looked at Mistress Mattie who was looking like she was about to faint.

Mistress Mattie grabbed hold of Hattie Mae's hand and said, "My Lord Hattie Mae, has Young Charles been drinking? Lord, please don't let his speech turn out like the one he gave at my wedding. We both know that was a catastrophe."

Hattie Mae just held on to Mistress Mattie. They didn't know where Young Charles's speech was leading up to. Hell Robert Lee was dead and, unless Young Charles had the gift to bring life back, Hattie Mae didn't know how he was going to repay her with the gift of life.

Young Charles said, "After Robert Lee was killed in battle, I received a letter. In the letter the man spoke of Robert Lee as a friend. He said he'd spent his last days with Robert Lee; while he was dying, Robert Lee spoke of his family. The man said in their conversation, they figured out they had something in common."

Young Charles looked at Hattie Mae and smiled.

Young Charles said, "That man said he would like to meet me one day. So when I came to New York, I arranged a meeting with him."

Young Charles seemed to be very impressed with himself. He was like a kid in a candy store. Whatever he wanted to say was bursting to get out.

Young Charles continued. He said, "So, in honor of Madame Fo'Rae and all she has done for my family and me, I've invited a special guest to dinner this evening."

Young Charles looked at the maid and said, "Please show our special guest to the living room."

Mistress Mattie clutched her pearls and said, "Oh my how I fucking hate surprises."

Hattie Mae just stood there. She couldn't imagine who could possibly be that special, especially to her. Hell everybody she loved was in France or standing in that room.

Young Charles stood next to Hattie Mae as the gentleman entered the room.

Young Charles smiled and said, "Madame, allow me to present to you, Doctor Claude Fo'Rae."

Hattie Mae felt her body go frozen. It was as if she was stuck to that spot. Her heart was filled with love. She couldn't move. "Dr. Claude Fo'Rae," Hattie Mae mumbled.

Young Charles said, "Yes, your son that was stolen from you at birth."

Claude Fo'Rae walked towards Hattie Mae.

Hattie Mae didn't know what to do. She looked over at Mistress Mattie, who was still holding Hattie Mae's hand.

Mistress Mattie walked Hattie Mae closer to Claude Fo'Rae.

Claude Fo'Rae was the spitting image of Savannah.

Hattie Mae smiled when she thought about Savannah being just a shade lighter than Claude.

Hattie Mae tried to compose herself.

As Claude Fo'Rae put his arms around her and uttered the words "I've always wanted to meet you, Mama."

Hattie Mae fell apart. Tears ran down her cheeks and the love she felt for her son consumed her. She held on tight to him.

Hattie Mae let him go and backed up.

Hattie Mae said, "My son."

There wasn't a dry eye in the room.

Claude Fo'Rae said, "Mama I've bought some people to meet you."

Claude Fo'Rae called for his family. He said, "Mama this is my wife and my three sons."

Hattie Mae looked at the beautiful lady standing in front of her and the three small children, one who the wife held in her arms.

Hattie Mae had a feeling she'd never experienced before. She never in life thought she'd see her son again.

Hattie Mae said, "Please tell me how all of this is possible."

Claude Fo'Rae said, "Well, when the war started signing Negros up, I signed up to use my skills as a doctor for the Negro troops. While I was working, I met your husband Robert Lee, who had the exact sir name as me "Fo'Rae." Through our conversation, we figured out his wife, Hattie Mae FoRae was my mother. In his last days, he told me all about you. How your family had escaped to freedom. How you were this powerful Voodoo Queen."

Claude Fo'Rae smiled and said, "I guess that's where I get the gift of medicine from."

Claude Fo'Rae told Hattie Mae about how he was raised by a couple of free Negros and all about his life in New York. He said he'd gone to medical school and met his wife. Hattie Mae was trying to soak all of what he said in. Hattie Mae felt faint. She stood by the fireplace to warm herself. Claude Fo'Rae handed Hattie Mae a leather bag with all Robert Lee's belongings in it.

Claude Fo'Rae said, "I promised him I would find you. That's how I found Charles Fo'Rae who told me all the wonderful stories of his childhood."

Hattie Mae stood there looking at the fire, and she said, "Son I'm sorry I wasn't there for you as a child like I was for Young Charles."

Claude Fo'Rae replied, "No, you need not apologize to me. I've had a full happy life. I have a wife and children who love me. The people whom I refer to as mother and father gave me all the love and knowledge they had. My dear mother, Claude Fo'Rae, my natural father, did me a favor when he left me with them. I hold no animosity or malice towards you. I only desire to know you."

Hattie Mae smiled and said, "So, it shall be."

Hattie Mae stood by the fire and watched Claude Fo'Rae and his family interact with Legacy and the rest of the Fo'Rae bunch.

Legacy came over and stood by Hattie Mae. Legacy smiled and said, "Brace yourself, Madame Fo'Rae. This is getting ready to get extremely good!"

Hattie Mae looked at Legacy and replied, "Whatever are you talking about child?"

Before Hattie Mae could finish her sentence, she heard Claude Fo'Rae say, "Madame Fo'Rae, I would like for you to meet someone else."

Hattie Mae assumed he wanted her to meet his parents that raised him. Hattie Mae was okay with that. She wanted to thank them for raising such a strong man.

Hattie Mae said, "Please tell me you brought your parents. I'd like to thank them."

Claude Fo'Rae replied, "Well, my mother died a few years ago. She was a God-fearing woman who loved the Lord, but I did bring my father. My father has been my rock; he taught me everything I know. He taught me how to love, how to be a great warrior and to respect my ancestors."

Hattie Mae was a little shocked by Claude's words. She said, "Your ancestors? What do you know about your ancestors?"

Hattie Mae figured Claude Fo'Rae was raised to believe in God since he said that his mother was a God-fearing woman.

Claude Fo'Rae smiled and said, "My mother was a God-fearing Christian. However, my father didn't believe in her God. He believed in the ancestors of his people, and he taught me all about them. He's here, and I would love for you to meet him."

Hattie Mae shook her head yes and said, "I would love to meet your father."

Claude Fo'Rae left the room to retrieve his father, who was standing outside.

Legacy stood right next to Hattie Mae. Hattie Mae knew she was avoiding Young Charles.

Claude Fo'Rae came into the room. He had a tall very handsome gentleman with him.

Claude Fo'Rae said, "Please allow me to introduce my father, Bactou."

Hattie Mae couldn't believe her eyes and ears. She gasped for breath and fell to the floor. Legacy bent down to help her up, but Hattie Mae couldn't compose herself. She just kneeled there on her hands and knees.

Hattie Mae closed her eyes and said to herself, *Oh great spirits from the beyond, please don't deceive my eyes and ears.*

Tears washed Hattie Mae's face.

Claude Fo'Rae said, "Allow me to help you. Please forgive me, Mama, I didn't mean to overwhelm you. I beg your forgiveness."

Hattie Mae pulled herself together and mumbled, "Please bring your father to me!"

Claude Fo'Rae replied, "Yes, but please allow me to help you to your feet first!"

Hattie Mae took a deep breath and slowly composed herself.
Hattie Mae's lips trembled, she said, "Please bring your father to me."

Mistress Mattie walked over to Hattie Mae in utter disgust and whispered, "Hattie Mae, this is no way to behave in front of company. Please rise to your feet and conduct yourself in a civilized manner."

Then Mistress Mattie bent down to Hattie Mae and smiled. She said, "I do declare you have got to be the luckiest women in the entire world. I must admit I'm powerfully jealous. Yes, I do remember your true love's name and if I'm not mistaken that delicious specimen of a man standing over there is him. I don't know how, but the good Lord himself has delivered him to you."

Claude Fo'Rae brought Bactou in front of Hattie Mae, who was still on her hands and knees.

Bactou said, "I'm sorry, ma'am, if my presence has offended you in any way. I will leave if that's your wish."

Hattie Mae arose to her feet. She gathered herself together.

Hattie Mae looked at Bactou standing there looking like the brave warrior she remembered him to be. He had aged well. He was beautiful. His skin was a dark colored brown, he had deep eyes and full lips and a strong nose.

The hints of grey hair around his temples amplified his attractiveness. He spoke with the accent of her homeland. Hattie Mae had to catch herself from reaching out to grab him. In that instance, the love she felt for Robert

Lee and DeMarco was overshadowed by the love she'd held in her heart for Bactou all these years. She thought he was dead. How could he be standing in front of her?

Hattie Mae said, "No, I could never send you away my fearless warrior."

The sound of Hattie Mae's voice seemed to confuse Bactou.

Hattie Mae said, "Long years ago in a country far away from here, two young innocent souls were snatched from their homeland. They snuck away from their village. One was a young, fearless warrior who was in pain, the other a young girl who practiced medicine. Some white men captured them. A ship carried them across the ocean headed for America. The warrior got loose and tried to free the girl. When he couldn't, he jumped overboard to his death. Or so the young girl thought."

The entire room was silent. You could hear the pounding of Hattie Mae's heart. Tears ran down Bactou's face.

Hattie Mae said, "Tell me how that warrior could be standing at my feet on this day?"

Bactou stumbled back in confusion. He slowly replied, "That warrior fell into the sea, not jumped. The ocean was strong and it swiftly carried him miles away from the ship. He felt as if he would drown to death on that very day. He drifted on a piece of wood that had fallen off the ship with him. He prayed for the ancestors to have mercy on his soul. Then he passed out. He woke up on the shores of what the Americans called South Carolina. A group of white Christians found him. Apparently, they did not believe in slavery. They hid him in their wagon and took him to New York.

There they taught him how to read and write in English. They gave him a job as a woodcutter. He lived on their property for three years until he met a young lady he was taken with. However, he held another love in his heart for the young girl who he left behind on the ship. For many years, he made secret trips to the south to find her, but with no luck. Everyone told him he would never find her. They told him awful stories about the south. Stories he witnessed first-hand on his secret trips. He prayed that the ancestors had taken her life and spared her such humiliation. One day, when he came back from one of his trips, his wife told him a strange white man had given her a baby. He had a tag on his toe that said, "Claude Fo'Rae, Jr." We raised him as our own. After my wife had our first baby, she begged me to stop looking for this young lady I longed for. Over the years, I never forgot her. I've prayed to the ancestors to bring her to me every day!"

Hattie Mae lifted the veil to reveal her face.

Hattie Mae softly said, "The ancestors have heard your cries and have brought me to you."

Hattie Mae slowly rubbed her hands across Bactou's face.

Hattie Mae said, "My brave warrior, it is I, the one you've sought for so many years."

Bactou fell to his knees at Hattie Mae's feet.

Bactou said, "This is but a dream. You cannot be real. I've questioned every runaway slave I ever encountered; I've searched the entire country for you. How can this be?"

Bactou cried out to the ancestors to remove such a cruel illusion from his sight.

Hattie Mae bent down and rubbed Bactou's face. She said, "I am no illusion. I am here. Flesh and blood and the ancestors have played no tricks. They have brought us together on this day. And for that, I'm truly thankful."

Bactou threw his arms around Hattie Mae, and they both sat on the floor and cried.

Mistress Mattie walked over to Hattie Mae and Bactou on the floor crying together.

Mistress Mattie looked at Hattie Mae with those big blue, piercing eyes and bucked them out.

Mistress Mattie said sarcastically, "Such a riveting tale. However, you do realize there are other people in this room with you. Would you two like some privacy?"

Collin Fo'Rae said, "Yes, that's a good idea, let's all give them a moment."

Everyone cleared the room and Hattie Mae and Bactou just laid on the floor together.

After dinner, Mistress Mattie insisted that Hattie Mae retire to her room. Mistress Mattie said that Hattie Mae had an extremely emotional day and she needed to rest.

Hattie Mae hated to agree with Mistress Mattie. However, Mistress Mattie was right she was exhausted. Hattie Mae hated to say goodbye to Bactou: In fear she'd never see him again.

Mistress Mattie fixed that. She insisted that Bactou spend the night in one of the guest rooms. She said it was no way that Hattie Mae could get any proper rest if she was worrying about not seeing him again. Mistress Mattie rushed Hattie Mae away after she said her goodnights to the family.

As Mistress Mattie and Hattie Mae walked to Hattie Mae's room, Mistress Mattie said, "Walk fast, keep your head down and don't look in the mirrors."

Hattie Mae was silent until she got to the room. When they entered the room, Mistress Mattie took a dark towel and covered the mirror that was over the face bowl in Hattie Mae's room.

Hattie Mae said, "What in the world is going on?"

Mistress Mattie was shaking like a leaf.

Mistress Mattie pointed to the mirror and said, "I saw him."

Hattie Mae was confused.

She said, "You saw who?"

Mistress Mattie whispered, "Master Fo'Rae. I saw him, here in this house in the mirror in the hallway. He was there looking."

Hattie Mae replied, "Are you sure? Or are you just imagining that because we are back in the states?"

Mistress Mattie said, "Hattie Mae, as sure as I sit here I tell you I seen him. When I was talking to that piece of trash my son calls his wife, she was standing with her back to the mirror rubbing that hideous baby bump, and I saw two reflections. Master Fo'Rae's and hers."

Mistress Mattie seemed to be terrified.

Hattie Mae said, "How many times do I have to tell you that you never have to fear the dead. They can not hurt you."

Mistress Mattie replied, "Yes, but whatever could he want in this house. Nobody here loves him. Not even his brother Collin Fo'Rae."

Hattie Mae had an idea of what he wanted, but she couldn't understand how he thought he could get away with it.

Hattie Mae sat up with Mistress Mattie until she fell asleep.

Right before Mistress Mattie fell asleep, she said, "Madame Fo'Rae, do not look into the mirrors. Even when you sneak off to be with your beautiful lover Bactou."

Hattie Mae rolled her eyes at Mistress Mattie and replied, "I'm not you, and I would never do such a thing. I have way to much respect for myself."

Mistress Mattie responded, "Well, I tell you what. If I'd lost half of my life to slavery, lost a husband that loved me more than himself, and lost a good-looking man like Demarco only to discover that the love of my life, whom I thought was dead was actually alive and had been searching for me for years, laid sleeping two doors down, I'd say to hell with proper etiquette and go get my man. But, that's just me. You sleep tight with your self-respect. Let's see how warm that keeps you."

Hattie Mae just rolled her eyes at Mistress Mattie and covered her head.

After hours of not being able to sleep, Hattie Mae couldn't help herself. She sneaked out of bed and went to Bactou. He welcomed her with open arms. No words were spoken. They'd already done enough talking.

Hattie Mae had to admit that Mistress Mattie was most definitely right. Sleeping next to Bactou was the best thing ever. Bactou was an amazing lover.

In the wee hours of the morning, Hattie Mae snuck back into her room. Only to find Mistress Mattie wide-awake with a bottle of wine, two wine glasses, and two cigars.

Mistress Mattie smiled at Hattie Mae and said, "Why you little tramp."

Mistress Mattie patted the chair and said, "Do come sit and chat with me. Tell me all about your rendezvous with the love of your life."

Chapter Eighteen:
Welcome Back

Over the weeks, Bactou and Hattie Mae grew closer. Hattie Mae had never experienced love like that. They planned on marrying after Hattie Mae's year of mourning was over.

Hattie Mae and her son Claude Fo'Rae were developing a beautiful relationship. However, the war wasn't over and Hattie Mae knew both her son and Young Charles had to go back to the battlefield. This made no sense at all since President Lincoln had already freed the slaves; the only problem was they didn't know yet.

Hattie Mae missed Savannah dearly. However, Savannah had refused to come to America. Savannah wrote that she'd given birth to a healthy baby boy. She also said that DeMarco disappeared the day Hattie Mae left. Hattie Mae remembered what DeMarco said to her about not having her in this life, but he shall have her in another. It was almost like he knew she wouldn't return to him. Hattie Mae also remembered him talking to Legacy the day they left. Plus Hattie Mae thought about what Legacy said the night Bactou came back.

Hattie Mae went to find Legacy. She knew Legacy was keeping a secret.

As Hattie Mae walked through the house looking for Legacy, she thought about why Master Fo'Rae might be lingering around in the mirrors. The only thing she could think of was he was trying to get back through Young Charles' unborn child. The ancestors believed that if you die without learning your lesson or fulfilling your purpose in life, you have to come back. The only way to get back was to be reborn. Hattie Mae figured Master Fo'Rae was trying to be reborn through Young Charles' unborn child. However, Hattie Mae had a strange feeling that Baby Girl One, now known as Sara, had the same idea.

Hattie Mae found Legacy writing in her journals.

Hattie Mae said, "One day someone's going to read those and think us foolish for sure."

Legacy laughed and replied, "Well, only an outsider without the gift would think us foolish."

Hattie Mae laughed and said, "This is an amazing life we seem to have, despite all the struggles."

Legacy replied, "I would agree."

Hattie Mae sat next to Legacy and said, "I often write about DeMarco and my encounters with him. Do you ever write about him?"

Legacy replied, "Not really, well maybe just a small section is about him."

Hattie Mae said, "Did you write about the last conversation you had with him?"

Legacy smiled at Hattie Mae and said, "If you want to know what I told him the last time I spoke with him, it's simple; I told him that I'd seen your future and he wasn't a part of it. His response to me was that maybe he wasn't a part of your future in this lifetime. He said he'd wait a thousand years to love you. He backed away gracefully."

Hattie Mae said, "Oh, well please tell me what you saw."

Legacy said, "I saw you living a wonderful life with Bactou; Happier than you've ever been. I saw me with Charles and our children. I've also seen some ugly things Madame Fo'Rae. Just because the slaves are free means nothing; some things will never change."

Hattie Mae replied, "Well, enough about what might be. Let's talk about what is. Mistress Mattie swears she saw Master Fo'Rae in the mirror."

Legacy responded, "She did, even though I never met him, I can feel his spirit. But, don't worry he will never enter this world again, At least not through a baby. Babies are innocent. Only the pure at heart can come back through a baby."

Hattie Mae got a glimpse of Young Charles' wife walking through the house. It seemed she was always talking with the Negro servants: one in particular, a young cook who happened to be a strong young buck.

Hattie Mae said, "Speaking of pure at heart. What do you think of Mrs. Fo'Rae?"

Legacy replied, "I don't think anything of her. She's irrelevant as far as I'm concerned. All her ways will soon be revealed."

Hattie Mae sat with Legacy for a while. Legacy was such a humble young lady. As powerful as she was, all she wanted to do was help others. She spent hours on the streets curing the poor with Hattie Mae.

Mistress Mattie was finally out of her mourning period. It was so nice to see her back to her usual southern bell charms.

Mistress Mattie had already snatched for herself a proper gentleman caller.

Hattie Mae was never amazed at how fast Mistress Mattie snagged a man. In weeks after courting him, Mistress Mattie announced that they would be married.

Collin Fo'Rae was reunited with his lover. It seems he couldn't live without her. He kept her hidden away as usual, while he plotted and schemed Young Charles' future. He was dead set on Young Charles becoming something political. Young Charles wife's daddy was a political man with a lot of power.

Young Charles and Hattie Mae had several discussions on what they would do if the baby his wife was carrying were to come out Negro. The possibility was strong seeing Young Charles was half Negro. Young Charles had concluded that if the baby were to come out Negro, they would tell his wife the baby died minutes after it was born. Young Charles planned to give the child to Hattie Mae's son Claude Fo'Rae to raise as his own. Claude Fo'Rae and his wife went along with the plan, as well as the rest of the Fo'Rae's. The plan was, if the baby came out Negro, Hattie Mae would fix Young Charles' wife so that she couldn't have any more babies. Hattie Mae was hesitant about that plan. She felt like it was cruel to do such a thing. They were already going to steal her baby if it came out Negro.

Hattie Mae told Young Charles's wife that when the time came to have the baby, only she and Hattie Mae could be in the room. Hattie Mae told her that too many people would put the baby at risk of contracting diseases. Young Charles' wife went along with the idea with no argument. She even suggested that they hold off telling her parents she was in labor until after the baby was born. Young Charles' wife said that her parents would only fuss over her and make the delivery more stressful.

Hattie Mae had a strange feeling that Young Charles's wife's reasoning for her parents not being there when she had the baby was not the entire truth. However, Hattie Mae went along with it.

One morning, Hattie Mae woke up to find all the servants gone. Legacy said Young Charles's wife had told them to leave. Mistress Mattie was out with her gentleman caller and Young Charles was pacing back and forth in the hallway.

Young Charles told Hattie Mae that he believed his wife was in labor. However, she wouldn't allow him in the room.

Hattie Mae went into the room where Mrs. Fo'Rae was in the bed apparently suffering from labor pains. Hattie Mae had a feeling something was going on. Mrs. Fo'Rae had at least another month before she was supposed to deliver.

Hattie Mae called for Legacy to bring her hot water and towels. It was evident that this baby was coming today.

As Hattie Mae wiped Mrs. Fo'Rae's head, she saw Baby Girl One, now known as Sara, looking at them through the mirror.

Hattie Mae looked at Baby Girl One, now known as Sara, and said, "If you plan on coming through this baby, I suggest you come now. This baby is coming soon.

Baby Girl One shook her head back and forth as if she was saying "No."

Hattie Mae didn't have time to chat with Baby Girl One. That baby was coming. The baby's head was crowning.

Hattie Mae looked back in the mirror to see Master Fo'Rae looking at her and laughing.

Master Fo'Rae said devilishly, "Good old Hattie Mae, I'll be seeing you real soon."

Then he smiled and disappeared.
Just like Hattie Mae had suspected, Master Fo'Rae was trying to come back through Young Charles' baby.

Hattie Mae screamed for Legacy. Hattie Mae told Legacy what she had seen. However, Legacy didn't seem worried.

Hattie Mae put a wooden spoon in Mrs. Fo'Rae's mouth and told her to bite down and push.

After two strong pushes, Mrs. Fo'Rae pushed out a big Negro baby girl.

Legacy looked at Hattie Mae, and Hattie Mae gave the signal for Legacy to put the smelling sauce under Mrs. Fo'Rae's nose. It would knock her out for a few minutes until Hattie Mae and Legacy could get the baby out of there.

Hattie Mae had to laugh. She looked at Legacy and said, "Well, one thing is for sure, Master Fo'Rae came back as his favorite thing on the planet, a Negro girl." Both ladies laughed.

Hattie Mae cleaned the baby up and was about to fix Mrs. FoRae so she couldn't have any more babies, when Legacy convinced her not to.

Hattie Mae and Legacy laid the baby in the bassinet next to the bed. Hattie Mae figured that Mrs. Fo'Rae would be out for at least a couple of hours.

That gave her time to get that baby girl to Claude Fo'Rae and get her story together. Hattie Mae's story was going to be that the baby was born stillborn and deformed. She was going to tell Mrs. Fo'Rae that it was best that she never saw it.

Hattie Mae and Legacy went to get the plan in motion. Young Charles went to say his goodbyes to his daughter.

Hattie Mae heard a scream from Young Charles that rocked her to her knees.

Hattie Mae took off running to the room.

Young Charles was standing there crying, and his wife was standing there holding a pillow.

Hattie Mae looked over to see the lifeless baby girl lying in the bassinet.

Hattie Mae didn't know what to think. Legacy said, "Would someone like to tell me what happened."

Young Charles could barely speak.

He said, "I walked in to check on the baby, and I found her standing there over the baby with that pillow. She put the pillow over the baby's face and killed her."

Young Charles fell to the ground.

He screamed, "Why would you do such a thing? How could you?"

What Mrs. Fo'Rae said next blew Hattie Mae away.

Young Charles wife coldly said, "That nigger baby is disgusting."

Hattie Mae was about to say something when Legacy looked at Hattie Mae and said, "Let the truth reveal itself!"

Hattie Mae stood there.

Mrs. Fo'Rae walked over to Young Charles and put on her best crying act. She said, "I didn't want to tell you this, but the cook forced himself on me. I was so scared I didn't know what to do."

Hattie Mae remembered all the times she'd seen Mrs. Fo'Rae talking with the cook. It didn't seem like he would do such a thing.

Legacy said, "Are you sure he forced himself on you?"

Mrs. Fo'Rae stood up. She had the same deceitful look Mistress Mattie always had when she'd done some God awful thing.

Mrs. Fo'Rae replied, "How dare you call me a liar. He raped me and put this awful monstrosity inside me."

Mrs. Fo'Rae looked at Young Charles, who was still sitting on the floor with his head in his lap.

Mrs. Fo'Rae said, "My love, we can get through this. We don't have to tell anyone. It could be our secret. We can always have another baby."

Young Charles stood up. He said, "And what do you suggest we do with the cook who raped you?"

Mrs. Fo'Rae said, "We don't want to involve anyone else. We'll just send him on his way and keep this between us. No one has to know. We'll tell everyone I miscarried. No one will be the wiser. I just want to put all this behind us."

The look of rage on Young Charles' face was frightening. It sent chills down Hattie Mae's spine.

Young Charles raced towards his wife. He grabbed her by the neck and squeezed his thumb in her throat. She was gasping for air.

Young Charles threw her across the room. He screamed, "You dirty, lying

363

low down whore. How dare you lie to my face as if I were a fool? I got the right mind to strangle you with my bare hands. Never would I believe that the cook raped you and you said nothing of it."

Mrs. Fo'Rae looked as if she couldn't believe what was happening. She couldn't believe her lies weren't working with Young Charles.

Mrs. Fo'Rae said, "Are you calling me a liar? Well, I never. You would go against me for a nigger?"

Young Charles got close and in her face.

Young Charles said, "Would it surprise you to know that for years you've been sleeping with a nigger and that nigger baby who you just killed could possibly had been mine?"

Mrs. Fo'Rae's eyes grew big as coins. She said, "What did you say? Lies, I don't believe you. How can you be a nigger?"

Young Charles said, "What does it matter, you are a killer."

Young Charles wrapped the baby up in a blanket.

He turned with the coldest stare. He said, "I want you out of this house and out of my eyesight before nightfall. I don't care where you go or what you do. I never want to set eyes on you again. You disgust me."

Young Charles ran out of the room holding the dead baby in his arms.

Legacy ran behind him leaving just Hattie Mae and Mrs. Fo'Rae in the room.

Hattie Mae looked down at the floor. Mrs. Fo'Rae was standing in a pool of blood.

Hattie Mae calmly said, "It appears that you are losing a lot of blood. I'd suggest you allow me to help you to your bed and stop the bleeding. Or I can take my stuff and be on my nigger way."

Mrs. Fo'Rae stretched out her arms to Hattie Mae.

Hattie Mae helped her to the bed.

Hattie Mae cleaned her up and stopped her bleeding. Hattie Mae gave her some herbs that would help her heal.

Hattie Mae sat next to the bed. She said, "It's clear to me that your heart is not in this marriage and you don't love your husband. So my question is, why did you marry him?"

Mrs. Fo'Rae didn't say a word; she just looked at the wall.

Hattie Mae said, "Well, you're not strong enough to walk to leave this house. So, here is where you will stay until you're better. You don't have to talk to me but, rest assured, you will answer to your husband's mother, Mistress Mattie."

Hattie Mae smiled and said, "Child, you are no match for that woman. This grievous action that you've committed against her son, well, child lets just say you are going to pay dearly for that. It doesn't matter who your father is."

Mrs. Fo'Rae looked at Hattie Mae and said, "What can I do. He hates me."

Hattie Mae said, "Well, first of all, you can pretend like you regret killing your child. I'll work the rest out with Young Charles later. But my advice to you is, stay away from Mistress Mattie."

As Hattie Mae stood in the hallway wrapping her mind around what had just happened, she glanced in the mirror. She saw Sara, formally known as Baby Girl One.

Hattie Mae said, "Did Mister Fo'Rae try to come back through that baby?"

Sara, formally known as Baby Girl One smirked and replied, "Yes he was able to get through, yet it appears he didn't last that long."

Hattie Mae smiled and said, "Apparently not!"

Hattie Mae hurried off to find Young Charles and Legacy. She found them outside on the back porch. They were in a heated conversation. Hattie Mae stood behind the door and listened.

Young Charles looked at Legacy and said, "I blame you! All that has happened is because of you!"

Legacy replied very calmly, "And how is that? I had nothing to do with the lies from your wife!"

Young Charles was furious.

He said, "Don't give me that innocent act. I know you! And I know you saw this in your stupid visions. You could have warned me of what was to come."

Young Charles unwrapped the dead baby girl and kissed her.

He looked back at Legacy and said, "Instead you came here to watch my heart break some more. As if you hadn't broke it and stomped on it years ago. What was this revenge, but why? I chose you years ago. And you chose to run off to France. God only knows what man had you over there."

Young Charles was hysterical. He was holding that dead baby and weeping like a child. He looked just like his crazy mama in that moment.

He said, "You were mine, and you ran off and left me. Now my baby is dead, and my wife is a whore and a monster."

Legacy put her arm around Young Charles' shoulders.

Legacy said, "Surely, you don't believe that!"

Young Charles held the dead baby close to him.

He said, "Surely I do! I hate all of you."

Legacy said, "That's just the hurt and anger talking. You know why I had to leave. I never saw this in my visions. However, you know perfectly well if I had, there was nothing I could do to stop it. I can not stop the future."

Young Charles replied, "You should have stayed and stood up to my mother and Uncle Collin. You should have fought for our love. Instead, you bought in to all the cousin stuff. We are no more cousins than anybody on the street, and you know it. I hate this dysfunctional family. My crazy mama, Mistress Mattie, married her cousin; Master Fo'Rae who stole your grandmother, Mama Hattie Mae from African then raped her for years and had your mama, Savannah. Then he raped his own daughter, Savannah and had you. And in the meantime my crazy Mama, Mistress Mattie, was forcing Hattie Mae's husband, Robert Lee to pleasure her and got pregnant with my sister and me. Then she killed my only sister."

Young Charles was screaming at the top of his lungs, crying and holding that dead baby. Snot and tears were running down his cheeks and spit hanging from his lips.

Young Charles said, "Did you hear how ridiculous that sounds. What kind of family is this? And to top it all off, my crazy mama and Uncle Collin made me pretend like I was white and I married this evil whore who killed my daughter. Now, do you see how this is all your fault?"

Legacy took a deep breath and said, "Now that you put it like that, you might have a point."

Legacy walked over to the outside bar and made both of them a drink.

Legacy said, "I've always loved you. Yes by blood we are cousins. But in the eyes of the world, I'm just a plantation baby and you are the master's son."

Young Charles sipped his drink. He calmed down and said, "Well, we would only be like third generation cousins, and we both know Master Fo'Rae ain't my father."

Legacy smiled and said, "Yes, third generation of a long line of crazy folks."

Young Charles smiled and said, "I really wanted to be a father. I would have loved my daughter."

Legacy replied, "Don't worry, you'll get your chance."

Legacy looked down at the ground.

She said, "And to answer your question about the men in France. Well, they're awfully handsome, but I've never known a man's touch. I've never met one that could replace you in my heart."

Hattie Mae had heard enough. She felt like the conversations they were about to have should be private between them.

Hattie Mae convinced Young Charles to give her the baby and to tell everybody that the baby was stillborn. Hattie Mae told Young Charles that it was best for everyone that people thought that. Hattie Mae promised they'd deal with Mrs. Fo'Rae at a later date.

Hattie Mae took the baby from Young Charles and sent word to Collin Fo'Rae to come to her at once.

Later on, when Mistress Mattie returned, Hattie Mae told Mistress Mattie the story she and Young Charles had agreed on.

Hattie Mae wasn't sure if Mistress Mattie bought it or not, but Mistress Mattie was too busy helping Young Charles through his grief. She didn't have time to dig too deep into the story.

Collin Fo'Rae notified Mrs. Fo'Rae's family about what happened. Collin Fo'Rae told her family he thought it was a good idea if they took her home with them for a while.

Hattie Mae told Collin Fo'Rae exactly what happened, which he used against the girl's father to secure Young Charles top position in the reconstruction of the south movement. Collin Fo'Rae convinced the girl's father that it was in all their best interest if she went away quietly and they dissolved the marriage based on irreconcilable differences.

Hattie Mae was sure somehow Mistress Mattie figured out the real story and took her revenge on Young Charles soon to be ex-wife. During the night on what would be Young Charles ex-wife last night in the house, all her hair seemed to fall out mysteriously, and after drinking her tea, her teeth were stained an awful shade of green.

Apparently, Legacy felt the need to teach her a lesson, too. Because all through the night, all you could hear was a baby crying and objects mysteriously moving around and bumping into walls.

Mrs. Fo'Rae was a nervous wreck the next day. She was crying and mumbling something about, "They did this to me" as she left in the carriage. Mistress Mattie pretended to have sympathy for her. Hattie Mae knew that Mistress Mattie wasn't finished issuing out her revenge on Mrs. Fo'Rae, she was just waiting for a more opportune time. As hateful as Mistress Mattie was, stained teeth and hair wasn't going to be enough. Mistress Mattie was out for blood. It didn't matter how far Mrs. Fo'Rae went, Hattie Mae knew Mistress Mattie was going to have her revenge.

Young Charles was quietly divorced from his wife. Finally, he ended up confessing his love for Legacy once again. This time, Collin Fo'Rae didn't stand in the way. Mistress Mattie was busy with her new husband and Hattie Mae was enjoying life with Bactou.

Hattie Mae never knew such happiness that she experienced with Bactou. She had always feared the best years of her life were gone. However, she now believed she was living the best years of her life.

Collin Fo'Rae moved back to the south to live a nice quiet life with his lover. He said on the Fo'Rae plantation he never had to explain his love for her.

Word finally got down south to the slaves that they were free.

Young Charles often went back and forth to the south on official business with the reconstruction of the south. During those trips, he passed for a white man.

Hattie Mae never stepped one foot in the south and neither did Legacy. The south seemed to be more dangerous than before they freed the slaves.

Legacy was pregnant with her first child and Young Charles was excited as ever, although they couldn't legally marry because Young Charles was still passing for a white man. They jumped the broom and considered themselves married.

As Legacy got bigger, Hattie Mae figured Legacy was having twins, which made perfect sense being that Young Charles was a twin.

Weeks before the birth of Legacy's first child, Savannah and her family came to America. Savannah had six girls and two boys in all, including Legacy.

Savannah said she could never let Legacy have a baby without her. Family should be together. And as much as she hated America, she loved Legacy more.

Hattie Mae was happy she had all her family with her. She had even grown close to her son Claude's children. However, none of them appeared to have the gift yet. But all Savannah's girls had the gift.

Hattie Mae prepared to deliver Legacy's twins. They all braced themselves. They didn't know what to expect. Hell, Legacy was one third Negro and Young Charles was half Negro, which Hattie Mae found to be funny because Young Charles was more Negro than Legacy, but Legacy was the darker one.

As Hattie Mae monitored Legacy's labor pains, she caught a glimpse of Baby Girl One, now known as Sara in the mirror.

Hattie Mae smiled and said, "Well, Baby Girl One, here's your chance. Apparently, you have two choices this time."

Baby Girl One, now known as Sara smiled and disappeared from the mirror.

Hattie Mae felt a strong wind brush past her and Legacy gave a loud scream.

Legacy gave a few pushes, and out popped a baby boy.

Hattie Mae handed the baby to Mistress Mattie.

Mistress Mattie smiled and said, "Well, he ain't too dark."

Hattie Mae just shook head at Mistress Mattie and said, "Dark or not, he is our grandson!"

Mistress Mattie smiled and replied, "Yes, he is our grandson. Why Hattie Mae that makes us real sisters now."

The baby boy was a shade of caramel candy.

Legacy was still in labor and the other baby was coming fast.

Legacy gave a loud scream and a hard push and out popped a baby girl.

Hattie Mae smiled and said, "If this ain't history repeating itself."

The baby girl was white as snow.

Hattie Mae handed the baby girl to Mistress Mattie.

Mistress Mattie held the baby in her arms. She said, "I'm gonna do right by you this time. I promise."

After they got the babies cleaned up, they gave them to Legacy to nurse.

Young Charles was downstairs handing out cigars. He was such a proud father.

That night, Hattie Mae went to check on the twins. Legacy was resting comfortably.

The boy twin, whom they'd named Robert Charles after Robert Lee was resting sound asleep.

The twin girl, whom they'd named Ba'gi after Baby Girl One, was wide awake and looking around as if she knew what she was looking at.

Hattie Mae picked her up and rocked her. Hattie Mae looked at her and smiled. Ba'gi looked just like Mistress Mattie except she had big brown eyes instead of big blue ones.

Hattie Mae smiled and said, "I know those eyes, little girl. Welcome back, Baby Girl One. We've missed you."

The End

Made in the USA
Middletown, DE
30 June 2020